2051

2051;
or The Emancipated Synthetic

L. Stanley

Ghost & Ribbon Publishing, Cardiff
www.ghostandribbon.com

First published 2018

ISBN 978 1 9999486 0 3 (print)
ISBN 978 1 9999486 1 0 (ebook)

Typesetting and Origination by Ghost & Ribbon Publishing
Printed by TJ International, Padstow, in the United Kingdom.

For my mum, Angela
(1965–2003)

*

Grief is the price we pay for love.
HRH Elizabeth II

In the year 2041, a law was passed stating that all crimes, debts and unfulfilled sentences could be traded for either the exchange of free labour, the exchange of personal favours for those in power, or for the increasingly popular exchange of a wholly domesticated existence measured by the severity of the outstanding liability.

With the criminal justice system all but abolished, this became a way of life in England, none challenging that which was the norm: trading life and time for gain, prosperity and the romance of fictitious emancipation.

For once in history, captivity and servitude were valued by all parties, and freedom was the myth and secret it was always thought to be.

Prologue

Ever since his wife died, he had wanted to replace her. Before that, even. She never lied when he wanted her to. And as a lawyer, lies were important to him. You didn't have to mean them, they could be brief or longstanding, but, in his mind, they were mandatory in order to retain relationships and, more importantly, to uphold a narrative or rhetoric.

In her opinion, his tie was always too blue or his shoes too dirty. The house was spotless, yet they needed to call the cleaner back again. Dinner plates were on fire or ice cold. On most days, she would be home when he arrived, and worst, she would be awake and waiting for him while their daughter slept, only to gripe and chastise when he headed straight to the study in his offensive brogues. The door closed behind him a little bit easier every time and it practically shut itself after nine years. His punishment was silence and hers was conversation.

Some candied deceit would have been welcomed, a brief kindness, pitiful intercourse or aesthetic commentary on his dress and demeanour could have meant that each torturous moment of his life could have been sweetened, although, he never knew what that was like. That was, until about a year after she left them. His first thought was, *How dare you? Brilliant. Leave me to raise our teenage daughter. Leave me alone at this point in my career. Perfect, perfect timing. Congratulations.*

Admittedly, after 'diagnosis: death', as they called it, was revealed, they took a moment to reflect on their unhappiness, concluding that her last seventeen months would be better than the last. When her energy waned and secret embraces under the sheets gave her comfort, he remembered her best things. When she was getting farther and farther away, and her heart was beating less, he wanted her desperately. The back of her neck and her rough red knees were his favourite places. He would trace her scars with curious fingertips and soft lips as she shivered at his touch. He bathed her every evening and made sure she ate a healthy breakfast in the mornings, even against her will. Aromatherapy treatments, massages, yoga, mindfulness, meditation – they tried it all. They tried and failed in sequence until he cremated her and gave her ashes to her parents.

Only now he knows that he wanted her for the wrong reason.

It was all for Sera, their old-at-heart, free-spirited creation. If he hadn't seen her come out of his wife, he would have never thought they were kin. Sera was nothing like her mother and he loved her more than he could ever understand. His daughter needed a mother, she deserved one. Doesn't every child have the right to be with the person who made and carried them for so long? And now she'll be miserable. He had seen it happen to others; losing someone close at such a young age ... They curl up, distressed and dark and alone. He didn't have time to be there for her, yet that was the way it had to be. With work and all that he had done, there was much to do and much to celebrate.

Years ago, he had an idea. What if justice didn't involve incarceration? What if no one felt useless, with skills and lives while they paid their price for their wrongdoing? What if, rather than wasting away doing nothing, people, *criminals,* had a purpose? It came to him one evening on an empty stomach while he listened to her watch a popular legal television show downstairs. She chuckled to herself once or twice, like usual, commenting to their four-year-old daughter on the proper proceedings in law.

He had heard a phrase: 'Spending six years rotting's the least I can do.' In immediate succession, he saw images of the future, and flashes of potential and vivid theories came into his mind. He scribbled notes and researched the precedent. There was nothing of this magnitude, with equal agreement, ever attempted. If he could persuade some members of parliament to see his point of view, this radical change could become reality, he had thought.

And it did. After years of protesting his positivity and expressing how much it would benefit those to whom others thought it exploited, it was finally agreed upon by both Houses and came into effect on the second day of March 2041.

Ten years later, the regret ate at him with every breath he took and he would be lying if he said he didn't wish that he could take it all back.

One

It is 21:57 and a young woman walks from the steaming kitchen and down the corridor in a black shirt and trousers, white pinafore, with heavy gold earrings in her ears and tight rings on her fingers. On her palm, she balances a silvery tray, a crystal glass and a decanter half-filled with whisky. She climbs two carpeted staircases, and stands waiting outside the large oak doors of the drawing room and waits.

Yi-Ling's eyes study the old faded wall clock until the large hand strikes twelve and it reads 22:00.

Instantly sticking the gum she is chewing in a safe place behind her upper right wisdom tooth, she enters the room, where, in the dim candlelight, the Right Honourable Prime Minister Wilson Frost sits musing. The forty-something-year-old man is a deep thinker, logical yet smug, enjoying the hanging silence in his cavernous surroundings, the paintings and portraits on the walls sitting vastly above him, a comfort inherited from the people who came before him. The air is hollow and shadowed, and the flickering of the single flame trickles over coarse cheekbones and round hazel eyes.

Setting down the tray on a mahogany side table, Yi-Ling pours the drink into the glass and carries it over to Frost, hands steady.

Parched, he takes it and sips.

On sore knees, the young woman begins an attempt to light the empty inglenook as words hang from Frost's lips.

He speaks: 'My mother was an anglophile. Fire,' he orders.

The fire takes and the flames rise, his rich brown skin glowing in the flickering light. Yi-Ling hauls herself off her knees with haste and listens quietly to her employer's tale beyond the shadow of the dark Chesterfield.

'Loved the English more than the fancy dresses she wore and the men she bought. England, not Britain. Tradition, not modernity or unity. Gentility. The Crown. The country. She even admired the little people, the 'hard-working, proud, grotty, hungry working class' who helped make up the mosaic of the democracy, the Dickens era of people she had read about years before. Sometimes she admired them. Probably how she tricked my poor father into impregnating her now that I think about it. Pretending to have a soul, you know? But there was nothing … there was nothing better than the pomp and luxury glorified by the media and centuries' worth of word of mouth. Her beautiful dark skin never held her back from her dreams, her pitiful background didn't dampen her greed. After he died, she chewed poverty up and spat it back out, spun lies and created traps, spending his money on rare and ancient crockery for afternoon teas, hired a cook purely for her ability to make bread and butter pudding, kitted out the help in painfully stereotypical garb and hired a Cambridge graduate to nurse and school me for seventeen years. Would she have been any less qualified if her alma mater were Birmingham, Manchester or Cardiff? Maybe. Maybe not. But her name was Grace. Glottal Stop Grace. How she would complain about the name my mother gave her! From her it was condescending but from me it was endearing. She loved me. You know, she was the one who taught me to walk and to talk and say 'please' and 'thank you', how to be a gentleman and how to be an exception in a violent and cursed town where nothing good happened. Now look at me.'

The drawing room at Number Ten is glorious. Ostentatious and spectacular, the room bleeds luxury and elegance. It oozes out of the walls and up through the floorboards. It sparkles from the glass chandelier as it gleams on the ceiling, shedding light onto the soft crushed velvet chairs and large mink rug. History is at every corner, on the faces of his predecessors on the walls, to the cornices and alcoves and the aged alcohol in his hands.

Although not his style, Frost fits into the extravagance of his surroundings, dressed in a brand-new Stefano Ricci, sipping on his whisky. All he needed was a cigar and a revolver to remind any onlooker of a 1930's gangster film.

He continues, solemn, after emptying the rest of the drink from his glass. 'My mother … She taught me nothing. We literally spoke different languages. Her tongue was Afrikaans and I was forbidden to speak it. When we lived down in South Africa, I learnt a few phrases from Grace, picked it up a little at the library or at the supermarket but I dare not tell her that I could understand her cursing. So we lived separate lives until I came back here to study for my degrees.

'But by accepting myself and letting others worry about where I fit, I studied, lied, cheated, polished up my language to fit in with the rest and was clever enough to be where I am sat right now, drinking with my favourite housekeeper. Before I was voted in – do you remember? – there was all of this talk about who I was and whether or not I deserved to be here, whether or not it mattered about the colour of my skin and where I was born, who my family was. Does any of it matter? Am I not your favourite? Do I not break barriers, giving hope to the poor, the ethnically diverse, the male, the new, the foreign, the challenged? Am I the new wave?' he asks himself.

He pauses, reminiscent of the lonely evening eating alone as a child while his mother went out to parties, of the forced schooling and lonely upbringing, his struggle and rise into his education and political career. He received no praise, motivation, encouragement nor love from the one person with whom it was supposed to be natural and found no new arms to belong to.

'And what was the one thing I've learned that I'll never forget for the rest of my miserable and cursed days?'

It took a moment for Yi-Ling to realise that he was speaking to her.

She stumbles a little. 'Don't have children ... Sir?'

Despite his annoyance, Frost is in silent agreement.

'Nothing ever comes for free,' Yi-Ling recites.

'No, it certainly doesn't, Yi-Ling. We've both learnt that the hard way.' He looks at her for the first time. 'Haven't we?'

'The only way we know.'

Frost laughs, chilling, making her jump. 'That's right.'

Patient, she asks, 'Was there anything else, Sir?'

Frost says nothing and gazes back into the glowing flames, entranced by their beauty.

Yi-Ling, taking the tray with her, exits the room and heads to the kitchen, back from where she came.

Inside, a middle-aged man covered in storytelling scars, wipes down surfaces with an old rag, cleaning up after the evening meal he had prepared hours earlier, routinely winding down after the day's work. He has grey bristly facial hair but the hair on his head is dark. Veins ripple his arms as he scrubs. He pays no heed to his colleague as she storms into the room, heated, slamming down the silver tray in a fit of rage.

He doesn't flinch despite the deafening clatter.

'I cannot stand that man.'

Still focused on cleaning, he utters, 'Quiet.'

'Oh, he's had it so tough! He's literally sipping five-hundred-pound whisky from a crystal glass off a tray made of precious metal and he's complaining about his first-world problems?'

'Was it the same story?' he asks. 'Mother dearest and her—'

'The same story.'

'Oh, it's a hit this week.'

'The neglected child. The cold and vacant mother. For the love of—! All woe-is-me. I'm sick of it, Cliff. I really am. You know, I could tell that story a thousand times. In my sleep. With a gun to my head. "My mother was an anglophile." If I hear it again, I swear …' She sits on the side of the surface that Cliff has just wiped down.

'You'll what?' he challenges. 'Knock him off mid-whisky, all for another round at Auction where you'll be sold off to the next rich spanner doing the dishes or raising the kids? Smart, Ling, really ace.'

She sighs. 'I'm not known for my ability to think ahead.'

'If you were, you'd have known he'd tell the story again.'

'Yeah, I suppose this is what my degree was for. To end up here in servitude listening to his delightful tales,' Yi-Ling decides, grim.

'Like he has every night for the past fortnight.'

'I get it! I was just hoping for the graduation one. Or the unlucky in love complaint, you know? Something new.'

Cliff smiles. 'Nothing ever comes for free.'

'I'll give you a slap for free in a minute,' she jokes, going for him. Jumping off the furniture, Yi-Ling leaves the room and heads to bed.

'Goodnight,' Cliff says, laughing.

'Night!' she calls, just before she is out of sight.

A modern apartment in a suburban area is engulfed by quiet streets and darkness until a landline rings. The woman in bed stirs angrily beneath the duvet. Beside the clock reading 23:11, a hand emerges from the covers, lifting and hanging up the phone.

The hand disappears again.

She flinches as her mobile phone rings loudly, a jaunty tune, vibrating across the bedside table. The noise ceases.

Across the room, another phone – her work phone – rings in a monotonous tone.

Mason, stunningly plain, stern and unashamedly hard-working, emerges from the sheets with mousy brown hair over her face, hands creeping over the surfaces, searching. Her eyes are still jammed closed yet she dives blindly to find the phone underneath the bottom end of her bed, body hanging delicately, inches from the cold wood.

A private number glows on the screen.

'Shit,' she mutters, falling onto the floor. 'Yes?'

'Is it done?'

'Not yet.'

'When I tell you to do something, I generally mean now, Mason.' The voice belongs to the prime minister, sitting in the same armchair, having not moved since. 'Not when you feel like it. The Budget won't wait for you to find the right time.'

'Will it wait for me to be awake?'

'I called your office. You weren't there.'

She sits on the edge of the bed with a hand in her hair, clinging to the only rest she has been able to get all day. She tries to ignore the 4 a.m. start she has ahead of her.

'Despite popular belief, I don't actually live there, so …'

Frost is silent for a moment. 'Were you sleeping?' he asks, unapologetic.

t's what people do at home, Sir.'

at did I say? You can't talk to me like that until you fire Mr Briscoe.'

They have an interesting relationship, a vague understanding that makes their distaste for one another manageable. Yet, just the sound of his name makes her guard fall down like a brick wall. Her insides squirm and her heart stops for a moment.

'Do I have to?' she whispers into the phone, child-like.

'We can no longer afford a solicitor general, no matter the history, no matter the importance or necessity. Trust me, it – it's nothing personal. We'd fire whoever was in the position,' he says without feeling.

'But it is personal. Briscoe is my friend and he's a damn good worker. Always has my back. If you could just think for a second – I need him. I really do.'

'We're all feeling the cuts, Mason, with the deepest knife. And I know that it's hard. It's breaking my heart, it really is, but look at it this way. As your workload increases, so do your wages. By forty percent.'

'I'm bursting with joy.'

'Thirty percent. Tomorrow.'

'Bye.'

He hangs up before she finishes her valediction, leaving her to throw herself onto her mountain of sheets, upset, angry and in despair.

There is nothing that Mason wants more than to be surrounded by friends in such depressing times. She had hoped that she could be inundated with allies rather than enemies, yet recently the constant shuffling of the legal department in His Majesty's Justice darkens her days and haunts her footsteps. At every turn, she expects a knife in the back or a dagger to the heart from the people she trusts the most. And, case in point, Mason is expected to lay off her closest friend and her colleague, extinguishing their twenty-year friendship and a strong longstanding partnership in one fell swoop.

She first spotted Briscoe while attempting to stash away a very old facsimile in Gray's Inn library two decades ago after she had lathered it with thick, red, tomato pasta sauce. Although food was prohibited, Mason had fallen asleep with the plastic pot hanging over the page and managed to leave a rather nice, rich stain on the pages and a sweet smell in the air. Leaning her shoulder over the worn pages, her useless tissue dabbed at the crumbling pages, creating more harm than good. Both studying under the pupillage of experienced barristers – or 'better barristers' as she often called them – Mason and Briscoe understood the consequences of defacing coveted texts and so he had offered his assistance. Naturally, they stifled chuckles and thought of masterful ways to hide it, a coup to blame the library assistant, and thirty-two different ways to get away with it in court – which included 'pleading penne'.

Briscoe was reprimanded for it, being 'a real gent', after which Mason decided she wouldn't have anything to do with someone who lied so easily. Of course, they argued about what had happened, she threatened to own up and even to quit but he convinced her that she had a shining future ahead of her, one that was sure to be greater than his own. Never finding a way to call it square, she agreed to help him study for every exam and court case, providing food, company, revision material, playlists and distractions where necessary. She even showed him her breast once when he started to tire.

Admittedly, he was as unreliable as she guessed and Briscoe would not turn up to late-night study sessions, only visited her once when she went home to Derby during the summer and went off to practice law in Kent while she stayed in London, the cause of their hiatus after graduating.

The occasion in which he did visit her was Summer 2033

during the Floods and, lucky for him, he could not leave until the sixth day came and it was safe to open the doors.

'You planned this,' he had said grumpily, over the dinner table with her parents.

'I don't know what you're talking about,' she smirked, pushing around her mashed potatoes.

'If she could control the weather she could,' Mr Mason bellowed under his moustache.

Despite being in such legal standing, Mason admits to herself that she does not have the power to save a job, an important job at that. Even without the fact that her best friend is in the role, solicitor general is the attorney general's number two, the helping hand in advising the King and running the Crown Prosecution Service with the ambitious director of public prosecutions, Sidra Tall.

Three hours feels like three minutes, and Mason drags her worn body out of the sheets and into the hot shower. She lives in a modest two-bedroom apartment, inexpensive for the time, yet spacious. No one would have known that one of the highest paid barristers lives in a place like this and that is the way she wants it. No danger is posed to her here as crime is at a low level and many professionals live in the same building. Doctors, bankers, teachers – they have them all. The interior is sleek yet simple, with warm colours reminding her of home and comfort. The floors are black and shiny and the walls are terracotta in the open living space, soft rugs and mood lighting to match. Beside the candles are bowls of pot pourri and old artwork resembling bones, along with stone to decorate the large bedroom.

Standing in the open shower, Mason runs through her duties for the day. Office. Meeting. Paperwork. Briscoe. CPS. Lincoln's. Office. Work. Work. Hassle. Strain. Et cetera.

While pouring freshly made coffee into her thermos, she

checks her Organiser X3 for her emails and legal updates. The micro-thin, electronic pocket organiser is no bigger than a sheet of A5 paper with a reflective mirror over the touchscreen. Eye recognition makes it so that only she can see the classified and protected documentation she holds on her device.

Giving herself a worried smile in the silver glass, she hauls her bag over her shoulder and grabs her black case full of books and reference material. Mason closes the door behind her and turns, pressing her thumb and third finger into the print lock, then walks downstairs, sipping her coffee.

The office is not far away so she ignores her six-year-old Renault and walks for almost half an hour along the quiet grassland and dirt tracks through the city. With all of the transport living belowground for the past fifteen years, life on the surface is as tranquil as it can be. Starbucks and McDonalds still impose themselves on pedestrians, yet the hustle and bustle of a time she remembers is absent. Bikes roll along without the threat of motor vehicles, in a care-free and respectful manner. Road markings and standardised signs highlight where entrances to bus stops, taxi ranks, trains and ventilation systems are placed and the Underground's descending steps remained. Neat pathways, rubbish bins, parks, fountains and other such typical things surround all of the old and new buildings. Everything is the same – except no loud horns, controlled and converted emissions, less vehicles thefts and manageable traffic.

Colleagues say 'Good morning' to Mason as she arrives, pushing her finger into a touchpad on entry.

'Morning Padraig,' she whispers.

'Tired?' he asks, knowing the answer.

'It's strange how much friendlier people are at this time of day.'

'Why is that?'

'I feel like murdering someone.'

He laughs. 'Don't say that here, Mason.'

'The worst thing that could happen is that I prosecute myself.' She starts towards the lift, contemplating the thought.

'Now that would be interesting,' Padraig calls. 'Have a good one.' She raises a hand in response, running to squeeze in through the closing doors of the elevator. 'And don't leave too late this evening. I can't leave until you do.'

Being a workaholic was not something Mason intended; she wanted to be the best and would preferably do so while doing as little work as possible. Briscoe would joke about how lazy she was and he was not the first. All of her friends had seen it in her – the lack of intent and constant procrastination would have been her downfall if not for her joy of winning.

This being said, attorney general was a role given to her by default. Vaughan Stredwick, the pillock they had hired (responsible for losing several cases that a wild orangutan could win, for money), who served for a grand total of three weeks, was robbed at knifepoint and suffered a massive asthma attack because of it. The first thing Mason was asked to do in her interim-turned-permanent role was to comment on the current state of the 'supposed safety in the streets' since the legal reform, in light of his terrible and unforeseen passing.

Word for word, she had said, in monotone: 'The late Right Honourable Vaughan Stredwick KC, while abiding and promoting the law, was not bound to it nor was he immune. It would render him superhuman to say that he could not fall victim to a random attack, if it was such, and therefore we should not treat this situation with any extraordinary measures on his account for his occupation and certainly not his death. Nothing can bring him back at this point and, as of his last breath, I am the Attorney General for England. Nothing makes me more sorrowful than to elevate in such a circumstance, however, it does not prevent me from doing the job I have been appointed for this country. Crime is not 'at a high' because one man was threatened with a penknife. One man, one citizen, is dead because he had a stubborn and temperamental breathing condition, which, under stress, caused him to suffer cardiac arrest. I'm not making this up, it's all on the Coroner's report. It could have happened at any time, in any place, watching the football or during sex with his wife. I would not worry about the fear of violence and an upsurge in rioting or whatever else it is that you are afraid of. Terrible things are happening now. Famine, hunger, poverty, homelessness, terminal diseases, starvation. Yet, here we are speaking of one man in privilege? I don't care about him or his corpse. I care about my job to protect the living and claim justice for those who have passed in unsettling conditions. I don't know what he cared about and we certainly cannot ask him now, but from what I knew of him and the conversations we had, he would be really happy to know that we were spending our precious time talking about his life and death and everything that made him so special.'

She has a distinct way with words. It was all anyone could talk about for the next few months at least, behind her back of course, but gossip was not important to her. It still isn't. The speech gave her balls and still puts fear into interns and newbies to this day. The attorney general who makes a mockery of the dead is a force to be reckoned with.

The seventh floor of Victory House bustles come seven thirty on any day of the week, but before five there is a sweet lull of calm in the air. Mason glides through the offices and cubicles toward the wall of windows at the back, turning right into her large office. Her name is emblazoned on the door in large print:

THE RIGHT HONOURABLE
DOLLY MASON KC MP
ATTORNEY GENERAL OF ENGLAND

She rolls her eyes at it and enters her office exactly the way she left it; the blinds are closed and the desk lamp still glowing above a half-eaten box of takeaway pizza and a warm glass of water. Black court shoes are tucked under the desk and a curved computer is on top amongst pencils and pens and sheets of paper she had been jotting notes down on. Theories and minutes swim on the pages amongst reminders to get the dry cleaning and items for her shopping list: carrots, peaches, pasta, shampoo, and so on.

Her body finds the cream swivel chair easily and she swings around once and then gets to grips with her gargantuan list of duties. Mason starts at the top, typing through the hours, thinking hard, case by case, detailing and whiling away time with emails and a meeting until Kevin Briscoe arrives in the building to start the day's work.

Two and a half hours later, Mason grabs her lip balm and runs it over both lips, bottom then top. She presses her lips together impatiently while looking at her friend. Usually a jovial and lovable man with a rounded happy face and a great set of teeth, he now tries to repress how pissed off he is by applying a deep set of lines to his brow.

'Are you kidding me?'

'I'm not, no.' Outside the room, the office is blossoming, the desks filling. She drags her eyes back to Briscoe, uneasy.

'Are you actually kidding me?

Taking a deep breath and holding her hands together, she says, 'Listen, Kevin, it's nothing personal. We just can't afford a solicitor general anymore. I'm not saying anything against your performance and dedication and your consistency—'

Briscoe tries to calm himself, but instead looks as though he has reached boiling point. 'Don't, Doll.'

'I told you, don't call—'

'I don't care about the money you're – he's giving me to

leave.'

'It's good money.'

'I thought we were friends.'

The only word that she can form falls out of her soft lips, 'Yes.'

'Where was I when you needed my arse in court for the third time running because you had too much on your plate? What the hell was I doing three months ago when I should have been running my own cases? I was helping you wrangle the CPS runaways. And when I have to stay late—'

'Kevin, I know all of this.'

At this point, he can't look at her. 'And when I have to stay late, I always do because I don't care about losing sleep, I care about the both of us – including me – not losing our jobs and the careers we spent years grafting for.'

The look they share is one of family and heartbreak. He doesn't have to tell her about grafting.

'I – I tried to help you.' She pauses and tries to find his eyes. 'This is it, Kevin.'

Shaking his head, he accepts. 'Well, I suppose there's not much you could do, Dolls. Am I, at least, still invited to the pity party later?'

She tries to hide her relief. 'Of course. Food per head's already been paid for.'

'Shouldn't be awkward at all.'

Mason turns to her computer and places her black glasses on her nose. 'What shouldn't be awkward?'

'Me being fired would make interesting conversation. Could you imagine—?'

Amid his gloomy words, there was a brief knock on the door and a tall, dark-haired forty-year-old woman of South Asian descent enters. The woman is Sidra Tall, shorter than her name implies yet she beholds a long neck, strong cheekbones and rich brown eyes.

Tall's surprised glare meets Briscoe's and she freezes.

'This is a bad time,' Mason says to her, dull.

Tall's arm floats to Briscoe's shoulder. 'Briscoe, I'm so sorry.'

'Are you really?' He looks at her, disbelieving.

'Of course, I mean, I don't know why anyone in their right mind would get rid of a lovely man like you, Kevin.'

'Too much, Sidra,' he replies, turning away.

Mason, still typing away, says, 'You wanted something?'

Tall addresses Mason. 'Just a general query. We're not getting many fraud cases. Could be a problem as we know for sure that it's been on the rise for the past ten years. It's definitely a problem. I smell a cover-up so I just thought we should discuss it before the meeting next week.'

'Briscoe.'

He stands. 'I'll let myself out then.'

Sourly, he heads for the door.

'I'll see you later,' Mason bids as he exits to his office to pack away his things in silence.

Tall lumbers into the empty seat Briscoe has left, unable to contain her excitement.

'Does this mean what I think it means?'

'No.'

'How do you know what I'm thinking?' Tall inquires.

'You want his job and you're not getting it. You, Briscoe and me were the most senior lawyers in Prosecution. And now it'll be just me and you. Sisters doing it for themselves or whatever,' she adds bitterly.

Tall deflates. 'That's not really how feminism works.'

'What?'

'Equality, not man-bashing. Or man-firing. Never mind.'

'Feminism doesn't work if the people don't, and if the law

doesn't, it's because it's not being enforced correctly, therefore the government try to appease people when it comes to social injustice even though it has a redundant cause and effect. Why else to people protest and riot about all kinds of equality? It's because the law is failing and some people and their old-fashioned ideas will never change.' She pauses. 'And it wasn't my decision. This is strictly a male-on-male issue.'

'So, first, the staff is downsized by seventy-two percent, then less funding and now no solicitor general? What is Frost playing at?'

'Actually, the first thing was upending criminal justice in England, remember? Less crime and convicted criminals on the streets doing their bit. Leaves us a lot less to prosecute.'

Tall holds up the paper in her hand. 'Record lows. Also, notes on current appeals.'

'Talk to me.' Mason grabs a pen and paper.

'Oh and don't forget we've got to be at the Commons in an hour and twenty.'

Mason picks up the phone and hits the button to connect to her assistant. 'George. Coffee.'

'The Question submitted today is by Renata Gibb, Deputy Prime Minister.'

'Thank you, Mr Speaker. I speak today on the consideration to vote on amendments to the Housing Act 2044 and is as follows: 'How can homelessness be reduced en masse by the refurbishment and reallocation of public institutions and should be poor be prosecuted for taking up homes in the streets?

'A vast statement, this is true, however, since 2038, fifty-five percent of prisons, schools and hospitals have been closed. Seventy percent of schools have been merged and/or relocated to derelict and unkempt prisons, and hospitals have done the same, having to suffer from closures and unsafe living and working conditions.

'Having spoken with the minister for health and the chair of Public Health England recently, it is widely known that the rate of infection has more than doubled, leading to more complications during and after surgery – even death. Supplies and surgical instruments have been in low supply for the past three years, causing a cap on non-urgent surgeries and a rise in new-age barbers and backstreet operations in highly populated communities. People are dying in the streets and no one is immune, neither the rich nor the poor and needy.'

People move about in the Commons, some leaving, yet Mason sits patiently, listening.

Renata Gibb continues: 'It is not up to members of parliament to vacillate on blatant and unparalleled poverty within our own health service and within our communities. The Housing Act 2044 voted on the relocation of vital institutions in this country for cost-effectiveness only but not for the good of its people. I did not vote for this although our Prime Minister forced his hand ...'

The crowd boos.

'He forced his hand. Even if he thinks this is for the good of all, this much is clear to me and should be to you all: we must save our institutions and enforce a step-by step plan to alleviate the pressure from hospitals, improve care and budgeting, assure parents that their children are having a full education despite the massive changes schools have been subjected to, increase teaching and support staff and reduce fees and institutional prestige, all in an effort to reduce the risk of consequence and decay which will affect us all vastly in the coming years. We need to seriously think about changing the quality of care by re-evaluating the Housing Act to include the homeless to house people who have nowhere to go. And while we're at it, we need to take a good long look at the Criminal Justice Act too.'

'Hear, hear.' A third of the room agree with her, Mason too although she doesn't voice it.

Another MP stands, addressing Gibb with a poised mouth and a smart attitude. 'I understand your view on the dire nature of the hospitals and education, however, you cannot deny the increase in efficiency, cohesiveness and the overall safety the compatibility of this program has brought with it and in full force.'

'Fiddlesticks, Henry, crime still happens every day. Putting people into a forced, glorified community service does not forestall reoffending. It just provides a false sense of security. And you would think that with more space the hospitals and schools would benefit but it doesn't and what, tell me, what was the point if the young and the sick suffer?'

Joseph Henry, MP for the constituency of Derbyshire Dales takes a seat as the others applaud her. Split fifty-fifty, half of the room look on sourly.

Mason ponders Gibb's idea, questioning herself and her actions as they do in the Commons wherever there is need.

'What do you think?' Mason whispers to Tall, who is sat on her right.

She shrugs. 'Good point but no ears.'

Mason gazes around. Not many people showed up today, clearly with better things to do. She tries to make it when she can, for the people of Vauxhall, lest they forget who she is, lest she forget they exist because of her busy schedule. During this debate, her presence almost means nothing. Today, there is no one here to take the deputy seriously, not the minister for health nor the prime minister himself.

Despite her power, Renata Gibb is still at the mercy of democracy while democracy is at the mercy of revolution.

Two

Beneath the changing sky, the City winds down and light raindrops hit the clean pavements, washing away the smokescreen of a society united by reform, a shadow of the time before. The sunset reveals the reality of corruption. Quietly, citizens walk around with a hint of distrust and suspicion, eyes downcast. Cars roll along the underground roads, orderly and patient despite mild traffic jams. The streets empty and people seek solace in their homes, locking up once, twice and three times to ease their fears in attempts to keep the evil out.

A large umbrella rises from the steps of Covent Garden Underground and the two people beneath it head for the Inner London Crown Court. A father in his early fifties, proud, respectful and in black and white dress, the justice minister and president of the New Supreme Court, the Right Honourable Justice, Lord Daniel Reid KC MP shelters his insular and mature fifteen-year-old daughter, Seraphim, from the weather.

As they walk towards His Majesty's Crown Court, Sera watches a slightly overweight young homeless man look longingly into a crowded restaurant through the large windows. She feels sympathy, which soon includes a hint of pity. Their eyes meet for a moment, but Justice Reid beckons her inside.

Six people in grey jumpsuits – individual national insurance numbers printed on the breast pocket – stand in the juror bay, dirty silver manacles and chains on their wrists and ankles, waiting for the Auction to begin.

Rows of eager and varied faces are in the audience. They are clearly wealthy, with expensive taste in apparel, and they chatter away quietly opposite the judge and auctioneer, some staring down at tablets that display information on each criminal for sale.

A homely, brunette housewife and mother of six is in the witness box, with TR152P printed on her faded clothing.

The gavel falls.

'And Lot TR152P is sold to buyer 1435,' bellows Judge Scott.

The woman is led out of the room by the members of security while Buyer 1435 is overwhelmed with happiness at their purchase. The next item in line, Lot AM277S, is taken to the witness box for their judgement. There are two people behind him, yet to be displayed. One is a tattooed gentleman, RP018N, and the other is a twenty-four-year-old female named Lot CA45JM. Her full brown eyes stay on the ground.

Judge Scott taps his master tablet and all of the others in the room change at his command, displaying the lot number, picture, age, price and other details.

He continues with an abhorrent drawl, looking weakly through reading glasses. 'The next item. Lot AM277S. National insurance as the same. Twenty-six-year-old black male, Alexander Sp— Well, you can give him any name you wish …'

At the back of the room, Reid and his daughter are welcomed, given a tablet to share and a buyer number. They seat themselves.

'… one hundred and seventy pounds, six foot five. Clean bill of health. Polite, educated young chap. Doesn't owe much. Starting bid at four thousand for a four-year service. Do I have four thousand pounds?'

An elderly male bidder puts up his sign. 'Four thousand.'

'Four thousand,' Scott confirms. 'Five thousand pounds anyone?'

Nothing.

'Come on, ladies. He's young, fit, has great hair, great eyes …'

AM277S is seething at this point, remembering Scott's well-known reputation for doing anything for a sale.

'And he's a Pisces, so we all know what that means,' he says, looking at him with small watery eyes. He winks and the crowd chuckle lightly.

'Four and a half, then?'

A woman in cashmere folds. 'Four and a half.'

The elderly male is back in. 'Five thousand!'

'Five thousand,' the judge calls. 'And a half?'

Another woman with sharp red nails decides she wants AM277S. She nods.

'And half. Six thousand?' Scott asks the old man. He shakes his head but the Cashmere woman leaps in. The ping pong bidding between the two females continues until the second comes victorious.

'Final offer of nine thousand pounds sterling to this lovely lady. Anymore? Last chance to snap up this young man. He's not dangerous. Will make a lovely addition to your home or business. No? Nine thousand pounds. Final offer. Nine thousand over here. Nine thousand. That's it.' The gavel falls. 'Sold. Nine thousand pounds to 3363. Well done on your purchase.'

3363 cackles and fans herself down while AM277S sighs.

He runs a hand through his black hair, hopeless. Meanwhile, Sera eyes CA45JM as RP018N is being prepared for sale.

'We'll see,' her father says quietly, a secret smile on his lips.

Bare feet and coffee on her desk, Mason's studious eyes move quickly behind a pair of glasses. Beyond her laptop, her hand drags a pen's trail across a rough piece of paper. She is waist-deep in work, as usual, contemplating three cases petitioning for retrial and reviewing the last twelve cases quashed in her jurisdiction.

The defendant is a forty-year-old homeless woman who broke into a bedding store for a night's sleep. She was charged with burglary once and was given a suspended sentence of six months. Two months later, she steals a bag of oranges from a market stall, handing them back once caught. She was charged with theft and looking at a year of service, her lawyer pinning their hopes on the retrial. For now, the defendant is happy with a warm bed and a meal in the cells.

Mason is tempted to deny the retrial, if not just to give the woman a potential year of comfort.

She sighs and looks to the next.

A man kills his swimming coach in the pool in front of twenty-two witnesses and none testify. Could be fear, but with inconclusive evidence, eyewitnesses, a very good alibi and pre-existing heart condition, it looks as though he will get away with it. He was sentenced but the decision then quashed with pressure from the New House of Lords and their fears of how 'it would look'. Another one of many who escape justice…

Mason wonders what that means these days. Even if someone is prosecuted, there is no mandatory sentencing, therefore, the passive rehabilitation focuses solely on an attempt at social integration where it may not be due or safe. Risk is a huge factor yet ten years of quiet seemed to justify the system further.

Baffled as to why anyone wanted this and whether this was predicted, Mason wonders quietly whether her experience, as well as her legal and political knowledge, have failed her. How does this continue on with no real direction or cause and with no one doubting the subtle terror and mindless character of those in power?

Is this justice or brainwashing?

The door knocks.

George enters, smiling. 'You're still here.'

She checks her watch. 'It's only nine.'

George floats around the room, fixing things, putting books onto the shelves, picking things off the floor and throwing waste into the bin.

As he waters her plant with the glass of warm water, he utters, 'Don't you have somewhere to be?'

Mason frowns. She hates when he is cryptic. 'Not that I'm aware.'

He stares at her, begging to differ.

After thirteen seconds, it clicks.

'I love you, Georgie,' Mason gushes, shoving her feet into her shoes for the tenth time that day. She grabs her suit jacket and bag, kisses his cheek and runs out of the office with haste.

George turns to the freshly dry-cleaned and pressed midnight blue evening gown hung on the wall and takes it with him, switching the lights off as he goes.

Streets away, the Auction continues. The crowd is now quite sparse. The gavel falls.

'No sale,' Judge Scott calls. He presses the appropriate buttons on his tablet. RP018N suppresses a smile as he is led out and back to the holding cells by a security guard.

Quiet and unchanged, CA45JM is taken to the stand and showed to the people. Her hair is tied back into one long plait hanging down the back of the torn grey jumpsuit, plain and harmless as her face, which bears no make-up nor expression. She rests her manacled hands softly on the side to ground herself, staring at the floor, just a few feet ahead of the first row of faces.

For the last time that evening, Scott calls to the people. 'And the final sale. Lot CA45JM. National Insurance as the same. Unnamed – or rather, listed with several. Permission to name as desired. Twenty-four-year-old woman. Five foot five. One hundred and thirty-eight pounds. Owes quite a lot. Steep debt. One hundred thousand pounds.' The crowd gasp. 'Mostly accumulated whilst evading arrest. I'll start the bidding at a quarter of a million, shall I?'

No one bids and the air suddenly feels thin and cold.

'She is a commodity,' Scott expresses with much effort. 'Smart too, streetwise. Logical. She has some serious travel under her belt too. Italy, France, Canada, India, Japan – so quite cultured. Despite her ignorance and failure to adhere to the rules, she is polite and as close to trustworthy as any criminal can get without being free. Could work well as a secretary, tutor, cleaner, cook, surrogate, wife even. She is the definition of multifunctional and would be forever in your debt, totalling a very rare and never-before-offered, mind-blowing life service in your care. Do I have any bids, ladies and gentleman?'

The first and only voice cuts through CA45JM like a blunt blade to the stomach.

'Two hundred and fifty thousand,' Reid calls. Sera beams beside him.

Instantly, Judge Scott recognises him. 'Excellent! Excellent choice, Lord Reid. Hope you're having a good evening.' Reid nods kindly. 'Any more bids? Didn't think so. Sold!'

He bangs the gavel, keen to leave for the evening. 'Buyers make your way to the reception area to organise payment and delivery. Thank you everyone for attending tonight. The next evening sale is on Tuesday week.'

'Come on.' A short and rotund security guard leads CA45JM down the steps of the witness box, through the secure doors and down the narrow corridor to the holding cells, not before she caught a glance of a young teenage girl hugging the man who bought her, clearly overjoyed with their brand-new purchase.

In the back of a slow black Hackney Carriage, the night sky and bright lights whiz by and Mason's nerves continue to build. After checking her phone and swallowing a Trebor extra-large peppermint whole, she pulls her medium-length hair down over her ear, checks her mirror and flattens down her trouser suit.

After a moment of consideration, she undoes the top button of her white blouse. Better.

Checking her image again in her compact mirror, she decides to tie her hair up again and that she should never show her soul on an occasion such as this, lest she should be eaten alive by the masses.

'Would you mind stepping on it?' she calls to the driver through the glass.

'Don't worry, we'll be there in five minutes. Jesus,' he mutters under his breath hotly.

As they approach the hotel, Mason spots other people in evening dress arriving, swanning inside in any old fashion, cool and vague and without haste.

'Oh good, I'm not late.'

The men and women, MPs, judges and other important members of the judiciary and executive bodies, exit fancy cars and limousines, mostly with smiles on their faces and money in their pockets.

'How much?' she asks, looking at the driver. From her place to this side of town, it was no more than fifty.

'Sixty-two.'

Annoyed, Mason swipes her card into a machine fixed to an interior armrest and exits the car to join the seductive and the sparkling. She does not have time to argue this evening.

On the adjacent dark street, Briscoe, in all of his expensive and wasted attire, parks his car, gets out and helps his date, Celeste Landau, newsreader and journalist, out of her side. She is youthful, deceptive, albeit slightly dim, unconventionally striking and is enhanced by her glamourous evening gown made of white silk.

She thanks her date for the assistance and takes his arm in the same moment that he notices Mason walk by the photographers scathingly and towards security by the hotel entrance. She stops and gazes at the building and Briscoe watches her contemplate whether or not to go in after coming all this way.

'Come on.' He beckons Celeste over gently and they walk over to Mason, blinded by cameras as they go.

'Showing some skin, I see,' Briscoe says, referencing Mason's trouser suit.

She notices the pair of them and applies a look of feigned interest.

'Then what are you?'

'Well-dressed. You really know how to—' He touches the cuff of her jacket and looks her over. 'My God, did you even try? This really is a party. They weren't joking.'

'I'm not here to celebrate.' Mason yanks back her arm. 'Who's your date?' she asks, not once looking at her.

'I'm sorry. My manners are clearly … Celeste, Dolly. Dolly, Celeste.'

Mason cringes slightly at her name and corrects Briscoe as she shakes Celeste's moisturised hand. It has a peachy scent.

'Mason.'

'Lovely to meet you,' Celeste responds. Mason raises an eyebrow, humoured by this woman's soft if not painfully stereotypical demeanour. Mason has it in her mind that this is not the twentieth century and has to stop herself from saying so aloud.

Briscoe turns to his date. 'Dolly and I … We go way back.'

Celeste makes a noise sounding like agreement.

'I'm glad you came,' Mason says, ignoring the third party.

'Thought I'd show my face. If not just to pretend to the PM that I'm not pissed but also because of the free booze. May as well drown my sorrows with the expensive stuff.'

'Did you run out of the supermarket own-brand boxed wine already, then?'

They both snigger while Celeste is stony-faced.

'No, I just resigned myself to the thought of spending my days self-analysing and editing Wikipedia pages for fun.'

'Classy,' Mason jibes.

'Might even take a holiday,' Briscoe says, hopeful. 'Maybe Paris or something like that.'

'What did you say? Powys?' Mason laughs. 'Seems more your budget.'

'Good point. I'm on pennies now that I'm just an MP,' he chuckles. 'Please attempt to have a little fun tonight.'

'Why should I?' Mason retorts, her tone changing. 'It's my job to be here and that is all. It's not my place to have an opinion, remember? And, anyway, even if I did have an opinion, this isn't the place to say it. I'm not stupid. I say one thing out of place and I'm dragged through some ridiculous media circus, the civil courts are on my back, defamation, slander, all sorts and I'm signing on every other week.'

'Lawyer through and through.'

'Well, I didn't pass the Bar for kicks, Kevin.'

'You're a lawyer?' Celeste chimes, glad to be part of the conversation.

Mason frowns and blinks twice at her. 'I'm the attorney general.'

'Yes.'

'You read the news Miss Lander. It might be—'

'Landau like Spandau, not—'

'As I was saying, Miss Lander, it might be great if you actually paid attention to the news once in a while.'

'Well, it was an easy mistake to make. Your face just isn't that memorable, that's all.'

'It's not my job to be seen. I can do it without wardrobe, hair and make-up beforehand.'

'I see that.'

Mason smirks, staggered by her attitude.

Briscoe attempts to slay the tension. 'Shall we go insi—?'

'I thought lawyers were all but out of work,' Celeste comments.

'Not me.'

'Congratulations.' She turns to Briscoe and stares directly into his eyes, beckoning. 'Let's go.'

Celeste leads him to security not before he turns back to Mason, smiling about the confrontation. Mason smiles back at him and summons to courage to follow them inside.

The dinner party is in full swing, music, hundreds of flutes of champagne, fancy hor d'oeurves and round tables to seat many. On the stage there is a microphone and a podium and, above it, an elaborate banner reading, 'TEN SUCCESSFUL TRADING YEARS.'

Beyond, various MPs, Justices, police officers, and people who work in government, legislative and judicial organisations dine and network at the tables and on the dancefloor, including Frost, currently at optimum satisfaction conversing joyously with Sidra Tall, wowing all in a backless green evening gown.

Others are present, Judges Cunningham and Scott, old and traditional men, a thick moustache and a beer belly respectively and, entering, Lord Reid, looking very pleased and very professional.

'Evening.' Reid greets Frost with vigour and Tall with a soft kiss and joins them with a glass of champagne.

Frost eventually takes to the stage and people gather around him.

'Yes … well, first off, I'd like to welcome you all and thank you for coming tonight. Thank you for taking the time to be here and thank you to all of the juniors and assistants doing all of our work at this present time.' There is a chuckle from the audience. 'We all know why we're here, to commemorate and enjoy the ten years since we changed this country for the better. Change and success. Every moment of hard work led to this moment, the moment where we look back and realise we did things in the right way. We're standing on the precipice of glory, honestly because there was no real life a decade ago. Now we are living. But enough of me. I'd like to give the honour of toasting our greatness to the minister for justice, the president of the New Supreme Court, my friend and one of the key founders of our utopia, Lord Daniel Reid.'

After lengthy applause, Reid gently climbs onto the stage, nimble and athletic, ignorant of the steps to his left. He smiles a cheeky smile and then applies a serious face.

'Ask anybody here, crime has never been so controlled and the pledge for safety has never been so secure. The Criminal Justice Act 2041 states, "Be it enacted by the King's most excellent Majesty … by and with the consent of the

Lords Spiritual and Temporal, and Commons, in this present Parliament assembled, and by the authority of the same ..."
We did this. Together. This Act, and all who endorsed it, made provisions on the swift and vital amendment and revision of the criminal justice system, a system that has failed its citizens in the past, all for the good of the people. The dissolution of the jurisdiction of criminal courts had never been attempted, except here, in England. It is unprecedented and future generations will thank us when they live in a fearless country, one we have not known for long. We've put in place such a system, such a phenomenon and, best of all, everyone benefits. No prison overcrowding, more schools, more hospitals, a just society with clean streets and a regiment created to offer freedom to every citizen without prejudice or judgement, releasing the constraints of a dated and archaic system. I have every hope that the next ten years will be as successful.' He raises his glass. 'Here's to freedom.'

The guests raise theirs too, leaving sparkling lights around the room. 'Freedom.'

Minutes later, the chatting and mingling continues.

With his wife on his arm, Judge Clarence Cunningham approaches Reid through the crowd.

'Mr Reid,' he says, condescending.

'Cunningham.'

'Nice speech, Sir,' he shakes his hand, grip tight. Reid moves on and kisses Mrs Cunningham's cheek politely.

Back to Cunningham, he states, 'Good haul last week.'

'Yes, yes ... one hundred and fifty in, thirty-seven out. The remainder will be gone by sunrise, I expect. Evening sell. Where Scott says the bargains are made.'

'Profits?' Reid asks.

'Forty-three percent, I'm told. Down since last month. But I'd like to congratulate you on your purchase. Scott mentioned

it while I was getting the wife a martini. The donation you
made was very generous.'

'It was for my daughter. What Sera wants, Sera gets, no
questions asked.'

Mrs Cunningham's face is unreadable, red cheeks as glossy
as her lipstick. She smiles, cheek to cheek, but her mouth says,
'I do have a question, if I may.'

Reid waits. 'Go on.'

'How could you possibly let someone so dangerous around
your only child?'

'Not that I need to answer to you –' Cunningham is astounded
by the tone Reid is using with his wife but does nothing. '– but
no person poses any threat toward me or my daughter. That's
the way it works. It's a mutual agreement, made to set these
people on the path to true emancipation, while being useful
and gaining skills. More importantly, they stay social and in
the world that changes so vastly.'

'Danger is a matter of perspective,' she retorts.

'Exactly,' Reid agrees. 'If anything, we're the least likely to
be harmed.'

Mrs Cunningham isn't convinced, so her husband cuts the
tension.

'That's what's so beautiful about it. Unity and harmony.'

Subject-changing, Reid demands, 'Now, how are you and
the rest of the judges on the Foundation planning to get those
profits up?'

Talking, the three sit at a table, deep in conversation.

Across the room, Reid spots Mason and Briscoe at a table
alone, talking and laughing. He watches Mason with subtle
interest and she does not notice, so continues on animatedly.

On the dancefloor, Celeste dances in the arms of a nameless
man. She waves to Briscoe and he smiles back with a thumbs-up.

Mason raises an eyebrow. 'Bet you feel like the luckiest man in the world, having a catch like that on your arm.'

'You know, it didn't really occur to me,' he mutters, coy.

'I'm sure. Where is the food?'

'So … how's work been treating you since my departure?'

'Well in those eleven hours, it has been just as hectic as usual. Honestly, I don't feel in charge of anything. The CPS, the SFO, they run themselves and I can feel them pushing me out.'

'Who is?'

'You know who,' she scolds. 'All of them. Tall and the rest of her lot. She thinks she can kiss up to me when the first thing she was after this morning was your job. I'd rather die than give in to them.'

They watch Tall as she networks with Frost and the other MPs.

'They're trying to get me out,' she repeats. 'They can feel my hesitancy.'

'Do you really think so?' He is only half-listening. 'You're a little paranoid, you know.'

'And then there's our dear prime minister.'

'Don't start …'

'He got rid of you, Kevin!'

'All the more reason to stay quiet. He has people everywhere and tonight they don't even have to hide.'

They both look around.

'Well, look at Reid. He's been sucked into this thing from day one, so blind to the truth that we're no better with the new system than we were ten years ago. In fact, we're worse off. So much worse.'

'Dolly …'

'Seriously, Kevin, do not call me that. Amending the Criminal—'

'And it's my fault your parents are partial to American country music?'

'Amending the Criminal Justice Act so drastically has made

the country worse. Criminals are on the streets. Worse, they're in people's homes and in their lives. Hospitals are running out of materials and staffing is low. Like that helps cancer patients and spreading pandemics! They have a surplus of beds because people are too broke to pay for care since the NHS was shut down, leaving sick people to fend for themselves with backstreet barbers and dealers and whoever else they can find. People are being sold like livestock. I mean, this isn't healthy. And when the EU broke away from us rather than the other way around … you know we did something really wrong. Then there's the revolting Commonwealth. I'm all for freedom but they're blocking us left and right. We're low on imported goods, food, medical supplies and we're a tiny island who have lived for centuries off taking from others. I haven't seen a banana in months, Kevin. How will we survive? If we carry on this way, we'll turn into a second-world country for sure, if we're not already.'

'Quiet, Dolly. Mouthing off like this won't help any, especially if you think there's a conspiracy to get you out. Come to think of it, if there was, why haven't they just fired you?'

'I don't know. But it's really unsettling.'

She gulps a glass of champagne and Briscoe notices Reid watching her with suspicion.

'You know … I don't think Reid is entirely there.'

Mason turns to look at Reid and he looks away. 'How do you mean?' she asks.

'He says all of these things because he should, to please Frost, but I don't think his heart is in it. I don't think he believes in anything anymore.'

'I don't even think Frost believes half of the stuff he regurgitates.'

'If you were to ask me,' Briscoe states, 'it's Reid who's walking on thin ice.'

'No, he's got the sympathy vote, hasn't he?'

'Oh yes, I forget.'

'She was nice.'

'Must be, if you're complimenting her. Rarity.'

'She was?'

'No. You complimenting people.'

'What? She was a kick-ass barrister.'

'She gave you a run for your money.'

'No. She didn't, but her death definitely saved his job. Wish I had a dead husband. People might give me a break.'

Second glass swallowed, she watches as waiters begin to appear, taking down order and bringing out trays of food.

'It's about time. I'm starving here.'

The scene is one of celebration, delight and honour. People settle down to their tables to eat. From the other side of the room, Tall and Celeste join Mason and Briscoe at their table.

'Not even a potato on the menu,' Mason complains. 'What is going on?'

'I heard that that up-and-coming chef from Norwich did the menu,' Tall says.

'And it's not his fault winter sucks and we can't import,' Briscoe titters.

'Who?' Mason asks, eyeing the menu.

'You know, that guy who's all over the television. I can't remember his name. Denn – Dawson? Began with a D, I think?'

'Norm Dillis,' says Celeste.

'That's him,' Tall agrees.

From the opposite side of the room, a pair of waiters walk towards the tables and cross each other, exchanging covered silver trays so quickly that no one notices. The waiter who receives the tray carries it to the buffet table and uncovers it to reveal a handgun and a grenade.

A guest, unaware and slight, sees the gun and panics,

screaming. 'Gun! Get down!'

A ripple of panic spreads. A gunshot and the lights are gone.

Blackout.

BANG. BANG.

Screams and rushed footsteps.

BANG. BANG. BANG.

A colossal explosion.

Three

B ANG. BANG.
    The camera topples, goes out of focus, shows passing,
running feet, is seemingly picked up and taken through the
screaming crown in a hurry, showing nothing more than faded
darkness, flashes of light, the occasional evening gown and
dirt-covered limbs.
    BANG. BANG. BANG.
    As the ceiling collapses, the video cuts off and prompts replay.
    Sera hits the replay button, nothing in her eyes, watching the
video show the arrival of the prime minister and other guests.
    She stands outside a hospital ward in a dark corridor with
concrete walls and floors, prison bars and security doors in
the distance. This hospital, like many others, had been created
inside an old and dilapidated prison. Each cell has a bed or
two, beds in corridors, barred doors in the open corridors and
guards on standby at huge protective doors. The doctors and
nurses wear various shades of black, grey and white. Despite
the vast number of beds lining the walls, there are piles of

opened and unopened air mail packages on top and beside them, aid from other countries, used needles, gauze and other basic medical supplies in waste bins, lying around, cluttering the limited space.

The suffering yell out in pain.

She turns away from the video on her phone to a woman in white wearing a name badge stating, 'Rosine Shaw, Nurse', who, pushing aside emotion and weakness, rinses out a cloth in bucket of water and places it back on the forehead of a shaking pneumonia patient.

The patient, dying, opens his tired eyes and takes Rosine's gloved hand with the slightest touch.

Rosine looks back with sympathy, understanding and even love.

Sera looks on in wonder as the patient goes limp and Rosine removes a pillow from beneath his head at a panicked yet controlled speed; she tries to save his life but before she can complete checking his airway, he is rigid and lifeless before Sera's eyes.

The nurse stands, numb, staring at the wall. Knowing that she is being watched, she turns to Sera but the young girl looks back to the video on her phone entitled 'MP shooting footage' before their eyes meet.

Sera lets a tear fall down her face silently, her nose growing stuffy.

Rosine covers the patient with a blanket and pushes the corpse towards the lift. She passes a room and, inside, lies Lord Reid and Sidra Tall, comatose and pale, parallel, entangled in a web of wires and tubes that ensure their survival.

The life support echoes the sound of two pulses.

In the corner of the room, injured and dirty, bedraggled and tired, are Mason and Briscoe.

It had taken Mason three hours to get away from the hotel.

Somehow, she had emerged from beneath the white tablecloth and the upended table that came with it and out of the swinging doors. She did not even notice the bodies she had to step over to do it. Someone's hand guided her down all those flights of stairs to the ground floor. She did not even notice the scratches on her knuckles and knees and the bruise on her cheek. On the street, people scattered. It was a disaster, and screams hurled out of people's mouths and panic and debris polluted the air. She had been sitting with a crying Celeste for thirty-five minutes while Briscoe went back inside to help, stroking her head quietly and occasionally telling the paparazzi to piss off. The police, the bomb squad and ambulances descended in vast numbers, the soldiers in black raiding the building, relieving survivors, noting the dead and searching for those they thought responsible.

A paramedic tended to Celeste's sprained wrist and then she waited for Briscoe, crashing into his arms when he finally got back to them. Sure that Mason was alright, he left to take his girlfriend home, promising to see her later. Sat on the back of the ambulance while getting her vitals taken, Mason had seen Frost being carted off in a huge black van by his security and witnessed various members of parliament leave the scene. Others stayed to wait for their friends and colleagues, others cried for the dead. Mason had seen at least three body bags at this point and feared who they might be.

Her hands had gone over her mouth when she had seen people being taken out of the building like pieces of meat. At first, Mason thought they were dead. Now she knows that they may as well be.

'If you live by the word, you die by the word,' Mason whispers.

'What word?' Briscoe asks.

'Compliance. Ignorance. Greed. Subservience. Fear.'

'That's not fair.'

'Stupidity. Neglect. All of the above,' she adds. 'Where is she?'

Briscoe nods towards Sera in the corridor and Mason walks out to her.

'Do you have anywhere to stay?'

'Oh, but we just met, Ms Attorney General.'

'You know who I am.'

'Yes.'

'Your dad's gonna be okay, you know.' She did not know what else to say.

'That's what they said about my mum and that was a lie. Are you a liar?'

Mason, again stumped, stands and looks over to Briscoe, consumed with both horror and relief. She leaves and heads home without another word.

Back at headquarters, Mason walks through the corridors, eyes downcast. People in other offices watch her with concern and curiosity as she sweeps towards her office.

George can be heard at his desk nearby, talking sternly into the telephone. 'Haven't you seen the news? Well, if you turn your television on, you'll see that there has been a slight political hiccup, and when I say 'slight', I do mean potentially cataclysmic, Mr Dunn. Mr Dunn, Ms Mason is very busy at the moment. Yes, at this specific moment. If you flick to channel one, you'll – Yes … Listen, fax and BCC all of the treason documents to our machine and to the PM's office and we'll be good to go and all without bothering Ms Mason. Well, how many do you have?'

Mason walks by, jaded. 'Evening,' she whispers.

Into the phone, he questions, 'Twenty-three? Evening,' he

replies to his boss. He notices that she is upset and stunned, especially when she closes the door to her office behind her. He instantly puts the phone down.

When he enters, Mason is slumped in her chair, gazing up at the ceiling, occasionally spinning in her chair.

'George, what am I doing here?'

'Took the words right out of my mouth.' He gazes at her, not recognising the woman before him. 'Are you alright? I called you about a hundred times.'

'I thought I told you to never ask me that.' She attempts a smile.

'I think an assassination attempt qualifies for a change in protocol every now and again. So?'

'So, I've never been more scared in my life.'

'Well, I'm glad to see you anyway.' She smiles as he picks up her tablet from her desk, going into her appointments. 'Lauren and Becky saw it first. The news. Got it up on the computer, then Toby called me—'

'Who?'

'Toby. Toby Basilden. CPS admin.'

'Of course,' Mason replies, lying.

'So, Toby called and I used my God-given initiative to push all of your morning appointments to the afternoon, I've blocked some of the phone lines for twenty-four hours so that only head offices can contact you and as soon as the tabloids started harassing us – which was literally ten seconds after the last gunshot – I gave them a false trail saying that you were being treated at a hospital in Essex.'

'And you did all of this assuming that I was alive?'

'I really hoped so. If not for the recognition of my skill during a crisis but because I actually like you, Ms Mason.'

'Are you okay, George?'

'I'm okay now.'

'Do you know what? Take the night off. If you like.'

'No, I need the money. And I'm supposed to be here. You're not.'

'George, I have to keep busy. I can't just sit at home.'

George stares at her as she sits up and looks at the things on her desk without conviction or purpose.

'Could you … give me a minute?' she asks.

'I'll be at my desk.'

He excuses himself and leaves.

As soon as he disappears, Mason dissolves into her own version of complete sorrow, hand clutching her chest with her eyes closed yet she is focused on coming back. She has to return to reality.

After a moment, she hears George talking to Briscoe outside her door. 'Do not go in there, Mr Briscoe. Mr Briscoe, please. She wants to be—'

'Understandable, but she's fine, George. I have news.'

The attorney general puts herself back together, sits up straight, fixes her hair and puts on her glasses.

Outside, George persists. 'I think we've all had enough news for today, so if you wouldn't mind making an appointment or calling in in the morning ...'

Mason begins to read the first piece of paper she can reach.

'Trust me, she'll want –' Briscoe enters, phone in hand. '– to hear this.' He smiles at her. 'Guess which video got fifty thousand hits in only ten minutes online? Guess?' Like her, he is still covered in dust.

'Don't tell me. A breakdancing baby.'

'No.'

'I do miss those videos.'

'Survivor footage. Well, it was meant to document the celebrations. A cameraman uploaded a glorious four-minute segment. Better than selling it. Instant notoriety. And social media's gone crazy. "Hashtag Pray for MPs." Not that most of these people online believe in anything.'

He hands her the phone but she doesn't take it.

'Somehow, I doubt that the three dead MPs and twelve seriously injured guests would call this glorious. You do realise that this is the biggest slaughter of MPs and the like in history. This is a very huge deal. I was on the Tube the other day and there was a woman on the phone, Eastern Asian, I think. She was speaking to someone and laughing about something in particular. And then this other woman goes over to her and taps her on the shoulder and says, "I know you're talking about me and how I'm dressed. I speak Mandarin too. I teach it actually." Her face fell. She assumed that just because she didn't look like she knew Mandarin, that she didn't know Mandarin. Do you see what I'm saying?'

'Absolutely not.'

'Jeez, Kevin, I'm saying you have to be careful who's listening!'

He sighs. 'Go on then.'

'What?'

'Tell me.'

'Tell you what, Kevin?'

'I know you're bursting with a theory or two, so come on. Hit me.'

'No theories necessary. They were after Frost. It is way too much of a coincidence that the two people Frost was talking to all night happened to be hurt in a pretty critical way.'

'But others were actually killed, so what is your point here? I thought you said they were after you.'

'Unless Frost fixed it, of course.'

'Hey, you cannot accuse the prime minister of attempted murder.'

'And conspiracy to overthrow the government,' she adds.

'His own government? Really? Dolly.'

'For his own gain. Tonight was all about sending a message.'

'We'll never know that!'

'Well, no, not for sure. I couldn't see. You shoved me under the table.'

'Would you rather I let you—?'

'Help people? Be a witness?!'

'By getting killed?! That helps no one!'

'No one but Frost and his rabble of miscreants. Just talking about them puts a bad taste in my mouth.'

'So don't work for the guy, Dolly. Leave.'

'I've never worked for him, Kevin. I'm here for the people, to get justice for all of the injustice his system has created, for all of the innocent lives criminals have taken and imposed themselves upon and those wrongly convicted, sentenced and sold for the past decade. It is wrong. As soon as I heard about the idea of it, I knew it was wrong. I appreciate your concern but this isn't about me or you.'

'I care about you, idiot! Is that a crime?'

'Kevin, you're not my big brother or anything like that so please stop acting like it. I can take care of myself.'

'Fine.' Clearly hurt, he leaves.

'Shit,' Mason curses. She rushes after him and into the oddly busy office – clearly the events of the evening had drawn in the early workers.

Once she reaches him, she taps his shoulder and he faces her.

'How would you like to work under me again?' she blurts.

'As long as I don't have to care for you.'

Mason is the one who is hurt now but covers it smartly with joy. 'It seems we're in need of a new DPP.' Briscoe says nothing. 'Okay then. I'll see you at Sidra's desk tomorrow.'

He nods, surrendering, and leaves.

Relieved, Mason finally breathes and then notices that the

others in the office had been watching the whole incident.

'Did I disturb you?'

They all get back to work in a hurry.

Security guards, one very heavy, the other very lazy, patrol the corridors of a dimly lit row of cells, guns in their belts. The night has set in, as well as fatigue, and they sit languidly against the walls.

Inside the farthest cell, CA45JM sits with her head against the concrete wall, knees to her chest and Lord Reid's face in her mind – that, coupled with the look of joy she witnessed on his daughter's face. She stifles her sadness and fury.

Sharing the holding cell with her are TR152P and AM277S, few of the many sold that evening for their actions.

TR152P pushes her light hair behind her ears and places her hands over her mouth. 'Christ.' She stares at the ground, hopeless. 'Christ. This is it.'

On the other side, AM277S stands awkward, nonplussed and vague. 'Didn't I tell you that we'd all go? I said that. Was only a matter of time. I bet the No-Sales are having a party right about now. "Break out the bunting, no slave labour tonight!" And, at the end of it all, my life is worth nine thousand pounds.'

Out of her daze, CA45JM says, 'Just your freedom, Alex.'

'The only consolation is the fact that our debts are clear, I suppose,' TR152P utters, solemn.

'Except now I have to spend four years of my life with some random woman in whatever role she chooses all because I couldn't afford my council tax,' says AM277S.

'All I'm guilty of is trying to send my children to school,' TR152P states.

'What happened?' CA45JM asks.

'I have six children. I started young and they're mostly all grown up and gone, got careers and made the most of themselves before all of this. My youngest two are five and nine. My nine-year-old, Joseph, went to our local school for free for years. Years. But, by the time it was Nick's turn, the school had been closed, merged with two other schools and relocated to the Old Eastway prison. All in the space of four years. And they were charging five hundred pounds a term per child. I know some people can afford it and more, but I just couldn't. And I worked two jobs so it wasn't like I could teach them at home. There weren't enough hours in the day. But I tried. I got a third job at the sweatshop factory, paid my niece to childmind after school. But she got married and left the country as soon as she could with her new husband. Brazil or something. The next thing I knew, I was sent bill after bill from the school and I tried to pay and then I had to pull them both out of school and then I got an eviction notice from my landlord and then I was dragged out onto the street by the police and I haven't seen Joe and Nick since. Probably in some grotty care home wondering where I am, scared out of their minds.'

Her mouth trembles.

'How long has it been?' CA45JM asks quietly.

'I don't remember. A few months?' She begins to cry, hard and AM277S comforts her. 'I just know it's been too long.'

AM277S rubs her arm slowly. 'What about you?' he asks CA45JM. 'You never told us.'

'It's stupid. Anyway, I don't plan to be at the beck and call of some Lord or whatever because of it.'

'Two hundred and fifty thousand pounds …' AM277S muses. 'Who would pay that?'

'I'm sure that was meant as a compliment,' CA45JM replies.

'No, I honestly don't think anyone has ever been sold for that much. It's like a house record or something. Then again, I don't think they've ever caught anyone with as much debt as you. It's all dependent on that, isn't it? So that it's fair.'

'It's not a big deal. And fair isn't a word I'd use. They're out there. Hundreds of people with more money troubles than Europe. Difference is, they have the means to stay unnoticed. In plain sight. I was just unlucky.'

TR152P resurfaces and wipes her eyes. 'Unlucky how?'

Ignoring her, she stares at the security guards and mutters, 'Did you notice that, every hour and twelve minutes, give or take, Security Guard One goes for coffee, which means that Number Two goes to the bathroom every half an hour and Three switches out with The One Who Looks Like A Lumberjack every Friday at midnight, leaving seven minutes of opportunity?'

'Meaning?' the mother of six questions.

'The Lumberjack wouldn't be able to run very fast.'

'Yes, but neither would I,' TR152P counters.

'It's almost Saturday,' CA45JM observes, looking the happiest she had been since they met her. She pulls out and key fob she had been hiding in her shoe and checks the wall clock and watches as the hands point towards midnight.

'Where did you get that?,' AM277S asks her, excited.

'Someone dropped it, obviously. No one said security guards had to have high IQs to do their jobs.'

'Rude,' AM277S utters. 'You know what this means, if we go?'

'I don't think I can do it,' TR152P interjects. 'I can't run. I can't do this. What if it just makes it worse? They'll just throw us back in here, only for life.'

'You're forgetting they don't do that anymore,' CA45JM reminds her. 'And they can't take our lives if they can't get to us. I have spent years trying to get away from these people and you can be sure that I am not going to let them steal my life. I refuse. Now are you coming or not? Because I'm leaving, with or without you.'

Mason muses by the coffee machine, thinking about what to do next. She waits for her cup to fill with the instant coffee she likes. No doubt, there will be a full-scale investigation into the attack and already the media had begun to chase their bone. Milk. The television and the radio yell things like terror and panic, yet Mason knows this threat is not from outside the UK. It smells local and it feels like a fight to the death.

A sprinkle of sugar and she knows that she has to prepare for the court case of her career if the police catch the perpetrators. She makes a note to herself to contact the most laidback son of a bitch she knows, the commissioner of the City of London police.

George yells, 'Urgent call from the prime minister, Ms Mason.'

The office freezes.

'George …'

'No excuses, I'm putting you through.'

'Fine. I'll take it in my office.' She skips back through to the desk, slamming the door behind her. After a moment, the phone rings and she answers.

'Good evening, Prime Minister.'

An unconscious security guard lays in the cell, the bars closed and locked. Some prisoners in the other cells cheer CA45JM, AM277S and TR152P on, some are sour and jealous. The three escapees sprint down the corridor, CA45JM with a mass of key fobs and a swollen fist, as the alarm is sounded and the lights flash. They freeze, for a moment, and then continue to run towards the atrium.

Two members of security appear behind them. AM277S

throws a chair and they fall down, one passing out. CA45JM kicks the other, knocking him out and taking his gun.

Another guard sees this and pursues them; they are forced into one of the courtrooms, which CA45JM quickly opens with a key fob, the second of three.

They enter the cold courtroom. It is ghostly quiet and eerie. All seats lay vacant and shadows cover the dark wood, ominous. There is an emergency exit on the other side of the room that they immediately head for.

The security guard, having followed them in, catches AM277S by the arm and holds a gun to his back.

CA45JM tries to shoot but it jams.

The gun safety is removed by trembling fingers.

No matter how much CA45JM cares for AM277S, she cannot shoot the security guard, despite his eyes begging. She fires a warning shot into the air instead, causing chips of wood to fall on top of them.

More security flood in behind them through the door and, during this distraction, TR152P throws one of her shoes at the security guard and AM277S tackles him to the ground, a knee smashing into the guard's forehead.

CA45JM drops the gun.

They run for the emergency exit and rush out under a hail of bullets.

Photographers, cameramen, journalists and security line the entrance of the hospital. The prime minister gets out of his car and begins the journey inside through the incessant crowd.

'Good evening?' he half-yells down the phone. His headset hangs from his ear as he wades through the crowds with three heavy bodyguards. 'Four MPs – so far – are dead, dozens injured, two critical …'

Journalists shout and call to Frost as he walks towards the doors.

'Prime Minister, do you have any comments on the events of this evening?'

'Do you admit to any responsibility for this tragedy?'

'Back it up. Please,' his bodyguard hollers.

'Mr Frost, how will the guilty parties be punished if you can ever find them?'

Frost walks through the dilapidated halls of the old hospital, through the typhoid and cancer patients in beds lining the halls, some nurses wearing masks over their mouths and noses. He goes through various secure doorways, requesting a mask of his own.

'What happened?' Frost questions.

'Have you tried the Internet, Sir?' Mason responds.

'Do you think this is a joke?'

'I know what this is,' she counters. 'Back in the day, they called it rebellion. And this needs to be handled like it was before. Trial by jury in the Crown Court followed by a very heavy and very final mandatory prison sentence.'

As she speaks, Frost stops outside a small private room in the Intensive Care Unit, watching a doctor check over Tall. On the other side of the room is Reid; the hospital is too small and overworked for separate rooms yet the doctors claim it is to reduce media exposure to keep them secure and enclosed.

'You seem to be forgetting that it is 2051 and that the law has changed, Ms Mason. And with the law, people change and lives change.' He turns away from the victims. 'I actually called you for a reason.'

'Yeah?'

'I just received a call from the security at the Crown. Not only are we dealing with conspirators and killers, but an unknown number of prisoners are attempting to escape the holding cells at the Crown Court. Four people have been injured, one prisoner shot dead.'

Lying in the doorway of the emergency exit is TR152P, with a bullet hole in the back and taking shallow breaths as she dies. CA45JM looks on in horror.

'Come on!' AM277S yells at her. 'Move it!'

'What do you need?' Mason asks.

'I need you to contact the Yard and see what they're doing to get these conspirators while I handle the fallout.'

'Murder is worse than conspiring, Frost.'

'Not from where I'm standing. We need to find out who they were after and who sent them. This is a matter of great importance and way beyond the police's power and experience to handle. Take a team and get your arse down there if you need to. Report to me in six hours. Downing Street.'

'Okay.' She pauses, thinking. 'What happens if these prisoners escape?'

'They were meant to pay their debt to society. And they will pay, even if I have to hunt every one of them down myself.'

'A bit dramatic, don't you think?'

'Hardly.'

He hangs up.

A few streets away from the Crown Court, CA45JM and AM277S rush into a dark alley overgrown with bushes and thickets, with all intentions of running through and to the other side to find shelter and sanctuary, however CA45JM slows down and holds her chest. Sirens ring out.

'I can't breathe. I can't … Stop …'

She stops and doubles over, breathing deeply.

AM277S turns to her, impatient. 'We need to go.'

'No, no, Alex … I can't run.'

'They will catch us if we don't keep moving. You don't want to end up like—'

'I didn't think any of us would die! Do you honestly think I would have done this otherwise? I thought, if we failed, they'd just take us back, I thought they'd play by the rules.'

'What rules? There are no rules anymore.'

'I know that, Alex. But she never got to see her children and it's all my fault.'

'No, it's their fault.'

'It's mine.'

'Fight your conscience elsewhere. We don't have the time.'

'We didn't think this through. Where will we go? How can we possible avoid being caught when the entire police force and every member of the public will be searching for us?'

'I don't know. We just lie low, maybe? Keep out of sight.'

'Amazing plan.'

'You're the one who's done this before! We're out. Focus on that. We're not being sold off to anybody. We're free.'

'That depends on your definition of freedom.'

'Do you see any locks or bars?' AM277S asks.

'No.'

'Well, I call that freedom.'

'I call it time,' CA45JM says.

'I'm glad you realised. We have to go now or all of this will be for nothing.'

'Where?'

'A friend of mine, well, an associate, lives about thirty miles from here. Ellis Grier. Fraud guy. Moonlights as a farmer during the day, helping out his parents.' He chuckles.

'And?'

'We need passports, ID, bank accounts …'

'Great. More illegality.'

'What did you expect? We can't just go on the run. We have to blend in.'

She pauses for a moment to consider the logic of his argument. The authorities would be looking for two homeless, bedraggled and starving jailbreaks, but if they could survive and get money, a house and even a job, they could fool everyone. Last time, she had done things differently.

'Okay.'

'Okay. So, we've broken out of a Crown Court, avoided a life of servitude and escaped death together. Do you think you might bless me with a name?'

'What name?'

'Your name.'

'CA45JM.'

'No, I meant your real name.'

'If it suits the system, it can suit you too, Alex.'

'Well it doesn't suit me. I told you all about me.'

'We have to go, remember?'

She runs out of the alley and he follows her until they reach the side entrance of a charity shop. She breaks the weak padlock on the shutters with a grotty brick and rolls them up.

'People are so poor these days they don't bother with decent security. Least of all charity shops.'

'I see,' Alex comments.

CA45JM uses the same brick to smash through the glass window in the door and enters.

The air is hollow and dusty inside, rack of clothes to the left and shelving all around. They instantly head towards the displays and change quickly without talking about it, removing their grey jumpsuits and thumbing through hangers for new clothes.

'So where does your friend live?' CA45JM asks.

'Just out of the city. The last I knew he was around the corner from a farmer's market just after a garden centre. But he has a flat which he rent from his parents above a café between a charity shop and a bakery in the centre of Surrey.'

'Could this friend do anything about our tattoos?' She was referring to the small infinity symbol on the insides of their wrists and the wrists of everyone who has ever been forced into servitude. This way, everyone would know what they had done and what they had been through. 'We're branded, remember? Easiest way to get caught, handing money over in a shop, flagging down a bus or a taxi … going sleeveless …'

'Maybe. No harm in … asking …' Alex is distracted, looking into the sky through the window.

'There aren't any helicopters.' She pulls on a dark grey jumper and a beanie hat.

'Yeah? What's that then?'

A helicopter circles, trying to be as discreet as possible and she runs over to the window to get a better look. There is no search light but the hum of the blades are quite clear.

'Which means the police aren't far behind,' Alex deduces.

'Look,' CA45JM points.

They both glance at the police cars and vans which stop outside in the alley. They panic, hearts beating fast, stepping away from the front of the shop.

'There has to be another way out,' she stutters. 'Employee entrance? Delivery bay?' She rushes to the back of the shop without hesitation as the police enter. She freezes, noticing that Alex is not right behind her.

'Alex!' she whispers.

Guns and light pour in all directions in search of the two escapees.

'On the ground! Now!'

'On the ground!'

'Don't move!'

'Hands behind your head!'

Alex puts up his hands, stunned and unable to see. He is tackled to the ground with guns pointed at him.

CA45JM hears the commotion and sprints to the back of the shop, heart hammering in her ribs.

'Where's the other one?'

A police officer notices two sets of jumpsuits on the ground and nods towards the back exit. A door beyond slams as it swings shut and CA45JM runs like her life depends on it although her chest aches.

She is unsure of if she hears footsteps behind her. Meanwhile, Alex is behind, handcuffed, upset and angry, although dazed.

'Did you hear that?' the tall shadowed men ask each other.

'Hurry up!'

A group of them run to the back of the shop and out of the doors only to find nothing in the darkness as CA45JM runs until she has no feeling left.

05.21 a.m. Breaking news with Celeste Landau. She is sitting at the news desk reading the words from the teleprompter, her bandaged wrist and bruised forehead on full display.

'The country has been put on alert after the escape and attempted escape of three prisoners from the Crown Court. The three had been sold at Auction early this evening and were to be delivered to sellers the following morning, but fought their way out of the building using physical force and assorted weaponry …'

In Briscoe's constituency of Richmond Park, he walks from his office within his modest apartment, walls aptly covering with certificates and other declarations, to his bedroom with a cup of coffee, were the television is on and the breaking news is being reported on the large screen. The blue banner states the words, 'BREAKOUT: PRISONER ESCAPES CROWN COURT AUCTION.' Briscoe watches eagerly, watching his girlfriend's plain face as she speaks in her best broadcasting voice.

'… with one prisoner killed on site and the other detained after the escape had taken place. The final prisoner, described as a five-foot-five black female in her mid-twenties, has evaded arrest, her whereabouts currently unknown …'

After a long shift at the hospital, Rosine finally pulls up in the large family car onto the driveway at home. Exhausted, she locks her car, places the keys in the front door and goes inside, looking forward to the warmth and the rest.

She takes off her jacket and shoes and puts them in their usual place, narrowly avoiding the wheelchair folded at the bottom of the stairs. The keys go into the bowl on the table and, with her bag on her shoulder, Rosine squeezes past a stairlift and then drags herself up thirteen steps. First, she checks on her son, Edwin, the teen asleep in his bed and then carries on to her own.

Her side of the bed warmly welcomes her and she settles next to her sleeping husband, Rex, and, while getting changed out of her bloodstained white uniform, she switches the television on with the remote control. He stirs and she instantly turns the volume down to soothe him.

The breaking news continues.

'Coroners confirm the death of one prisoner in the early hours of this morning, which police describe as a 'necessary action enforced to maintain a better society.' In keeping with the UK's criminal law, the detainees were treated as hostile upon their attempt of freedom ...'

Rex rolls over to watch the television, half-asleep.

'Hey,' he whispers.

'Hi.' She kisses his cheek.

'What happened?'

Rosine nods towards the TV and they watch together.

'... authorities decide on the best course of action. For now, a nationwide search has been put into operation in order to find the inmate identified as CA45JM, last seen at a charity shop west of Covent Garden, no longer in a grey jumpsuit.' An artist's drawing appears on the screen, bearing a likeness to CA45JM, along with a hotline phone number. 'Here is an artist's sketch of the prisoner. Please call this number or the police if you see anyone who bears any resemblance to this woman. The prime minister has stated that those who try to evade reparation will be stopped and brought to justice ...'

Mason is out on a morning run, earlier than usual to stop the noise in her head, listening to the news on the radio through wireless earphones as she powers down the street at an easy pace.

'The prime minister has authorised a manhunt for the escaped prisoner with full haste. We will have the commissioner of the City of London police, Bhavesh Shah, who organised the retention of the second escapee, speaking to us live in an hour and updated reports will continue. The MP shooting, which occurred yesterday, is said to not be linked to the Crown Court escape at this stage. The shooting has awakened the House of Parliament following the deaths of four MPs at a city hotel where a dinner was being held. Countless others were injured when an unknown number of conspirators engaged in what seemed like an orchestrated attack on members of parliament, judges and those in legal and political standing as they celebrated the first decade of the reformed criminal justice system.'

Mason runs back to her flat, up the steps and to the front door. She wipes her forehead angrily.

'The prime minister, attorney general and members of the New Supreme Court were also present. The names of the dead have not yet been released but families have been notified. Some have said and others will agree that this has been a trying day for England, both events of the tonight shocking the nation. It is 5.30 a.m. Stay tuned for more news.'

She locks the front door and undresses, heading to the shower.

Four

Loneliness is her forte, or so she thought. Day one is the hardest, they say, but days two, three, four and all of the rest are achingly lengthy, where minutes feel like hours, hours like days, days are weeks and time never ends. Or so they say.

It is five hours since she left Alex behind and the sun has not yet risen. The air is cold and the darkness is deep. The best places are in the shadows so she starts on the stretching planes of Aboveground, keeping away from the bright lights and cars Below. The risk, as always, is the open air without shelter. This domain is what they all dreamed of, open land for play and pleasure, where birds can fly and sing and live and children and the elderly alike can roam without the threat of cars and smoke and the daily rush of life at nine and five.

Left, right, one step in front of the other and she tries to remember what it is like to chew and swallow and feel content. Her stomach groans, having missed the small evening meal of bland rice pudding that she often looked forward to. One step and then the next and she walks towards a large patch of parkland and wonders around for a place to sleep for the night and, perhaps, into most of the day to take her mind off her unrelenting hunger.

'Shut up,' she tells her stomach forcefully. 'Don't embarrass me around all these people.' Her only company is the night sky above her and the twinkling lights blanketed within. They remind her of the star signs and the cliché of gazing with a lover, something she had never done. It was like making shapes out of clouds and castles out of sand, a means of killing time. She has a lot, or very little but she wishes she knew which.

Her plan is to walk, to walk as far as she can every day, rest and then walk again. With no wish to find a permanent abode, she wants to walk to the far stretches of the earth and back, to keep going and to survive.

Focusing on the crunch of leaves underfoot, counting each one, she walks until she reaches the next entrance to Belowground. Honking horns and the skidding of tyres against gravel can be heard, growing louder with every step and the glowing lights cut through the air. She hadn't seen it in so long and the temptation was rife.

Cautious, she looks over the edge at the tiled walls along the route below.

'Sorry.' Behind her, a man on a bike that she had not seen coming bumps into her during his dismount. Swiftly, he places his bicycle over his shoulder and rushes down the solid steps towards the transport systems of the city.

Curiosity tempts her forward.

She goes down the steps into a hollowed-out pathway, like an underpass or subway walkthrough or the route between London's tubes. Along the walls are various signs for Underground stations, train stations, bus stops, road markings and the next exit and/or local landmarks and street signs. A one-way walking system is in place as well as a 'No Loitering' sign.

Noticing a camera at the end of the tunnel, she turns away from it and is forced to stare upon a lonely old, grey man sat down on the ground with a blanket and a can of corned beef in his hand. Tucking her long plait safely under her hat, she approaches him, silent.

'There any chance you've got a tin opener?' he asks kindly.

She shakes her head and looks him over. Skinny and dirty; she could have been looking in a mirror. The poor all looked the same and could not be missed in a crowd. They were usually the ones on the floor begging or on the floor dying.

The dents in the top of the can show that he has been trying to break through for a long time. Maybe he was too weak to give it a real go, she did not know, but she takes the tin anyway, steps on it hard with her thick black boots and the lid gives way enough for her to prise it open for him without cutting herself too badly. The pink meat oozes out uncomfortably.

He scoffs the whole thing down within half a minute, forgetting she is watching.

He freezes. 'I'm sorry. I'm – I didn't ...'

'I've eaten.'

There is no breeze down there yet it is stone cold on the ground. She smiles at him with earnest and he smiles back.

After a moment, he leans over and covers her with the blanket. 'It'll go below freezing in about two hours.'

'Thank you.'

She talks to him, asks him his story and he replies with a tale of hard times and loss. He has a job working in the sweatshop that manufactures the grey prison jumpsuits amongst other things. He pays for his mother's bed in her nursing home and he pays for his corned beef. Sacrifice is the compromise of the day and he has to choose between one or the other; he chooses the woman who gave him the air in his lungs.

Once he sleeps, she tucks him in tight with his blanket,

stretches her tired muscles and starts again, hoping that just with pure will she can make it from night to night. She forgets that she had done this before, only before she had money and she had no idea what it was like to live without it.

An open-ended truck is pelting down an empty country road, mud slashing in its wake as a heavily pregnant Irish woman screams in the back. Wind blowing in her face, she is in unimaginable pain. Her legs are splayed as she desperately clutches at her stomach and the ropes and crates around her. Her sweating husband occasionally glances back at his screaming wife as he drives with less than the optimal amount of focus over bumps and through ditches.

'Only seven more miles, my love. Please hang on.'

'Seven?! Paul, can't you go any faster? Please!' Edith screams painfully and cries. 'This thing is coming out now. Right now!'

'Six and a half! I meant six and a half miles. I think. We just need to go past the school and across the river and that should only take a few minutes. Just – just hold it in until we get to the doctor.'

'Hold it in?! I can't. I physically can't. Please just hurry up!'

Her toes curl and her hands grasp the side of the truck.

Paul panics. 'Oh God. Oh God, I knew we should have found a doctor who didn't practise so far away. I told you. I told you.' He turns to her as she sobs. 'I told you, Edith, that something like this could happen. But just hang on. I can go faster if you—'

Edith bashes the side of the truck forcefully.

'Watch where you're driving!'

Paul turns to the road. They have driven off the road and onto the grassy fields and farmland. He swerves back onto the narrow lane, causing them both to tumble around.

'Sorry!'

'Stop the car.' She screams a long scream and her legs quiver uncontrollably.

'What?'

'Stop the damn car!'

He stamps onto the brake and the truck skids and eventually stops by falling into a ditch. The engine and radiator begin to emit steam.

Paul tries the ignition. It does not start up.

'I think I broke the truck.'

He climbs into the back next to a silent Edith, crouching beside her.

'What is it?'

He looks down as his wife shows him something in a bundle of blankets. She sets aside a pair of grotty scissors. Exhausted, she lays back in order to breathe for a moment. Paul smiles affectionately and picks up his baby.

'A girl?'

Edith nods and glances at her husband and daughter.

Paul's face suddenly drops and changes to worry and intense panic.

'She's not breathing. She's not breathing.'

'What? How can she—?'

Edith looks at her small daughter, terrified.

'I – I didn't do anything. She just went limp and she's not breathing. Edie, what do I do? What do I do? She's losing colour.'

Their hearts race, tears well up and their bodies shake.

'I don't know!'

'What do I do? She's—'

'We need a doctor! Now.'

Edith takes the baby and begins to rock her as she lay next to her heart. Paul jumps off the back of the truck.

'It's less than a mile to the next town. There'll be a phone. I can run.'

'Okay, well go! But you get there and back as fast as you possibly can.'

Paul takes off sprinting southbound, almost disappearing in the darkness.

Edith holds her daughter desperately. 'Come on, baby. Come on, little girl. Daddy's gone for help. Breathe, please. Breathe for me. Come on.'

There is an audible pause. Something like fifteen seconds passes with nothing but Edith staring at her daughter in fear. And, just like that, the baby takes a breath and wails lightly, clearing her little lungs. Edith sighs happily, expressing complete happiness and smiles appreciatively.

'Yes. Yes, breathe … Thank God. Paul!'

Struggling, Edith pushes herself off the back of the truck slowly, holding her daughter in one arm and turns towards where Paul was running.

'Paul! Paul, come back to the car and look! You don't need—!'

As she walks closer, Edith sees, to her horror, a pile in the road. She begins to walk towards it and realises that the pile is her husband, crumpled and face down.

She screams far worse than she had done before and stumbles to him as her baby cries in response to her yelling.

He has the most impressive beard and matching moustache, smooth dark chestnut, wavy and well-oiled. Bhavesh Shah is older than she is yet more stylish – although that was not difficult. He has a dark bun tied at the back of his head, yet he looks suave and manly in his emerald tie, midnight blue shirt and grey suit, smouldering and brooding almost.

If Mason had time for love, he would be the perfect candidate. His teeth are uniform, white and complete, his office immaculate and, considering his role, an optimistic man with a kind nature. It was a shame that she finds him throwing a mini basketball into its equally mini-sized net in his socks, flexing his jaw as he leapt.

He cheers for himself after the ball flies across the length of the room.

She claps, sarcastic.

'Now you need to do as good a job at finding bad people.'

He turns. 'Oh, it's you!' he says, smiling. 'Come to suck the life's blood out of me? Well, try your best, Ms Mason, because I'm actually in a good mood today and –'

'When are you never?'

'– you're not going to ruin it.'

'I'll do my best.'

'Take a seat.' He sits down at his impressive desk, his old officer uniform framed on the wall and the hat propped on a stand beside it.

'I'd rather stand. This won't take long.'

He shrugs. 'Your choice. You came to talk about the biggest investigation this office has seen since 2040.'

'You could have fooled me, Commissioner. Not one person in here is bustling around anymore than they do usually.'

'But not any less, you'd agree?'

'Where are the bulletin boards and marker pens and drawing pins with maps and string?'

'Safely where they belong in the films. We're not just sitting on our arses, Mason. I've got fifty men searching the streets, the Internet, I've got help from MI5 and GCHQ on this, and it's not as though I can tell you anything anyway.' He smiles.

'Me?' She folds her arms angrily. 'You can't tell the attorney general the progress of an investigation that she could have been victim to?'

'You're not going to go all 'Swing Low, Sweet Chariot' on me, are you?'

'This is a pile of shit, Bhav. Who do I need to talk to to get someone to use their big words and explain what is happening with this country? The prime minister sent me here to—'

'Well, that is another story entirely.'

'Yes, I thought it might be.'

'Why didn't you say Old Frostie sent you?'

'I didn't think I had to. I have as much authority if not more than he does here, as lawyer to the Crown, whom I have a meeting with at the end of this week.'

'I never thought you were one to namedrop, yet here they all come, thick and fast ...'

'I never usually have to. Over the past year, things have, shall we say, changed.'

'Change is the word of the season, the name of the day, Mason. It's inevitable.'

'That's the problem. If only things could stay the same. Not as they are now but as they were. Don't get me wrong, there are elements of this new life which are great. Crime rates are phenomenal. But the poverty and the homelessness? Is it really worth it?'

'You're the MP, you voted for it.'

'I didn't. Majority rules.'

'Come here.' He stands and goes to his high-rise window from where you can see the whole City. She joins him, gazing at the hypnotic landscape. 'The view from Scotland Yard is a rare one.' He takes her shoulders. 'Don't forget, it's the minority that rule. People like Frosted Flake and you and I. There are millions of others out there without a voice, so use yours.'

'And this is what they call democracy.'

'Crazy, isn't it?' He sits again. 'So, how's things?'

'Good.'

'Your parents?'

'Still alive. Yours?'

'Still dead.' He smiles at her, glancing at her soft mouth. 'We should go for coffee. Or wine.'

'How many times have I told you that I'm not attracted to you?'

'Well, first of all, that is a lie. And second … well, there is no second point but I'm sure if you try it, it won't be as bad as you think. How long has it been?'

She gives him a look of discontent. 'Since what?'

He raises his eyebrows and laughs uncontrollably once she catches on.

'You cheeky bastard.'

'Listen, all I can do is try. I can only ask again in another few months when you come to see me again.'

'That could be sooner than you think, Bhav.'

'Is that a threat?'

'Just a friendly warning.'

'Nothing's friendly when Frost is involved. And since when did you go around like his servant-girl checking up on people at his command?'

'I don't.'

'Then what is this, Mason? A social call? You finally giving in to me?'

'He mentioned it but I'm mostly here for my own agenda.'

'Oh, crossed, double-crossed!'

'What are you talking about?'

'You're not sleeping with him, are you?' He winces.

'I'd rather die, Bhavesh.'

'Good.'

'Are you going to tell me your progress or not? I'm not Frost's bitch – that much is clear. And the King will want to know that something is being done and that His family is safe. And, God knows, I do not have the time for all of this glorious yet time-consuming banter. I have a pile of work waiting for me back at the office that needs to be done and the clock is ticking.'

'You really want to know?'

'Yes.'

'You really, really want to know?'

'Bhav.'

He leans back in this chair and the smile drops from his face. 'We have intelligence that this was an orchestrated attack planned from within the UK rather than outside. If it was Middle East, Russia, the strategy would be clear and you'd be debating this in Commons by now. But this seems to be just some nutter with issues. No one has been after politicians like this since Guy Fawkes and no one has been this successful. My guys have found no DNA but the cameras show that there could have been multiple waiters involved, so we're in the process of trawling through the agency's employment records to try and find links to criminals in our database, but obviously—'

'If it's someone clever, they might get people without a record to do the dirty work, fake names as well maybe.'

'Exactly. So, I have a small team doing that, as we have to cover all bases, and then another going through social media, newspapers, anything out of the ordinary that even smells like a distaste of politicians.'

'Let me guess, there's too much to go through.'

'Massively. There have been so many riots and protests in the last decade, I can't keep track. I don't know about you.' Mason nods. 'We've got our eye on anti-establishment groups, anyone who has written anything against the politics of today, bloggers, vloggers, journalists, professors, activists, trying to work by elimination.'

'Eliminating 75 million, one by one.'

'We have to start somewhere.'

'So, you're saying it's early days, come back in a fortnight?'

'You read my mind. Maybe we can meet over a cold beer and a bag of Doritos.'

'Never.'

'See how you feel.' She stands and shakes his hand but he lifts it and places a soft kiss on her skin. 'You know where to find me.'

'Always a pleasure,' Mason says.

There was something about him that makes her stomach lurch in that sweet way it does, however the amount of time it takes to get to the point with that man is not always worth it. He is tight with information, as he should be, fronting with a comfortable and chilled attitude. She always enjoys working with him, something which she suspects he already worked out.

Mason exits his office, saying goodbye to his counterfeit-blonde and unattractive personal assistant on the way out. Once down in the reception area, she is signed out and hops straight into her car where George is waiting in the driving seat, listening to the radio.

'How was it?'

'A bullet in the dark.'

'Oh crap.'

'Yeah.'

The journey to Downing Street does not take them long, no more than thirty minutes; the Belowground did not reduce London traffic as much as people though it would. Cyclists still rode beside the other vehicles, only there are less pedestrians using crossings and stalling the constant flow of movement.

When they arrive, various news broadcasters are lined up outside, no doubt covering the recent killings, the prison outbreak and questioning the running of the country in general.

Mason and George stop nearer the end of the road in a designated parking space and walk to the black door, waiting for security to clear them. Mason keeps her eyes low and does not satisfy the lingering prowess of the journalists surrounding them.

After a moment, they step inside, are searched and earn their way into the prestigious house.

'I'll wait here,' George says and he sits with the security, making conversation as he always does, running through vague details of the work he has to do, never saying too much when they ask how things are.

Mason is escorted to the prime minister with a clear badge on her chest, stating, 'Dolly Mason KC MP, Attorney General for England.'

As soon as they are left alone, she takes the badge off and puts it in her jacket pocket.

Frost is sat nestled in the window seat a significant other might occupy, on salmon pink buttoned velvet material with murder on his mind and a pen in hand.

'News?'

'Nothing happens overnight.'

'Did you know that my grandparents were homeless all of their lives?'

'Yes.'

'They lived near the shacks and hills and bordered the inner city of Soweto, in a half-made thing that gave them no real shelter. Homelessness is a matter of perspective but they felt that they had nowhere to house their new baby when she arrived.' Mason says nothing, waiting patiently. 'That must be why my mother resented them. And me. They were borne of poverty and me of privilege thanks to my dad, something she had not earned herself and only appropriated through greed and manipulation. They were so humble and nice. But I never saw them past the age of eight. My mother barely let me see them anyway and cut off all contact because of one argument. When I was eleven, Gramps passed and seven months later so did Grandma. She needed the company. She didn't die of a broken heart, she died of loneliness that only a family could give after losing her partner. You see, they were never married. She needed the support my mother failed to provide. If they'd have lived now, I'd have given them everything they needed and they'd never look back at the shack and the empty stomachs and a wailing baby and rainwater dripping through the roof and the sickness and the heartache.'

'There are people still in similar conditions that you could help.'

It takes him a moment to remember that she is still there but he turns to her softly.

'Glad you could make it. No progress from Shah, then?'

'He has ideas. But ideas –'

'Don't keep me warm at night.' No one kept him warm at night. He was alone in the cold.

'– don't keep the City safe.'

'And here I thought you'd be harping on about criminals on the street not making anything safe.'

'Took the words out of my mouth, Prime Minister.'

'On the contrary, Ms Mason. I plead for the affirmative. Giving freedom where detention took reign turns tables. People will not commit crimes if they have to really pay for their wrongdoings.'

'Or they reoffend because the price they pay is too low.'

'My staff hate me. All criminals, the lot of them. Mostly. They hate that they have to serve and would never commit another crime to avoid this kind of lifestyle.'

'You feel safe around them?'

'I have security.'

'Normal people don't.'

'You don't think I'm normal?'

Mason says nothing. She walks to the window to face him and he looks at her for the first time.

'Are you alright, Wilson?'

He really looks at her now, in a strange and timid way.

'I'm sorry?'

'What happened the other day was really, really close. You know I don't get scared but I was. I still am. As humans, we fear what we don't know or understand and we are fighting an elusive force with no name or face. They could have blown us all up with the touch of a button but they didn't. They shot people down in the most horrific and bloodthirsty way to make us stand up and take a good look. The terror we are used to targets civilians, not us. They'll try again.'

He says nothing.

'Wilson!'

'Do you think I'm stupid? I know how dangerous it is to be me right now. Don't think I don't. The best course of action right now would be to lie low and not let this change our duty. We find the perpetrators and bring them to justice. And we find the escaped prisoner.'

'Who?'

'They call her the Crown Court Convict. In the tabloids anyway.' He checks his watch. 'I have a meeting with Cunningham in ten minutes …'

'Sorry, I haven't had time to read up on anything properly.'

He clicks his tongue. 'Disappointing. Young girl with the largest debt known to man escaped the Crown Court at the same time as the shooting.'

'And you don't think it's a coincidence.'

'Not when she was just sold to the justice minister.'

Mason suppresses her shock. 'Reid bought her? For what?

As what?'

'I'm not one to speculate but it seems his daughter is in need of a new mother. Especially now.'

'So you're saying that she may be part of the whole scheme, to—'

'A plan to avoid a lifetime of servitude with a man she doesn't know and a child who isn't her own.'

'Have you replaced him yet?'

'Judge Scott is taking over the courts and Cunningham is advising me on legal matters but there is no replacement. Reid's not dead yet. He was my right-hand man. Find this woman and we break this whole thing.' He shoves a copy of *The Independent* into her hands. 'Page seven about sums it up. Anything else?'

'No, Sir.'

Mason leaves the grand living room cradling the newspaper delicately. Upon seeing her, George stands.

A security guard, Truman, stops her.

'You know who I am,' she complains. 'Hang on.' She searches her pockets and pulls out her visitor badge. 'There you go. Come on,' she says to George.

Ignoring questions from eager reporters once more, they walk calmly to the car and head back to the office.

Mason opens her X3 and sends a secure email to Shah with the words 'Crown Court Convict.' Within a few seconds, he sends back a sad face image. That meant he is on top of it.

She opens the paper and reads the article aloud to George: 'Listen to this. "Most Valuable Convict Escapes Justice. Aside from the tragic deaths at the Marsh Manor Hotel, in the early hours of Saturday morning a criminal due for justice escaped custody just hours after being sold to one of the victims of the attack. Lord Daniel Reid, a senior member of the New Supreme Court, was left in a coma after being shot three times by unknown attackers." Three times?'

George shrugs. 'Must have gotten the information from a nurse or somebody at the hospital.'

Mason looks solemn. She continues. '"The young woman due to serve Lord Reid is twenty-four years old and is named CA45JM. Her true identity has not been given. She was last seen in a charity shop near the Crown Court changing into a dark jacket and trousers and a woollen hat. She will have been branded with the infinity mark on her inner left wrist. Please be warned that she is dangerous. The police have not yet released details on her crimes but she has the highest debt since this system began a decade ago and was sold for a quarter of a million pounds, beating the record of jewel thief Marcell Syd, bought for one hundred and fifty thousand pounds by the jeweller he stole from. He was bought to become their Theft Awareness Officer to ensure the safety of their stock and to rehabilitate him in the hopes that he will not attempt the theft again once he finishes his fifty-year sentence with the company. CA45JM has a life sentence to serve and has not yet been seen since the escape. Searches have begun in Central London and the surrounding London boroughs. If anyone has seen CA45JM please –" call on this number, 020, blah, blah, blah. The world's gone mad.'

'Why do you say that?'

'Chasing after a young girl for this killing feels wrong to me. She wasn't even there.'

'Doesn't mean that she can't have known about it.'

'But she wouldn't have been stupid enough to escape on the same night so that everyone points the finger.'

'Or that was anticipated and she is doing what she shouldn't to lessen the suspicion.'

'Touché, Mr Prosecutor,' Mason commends lightly. 'But honestly, George, this feels like a wild goose.'

'A wild goose chase, you mean.'

'Whatever, but I don't like it. At all. And if they were to ask me if I agree, I'd say no.'

'So why are you going along with it?'

'I wouldn't be doing my job if I didn't investigate every avenue while equally following the crowd to throw them off the scent of my investigation.'

'Didn't think that was your style.'

'It's not.'

George shakes his head as they continue on to their office. 'Why do you do that?'

'Do what?'

'Pretend as though you care so much and then eventually do nothing about it?'

'If you must know, I don't do nothing. I'm just gathering the evidence like the lawyer that I am and just … waiting …'

It is raining outside. Rosine comes through the back door and sits at the dining table, tired. There is a tea towel patterned with country chickens and a half-eaten bowl of cereal on the table. She does not touch it, only rolls her eyes at the mess.

Rex comes in through the front door of the house, keys thrown onto the side table in the hallway and meets her at the creaking dining table, angry.

'Could you put the kettle on?' she asks.

He looks at her.

She gets up and puts it on herself, taking out two mugs, the Miami mug and the World's Best Daughter one, dropping a teabag in each.

She sits as the kettle boils.

'Ed wanted to see you before he went to school.'

'It's called a night shift for a reason, Rex. I leave after sunset.

I get back after sunrise. It's not my fault I only see my son for three hours, on a good day, nor is it my fault that the bailiffs are hanging over my shoulders ready to take away all that I own and more.'

'Hanging over our shoulders.'

'Let's not pretend this isn't your fault, Rex. This is all your fault.'

He sounds ashamed, although she cannot work out if it is genuine. 'I didn't ask for your help.'

There is a sharp click and the sound of boiling water. The kettle is done but no one moves.

'I know. But what did you expect me to—?'

'I expected you take care of Ed. I expected you to want to take care of Ed.'

'That is exactly what I'm doing.'

'No, instead you complain as though it's such a hard job to be a mother to your own child.'

'How dare you say that to me?! I am the only one who does anything around here. The working, the cleaning, the cooking, the parenting. All you do is mope about and accuse! Are you saying that I should have left you there? Wait for them to subject you to some other kind of terror, miles away from me and our son, being anything from a house cleaner to a husband to some other woman?'

'You should have left me, Rosie.'

'I should have left you. But I didn't. With the amount of complaining you do, I don't know if it's worth it. But I love you. And I hardly think my late shift compares to the twenty-five-thousand-pound debt you've left me with.'

Rosine gets up and prepares the two teas while Rex stands quietly. A drop of coconut milk and no sugar. Two glugs of milk, half a sugar, like always.

He hates the sound the spoon makes against the cup.

When she places the drinks on the table they sit opposite each other.

'I'm sorry,' Rex says. 'I've said it before. I knew this could happen. I forced it on the two of you. And, honestly, I deserved what I got. But you saved me Rosie. I didn't ask for it, but you bought me out.' He takes her hand. 'You've got to find a positive in this. We're together.'

She says nothing.

'Rosie.'

'A woman came into the hospital last night. Pregnant. She was in so much pain. Came into Triage barely saying a word. I overheard Karis and Millie on reception talking about the cuts. Again. They said Psych don't need money for new long chairs, clipboards or padded walls.

'"The government messed people up."' We have two women to a room at the moment on weekdays, more at the weekends and barely any bedding … It's disgusting, Rex. So, anyway, I help out in maternity 'cause of the staff shortage for an extra few pounds an hour. Just check-ups. And there was a woman who was holding in all of her pain. Karis and Millie thought she was lying just for a bed, but she had her son an hour later.

'After she had him, I went to check her IV and she was sat in there flicking through a magazine as he slept in his little cot beside her. She wouldn't even look at him. I told her he was beautiful because he was. Gorgeous little thing. But she said nothing. It was like I wasn't even there. So I asked her how she was, how she was feeling. She said she was better and asked if she was still dehydrated. I said no and that they could go home in the morning, if all was well.

'And then she said, "Social Services will be here soon." I was shocked so I asked her to repeat herself, just to be certain. "Social Services," she repeats. They were going to take him. And I went ballistic. You know, I was asking her if she'd really thought about what this might mean and if she just held him, she might change her mind. But she said she was gonna give him up and that no nurse was gonna convince her otherwise and no woman with a "cosy job" is telling her what to do. And then she broke. She cried like a mother.

'The week before, her boyfriend was in a car crash and had a severe brain injury. He's twenty-nine and there's no NHS beds for fifty miles to keep him so they temporarily fixed him up and send him somewhere else. Somewhere that charges thousands. They can't afford a thing, not the operation, let alone the baby. He was a bartender and she volunteered at a hospice, so God knows what she's gonna do now that he's had his injury. So, she said she had to give up her son because someone will pay for him.

"That's what they do these days. A body for cash." She was hoping that some rich family will take him in and love him so that she can survive and pay for her boyfriend to live. I didn't understand before, but I got it then. I left her alone, wondering how anyone could do such a thing, but … she had to. So, I went back in with a leaflet for a therapy-type group for new mothers. Thought it might help if she talked to other women.

'She didn't have a choice in all of this like so many others. It's a common thing now, at the hospital. Giving up your child is common. That mother did not bring this on herself. She didn't ask her boyfriend to get into a car accident. Now he won't know his son because she saved him. That is a sacrifice. But you? You felt like seeing a prostitute. So, yes, you brought this upon yourself and I should have left you.'

Picking up her tea, Rosine leaves the room.

'I think you'll find the role slightly different,' Mason advises Briscoe at the coffee machine, her safe haven and her place of joy.

'Piece o' cake.' He stirs in three sugars and sips as she fixes hers. He then allows her to follow him into his new office, which is across the hall from hers, almost opposite. His previous sign, which read 'SOLICTOR GENERAL', had been changed to read:

THE RIGHT HONOURABLE
KEVIN BRISCOE KC MP
DIRECTOR OF PUBLIC PROSECUTIONS

'Now we can wave to each other while we read our morning emails,' he gushes.

Mason frowns at him. 'We just need to get back to normal as soon as possible.'

'If possible,' Briscoe adjusts. 'I thought I'd never find a job.'

Mason frowns. 'You weren't even gone long enough to worry about that. And you're still an MP.'

'I'm used to doubling up. It's all I know now. And what would you do? I was scared out of my mind that I'd have to retrain as a solicitor.'

'I hate solicitors,' Mason adds bitterly.

'Plenty of work for them, what with the increase in divorces and adoptions. Then there's property, employment law and everything else. The civil courts are loving this new system.' Mason makes an agreeing noise as she sips her coffee. 'You weren't in yesterday morning, were you? The funerals are a week Monday.'

'Funerals?' She lowers her mug.

'Yeah. Televised. Surprised the families went for it, to be honest.'

'Why so long?'

'Have to wait until after the autopsies, you know? Hopefully there won't be any more to add.'

'Meaning?'

'I hope no one else dies,' he says as though it were obvious. It was. Briscoe takes out a framed picture of Celeste posing in front of a waterfall in a canary yellow bikini and places it carefully on his desk. 'I hear Reid isn't doing too well.'

'He is in a coma.'

'Yeah. All I'm saying is what goes around comes around.'

'You've changed your tune. No one deserves to go through what he has, no matter how terrible they are at their jobs.'

'And Reid was terrible,' Briscoe counters. 'Anyway, what happened to "you live by the word, you die by the word?"'

'Be that as it may … Listen, I'm sending a team of four to Scotland Yard – Friel, Michaels, Wendle and Waltz probably, if you can spare your new assistant – to advise Shah's lot and keep tabs on the investigation for me. Don't you have cases to work on?'

'I was going to mention one …'

'Rissington?'

'How did you know?' Mason smiles at him.

'The Rissington family own a string of private clinics, very well-known surgeons with steep prices. They perform the most heinous and unlicensed operations there are. They cut off limbs, perform abortions, plastic surgery and even the poor seem to be going for them.'

'How do they even afford it?' he questions.

'The way everyone does these days. Exchange.'

Exchange is the way of life. The poor, cash-strapped and dissonant barter and trade for the items they lived on, the food they ate, the drink they drank and the lives they lived. Trade is a fluid concept. Physical cash has not been in circulation since 2029 and only the well-off, wealthy and elite have the means to acquire credit. Most people get by on growing their own vegetables and baking their own bread after trading shoes, heirlooms and antique tables to fund seeds and grain; farming became a popular occupation, animal supply fell, vegetarianism and veganism became less of a life choice, retail and clothing shops bottomed; with people making their own wardrobes, only few shops remained, heavily priced and reserved for those who had good enough jobs and some inheritance from a rich dead relative. If you had a credit card these days, it was a symbol of power and/or wealth.

'But how do they make money from that?'

'They don't have to. They get enough money from the super-rich who want breast augmentations or experimental treatments for incurable diseases. The worst thing is, they actually have helped cure some people … It's shit really. Good luck to you.'

'Now that's a pep talk,' he utters sarcastically.

'Any time. How have you got on with research?'

'There's really no precedent for it,' Briscoe says flicking through his small pile of notes.

'Never is these days. Things have gone so effing topsy turvy I don't even know what day of the week it is.'

'Thursday.'

'Shit.' Mason darts out of the office and runs into George. 'Sorry – erm – when was my meeting with the King?'

'Lunch today but he rescheduled. I said this morning.'

She casts her mind back and vaguely remembers something about a diary change, which she scribbled down nonchalantly in pencil.

'Oh God, yeah. I'm sorry.'

'No, it's what I'm here for.' He had not taken his eyes off his computer.

'I do love you, Georgie.'

Blushing, he glances at her over his monitor. 'You have mentioned that once or twice.'

Grinning, she strides back into Briscoe's office with a small smile. She sits on his desk and stretches languidly.

'You were saying?' Briscoe asked.

'Good luck and don't drag my department further into the dirt?'

This is not his intention. Briscoe had already been close to losing his career once and, as far as he is concerned, he had been handed a miracle on a platter and was the luckiest person alive. He has a beautiful girlfriend, the most adored woman of all of the newsreaders on the six television stations they had (three for those who couldn't afford it). Somehow, he still retains a position of power and with it a salary that could maintain his home and lifestyle, and he was spending every day with his best friend of all. Although she will never admit it, she loves him as much as he loves her.

Five

The funeral cars arrived at Westminster Abbey at noon and, with it, the cries of loved ones. Everyone is dressed in monochrome, reflecting how they feel inside: dark, colourless and lonely. The loud clanging of the bell masks the scuffling of a hundred footsteps as people line the passage to the door and the pallbearers prepare themselves for lift-off.

The smell of fresh flowers fills the air when the cars are opened; lilies, roses, chrysanthemums and daisies spelling out things like 'Dad', 'Mum'. 'Grandpa', 'Friend' and 'Kris', flowers by the doorway, flowers in the arms of the mourners accompanied by their handkerchiefs and gnarly damp tissues.

One by one, the dead cross the threshold, ignorant of the cameras, the greasy reporters and the hovering helicopter overhead. Inside people's homes, there is a running commentary emanating from the television speakers, reminding viewers of the names of the dead: Phillip Pagett, Orla Victoria Archer, Kris Abdo and Ezra J Tuminez.

Phillip Pagett was the eldest of the four, a grandfather of

six small-to-medium children and had been around during the better days. Born in '79, he seemed wiser and more worldly than others, clearly in remembrance of the days of incarceration. The world was a different place when he grew up and he was a huge advocate of reform. He voted 'No' for the Criminal Justice Act amendment and everyone knew it. Every week in Parliament, if he could, he would mention another thing that aggravated him about it, so much so that people almost ignored him because they already knew what he would say. 'Never in my day…' was the phrase.

Mrs Archer was not a particularly nice woman. Most people in her job were the same, but she played her part well. She graduated from Bangor University with an outstanding Political Science degree and went on to study International Studies, Anthropology and Economics at Masters level. No one knew, but she was planning on leaving the Commons to lecture at King's College for a quieter, more academic lifestyle where she would not need to rip her hair out every night over big decisions and where she would not have to fear for her safety.

Kris was fairly unknown, although not anymore. He had been an MP for only a year, tried his best to reflect his constituency in Bath with the utmost honesty and cause, as his father had before him. At thirty-five, he had welcomed his first son into the world, a small, fat three-month-old now clutched tightly in the arms of his mother who wept salty tears onto his little white shirt.

Ezra's constituency was in the heart of bedlam within the streets of the city of Liverpool, stuck with poverty and pain where life was not as easy as it had been half a decade previously. He had made it his mission to improve dire conditions and rising unemployment, to give his people a better lifestyle and more chances of survival. Mortality rates were lower the farther north you went and the colder the temperature was. Scotland had gained their independence and were governed separately from England and there was not Great Britain or the United Kingdom, just England, Ireland, Scotland and Wales using their own resources and making the most of their budgets and national freedom.

Mason is not one for funerals but she had turned up nonetheless in a simple black dress cut to the knees and a black jacket that looks frighteningly similar to the one she wears to work. She stands silently between George and Briscoe, awaiting their turn to go in after the families and friends and the prime minister.

Chatter begins among the reporters at the sight of Frost, who looks grim as usual, perfect for the occasion, dressed head to toe in black; black suit, black shirt, black tie. As they go in after him, they pass Celeste in a black and white blouse and black skirt, her hair styled like Jackie Kennedy. Upon seeing her boyfriend, she shoves her microphone alarmingly quickly towards him.

He flinches.

'For God's sake, Celeste, no,' Briscoe utters angrily.

Mason makes sure that Celeste sees her smile at her embarrassment.

Flustered, she turns back to the camera and states solemnly, 'The prime minister there and other members of parliament heading into the Abbey …'

The service is longer than usual, three times as long with four times the people, and the Abbey is jam-packed with some standing outside, watching on monitors that line Abingdon Street. The cremations follow – burials yet another outdated practice – and the memorials are revealed outside Westminster Abbey on four shiny brass plaques. The crowds gather at an unimportant hotel where food and drinks had been paid for by the tax payer and the media are shut out at the end of the road by large barriers and equally large men.

Mason, Briscoe and George are sat at the bar away from the small crowd hovering around Frost. Most never really saw him and so the civilians who were mourning thought it to be an honour to meet him in person. His security guards are on standby.

'Thank you for coming,' Mrs Abdo whispers. She shakes Frost's hand with her right while her left rocks her son's pushchair backwards and forwards softly.

'I wouldn't dream of being anywhere else, Mrs Abdo.' Frost replies, as though he has a soul. 'Kris was an inspiring man.'

'Thank you' is all she can say before she is reduced to tears again. The Archers and the Pagetts gather close by.

'Bollocks,' Briscoe says, overhearing. 'I bet he never even met him.'

'Be quiet,' Mason commands. She takes the glass of Jack Daniels from his grasp and slides it across the bar. 'It's only just gone three, for goodness sake.' She hands him her glass of water and he gulps it down. 'Orange juice, please,' she requests from the bartender. 'Want anything?' she asks George. He shakes his head.

'We have the day off,' Briscoe complains.

'You might have, but I've still got things to do.'

'I thought you said you weren't going to the office,' George queries.

'No, I'll do it at home. May as well use the space. The apartment gets lonely without me.' She laughs to herself as she pays for her juice and sips. 'Just some case material to read and a few reports to do.'

'I did the SPO figures and emailed them to you,' George reminds her.

'Thanks. I was dreading that.'

'No problem.'

'What are you doing today?'

'Nothing really. Was considering seeing my dad but he's busy,' George says.

'Him and the rest of us.'

'Can you believe Celeste?' Briscoe splutters.

'Yes,' Mason and George chorus.

'And I bet the first thing she'll do is complain that I didn't get her in here. You have to be invited, Celeste. It's not a bloody wedding, we don't get plus ones.'

Mason smiles. 'Did you know she was a reporter before you started sleeping with her?'

'Funny,' he responds, not laughing.

'Reporter and newsreader,' George corrects. 'Does she get more money for having to do two jobs?'

'I don't think so,' he replies. 'It's just like with everyone else having to pull double-duty. But the way she goes on like she's broke sometimes …'

'Of course she does,' Mason mutters under her breath.

'What?'

'All I'm saying, Kevin, is be careful. Don't let her use you for your occupation.'

'She's not after my money, Dolly.'

'I meant your position. Within a week you've been the solicitor general and the director of public prosecutions. You're on the inside. Literally.'

'Yes, I remember the clauses we all agreed to and non-disclosure or whatever else. I haven't told her anything about anything.'

'Then, by all means, have the time of your life,' Mason says, content.

When Briscoe arrives home that afternoon, Celeste is waiting for him, wearing nothing but her pride in the middle of the living room.

Briscoe stops dead.

He drops his keys and the Mars bar he was holding, almost choking on the chocolate, caramel and nougat in his throat. He coughs and swallows.

'Afternoon,' he says, eyes watering.

'Good afternoon, Mr Briscoe,' she says in a voice she considered to be seductive. It isn't, but he doesn't say anything.

'So … how was your day?'

'You know exactly how it was, Kevin.' She walks towards him and grabs his hair. 'You ignored me.'

'How … could I possible ignore you?' He grasps her shoulder and slowly moves down her arm and snakes around her waist as she leans into him.

'Do you love me, Kevin?'

'Of course.'

'If you loved me,' she whispers into his ear, 'you'd give me what I want and not ignore me during the biggest event of the year!'

Briscoe flinches at her change of pitch and leans away from her. 'What? What the hell are you talking about?'

'You said you'd comment for me but you treated me like crap today, like you didn't even know who I was.'

'The coffins weren't even inside, Celeste! It wasn't exactly the right time!'

'Do you know how difficult my job is? Do you?'

'Oh, here we go! "My life is so hard –"'

'I work all day long gathering my stories! I'm on the TV –'

'" – and I don't get anything my way –"'

'– and I'm out in the field –'

'" – even if I stamp my heels and throw a tantrum!"'

'And you said you'd help me where you could, Kevin!'

'Where I could, Celeste, I let you know information before we release it to other networks. Be grateful! I don't hand out invitations to strangers' funerals like it's a birthday party!'

'I am your girlfriend! I already got you on TV twice.'

'Did I ask you to do that? No!'

'Yes you did.'

'No.'

'Yes you did!'

'No. Wrong again! And, Jesus Christ, put some clothes on.'

'I can do whatever I like.'

'Not in my flat you can't.' He walks a few paces away from her.

'Then I'll move out.'

'When did you move in?!'

'When did you decide that I wasn't important to you, so much so that you absolutely humiliated me on live television in front of thousands of people while you were at your exclusive funeral with the prime minister and Polly –

'It's Dolly.'

'– and I was just left on the sidelines trying my best to tell the truth to the people who are left wondering what is even happening! They're scared … and I am too.'

He softens his voice and looks into her green eyes. 'We're doing everything we can to sort it. Dolly's got four of her team on it with Shah and he's already been—'

'Four? Which of her team did she send to Scotland Yard?' she says, inquisitive.

Briscoe freezes. 'Oh for goodness – Do not report that!'

'I wouldn't dare,' she says, prancing about the living room and ducking him as she skips to the bedroom.

'If I see even a hint of that on the news in the morning—!'

She kisses his lips before he can say anything, placing his hands on her behind. She walks them backwards onto the bed, cascading down, and pushes her legs in opposite directions.

The next morning, Celeste's producer, Steven Kingsbury, talks at her as her hair and make-up is being touched up before the midday broadcast.

'Just wonderful, simply amazeballs, Celeste. Tops lawyers are on the case with the nut-heads at Scotland Yard, which means that this is big, huge, absolutely mammoth. The threat to the MPs is real and to the prime minster, who clearly was the target of the attack. There will be blood. They'll be back again and we'll be in prime position for the next funeral. It's a shame he didn't have more to give you. No holding back now, Celeste, we – need – more. I knew sleeping with the solicitor general would reap benefits bigger than we could envisage. There was that defamation case he let slip about, the school slaughters as well. Does he know anything about the Crown Court Convict? That would really boost our ratings ...'

'We're the biggest broadcaster on television, Steve. We don't need to run around like lunatic interns at a cheesy tabloid magazine where our stories are more fiction than fact. We've already made it.'

'But there's the struggle to the top and the struggle to stay there. It'll be more embarrassing if we fall. We need stories that stun and strike the hearts of the rich as well as the poor ...'

'The rich don't have souls, Steve,' Celeste says with one eye closed as Fenella curls her eyelashes.

'And we won't join them until we go where no news station has gone before.'

'And where is that?'

'I don't know yet but it feels exciting. One minute,' he adds, having heard a queue from his earpiece.

'Okay,' Fenella responds, distressed. She dives into her case, adds a nude lipstick to Celeste's lips and then touches up on her foundation.

'Remember,' Steve says to Celeste, 'next assignment: Crown Court Convict.'

'Fine,' she mutters. He walks over to her and gives her a firm kiss on her mouth.

'Jesus, Steve, I just did her make-up,' Fenella complains. She reaches back into her case.

'Ten seconds,' he says to her while looking at Celeste.

Her eyes are fixed stonily on his maroon brogues.

' – if the request for funding from Europe and the Americas will come to pass as we desperately seek aid from our former allies to combat mass poverty.

'The country's top lawyers have joined the investigation to solve the mystery of the MP attacks, which occurred last week. The Attorney General for England, Dolly Mason, has reportedly dispatched her finest lawyers to assist in the ongoing search for the assassin or assassins, based currently at Scotland Yard. Sources say that the target of the attack was the prime minister himself although he has denied this speculation. Wilson Frost stated last week, "I take a threat like this very seriously. An attack on our politicians is an attack on our country and our way of life. The conspirators and any co-conspirators will be caught and they will be made accountable for their actions." The attack took place during the celebration of the ten-year anniversary of the amendment to the criminal justice act, killing five MPs and leaving two in intensive care. The Lord Chancellor, Daniel Reid and MP Sidra Tall, director of public prosecutions—"

'I don't even want to know how she got this out of you,' Mason says to Kevin over the phone as she drives in her car up the M4 near Swindon.

'Dolls, I'm so sorry. It slipped out and she swore she wouldn't say anything.'

'She said that the last time.' She sighs as she swings around onto the A419 to Stroud, deep in thought. 'How are things at work?'

'You chose a good day to take off. It's fairly quiet, in the grand scheme of things. Rissington prep, case reviews … same old.'

'Is George okay?'

'You've trained him well. Bossing everyone around with the utmost subtlety. Just enough force, just enough mean. Just like you like it.'

'Mmm,' she mutters. Her phone beeps, another call on the line. 'Hang on Kevin, Mum's on the phone.'

'I'll go. Give her my love.'

'Okay bye.' He hangs up and the call connects. 'Mum?'

'Hey, Dolly. Could you do me a favour and get—?'

'What do you need from the supermarket?'

Mrs Mason chortles. 'Just a few bits and pieces.'

After listing what she wants, Mrs Mason leaves her daughter to her detour. She talks as she drives, until she reaches the slip road she needs, merging slowly out of the darkness of the tunnel and into the light. Swinging by the local shop, Mason gathers the items and pays on her credit card, a privilege funded by her job, as others exchange televisions, pairs of shoes and clothing over the counter for menial items. Sighing, she continues on her journey placidly.

She knows she is back in Stroud by the halt in traffic, caused by nothing less than four of the two hundred and fifty free-roaming cows alongside Minchinhampton Common, the vast circle of greenery surrounding the thin line of cars waiting rather impatiently. The Cotswolds were too beautiful and costly to build the roads underground. After protests in the Lake District in 2030, most Areas of Outstanding Natural Beauty remained untouched and the cities and towns were subjected to the Underground roads. It was any wonder that more people did not relocate out here. Hills encroach all around, massive commanding figures above the people who live among them, a litter of houses set within the inclining ground, as though clinging to the hillsides for dear life. Chimneys emit smoke at intervals and other cows and farmyard animals can be seen in the distance, grazing on neighbouring farmland.

A Ford waits for a brown and white cow to slowly step from the middle of the road to the edge. It turns, looks to the other side and decides to go back from where it came with even less haste.

Mason spends her time taking in the fresh air and watches a couple of middle-aged men swing their clubs at tiny white golf-balls. She watched one fly over the scene, bird-like, and land far on the other side, close to his mark. The man grins happily and brags to his friend who is searching anxiously for his ball.

English countryside personified, Mason's Renault glides through the road quietly, avoiding a cow protectively scooting along a smaller version of itself across the road. She follows the line of green trees swaying softly in the distance and an adjacent stone wall, the path leading her to her parents' new home that they moved into shortly before Mason decided to up sticks to London during her thriving career as a barrister. This had occurred five years after the Flood had had its way with her childhood home and the corresponding damage could not be fixed after years of work and buckets of money. Happy with their choice, Mason never admitted that she preferred this house a lot more than she had her own, and the lifestyle that came with it, irritated by the fact that she never got to grow up surrounded by such beauty the earth had bestowed upon Gloucestershire.

The younger of the female Masons turns up half an hour later than she intended, closer to midday, setting down broccoli, juice, eggs and dishwasher tablets on the kitchen worktop in her parents' kitchen. She was given a tight breathtaking hug upon sight, along with three light kisses.

'Oh, honey, are you alright?'

Ever since the shootings, her mum had taken to asking her more frequently whether she was alright, okay or alive at least once a day, and today, clearly, she is thrilled to see that she is in one piece.

Mason nods animatedly and is released.

It is light and smells of wood and herbs in the kitchen and breakfast room, plant pots on the window sills. The hanging clock with her face on it – yellow party hat on her head and her eyes crossed – had been in their possession since she had bought it for them for Christmas when she was five, an investment conjured by her late Aunt Belle. She had saved both her pocket money and birthday money and her parents had not taken it down since – except only to move from one house to another – although it had been thirty-six years.

'Where's Dad?' she asked looking at her mother's face.

'Out at Rick's, helping him fix his car.' Rick was a family friend and Mr Mason was a recently retired mechanic. 'Something to do with the alternator,' she said. 'He might have lunch there and then run a few errands. You should have said you were coming sooner than this morning.'

'Yeah, well, it beats the City. Plus, I'm owed the hours. Didn't take all of yesterday off like I was supposed to and HR have been on at me to actually use my accrued holiday leave for about three years now, so …'

Mason looks kindly upon her mother.

Mrs Mason, completely white-haired, dusted with light wrinkles and a handful of freckles looked back happily, although Mason can see the deep-seated stress lingering behind her small amber eyes. Her face resembles her own, in most respects. The eyes and the angular freckled nose, along with the tight-lipped mouth and bold expression mirrors her on a good day. Mrs Mason's white hair flows down her back to near her waist whereas Mason's is brunette and comfortable at her shoulders.

Her soft, wrinkled hand, with two jewelled silver rings on the appropriate finger, touches her shoulder. 'What is it?'

'I don't know how much longer I can go on like this,' Mason utters truthfully, running a hand through her hair. It is no surprise that the truth comes out when in her mother's critical presence, yet she holds back for a moment before she continues. 'Do I leave now and spare myself the hassle or do I try to achieve the impossible and fail?'

'That's fighting talk, Dolls,' Mrs Mason says sarcastically. 'You're not going to get far by being pessimistic.'

'You don't know what it's like, Mother. These people and this job ...' She only uses the term 'Mother' when she disagrees with her. 'If you were in my shoes, what would you do if the whole country was going to hell? What would you do if you had orders coming from the prime minister in one ear and your common sense in the other at complete polar opposites?'

'Well,' Mrs Mason started, 'I'm not a brain-box like you. I'd never be attorney general ...'

'True,' Mason said. They both smile.

'But, if I was, I'd go with my heart and not my head. What is your heart telling you?' Mrs Mason flicks the switch on the kettle and lets it boil while she gets two mugs, fixing up two coffees.

'It's telling me that something bad is going to happen. Tall and Reid are in intensive care still, fighting for their lives, five MPs are dead, the lunatic who did this is still out there and there's only a matter of time before there's riots! We have more reviews and retrials than actual cases. I'm almost tempted to wait for this all to break loose so that my job will be more interesting. But, when push comes to shove, I don't like this pile-of-crap Criminal Justice Act. It makes my skin crawl! No mandatory sentencing, no real means to show the people that we have any control. You don't know how many trials I've had where … well, ninety per cent of my cases are reoffenders and most of those are murderers and rapists who would fry in the chair if this were America …'

'Last I checked, this is definitely England,' Mrs Mason said, sipping her coffee.

'Not how I remember it.'

'Not how *I* remember it. The nineteen-nineties and the noughties were nothing to be inspired by but when these propositions came in when you were young … I doubt anyone really understood what was going to happen.'

'Because the government is full of liars and cheats. And the justice system! I doubt half of the population even understand now they're living it. And I feel like I'm caught in the middle. The hardest thing is, I'm actually happy that Tall is in hospital.'

'Why on earth would you be happy?' her mother asked, shocked.

'Because Frost made me fire Kevin the same day. And I did it too – hated every second. And then that happened … and I gave him the DPP job. He still won't look at me in the same way.'

'I'm sure he understands,' Mrs Mason assures.

'Mum, you know him. He holds a grudge. And the worst thing is, he's not even used to being betrayed. It's only ever been me who's let him down.'

'You pick him up too. You were there for him after his Mum passed.'

Mason remembered the tears. Kevin's father had died when he was younger but his mother's unexpected death in a house fire sent him into a rage only alcohol could soothe.

'This is different. We were supposed to l
other and I let Frost overrule me.'

'If anyone can, it's him. Surely Kevin sl
that.' Mason shrugs. 'How's the investigation

She frowns at her. 'You know I can't talk a

'Everyone else is.'

'It's … what it is. The sooner we get leads, the sooner everyone will be able to sleep at night.'

'You know that you can always come here if you need a break from things,' Mrs Mason offers for the hundredth time.

'I know, Mum.'

She never got to see her father on this occasion. He never returned before she headed off at about four in the afternoon. Fearful of the darkness, Mason called her father and asked him to stay at Rick's for the night – which he obliged – so that she could ensure that her mother locked the house up securely. They had shutters, a deadbolt and an alarm system like most people, protecting against the desperate homeless. Although not dangerous, their starvation had been the cause of various muggings and break-ins and Mrs Mason did not feel safe alone. It was always preferred that the place is locked up before sunset no matter who was home.

Mason set off after checking her Mum was okay, looking forward to the quiet drive home and the time to think without interruption.

Getting home late, she ate a bowl of cereal before retreating to bed, looking forward to the week ahead in the most sarcastic way possible.

It begins with a debate on terror in the Commons and the likelihood that another strike will occur. The severity of the shootings had finally called them all to action and the prospect of an empty House, or rather a House with blood on those lovely green seats, was something no one wanted to imagine.

rchy at its best is a society without order, although Mason is hard-pressed to believe that what they had now was order. Unresolved and pending, the debate ended with no conclusion and she went back to work uneasy. Next came three resignations in her department, one disciplinary hearing for sexual harassment, then a set date for the Rissington trial and a handover to her once Briscoe had done as much prep with his team as possible to see if she could add anything to his research. In exchange, he looked over a number of retrials for her as she delved deeper into the Rissingtons, finding more information than Briscoe could.

'Typical.' She thought that he would do a sub-standard job, that he would be struggling under his new position. It's always the way; it takes him about six weeks to get settled and then there's Celeste, making his work–home balance a struggle, but she refrains from mentioning it now, even though he is dying to talk to someone about it.

Eventually, he approaches George.

'Yes?' It is clear that he dislikes Briscoe to a certain extent, but he remains professional.

'I was just thinking …' Briscoe begins.

'About?'

'How do you say no … without saying yes?'

'I'm sorry?' George asks, confused.

'To a woman,' Briscoe reiterates.

'Oh … well, I don't know. Best thing to do is be honest and don't be a prat about things when they start to throw a fit or try to persuade you otherwise.' He pauses. 'Get it over with.'

'I will. I am.' He is slightly offended and unsure.

'Then break up with Celeste today and let's not beat around the bush. God knows it would give us all some peace,' George tells him, rising out of his chair and making his way to the men's toilets.

Six

The mouth is all he can focus on. Opening and closing
in succession, those off-white teeth and pink tongue,
vacant noise falling into the telephone. But it is far away. He
cannot hear what the man in the suit is saying, but he looks
professional, like he knows what he's doing. Dressed in a suit
that would have cost him most of his possessions to own, this
guy is the real deal.

Occasionally, his hand goes up and Judge Cunningham nods
in recognition, the price on his head rising, just white noise
buzzing in his ears as he attempts to concentrate on his fate.
Failing, he closes his eyes and waits, currently devoid of all
feeling; his attempt at freedom was long gone and wasted.

'SOLD!'

The dreaded words awake him from his stupor and the gavel
causes his head to beat a fraction faster.

He cannot remember being taken back to the cell, nor
sleeping, nor waking, nor the horrid porridge breakfast, nor the
security guard yelling at him for some sign of life before they

locked him in shackles, checked and scanned his infinity bar
code and was walked back into the thing dazzling sunshine.
For eleven seconds, he is bathed in it; despite the cold, it is an
amazing prickling on his pale skin and that is what he misses
once they shut the doors on it and the van rumbles into motion.

They arrive at their destination in less than half an hour, he
guesses, having stared at the palms of his hands for most of
the journey, counting on his fingers. He wonders if he would
ever taste chocolate spread again, enjoy a lavish Christmas
dinner with all of the trimmings, wonders if the person who
freed him of his incarceration would have pity on him and
not subject him to dire servitude and squalor. Then again, he
cannot complain. Surely anything is better than staring at the
bars that keep you in …

'Time to go.' Both guards are there to meet him when the
doors open.

There is less sun here, all three of them shrouded in shadows.
There is no wind. Alex looks around. They are stationed at a
back entrance to a lovely stone building. No rubbish litters the
ground, no chewing gum; it looks barely walked on or often
cleaned and cared for.

Great, he thinks. *Definitely rich.* That means his hope of
compassion is dashed. But he has been wrong before.

They wait at a door, which opens itself without knocking,
where Alex is transferred into the hands of a short stocky fair-
haired security guard, who, despite his size and age, looks as
though he could take on most if not all of the New Zealand
rugby team.

He hears one of the guards yell, 'Enjoy!' through the rolled
down window as the van reverses back down the road.

Grim, Alex waits as the door is closed and locked and
precious seconds pass slowly as his manacles are removed. It
feels almost surreal that he is now able to move about freely in

the real world. It is almost the same as before.

'Don't get any ideas,' the new guard warns, locking the chains away safely. 'These can go right back on if you misbehave. Follow me.'

Alex does as he is told and walks further into the warm basement level and through a wine cellar towards a staircase.

'May I ask what my role will be?'

For a moment, he does not receive an answer.

'You'll have to ask your employer,' he mutters.

'Okay,' Alex says, nervous. 'Well, is she nice?'

He doesn't expect the man's laughter. 'I'm Nico. And he is probably the most hated man in the country.'

The staircase leads to an empty kitchen, although Alex can see that some work had begun. A few pans are on the worktop in an unceremonious fashion and a box of eggs is open.

The wall clock reads eleven minutes past six.

They pass through without a sound, Alex enjoying swinging his arms, joyous of his perceived freedom, taking in everything his eyes encounter.

Upon their exit of the moderately-sized kitchen, his feet meet with a luxury oriental carpet in the hallway lined with pictures of men and women he did not know in gilded frames; an engraved glass mirror is on the wall in the hall. He frowns at his dirty reflection, not recognising the bags under his eyes nor his drained complexion.

Passing a number of reception rooms, they enter the farthest but one, a small snug reminiscent of a comfortable living room, with a large television on the wall and two mugs of coffee on the glass table. The long curtains had not yet been fully drawn. The seat nearest to where they stood was already filled, although all Alex can see is a grey sock on a raised foot.

'Thank you,' the man says.

Nico leaves quietly.

'Please take a seat, Alex.'

He does so, turning, seeing the face of Wilson Frost, his leg propped up by his other, no shoes on his feet. He doubts anyone had seen the prime minister like this, except very few people under this same roof.

'Do you like coffee?' he asks.

'I don't know.'

Wilson smiles. 'You've only been locked up for five months, Alex.'

'Feels like years. Is it good?' He motions towards the coffee.

'Not the best, but I like it.' Alex lifts the cup. 'It's strong. Hope you don't mind.'

'No.' He sips and the bitter flavour sinks into his tongue and swirls around his mouth, nouveau delicious, instantly energising. 'Thank you.'

Wilson observes him and the grey jumpsuit he has on his thin and sunken body.

'Do you know why you're here?'

'You tell me,' Alex responds, putting down the warm mug.

'A job. Something as simple and mundane as work. I know who you are, saw you on the television, was informed by Judge Cunningham and an inspector of the City of London police that you, Alexander Spade, tried to escape justice just a week ago, having only initially committed a menial crime, nothing to hang a man for, just the omission of council tax payment and poverty and perhaps a little pride. But then you made things worse for yourself. I don't need to go into that but your sentence has doubled, as I'm sure you're aware. I had to have you. You are made of the thing I wish most people were: courage. In the face of a life of misery, you sought a better life. Just like me, you had strived to make something better of yourself, to find another way. Although you failed, I still see a strength in your eyes which makes me quiver and sing. You don't give up. Half of my security have never even been in a fist-fight in a bar or a punch-up in a playground, but you have looked down the barrel of a gun and seen your life flash before you.'

'You want me as part of your security?' Alex cannot believe it. Perhaps this is not going to be as bad as he thought.

'Times are getting tough for me. Being prime minister is not all people think. I get death threats every other day, but none as real as what is happening now. You'll understand soon, once you watch the television and read the newspaper and browse the Internet, privileges you have not yet enjoyed since you've been freed. You'll see the fear that's spreading. You'll be second to Nico, no matter what the others say. He'll teach you how we do things and, I don't know, take you to the gym with him too.' Alex was on the not-so-muscly side since he had been arrested. 'Bravery is hard to come by and I need men and women who have glimpsed and evaded death so that I can live the long life that I need to in order to serve my country.'

'Right.' Alex still does not quite understand but saves his questions for another day, for Nico perhaps. He is rather tired and yawns. 'Okay.'

'Nico!'

Alex flinches as Nico re-enters.

'Take Alex to his room,' Frost orders.

Alex rises before he is asked and follows Nico out of the room, not before he is passed by a short dark-haired woman with heavy gold earrings hanging from her ears who is carrying a selection of pastries on a tray. She doesn't register his existence and serves the food to Frost.

Back on the basement level, Nico leads Alex to a small corridor with a heavily bolted door consisting of five rooms. They enter the first on the right, where a double bed is positioned beneath a high rectangular window. Beside it is a small chest of drawers, a wardrobe, and a dark rug is on the smooth wooden floors. Alex is surprised to see a small television on the wall and an en-suite shower room just opposite.

He cannot help but smile.

'Welcome to freedom, mate,' Nico says. 'Beats a prison cell, doesn't it?'

'What prison cell?' Alex responds, laughing.

'Main door locks automatically at ten and unlocks at five. All of the staff eat in the kitchen three times a day. Any time between six and eight, twelve and two and four and six, depending on your schedule. Unfortunately for security, ours changes all the time so you'll be lucky if you get regular meals but he always makes sure we eat, even if we're out somewhere, so don't worry.'

He isn't worried.

'Socialise as you want down here, but no going upstairs unless you're working or unless you're summoned. Alright?'

Alex nods firmly. 'Who was that girl upstairs?'

'Maid. Ling. She probably won't appreciate being called that. Well, I've got the rest of the day off – so do you. I'll be your mentor, so ... see you tomorrow? Early start.'

'Yeah, sure.'

'I'm off home.'

'You don't live here?' Alex asks, testing his new mattress.

'No, just you criminals live on site. I actually choose to work here, crazy as that is.' He chuckles. 'Enjoy your day,' he says sincerely, closing the door behind him.

The next morning, Alex awakes with a start at five in the morning, having had the best night's sleep for years. The sound of the doors unlocking drags him out of his slumber, reminding him of what had happened. He had drifted off shortly after arriving in his new home and, consequently, awoke with both an aching stomach and a dry mouth.

He checks the wall clock again and it is only quarter past

five. He can hear movement in the corridor but waits until the clock reads six before getting up, taking a long hot shower, changing into a shirt and trousers that he finds in the drawers and making his way upstairs.

The house is awake and the day has begun. There is tinkling in the kitchen and, above, he can hear footsteps, perhaps the footsteps of the maid and the cleaners tasked with preparing Frost for the day ahead. He is sure to be awake now and, truth be told, Alex is not entirely sure of what he has to do in his new role.

He ponders this as he enters the kitchen area. A thin and muscled man is carefully preparing two sets of breakfasts. One, decorative on a silver tray; eggs, toast, fruit, pastries and coffee as a choice. The other set is toast stacked unceremoniously, a bowl of scrambled eggs with a large spoon, a bowl of baked beans, again with a spoon and a tower of apples. Plates are on the side for self-serving.

The things Clifton Michael Bell had done in his life might have dictated the patterns his mind follows; the legal murders committed for the sake of King and Country might have made him cry at night and long for death, however, he took a different view on such things. He had been forced and moulded, turned into a different man. It was not his choice.

Having being detained for drug charges in his youth, he always had a hard life, but when he was his third time out of prison and found in possession of a handgun seven years ago, he was bought by an army corporal and drafted into the war with the Russian Federation. He focused all of his anger and pain into following the rules, hoping to go home to his son.

In 2047, he was sent home and then framed for a mugging, losing the trust of his only child and ex-wife. It was discovered that he often cooked meals for his comrades in Russia, had a talent for it and, all of a sudden, he was serving up four meals a day for Wilson Frost. If he was a paid employee, it would be a coveted role but he supposed cheap and free labour was a way to save taxpayer money. He accepts his sentence of six years and waits for 2053 to come with nothing but patience.

'Hi,' Alex says.

The man cannot hear him so he says it again, louder.

Cliff turns and surveys the young gentleman before him.

'Who are you?'

'You don't recognise me?' Alex expected his face to be all over the papers for what they had done.

'Are you famous?'

'No. Can I have some of this?' Cliff nods and Alex begins to help himself to breakfast. 'I just thought … I did something and …'

'That much is obvious. Wouldn't be here if you didn't do anything.'

'What did you do?' Alex asked. As soon as he did, he wanted to take it back. Cliff did not look like the kind of man to pickpocket. Murder was more like it. 'I tried to escape and got caught. Now, here I am.'

'Oh yes, I heard about that.'

'I thought you said you didn't recognise me.'

'Do I care what you look like? I heard some idiots tried to escape justice and failed. I hardly think that makes you worthy of my time or interest.'

Cliff crosses the kitchen with the tray and opens the door. Ling is in the doorway, hand outstretched.

'Thank you kindly,' she mutters, chewing gum. She sees Alex in the corner of her eyes and says, loudly, 'Who's your new friend?' to Cliff.

Cliff shrugs and gets back to work while Ling disappears upstairs.

An hour later, Nico collects Alex from his room and they

go to the security office on the ground floor. It was set at the back of the building, inconspicuous, his reporting place every morning. There, he would receive a reminder of the day's events and, every evening, a briefing on the day ahead. It is fairly self-explanatory. You go where the prime minister goes and make sure that no one gets within five feet of him and that he doesn't get shot or blown up.

'This, of course, comes with its limitations …' Nico lifts his shirt to show two scars sliced down his abdomen. 'So I'll need you to sign this before you start next week.'

Nico slides a small booklet and a pen over to him.

'What, sign my life away?' Alex mutters.

'You've already done that. This just makes it official.'

Sighing, Alex signs.

'You're not even going to read it?'

'You said it didn't matter.'

'Alright.' Nico takes the contract back and moves on to another topic, looking over Alex curiously. 'The gym is upstairs and we are allowed to use it whenever we're free so, for the rest of this week, we'll be doing some training and take it from there.'

Agreeing, Alex follows Nico upstairs, looking forward to taking his anger out on something other than himself.

The journey to Surrey is longer than she cares to admit. A bus or the train would take no time at all, but walking and trying not to be recognised by the public is difficult. Wearing a balaclava would not make her less conspicuous, only more so, and having her face on show, as clear as day, was not wise either.

She had cut her long wiry hair three nights ago. It was getting difficult to maintain anyway, she told herself, and she cut it short, but not too short, just small curly waves dusting over her ears. She stole a long brown straight-haired wig and wore this with a knitted grey hat pulled as far down as she could without blinding herself. It kept her head warm anyway.

Fingerless gloves on her fingers and a knitted scarf around her face shield her from the cold as well as the street cameras. She had also acquired a backpack from a skip outside Twickenham and she steadily began to fill it with bits of food she had managed to scavenge, a water bottle she had filled in a public toilet and streams she might pass, as well as three socks she found on the roadside, a pen she thought she might use as a defensive weapon and old coins from decades before that she had spotted glittering in the gutter; she would be able to exchange them for something if she found the right merchant who dealt in antique items.

Today, she had swapped coats with a woman she met briefly at a bus stop. Apparently the one CA45JM had taken from the charity shop was an outlet designer brand from five years ago, which this young woman had begged her mother for. She obligingly handed it over and put on the dark checked woollen coat, which was a lot warmer and smelt quite sweet.

Every other day, she is able to read pages of the newspaper and the bizarre items written inside it. Divorces and adoptions were on the rise, more cases of libel and slander, property prices were at a staggering high. Apparently, ten high court judges were to be investigated and around one hundred civil servants were staring at redundancy. Apparently, the conditions of two MPs fatally injured at the shootings a few weeks ago were worsening and there is not much hope left, it seemed. Doctors were trying their best, but with limited supplies and low funding, resources are limited as well as time. How long do they keep someone on life support? There is another piece on the funerals of the others who had died as a result of the shooting, a tawdry affair, masked with pomp and the genuine sorrow of family. She was in there too, within the first five pages usually for maximum effect, almost every time she scans the damp and faded pages she sees yet another piece on her disappearance, the lack of progress on the manhunt and how dangerous she is.

CA45JM had never considered herself dangerous. Then again, you never do until it is too late to see what you don't care to admit. There had been regrets and chances she wished she had taken, opportunities anew, but life seemed to regurgitate all of the shit in her life with every stroke of the clock. Ever since 2041, every choice she made seemed to cause her to spiral down a path of inconsistency and irrationality. She did not know herself. She was once a young girl who wanted to be a clinical psychologist, with every plan to graduate and make it all on her own. She made it over the threshold, but the shadows of the new world were too much to deal with and she had to drop out after two semesters, move back home with a mountain of debt, and sadness coupled with the loss of independence and everything that made her who she was. Decision after decision … and now she is just a number.

Somehow she had become one of those criminals you see on the TV – if you had one – ducking and diving the authorities for something she did not do and for her beliefs – namely, the belief that innocent people should not be bought like cattle. She has the feeling that it has become more than that, some scheme to feed money into the elite and their lifestyles but this was not important. She is now reading things that even her mother would cry at. Apparently, she was responsible for the shooting and the attempt on the prime minister's life. It's a theory, but theories and guesswork have worked before and seemed to be enough to convict her with a lifetime sentence of servitude.

She quite likes sleeping in the park. There is not as much food as if you found refuge at the back entrance of a restaurant. Here, there is usually a buffet available if you can wrestle it from the strays, but in the park she can see the stars and occasionally gaze into people's living rooms while she lays behind a cluster of bushes.

Coughing, she rolls onto her side and her eyes soak up the family of five in their Victorian three-storey home, a traditional old building. CA45JM imagines the heat most of all. She had developed a stubborn cough and would do anything for central heating and would definitely kill for an open fire. She tries not to think of hot chocolate and marshmallows and a warm bed to sleep in at night.

How would her life have turned out had she not escaped the Crown Court? Well, she would not be lying on the ground wondering where her next meal was coming from, because, let's face it, she would have been fed and kept alive with Lord Whatever-His-Name-Was.

She rolls over to find his name in an article she read earlier about his dwindling condition.

Reid. That was it. She would have been welcomed into the Reid household and probably have been made to cook and clean, but nevertheless would have been provided with a home, food and healthcare, rather than stealing on the streets.

Even though it's not fair, it doesn't mean that it's not right. No, she had not done what they said she had, but she certainly is not living a better life. Living a lie would keep her alive but she refuses to allow them the satisfaction of making her give in. She would never give in and would rather die than serve at the feet of some rich guy and his brat of a daughter.

The next morning is rainy. Bad for her cold, but good for coverage.

Having found an almost-new boxed microwave in a skip she

had also found an apple in, she walks to a shop down the street and enters.

She places the box on the desk.

'What do you want for it?' the hoarse man with the beer belly asks. She bet he smoked fifty a day by the smell of him.

'Wheels,' she utters. She keeps her head down in case he has cameras the police could request.

He spots the infinity symbol on her wrist and goes rigid. 'No cars, no bikes.'

'Not one bike?' she begs. 'There was one in the window!'

'Display only, honey. Sorry.' He doesn't sound it. 'Wouldn't get you the bike anyway.'

'But it's basically new.' She touches the microwave box protectively.

'New, but still a cheap model.' He shuffles from behind the desk and walks around the store to pick something up. 'Can get you this though.'

He is holding a skateboard.

'A skateboard.'

'You're not blind, I see.'

'That's really all you have?'

'Listen, you can go elsewhere, but there aren't any more swap shops for another three miles. Take it or leave it.'

Muttering under her breath, CA45JM accepts and swaps the microwave for the green and black skateboard.

At least it's easy to carry, she thinks to herself.

The only trouble is that she had not tried to skate in over a decade, and so she spent the next two days practicing at night where no one would see her and, by the third day, she was travelling at night almost twice as far as if she had walked. She is nocturnal now, sleeping in the sun and riding along at night where no one will laugh when she falls onto her face or scuffs her knee.

She actually begins to enjoy it, the wind rushing into her ears and even the challenges of swerving corners and thinking on your feet. She almost gets hit by three cyclists Aboveground and nearly rolls into two elderly women walking home from a book club but improves massively by the time a week passes.

Alex's instructions had been vague although she had not forgotten: he has a flat which he rent from his parents above a café between a charity shop and a bakery in the centre of Surrey …

She decides to start on Lower High Street and work outwards, rolling into the desolate street at around 23:32. There is nothing but the wind and the crushing darkness, an occasional plastic bag rolling along into the gutter and a shot from beyond reminds her that she is not alone.

There are hardly any charity shops, so she knew when she saw it that she had found the right place. It was hardly a back street, more of a secret dwelling, where the posh cafés gained favour from being a place you went to only if you knew about it, where the walls were sometimes coated in expensive fabrics and a chaise longue or two, setting the ambience under candlelight so the customers looked forward to the day they detested the place for giving into success, fame and commerciality. She can't imagine what would happen if coffee was ever split or someone said they were dissatisfied with service. The charity shop on the left is rather nice too, but nothing more than it is, the bakery on the other side has chairs and boasts fresh bakes every morning and deals with a hot beverage. Above all of these shops are flats lined with something like pale columns, painted and well-maintained.

Yellow light glows from the window above the café and, in this moment, CA45JM wonders and hopes that Alex was right. If she knocks on this door and he is not who she was looking for, he could recognise her for who the government had said she was and call the police straight over. She would be locked up within the hour, due to be sold off to whoever would have her. She only had one shot.

There is no visible intercom and so she shoves her skateboard under her arm and walks around the row of buildings until she finds a back entrance, cars parked in ceremony.

Breathing and thinking of a cover story, she buzzes for number 33A. The café had been number 33.

'Yello,' comes an animated voice through the speaker.

'Alex sent me. I need your help, Ellis.'

She is automatically buzzed in. she feels the warmth of the building encase her as she takes the stairs up to the flat.

The door is open when she gets there and she enters to a bright modern apartment with dark walls, a little messy, food cooking in the kitchen. The smell of meat and vegetables delights her nostrils.

Ellis closes the door behind her. 'And you are?' he asks, interested.

He is a short man, as men go, yet taller than she is. His hair is short, as though recently cut and brown stubble brushes his chin. He looks less impressive than she expected, in blue jeans and a t-shirt, yet it was in the evening when guests usually refrain from calling, so she forgives his decorum.

'Alex didn't tell you?' she responds, feigning confusion.

'I haven't spoken to him in … just less than a year? Said he might come. Instead I get you. Now, who are you?'

'He's my husband. We hadn't known each other long; I used to work at the bank and we just got talking. Next thing I knew, we were together and I couldn't have been happier. Anyway, life's short, so we got married and then … well, he's gone now. Sold off, I expect. I had a short sentence after I couldn't pay the bills.' She shows him her infinity mark on her wrist. He nods. 'Now I have nowhere to live and only the name he gave me the last time I saw him: your name.'

'Well, where's your wedding band?' Ellis queries.

'Do you honestly think I could afford to keep it?'

'I don't know. Some people tend not to sell something that means so much to them – that's why they're called keepsakes,' he argues.

'And some people don't know what it's like to have nothing when they live in the comfort of a home given to them by their parents.'

'Fair enough. Hungry?' he asks, going over to the open plan kitchen-dining area.

She follows, stomach aching.

He plates up small portions of pan-fried chicken and steamed vegetables, the first nutritious meal she has had in a long time.

'Thank you,' she utters between chews.

He tells her the story of how he had met Alex. Alex's best friend had been sold, served his time and released, yet it hindered his life afterwards. He was unable to find work and eventually killed himself.

'… so then I decided to help people transition from the life before and the life after. Adam came to me with an idea. He said that maybe, if he could get rid of his old life, he could start again. Alex thought it was brilliant but didn't really believe in it. I suppose he does now that he's been mixed up in all of this bullshit. Anyway, Adam killed himself within three weeks of us starting up.'

'I believe in it. And I need your help. I can't go on like this anymore. And … I want to get Alex out, if I can.'

'And you can't do it with that on your wrist?'

'No.'

He nods. 'Alright. I know someone who can sort your tattoo.'

'Wait, I thought you did that.'

'I can get you an identity but I'm no tattoo artist. And if you want my help, I say what happens. You can stay here for a few days, but once I have you sorted, you'll have to go. You can stay at my parents' farm. It's not too far from here but they won't even know you're there because they're on some cruise in the Med for six weeks. That okay?'

She nods. 'Thank you.'

'Don't worry about it, Mrs Spade.'

Seven

'Miss Reid, I just don't know what to say to you in order to get through to you. Not in my school nor in any other do you have the right to ignore the practices and standards of education we uphold here simply because you "don't feel like it". You do not, under any circumstance, ignore teachers and supporting staff when they explicitly tell you to do something nor do you leave school grounds unaccompanied without notifying anyone, scaring your housemistress half to death when you couldn't be found. You could have been hurt, or worse.'

Sera rolls her eyes.

'It was after sundown and none of your classmates had a clue where you'd gone. Maybe you forced them into silence, or they didn't know, or they're just loyal friends, but when your parents signed the agreement when you were enrolled, they agreed that you would follow the school rules and that includes our very clear code of conduct, which also includes the provision that you're not to stray off the school site without consent. Having a hard time is no excuse for uncouth behaviour. We have people here who can help you and we really want to. After your mother passed away, we gave you all the time you needed, allowed to go home and study from there and, when you gpot back, allowed you to have your own room and private study for three months. And now you have your own space again, given the situation, and I know that this isn't the same as that but, Seraphim, you must communicate with us if you need something.' The Headmistress pauses. 'Do you need something?'

Sera looks into her eyes and says nothing. Then her gaze travels to the window, where the girls outside are playing a very poor game of lacrosse.

'Pretending to be mute will only aggravate me further, Sera.' Sera does not move. 'Okay. Okay, I'll be sending a letter to your guardian requesting a meeting before the next exeat, so expect to see me again in the next few weeks. You're excused.'

Without taking another breath, Sera storms across the room and leaves, slamming the door behind her.

The journey back to her dorm is uninterrupted, so she has time to reflect on her behaviour, much to her disdain. She is never usually like this, keeps herself to herself. The only thing that remained the same was her lack of involvement in conversation. She was always a girl of two sides; she is opinionated and loud when she needs to be, but also can be a quiet girl, not wanting to get into other peoples' business. Now her silence is her weapon, infuriating staff and teachers to no end with her constant and incessant quiet.

They can hardly blame her. Two years ago, her mother had died after a long and terrible illness, something they all knew was coming, yet it was nothing they could prepare themselves for. Her father had been distant and almost unkind while she was forced to continue with school even though her heart was not in it. Her heart was at home since she had spent the last month of her mother's life by her side, simply talking and soaking in all of her features and habits before she forgot them weeks later.

Twelve years old and wizened beyond her wildest dreams, Sera saw life differently after that; she still does. To her, life is a game of time-wasting, occupying boredom and quelling procrastination until the end came, under the pretences of enjoyment and sanity. She had failed to see the point in most things, let alone education. Her father had abandoned her and their relationship deteriorated with every day that passed. Now, he is as good as gone. Left to rot, Sera thinks she may as well be dead too.

The grounds glow greenly through the window and she takes a detour out onto the grass before heading to bed. The Saturday afternoon busies itself with studying, long walks and extra-curriculars. She glances at the lacrosse game, which was drawing to a close, and thinks of the tennis game that she should be participating in.

I am so alone, she tells herself over and over. There might be some others who may have lost a parent, but no one was in her situation and she was not in theirs. This, she had to deal with alone. This, she had to fight. Her father is lying in a hospital bed with no signs of life and she is as empty and hollow as she imagines him to be. The father she knew is no longer in there, he is lost somewhere, waiting to return or to be freed.

Please come back, she hopes, tears welling in her eyes as she turns her back on the squealing girls as rain falls from the greying clouds.

Although she is in her fourth year, she had been allowed her own dorm again, given the circumstances. She throws herself onto the bed and buries her face into the pillow, long mousy brown hair cascading over the white cotton, stifling tears from her green eyes that never threatened appearance.

Lunch is in twenty minutes but she ignores the hungry call of her stomach, much like the pile of homework and prep on her desk and the advice of her peers and teachers.

No one sees her for most of the day, and when she does not arrive to her morning classes, panic ensues and her housemistress charges into her room to find her curled up in bed, watching the sky through the window.

'This has gone on long enough.' She leaves the room, livid, and the next thing Seraphim knows, she is marched onto the school bus with half of her things and taken back to her temporary home, a week and more before the exeat, to the home of Judge and Mrs Cunningham – their home, not hers.

Rotherfield Greys is a village Sera thought was quite bland when she first came here years ago, whereas others found it both picturesque and timely. It has a post office, a pub, a shop and a church, all a reminder of the years long passed and the people who lived and died there. Quiet, the village sits near the town of Henley-on-Thames, Sera thinks it has a rather 'school' feeling to it, reminding her largely of the place she dreaded, with its historical significance, weathered brickwork and smiling faces. The need to breathe in the green, green air was not much to her, yet it is always a good excuse when she wants to have time alone – which happens all of the time.

It is the first thing she tries when she arrives outside the two-hundred-and-fifty-year-old redbrick cottage the Cunninghams own. The long gravelled drive is bordered by a variety of shrubbery and a large garage stands beyond, housing cars more expensive than she can ever imagine. She had stayed there for three nights before going back to school weeks ago and recalled dreary memories of having to go to dinner parties with her parents and avoiding making small talk with the other lawyers' children. They all had names like Matilda Hyacinth and Walter Woodrow Henry; Seraphim Una did not go down well.

'Sounds like a fat baby,' nine-year-old Imelda Cordelia had spewed as she tantalised the platter of prawns she held out of reach of the others.

Nine herself, Sera had replied, cross-armed, 'That would be cherubim. And actually, it means "a creature from heaven."'

'Creature!' Reginald Auguste hollered, spraying his melon-mint mocktail. 'Creature!' He could barely hold in his chuckles and this spread to the other children, who mimicked one another until Sera was reduced to tears and left the room to sulk in the downstairs toilet.

Fond memories aside, Sera spots Mrs Cunningham waiting for her at the front door when the bus pulls in. Her red hair is lying perfectly on her shoulders, her face perfectly coated in light make-up and a cheery smile. She looked perfect, although her clothes said gardening. Sera, who has never seen this woman in anything but a cocktail dress is glad to see that she is in a pair of denim dungarees and a white shirt with the sleeves rolled up, a light sprinkling of dirt on her knees.

'I'll get your things,' the driver mentions quietly. He and his large stomach shuffle out of the doors and he begins unloading her suitcases and boxes.

Looking out of the window at her temporary carer, Sera feels nothing, even as she watches Mrs Cunningham say her name twice and beckon her over with a gloved hand.

Eventually, Mrs Cunningham strolls to the door and opens it.

'Sera! I was calling you.'

She knows.

'Hi, Mrs Cunningham,' she says with minimal enthusiasm.

'I'm great, thank you, dear,' she replies to an unspoken question. 'Mr Cunningham and I are very disappointed that you've been sent home early, but equally as glad to have you.'

She says this in earnest and then turns to the driver. 'Just inside the door would be great.'

He nods and struggles with the luggage.

'I've fixed a cold lunch if you're hungry. I didn't know what time you'd be arriving.'

'I'm not really in the mood for salad,' Sera says, jumping out of the van and thinking of sausages. 'I was just going to go for a walk maybe and get some—'

'Oh, lovely, I can join you. Been green-fingering the veggies and I could use a break.'

When she waggled her fingers while saying 'green-fingering', Sera held in the urge to projectile-vomit.

'Actually, Mrs Cunningham, I might stay inside. Looks like it might rain.' She remembers to glance at the sky and enters the house, the genteel lady behind her following.

Sera begins the climb up the wide staircase to her fake bedroom at the back of the house.

'Good call,' she says, closing the door on the driver without a thank you. 'There's some mixed nuts and hummus in the kitchen. And cucumber!' she adds, as though this made it all the tastier.

'No, thank you,' Sera mutters, closing the bedroom door.

The next few days are of little consequence. Her headphones remain either over her ears or around her neck for quick access whenever someone tries to speak with her about her supposed behaviour. Nothing makes her more pleased than to see the sour and frustrated faces of the kindly Cunninghams when she excuses herself from the room, pretends to need the lavatory or sinks into one of her favourite songs on top volume. Meals get more awkward by the day, so Sera decides not to attend on the ninth night.

She sits in her room, singing, missing her real one. Contemplating covering the walls in posters and adding fairy lights to the headboard and fireplace, she sees Mrs Cunningham enter through the reflective glass in the window. She is wearing a green cocktail dress and white heels.

Sera removes her headphones.

' – you she was coming to dinner tonight. It's like you don't even listen to me.'

She was getting annoyed, but Sera did not change her response even though she considered it. Mrs Cunningham isn't evil, after all.

'I don't have to listen to you.'

'No, but I asked you nicely to come to eat today as we have a guest who would like to say hello.'

'You didn't say that. Who is it?' She is interested.

'It's not my fault you can't hear over that music,' Mrs Cunningham says smartly. 'It's Ms Mason. Mr Cunningham invited her over for work and I managed to convince her to stay for dinner last week. She wants to say hello.'

Sera knew that Mrs Cunningham enjoyed entertaining far too much but she also knew that the last conversation she had with the attorney general was unfinished.

'Fine.'

Sera gets off the bed and makes to follow Mrs Cunningham downstairs.

'Are you – Don't you want to change?'

Sera is wearing leggings, a denim shirt and fluffy purple boot slippers. Her hair is tied up in an unceremonious bun.

'Not really, Mrs C.'

Ignoring the noise Mrs Cunningham made at her response, Sera tucks her iPod into the back of her leggings and joins the adults in the dining room where the chandelier is lit, the fire is roaring and platters of food wait to be served onto four plates.

Mason is sat opposite the judge in a suit, perhaps waiting for the silence to pass. Judge Cunningham removes his eyes from the buttons of her shirt as his wife enters.

'She rises!' Cunningham jokes, laughing. He wipes the sweat from his thick brown moustache, yet it shines on his bald patch.

Sera doesn't smile as she sits next to him. Instead, she decides that she is hungry and will have a bit of the lamb that is steaming on the table. She makes eye contact with Mason and says, 'Hello.'

'It's nice to see you Sera,' she replies, polite.

Sera notices that her cuts and bruises have healed. She nods.

Mrs Cunningham rushes around serving food directly onto plates as though she were feeding the starving, the people at the tabled saying 'Yes please' or 'No thank you' to vegetables and sauces when shoved under their noses by their host.

They eat and sip occasionally.

'I see you found somewhere to stay,' Mason says.

'No choice. They came for me and forced me against my will.'

Judge Cunningham sniffs rather loudly and then takes a gulp of wine. 'We've known you since you were a young girl. Leaving you alone in the hospital was not an option.'

'I'd rather be homeless.'

'I'd rather you alive,' Mrs Cunningham counters, upset. 'So I'll continue to inconvenience you by keeping you safe.'

'God knows, you've got nothing else to do,' Sera says before chewing and swallowing a large chunk of lamb.

Mrs Cunningham is stony-faced and her husband mutters, 'No, Shannah.'

'They're your godparents, Sera. What do you expect?' Mason states seriously. 'Your parents trusted them with you. That's got to count for something, no matter how annoying they are to you.'

Sera shrugs and starts on the roast potatoes. Mrs Cunningham had done a good job.

The table is silent for a further ten minutes.

'Mrs Foss called today to confirm the appointment tomorrow,' Mr Cunningham states.

Sera gives in. 'What appointment?'

'The meeting about you,' Mrs Cunningham fills in. 'We're going to get to the bottom of what's happening, once and for all.'

'It's obvious what's happening,' Mason says quietly. 'Thank you for inviting me here, but I have to say, your approach to this is all wrong. She hates everything right now so you're no different, let alone school. That much is clear. The best thing you can do to help her is to leave her alone. Both of her parents are gone at the moment, so you won't get anywhere trying to act like her mum and dad.'

Mrs Cunningham looks as though she is ready to bawl incessantly while Judge Cunningham is indifferent.

'We are charged with her care, not you. Your opinion is duly noted, but—'

'I want you to go to the meeting, not them,' Sera says.

'Excuse me?' Mason stumbles, with a cough following.

Mrs Cunningham sniffs behind her serviette and leaves the room.

'Seraphim, this is not a wise decision ...' Cunningham begins.

'But is it mine. I'll go to this stupid meeting with her, but not you two.'

Mason looks unsettled. 'Do you really want me to?'

Pudding arrives in the arms of a fresh-faced, red-eyed Mrs Cunningham, a summer fruit pavlova. 'Who wants dessert?'

Sera nods, avoiding the eyes of her new family.

'What time is it, then?' Mason says, taking out her pocket organiser.

Mason arrives at the cottage at eleven and not a minute after, muttering about the traffic and the need to get off quickly.

Conversation avoided, Sera slips into her car and they drive casually through the village and to the A road that leads to the Belowground roads. Mason is pleased to see that Sera is dressed in a plain black dress and jacket rather than jeans. Her aim was to get Sera off the hook with as little damage possible.

'Did you have breakfast?' she asks.

'Did you?' Sera questions.

'No.'

'Naughty, naughty.' Mason smiles despite herself. 'I had a bagel, thank you. Much to Mrs Cunningham's horror. She sees no place in the world for bread.'

'Yes, she used to be a lot bigger than she is now. Then she had an eating disorder a few years back.' Mason didn't hesitate with the truth today.

'That explains why she thinks she just pushed me out of the womb.'

'I'm sorry?'

'I'm assuming she can't have children,' Sera deduces. 'It explains the lack of air when I'm around her.'

Mason smiles sadly. 'Give her a break, Sera. She cares about you a lot. And, no, she hasn't had the opportunity to have her own children, but, trust me, she mothers everybody. You don't have to be fifteen to feel the wrath of Mrs Cunningham's kind heart. She practically reverse-psychologied me into coming to dinner and I didn't even realise it until I got to the front door. She is a hard woman to say no to. I admire your strength.'

They both chuckle as they approach the junction down into the tunnels. The sky disappears and the lights around them fly past as they shoot towards their destination. Mason watches Sera closely and then speaks with careful words, grasping the steering wheel securely.

'They didn't want to tell you this but Sidra Tall died yesterday morning. The other person who was in a coma. I used to work with her.'

Sera's throat tightens, yet she looks straight at Mason. 'But my dad's still okay? I haven't seen him all week.'

Mason nods. 'He's still here, don't worry. I just thought you should be kept up-to-date with any developments.'

'You sounded so lawyer-y just then.'

'Saying "developments" is lawyer-y?' Mason wonders.

Sera shrugs and smiles, scratching at the skin around her thumbnail. 'Thank you for telling me.'

'You would have found out on the Internet anyway.'

'Can't, Wi-Fi's out. Mrs Cunningham said she'd call about it.'

Mason laughs, 'Well, that sounds like a lie.'

'Yeah, it does, doesn't it? How dare she?' Sera turns on the radio and they listen to current tracks, Sera singing along as they drove to her school. Throughout the entire journey she assured Mason that she hated each song but still sung along because of the 'irreparable mind control the media insist on performing on today's youth.'

Mason asks what Mrs Foss was like far too late to be prepared and is nervous about meeting her for the final ten minutes of the journey, as though it was her education that depended on its outcome.

'I'm sorry, who are you?' Headmistress Foss asks when she opens the door to her study.

'Ms Mason, attorney general,' she says, with an unknown confidence.

'No, I meant who are you to Sera.'

'I'm her friend. I know her father. Mr and Mrs Cunningham agreed to my being here.' Mason sticks with facts.

They are sat down on soft sofas, offered tea, coffee and biscuits and then get down to the nitty gritty of Sera's future.

'I'm sure you're aware that Sera has no regard to school rules anymore, has been missing all of her classes and extra-curriculars, not turning up for all of her meals and, most dangerously, went into the village on her own, unattended, without permission.'

'Oh.' Mason looks at Sera as she blushes.

'I've never had a student like it. I understand that things are difficult but there is no excuse. And then there's the issue of the fees ...'

'What issue?'

'They haven't been paid?' Sera says, worried.

'Mr Reid paid for Sera's schooling termly and the last payment is long overdue for the next term. We can invoice in arrears, however, I have been advised by the finance team to ask about other forms of payment. I already asked Judge and Mrs Cunningham but they had no idea who was going to pay for this.'

'Well, no one can. I know how much the fees are here,' Mason says, thinking back to when independent education was just a couple of thousand a term. She glances at Sera who, silent, gives her blessing for the words coming out of her mouth. 'I'm afraid I'm going to have to withdraw Sera, effective immediately.'

'Yes!'

'I'm sorry?! That power lies with her parent or guardian!' Foss argues.

Mason stands and Sera copies.

'Her parents are currently unavailable and her godparents won't give you what you want. Either accept it or ... don't. Goodbye, Mrs Foss. Thanks for the tea.'

'I'm sorry, but I'll need that in writing if you think that—'

'Oh, piss off, Mrs Foss,' Sera says gleefully. 'I'm out of here.'

Leaving the elderly woman gobsmacked, Mason ushers Sera out of the room, shaking her head.

'You know, you'd've had to have left school after that anyway?'

Sera shrugs. 'It was worth it, though, wasn't it? You saw her face. Classic!'

'You understood why I did that?' Mason checked, while they gathered the rest of Sera's belongings and made their way off the premises for the last time.

'Course. Dad has a lot of money, so do you and the Cunninghams probably. But I'm not your problem and no one should have to pay that much money for little old me.'

Mason wanted to agree, but thought it would sound too mean if she said it out loud.

Sera groans as they get into the car and head back to Rotherfield Greys. 'Now back to the daily grind. Ignoring them is going to be even more pleasurable when they realise what we've done!'

'You'll have to go to school, Sera. That's the law.'

'Oh, I almost forgot you were a woman of the people.'

Mason laughs. 'I'm a human too!'

'You're better than Gavel and Stepford anyway.'

'Right…'

'You know, because he's a judge … and she's artificial …'

'I get it … Gosh, you three just might end up killing each other.'

'You could do it now. Spare me the pain of having to go back. Or top me off just after you explain that I don't go to school anymore. That should be hilarious.'

Dreading the thought, Mason is quiet for most of the drive. She wonders about Reid, about Daniel, and whether or not he would be happy that she was intervening in his daughter's life. Surely, he would be happy that she had stepped in just before all hell breaks loose at the Cunninghams'. Surely, she has to try and keep the relationship Sera has with them unified. Living with them is not the answer. Sera is already reckless and a rule-breaker, something the Cunninghams do not appreciate, and her mouth was only likely to get her into more trouble the longer she lives with them.

Mason pulls up outside the house, stalling, hoping that they didn't realise that they were back very early. It is just past one.

'I'm not a crazy person,' Mason begins.

Sera waits. 'You, kind of, sound it.'

'But do you want to live with me? In London. Temporarily.'

Sera's eyes go blank for a second.

'We can find you a school and – and your dad will be better soon, so …'

Sera smiles, almost embarrassed. 'I'll get my things.'

Mason waits in the car, heart beating fast. Ten minutes later, Sera gathers her things outside with Mrs Cunningham on her tail, talking irritably at her.

' – if Mr Cunningham were here, I would tell him to get you right back in that house, young lady. You can't go with her! Legally, you are not hers so keep and—'

'I'm no one's to keep! And it's my choice!'

'Please, Sera, we can pay for your schooling. I'll do anything, please just stay. I'm sorry about making you live here, I really am, but don't leave. I – I – I don't want you to go …'

Mason watches while Sera, uncharacteristically, drops her bags and hugs Mrs Cunningham. She gives them a minute and then she gets out of the car to help with the luggage.

'Look after her,' Mrs Cunningham says, holding in tears. 'There's a good girl in there somewhere.'

'I know,' Mason replies, in earnest. 'And I will, Shannah.'

They pack all of her things in and Mrs Cunningham waves them off as they go.

'I bet she's on the phone right now to her husband. In tears or cracking open the champagne, I don't know.' She laughs and Sera chuckles. 'No … What did she say to you?'

'She wants visitation rights.'

'And what did you say?'

'So, I said once a month is the best I can do. Got to give the old broad something for taking care of me while I was being such a bitch.'

'And here I thought you had no soul.'

Eight

New mother? Newly pregnant? A woman in need of support?
Come to the Railside Function Room at 7pm every Saturday
A safe place to talk
A place to discuss your options

Three women turn up this time, for fear of the illegality of the meeting. The flyer did not say much and the grottiness of the location creates necessary scepticism. Mother and baby support groups happen all of the time and talking is not a crime, but Molly doubts that the nurse had known what this was. If she had attended herself, she may not have been so quick to suggest it to others.

Shadows dancing along the brown concrete walls, they arrive at seven in the evening to a function room beside the hospital, a derelict building that does not seem occupied. It is only when the others arrive do they all venture inside, nervous and silent. The woman heading the group is intelligent and middle-aged, dark hair tied behind her round face. She introduces herself as they fill out name badges.

'I'm Dr India Rissington. I'm a surgeon and therapist and, obviously, invite women to share their experiences after childbirth or traumatic childbirth or pregnancies. That kind of thing. There's nothing to be afraid of, nothing will be shared. This is all confidential and completely non-discriminate. Obviously, you were referred because someone may have thought you needed to talk to somebody or you found out about us through word-of-mouth and our good work. That is all we're here to do, is talk. Is that okay?' She looks at them all happily. 'Who would like to go first?'

Molly, taciturn, raises her hand. Her story is short. She convinces herself that her son does not exist. He was taken away two weeks ago for greener pastures and a family with more money than she could fathom, to be brought up more comfortably and perhaps more ignorant of the real world than she would have liked. Her boyfriend is in hospital, recovering from a car accident with his life dwindling as they speak.

'My husband is similar.' Edith has her with her daughter. She is asleep in a carrier on her chest, sucking her tongue lightly against the warmth of her mother's chest. Secretly, she berates this grubby-looking woman. *How could anybody give up their child?* 'He needs surgery but I have no money.'

'Did they tell you about the thirty-day clause too?'

'Yes.'

'Absolute bollocks.' Molly tries not to stare at the writhing baby across the room. 'I didn't give up my son for this.'

'How much money did you get?' the third woman, the youngest, finally speaks.

'And what's your name?' Dr Rissington asks.

'Zoë. How much?' Her fingers tremble over the folders of her bulging cardigan.

'Not enough,' Molly replies. 'It's life-changing but not enough to save him in this day and age. I could rent a small house, start again in a new country, but what's the point in all of that? You know? He's sick and so am I for what I did. A sack full of cash for a baby. I'm not fine about it, before you all judge me.'

'And why are you here today, Zoë?' Dr Rissingon asks.

The room is silent until Zoë relays the tale of her unwanted pregnancy.

'I was his favourite for years. Loved him too, like a granddaughter should.' Her eyes gloss over. 'But anyway, when I was ten, Mum didn't want me to see him anymore – she never did really – and we moved away. I got back in touch when I was fourteen, thought I was doing the right thing, went round to see how he was because he had joint problems and things. Everything was fine for about three years. One day he must have just cracked. On Tuesdays, I help him with the gardening. He ... told me he would cut my throat if I didn't open my legs. So I did.'

'I am so sorry,' Dr Rissington says.

Edith takes Zoë's hand.

'Mum abandoned me once I told her what happened. She said I brought it on myself. And it turns out he's my father too, so ...'

'And you don't want it?' Dr Rissington asks her, looking at her stomach.

'Would you want this thing?'

The doctor bows her head. 'It's a difficult decision for anyone, Zoë. Thank you for sharing that.'

She shrugs, gripping Edith's hand.

'Now, I'm going to share my story, if I may,' the doctor states. 'Twenty-two years ago, I qualified as a psychiatric doctor, practicing dutifully and in line for promotion until I was on the brink of depression when my long-time partner – she was killed in a car accident. I took a hiatus. But by the time I was ready to see another patient, three years had gone by and there was talk of new laws and votes to change an already changed country. To feel useful again, I joined a protest group, offered support to people who had been mistreated by the police.

'Then I met Dr Rissington, an anaesthetist training to be a surgeon. He was and is the single most clever man I've ever met, with such radical and amazing ideas on right and wrong. And he was helping people, people such as yourselves where they couldn't afford it or had no other option. I think of how many lives he has saved and how many people would be dead right now without him and smile. He is a great man. So, in the end, I married him and have two beautiful sons. 2041 came and went and we were shut down while I was running my own department in the hospital. My most important achievement is the clinic we opened together six years ago. We've changed and made lives. People, just like yourselves, have come to us in their darkest hours and allowed us to help them. It may be unconventional and risky, but what else do we have? We provide a chance at living where the fucked-up doctors give you thirty days to agonise over a life, to say goodbye essentially. I'm amazed they give that long. Medicine is not what it used to be. I'm no longer blind to the strategies and corners cut by the people who claim to help and the politicians who rule instead of guide.

'I take care of myself, my husband, my children and every other person who asks me, as much as I possibly can. I know what it feels like to be let down and to want nothing more than to help those I love. I want to save your husband Edith and your boyfriend, Molly. And that child growing inside you grows inside the stomachs of every woman raped or every woman hurt in this world. I understand. I have options for you that we can discuss. We don't require money or payment.

Just your time and perhaps your help in exchange too. Here.'
She gives them all a card with the address of the clinic and a
telephone number. 'We can help but, I'm afraid, it's all of you
or none of you. We have housing and food. Make your decision
and give me a call.'

With that, she departs and they watch until the door closes.

'If you ask me, she's a bit of a nutter,' Molly says through the
silence. 'She really is a strange one.'

'Molly,' Edith says, rolling her eyes.

'I'm not saying that she's talking a load of crap because she
might not be, but that speech was horrific.'

'She's not talking crap,' Zoë reassures. 'The only reason
I came here was because I heard that some doctors this way
offered surgical help to those who can't afford it. Someone
from my area got some funny infection in his leg. Doctors told
him it was a lost cause but the Rissingtons removed it quick
and now he's okay.'

'It could be chance.' Edith says. The baby begins to complain
and she stands, pacing. 'I know sweetheart. I know that lady
was odd. Wasn't she?'

'I'm sick and tired of living in a grubby little hostel with
ten thousand other people,' Zoë says, upset. 'She has food and
somewhere to live and I can finally free myself of this thing. I
don't know you three but please help me. I already had nothing,
now I'm even less. I can't go back there tonight.'

'Come with me, then,' Molly suggests. 'At least so we can
think about what to do.'

'Until you dump me back in the hostel? I don't think so.'

'Listen, I don't dump people.'

'Just your baby,' Edith mutters under her breath.

'Since Oscar went into hospital our flat was taken away. I
couldn't bear to live there without him anyway. I'm living in a
hotel for now until I decide on my next move.'

'Thought you said you didn't want the money,' Edith says uncomfortably.

'I need to live if I'm going to help Oscar. You can come too if you want. Both of you.' She looks at Edith's baby. 'At least until we make our minds up. Then, if we go separate ways, we go separate ways. I know you think I'm the world's worst mother for what I did but I still have time to help you understand why if you'll let me.'

'Oh, I know why,' Edith says. 'It doesn't mean that I understand.'

'Please,' Molly says, looking at the ground. 'I know that this "everyone or nothing" thing is probably just a marketing ploy, but I don't really have many people at the moment.'

'Can't say I have either,' Zoë says.

'Me neither.' Edith tucks the card into her back pocket. 'Okay, Molly, show me what you're made of.'

'Is that a challenge?' The two women chuckle with her and head for the door in step.

It doesn't take long to collect Zoë's things from the hostel. She owns just a few bags and has nobody to say goodbye to. Built in a vacant alley in the centre of town, nobody notices the five-month-pregnant woman leaving with strangers.

Edith is so far away from home that she had already said goodbye to it a week ago when she returned for the baby's things they had saved for. She stores bottles and food in a backpack and suitcase, along with a secret supply of valuable items for hard times in a small house where she lodges.

The hotel is close to the hospital and no bigger than the hostel. The room Molly paid for is square, heated and has plenty of blankets for them all to share. The owners don't ask questions about the rooms new occupants, as she had hoped.

'Make yourselves at home.'

Clean and inviting with a red cushion on a sofa and matching curtains, they smile at the effort made by the hoteliers and sit down cautiously. Effort is rare these days.

'I have dinner all sorted.' Molly dives under the bed for a plastic box with a lid. She pulls items out. 'Cheddar and a lump of okay-ish bread, but I can toast it.' She rummages to light a candle on the coffee table. Beside it, is a stick and an open newspaper with old burnt crumbs scattered on top. 'And I save this for special occasions.' She pulls out a large bottle which is half-empty. 'Blackcurrant cordial!'

'Oh my God!' Edith says.

'Where the hell did you get that?' Zoë exclaims. 'I haven't seen a bottle of that stuff for about six months.'

'Thirteen, but who's counting?' Edith mutters. 'You really don't have to, Molly.'

'You know,' she responds, 'I haven't really had anybody since Oscar. My brothers didn't approve of him so I left home and I haven't really spoken to them since. They do okay, I think, but I wouldn't know, and since all of the world went to pot, I haven't been able to keep friends. It's everyone for themselves. Hence why I treated myself to this lovely bottle! I was looking for something stronger but this does the trick.'

She rushes to the bathroom with three empty water bottles and comes back shaking and mixing the cordial into the tap water.

'Here you go.'

After handing the drinks over, she starts on the evening meal, toasting bits of bread slowly and cutting the mature cheddar into small pieces.

Edith allows her daughter to drink from her breast while rocking her lightly and sipping on her fruit drink. 'Thank you,' she says in earnest as Molly passes her another piece of bread.

'No worries.'

'This is a lovely place,' Zoë says, sounding a lot more perky. 'The cushions and the sofa. Really classy.'

Molly laughs. 'Wow, you're really glad to get out, aren't you?'

'You have no idea. Only thing I had to look forward to was onion soup. For the seventieth night in a row.'

'Nice,' Molly says with cheese in her teeth.

'What's her name?' Zoë asks, turning to Edith and her daughter. She had fallen asleep across her chest and Edith carefully tucks her into her blanket carrier across her body.

'Well, I'm not sure,' she responds, touching her delicate skin. 'Haven't decided yet.'

'What about your mum's name or your husband's mum's name?' Zoë suggests.

'Trudy or Mary? Paul would be thrilled.'

'What about Paula?' Molly suggests.

'Paula …' Edith looks into her daughter's face and smiles. 'Maybe.'

'I called my son Oscar, after his dad. Maybe I shouldn't have.'

'No, maybe not,' Zoë states, worried. 'I'm not naming this. I don't want anything to do with it.'

'Honey, as much as you hate him, you can't hate the baby. They're innocent in all of this, perhaps more than you are,' Edith advises. 'Have you ever considered putting it up for adoption?'

'Of course I have. Especially with the nice settlement Molly got. But, on the other side of it, I just want it gone. I don't think I could last another twenty weeks, I really don't. I'd sooner jump off the closest bridge.'

Edith and Molly look at each other and say nothing more on the subject.

'So, what about your family, Edith? Still in Ireland?'

'Don't have any. All dead in the dust, unfortunately. Came to England in '38, met Paul at work and we've been together since in a little village near Bristol. Gloucester's the closest functioning hospital so here we are.'

'Dr Rissington operates out of Reading. Did you see that?' Zoë informs, looking at the business card with intrigue.

'Do you fancy moving to Reading?' Molly asks.

'I hear they're all stuck up their own arses. The ones who can afford to live well,' Edith says.

'Only most of them,' Molly chips in. 'But I do here things are better looked after over there. Could be a nice change.'

'I'd be far away from Paul. And you Oscar.'

'We'd maybe have to ask about that. Maybe they come with us or something.'

'I hope so,' Edith says quietly.

'Thanks for thinking about it, you guys,' Zoë mutters. 'It means a lot. Really. I just have the feeling that she could help us. I mean, how often do you see anybody have an abortion these days? They're practically unheard of.'

'Because they're illegal!' Molly yells. 'You get caught doing that …'

'I don't give a damn about the low population! I deserve the right to a choice. Just like you, Molly.'

'I didn't see it that way.'

'Well Edith doesn't agree with you. Differences aside, it's my decision.'

'Actually, it's ours,' Edith corrects. 'Without us, you don't get to do this.'

Zoë resorts to silence and stares moodily out of the window from her spot on the sofa.

'Alright, I have your gear. Two forms of ID,' Ellis closes the front door behind him and puts a National Insurance card and a white English passport in front of her at the dining table. 'You said your real initials are CM so I made your fake name the same. It's the last thing they'll expect. You have to hide in plain sight these days. Welcome to your new life, Clarke Manning.'

'I like it.' Clarke takes a look at her new passport photo and smiles, impressed. 'That'll do!'

'I don't do half measures. So you're a few years older than you are, just turned twenty-seven last month, so go with it. You're from Hastings originally and moved to London as a child. You were a self-employed photographer. Trust me, self-employed people are harder to trace.' He passes her an old camera. 'Your pride and joy. Now you do whatever it is you choose to do when you leave here. Get a job, sleep on the street, makes no difference to me.'

'Oh, I thought you cared!' She jokes sitting at the breakfast bar, stroking the bandage over her infinity tattoo where the artist had lovingly altered it to look like a daisy the day before. It had started to itch and she was beginning to get very irritable.

'Only enough to get you on your way. Perhaps drop the wig and go with the short hair? Up to you but it looks better without.'

'Thank you.' She strokes the back of her hair gently and looks at him as he clears away the plates she had left. Clarke shifts onto the sofa area and he joins her.

'You look good in my clothes,' he says, without looking.

She glances over at him, watching as he puts his hand through his hair and bites his nails. 'I've told you all about me, but you've said nothing about yourself.'

'Not what I'm here for.' He switches on the television and flicks mindlessly through the channels, anything to drown out the sound of her inquisitive voice. 'Why does it matter to you, anyway?'

'It doesn't, I'm just curious. It's only human, you know.'

'Is it really?' He decides on the news, although he hates it. 'This is so depressing these days.'

'Do you usually let people stay here? I mean, I've been here for a week.'

'Just as long as it takes. Then I send people on their merry way. Don't get too comfortable or get any ideas. You can leave as soon as your – Holy mother, Alex?'

Clarke's eyes hit the television faster than she can register, falling solely on Alex's face, clearly seen between the cluster of security guards and the prime minister in their wake. The headline is about the death of the director of public prosecutions and the widespread panic and fear among those in power. He is dressed head to toe in black with an earpiece in, looking very professional. With care, he escorts the prime minister into a car and follows him in eagerly.

'What the hell is he —?' Clarke begins. 'You don't think—?'

'I do.'

Despite the robotic nature of the bodyguards, Alex seems calm and had, in fact, smiled on camera. Both Ellis and Clarke can see the contentedness upon his face.

'Why would Wilson Frost buy Alex?' Ellis mulls.

'To find me,' Clarke says, heart pounding in her chest. Instantly, she heads for the spare room she had been sleeping in and shoves items into her backpack.

'What are you doing?' Ellis follows her into the room.

'Like you said, Ellis, I need to leave. It's only a matter of time before Frost finds me.'

'Alex wouldn't give you up.'

'Are you sure? Because I'm not!' She rushes back into the living area for her new identification. 'Listen, I do not have time for this. They could be on their way right now.'

'You have nowhere to go.'

'I don't care.'

'Clarke, stop.' He stands in the doorway and waits for her to stop moving. She gives in and waits. 'I'll admit, this is weird. If Frost finds you, he exposes me and the whole thing that I do here, which means he finds hundreds of former and current criminals in the process. I can take a look into this if you just wait. You said you want Alex back, don't you?'

Clarke nods stiffly.

'Okay, so here's the plan. You go to my parents' farm and wait there until I can see what I find out. Then I'll come and get you and—'

'But, Ellis, he—'

'But nothing. You cannot come with me to London. You'll be caught for sure.'

Clarke stands. 'Why are you going to London?'

'To see if I can suss out how much Frost knows.' He places his hand on her cheek softly. She examines it, taken aback. 'Please. Just go there and wait for me. Please.'

Clarke nods and continues to pack. It is decided that she leave immediately, for fear of capture and because she would not feel safe even if she was. Ellis provides plenty of food, warm clothes and a blanket, a torch and full directions to the farm twenty miles away and the shrouded entrance to the land through a public footpath.

Perhaps prematurely, Clarke peels off the plaster over her new tattoo and allows the cold night air to swim over it, both soothing and numbing as she travels alone in the dark, forgetting her imagined love for Alex, reminded of potential betrayal and the unrequited passion that she had hoped to receive from her newfound saviour.

'Kevin – now, don't get mad, but – I did a bad thing ...' He is stood outside her door with arms crossed and a distant smile creeps onto his lips.

'Yes, I did think that blue jeans weren't really you.' She is indeed wearing jeans and a vest and Briscoe looks her over with humour in his expression.

'Kevin, this isn't funny.'

He is standing just inside the doorframe now, chewing gum fervently with his hands in his pockets. The news of Tall's death has brought him on this Sunday morning, in the hope of discussing things away from the prying eyes and ears at the office. Instead, he is still on the doorstep after having knocked on the door three minutes ago.

'Why are you stalling? Let me in.'

'I'm hungry! Do you have any crisps?!' Sera yells from inside.

'Who is that?' Kevin says, his face dropping. He peers around Mason's casual figure into the apartment.

Mason's eyes are on the ground. 'Sera Reid.'

'Dolly!' He drops his voice. 'Why would you–? This is not the time to be nice!'

'That's just great, Kevin. What was I supposed to do? Her father is in a coma. She hates the Cunninghams, everyone does, and no one was going to pay for her to continue at that overpriced museum they call a school ...'

'And you are?'

'Of course not. I was thinking she could go to somewhere local around here.'

'State school? Reid's daughter? I can see that going down well,' he says sarcastic.

'She doesn't have a choice. And I'm sure when Reid is all better she can go back to her old school and everything will be back to normal.'

'How very optimistic of you.'

Mason stands aside and lets him in. To Sera, she says, 'Yes, I have some in the cupboard on the—'

'Found them,' Sera replies, crunching the food between her teeth. 'Is he your boyfriend?'

'Definitely not,' Mason confirms.

'I'm Kevin. I work with Dolly. I just came over for a quick chat and then I'll be out of your hair.'

'Oh, don't mind me, Kevin,' Sera utters cutely. 'I'll just sit here quietly and watch TV. Talk away.'

She grins and turns on the television, watching Sunday morning cartoons as she lounges on Mason's leather sofa.

Mason and Briscoe settle in the corner of the kitchen. Mason pours them both a coffee.

'Charming, isn't she?' Mason asks.

'She's her father's daughter. Clearly clever and doesn't take any crap from anyone.'

Mason makes a noise that sounds like agreement. 'It's weird that Sidra's gone.'

'I know. Even though I couldn't stand her at the best of times.'

'Me neither, but we were friends at one stage, really good friends. She started at the CPS a few months before me and showed me the ropes. Years down the line, friendly competition made us see the worst in each other. I swear, she couldn't even look at me when I got this job, even though she was DPP, it still hurt her.'

'I remember. She literally took it personally. She thought she got passed over. Your guilt won't help anything now though, Dolls. We just need to find whoever did this.'

'You mean, Shah needs to. That's not our job. We prosecute.'

'Yeah? And how is he doing so far? Last I heard, they were rounding up bosses from catering companies and interrogating them one by one, searching employment records as though the culprit would use their real name. These people are not stupid and Shah is treating them as though they are. We won't have anyone to prosecute at this rate.'

'Or maybe he's just counting on them being human. Everyone makes mistakes, Kevin. Especially emotional crazed murderers.'

'He hopes they'll make a mistake. Is it enough? Who knows. Most high-profile case in years and all the police have to say on it is "just give us a few more minutes to take our heads out of our arses …"'

'They're a good team,' Mason says. 'But it might just be too big a situation for them to deal with.'

'You think? If they still have nothing to go on, the media will start making things up.'

'With your girlfriend at the helm with her torch and pitchfork.' Mason laughs but Briscoe does not move. 'I just made a joke, Kevin. Feel free to laugh.' He says nothing. 'What is wrong with you?'

'It's not working between us. Celeste and I.'

Mason places a patronising hand on his back. 'Oh no. I didn't want to be right, Kevin, honestly. How did she react?'

He shrugs. 'We haven't discussed it yet. How can I? She's moved herself in and is getting all … comfortable …'

'Simple. Just tell her to get out. It'll be better for us all once you do.'

'You sound like George.'

'Of course. I made him. Listen, I know you're a lovely guy who probably can't say no to a blonde but it's time to take your own advice and remove your head from your arse too.'

'Okay,' he says unsure.

'And if that doesn't work, give yourself a deadline. Always works for me.'

'Yes, maybe.' He stands. 'Well, as much fun as this has been … I'm going to go to the gym. I've been slacking.'

'Oh, me too. Can I come?'

'Aren't you forgetting your new daughter?'

Mason's face falls and she ushers Briscoe out of the door with haste. Turning back to Sera, who is lying practically upside down on the sofa, she asks, 'What shall we do today then?'

The teenager shrugs and points at the TV, so Mason departs to her office, which is marginally cleaner than her one at work, spending her Sunday afternoon browsing and buying suits on the Internet and searching for potential schools for Sera. She makes a list of five for her to choose from, all very good schools with excellent results and plans to spring them on her at dinner.

There is a knock on the office door and Mason yells for her to come in.

'What are you doing in here?'

Mason hides her list. 'Just looking at clothes,' she says.

'Can we go and see my dad? Please?' Her frame is curled in and her hands cling to the doorframe as if terrified of rejection.

'Of course.' Mason checks her watch. 'We should be okay for the visiting hours if we hurry.'

Within minutes, they are in the car and they arrive at the hospital within half an hour. Stopping at the hospital shop for tulips, Mason follows a nervous Sera upstairs and into the room they are keeping her father.

It looks larger than before, now that Sidra's presence is gone and Reid is pale and frail in the corner of the room. Sera stops by the door and Mason gives her a moment. She can hear her breathing carefully in and out so decides to take the flowers from her trembling fingers. The empty vase on the bedside table welcomes the addition but only makes his depleting complexion look worse. Mason tries to hide her shock. She did not want to lie – again – and say that he looked better and that the odds were in their favour because that would have been unfair.

The embodiment of sickness, Reid's mouth is ajar with a tube stuck in his throat, making his chest move synthetically up and down. The machines say that everything is okay, but his still figure says otherwise. His face holds an emptiness that neither of them are used to and his rounded, happy face is pallid, as though it had had neither colour nor life. His head is wrapped gently with bandages and his right arm lays in a cast. If you had not known what had happened to him, you could not tell that he had been shot three times in the back.

Sera's eyes scream despair as she stands by his side, holding in tears. To her, he is unrecognisable, no longer the man who taught her to walk, who picked her up from school every day up until she was eleven, who knew which flavour ice cream would cheer her up depending on what the issue was, who promised her that they would be okay and that things would change for them since their lives were turned upside down. They did, but not in the way they had envisioned. Sera had been looking forward to having a mother figure at home finally. The last thing on her mind was the thought of having to pretend to be strong and now she has one of the most powerful women in the country looking after her and no father to speak of. She cannot complain yet Sera does not have time to be grateful that she got exactly what she wanted but at the cost of her father's life.

'Do you think he can hear us?' Sera asks timidly. She takes his hand.

'Maybe.'

She addresses her dad, nervous. 'I'm doing okay. Dad … Well, this feels stupid.'

'Say what you have to say,' Mason guides.

'I just wanted to let you know that I'm not alone. I have Mason looking after me while I wait for you. Just don't take too long.' She tries a laugh but stifles it awkwardly. 'He knows I hate waiting.'

'Miss Reid.' A voice comes from behind them, making Mason jump a little. A doctor in black scrubs enters. 'Who is this?'

'Hi. This is Ms Mason. She's my guardian.'

They shake hands. 'I'm Dr Spratt. I'm glad you're here as I wanted to discuss something with Miss Reid.'

'What is it?' Sera asks.

'Your father has been comatose for a few weeks now and we need to do some final neurology testing in order to see if this has developed into PVS.'

'What does that even mean?' Sera wonders aloud, clearly frustrated.

'It's a—' Dr Spratt begins.

'Persistent vegetative state. Let me guess, the next thing you're going to say is about the thirty-day clause.'

'No, the next thing was about seeing if we can wake Mr Reid up.'

'And then after that you want to talk about switching him off.'

'What?' Sera says, getting to her feet.

'Mr Reid is in a delicate condition and he—'

'Lord Reid, actually. And I don't appreciate you coming in here and dropping this on his fifteen-year-old child like it's the daily news bulletin.'

Dr Spratt sighs. 'I mean no ill will, Ms Mason, but she is his next of kin. This is hospital policy and I'm obligated to inform you that if the patient has not been marginally treated within thirty days, we cannot keep them and waste our resources when so many others are also sick. If it's alright with you, we want to run some tests on his heart and brain and try and take him off the ventilator today to see if there's been any progress. Is that okay with you, Miss Reid?'

Sera nods and Mason holds her shoulders, keeping her steady.

'It might take a few hours but feel free to stay.'

The doctor leaves the room and they are soon joined by two more members of hospital staff, who wheel Reid out of the room for testing. It all happens quickly and he re-joins Sera and Mason in what feels like five minutes' worth of time, docile as ever, Dr Spratt in tow along with Nurse Rosine.

'Are you ready for me to begin?' the doctor asks.

Sera mutters her blessing and they prepare Reid for their little experiment, steadily swapping the tubes down his throat for an artificial manual breathing unit.

They wait outside, but can see in through the window in the door.

'Sera, you don't have to watch,' Mason says as she takes a pause from her pacing.

'No, I want to see.' Mason places a hand on her shoulder and forces herself to watch alongside her. For a moment, the air is still, the only thing heard is the air bursting through the mechanical mask over his mouth and the nurse's hands are the only thing moving until Reid shifts. The doctor holds his wrist, listening to his heart but suddenly turns panicked as the machines beep frantically.

'I've got nothing. Get him back on.'

During the car journey home in the darkness, Sera's teeth make such a severe mark in her bottom lip that she cannot feel it at all.

'I'll sort it,' Mason promises.

Without prompt, she drives to her closest pizza takeaway, orders the largest, cheesiest pizza available and bundles it into the car. Sera waits in the car the whole time, her mind still on the events of the evening.

Once they arrive home, the first thing they do is begin shovelling the food down on the sofa in front of an unimportant film on the television.

'Feel any better?' Mason asks, when they are halfway through.

'Hang on, I don't think I've had just enough grease yet,' she responds, picking up another slice. 'Mrs Cunningham usually does duck or something on Sundays.'

'Well, I'm not Mrs Cunningham. And nothing beats pizza after a bad day.' Mason wipes her hands on a paper napkin and finally addresses the issue she had been skirting around all day. 'You'll need to be in school as soon as possible. This coming week if we can wrangle it.'

'I know,' Sera says, mundane.

'It won't be anything like the school you're used to.'

'I figured.'

'And you're okay with that?'

'Not really but I'm not okay about a lot of things. This is the least of my problems.'

Relaxed, Mason gives her the list for her to look over while she is at work the next day. 'Will you be okay, here on your own?'

'Yeah, I'll be fine. You have Internet access and food. That's all I need.'

'When I was your age, I was so different to you.' Mason looks into nothing, thinking back through the years.

'How?'

'You're confident and strong. I was nerdy and miserable.'

'Who said I'm not miserable?' Sera smiles at this and this is why Mason believes her.

'You've been through so much, Sera. No one would blame you if you were. I don't know how I would cope if it were me. At your age, my biggest problem was worrying if my parents would get a divorce.'

'Yeah, I have no sympathy for people in that situation. Your parents could be dead. If anything, kids in that situation should try to see the light: if your parents do divorce, at least they'll be happier than if they were bitching at each other at home all day. That and the fact that you get two houses to live in, maybe even more brothers and sisters if you're lucky.'

'Interesting perspective. They're still together at the moment.'

'You turned out okay though. Attorney General of England and all that …' Sera gulps down water. 'Top lawyer around town.'

'I suppose.'

'I think that's what a therapist would call minimisation. You've achieved a lot. Almost a figure to look up to.'

Mason smiles, her stomach turning. 'Can I ask you something?' Sera nods. 'Why did you two buy that woman at the court the other day?'

Sera sits up in her chair and puts down her pizza slice. 'I wanted a mother. Still do. Dad had been too busy with work to find someone he loved. Maybe he still loves Mum, but we thought that if he was part of giving us this weird system, we may as well benefit from it too.'

Mason smiles, understanding.

'I've been alone for a long time. Even with Dad around, I just didn't know what to call it. And it's strange because I was always closer to him than Mum, but when she died, the dynamic changed. And even though we didn't spend any less time with each other, it just wasn't the same. So, whenever we did talk, it was awkward but nice and eventually I told him how I felt … that I wasn't happy. So obviously, he suggested some therapist he could get through work but I just told him I needed him to move on and maybe find someone new. It had been years. Maybe I pushed him too hard because the next thing I knew, he was suggesting we get someone in for me to talk to at home. We just didn't realise that she would try to escape, obviously. Maybe not the best choice. Then again, I probably would in her position …' She picks up her pizza again and fills her mouth with the rest of the slice.

'Have you given any thought to what you want to do in the future?' Mason asks.

'Not a second. I don't even know what I'm doing next week.

I do not have time to figure out a five-year plan.'

'What do you like doing?'

'I like music …'

'Okay.'

'I know adults might says there's no money in it or the chances of making it are slim. I honestly don't know. Dad always wanted me to study law but I'm pretty sure I'd rather be a barista than a barrister.' Mason chuckles. 'Told myself I'd do women's studies just to piss him off. Mum and Dad always used to say, if you want to change things, go and do it: don't study it for years just to end up working in retail.'

They both laugh and Mason refrains from telling this young woman how much she enjoys her company and that she is the spitting image of both of her parents combined.

Nine

Paula wakes the group with her cries. Yawning, her mother changes her cloth nappy and settles her down with a milky breakfast, holding her gently in her arms.

Two days since their meeting, it had been decided last night that they would contact Dr Rissington and allow her to help them as much as possible. Edith and Molly, although unsure, have no other option and Zoë sees no other avenue that she can take. It is life or death.

After half a bowl of unsweetened porridge, Molly makes the call from the landline phone in the room.

'You've made the right decision,' Dr Rissington commends. 'We can relocate you all, Oscar and Paul included, to Reading tomorrow and begin the proceedings there.'

'That's very fast,' Molly says, frowning at the others. 'Why so soon?'

'Both men are in serious conditions, I gather, and we need to move quickly in order to assess and treat them.'

'Okay.'

'What is she saying?' Zoë whispers.

Molly holds up her hand.

'We'll pick them up first and then come for the three of you this evening, so sit tight and a car will be with you after sundown.'

Sitting tight was the hardest part. Edith and Molly had many questions still unanswered. How was Dr Rissington going to check out two very ill patients under the noses of the doctors and other medical professionals? Would she use force? Would they see their partners on the journey or would they be ahead of them? The illegality of the mission was the least of Zoë's problems. She was simply ecstatic about the fact that she was getting her way for once on life, revelling in the idea of an unencumbered future, dismissive of the warnings and advice the others were attempting to give her.

They badger her to think carefully because taking a life is serious. She throws back that rape is too. She had been led on and betrayed by someone she thought she knew while they were simply in love. She wants that feeling, that breathless feeling of loving someone and having them love you back. Edith argues that Paula provides her with that. Zoë hadn't meant it that way. She wants a family with a man she loves and maybe children in the far future, not so young, nor in such tragic circumstances. Molly tries to make her see reason but is shut down very quickly with a sharp comment about her being in no position to judge.

Three mothers in a room with different paths, they argue and snipe at one another for the decisions they made and the ones yet to come until the sun goes down beyond the windows and a SUV rolls to a stop across the street.

'Was that there before?' Zoë asks, glancing at it from behind the curtains.

'Get away from there, they might see us!' Edith whispers.

The phone rings and they all jump.

Zoë grabs it. 'Hello?'

'I'm outside. Bring your things and we'll be on our way.'

The line goes dead.

'It's her. Let's go.'

They begin to gather their belongings quickly. They had not packed earlier through fear of being let down, as well as slight hesitancy, and now have to rush in order to not leave Rissington waiting.

'Hold her for a second please?' Edith holds out her daughter and Molly opens her arms. 'Not you.'

Angry, Molly turns away and Zoë shuffles over, holding Paula as she sticks her tongue in and out. Zoë has her backpack and shoes on, positively glowing with excitement. She helps Edith slip her daughter into her carrier on her front and Molly takes one of Edith's bags down the stairs without a word.

Dr Rissington looks less professional than when they first met her. Her hair is tied back with her ponytail hanging out the back of a dark sports cap and she has a hoodie on under a dark jacket. Truth be told, she looks tired and drawn, as well as fairly nervous, waiting in the dark.

When they approach, they hear the car doors unlock and lumber in excitedly after placing their luggage in the back. Molly is sat in the front with the doctor and Edith, Paula and Zoë attempt to fill up the back seats.

To their surprise, the journey is silent. Perhaps none of them want to be the first to speak but they had expected Dr Rissington to explain what was going to happen. She does not.

They arrive outside an old warehouse in Berkshire a few hours later and follow the doctor inside. For a while, the only sound is the vacant snores of Paula's until they enter the building and hear light activity, the tinkering of metal instruments, springs compressing on mattresses, beeping machines and hushed whispers. Edith, Molly and Zoë are not shown the first two levels, so they guess that this is where the patients were operated on and recovering. Upstairs, there are small apartments and rooms just as nice and as basic as the hotel they were staying in. They are given a room for three and a baby; a crib is located at the end of one of the three single beds lined against the brick wall.

'Get some rest and I'll see you tomorrow.' Once more, Rissington leaves.

They stare at each other.

'Is it just me or did she seem off to you?' Molly asks the room while pushing her bag aside.

'Who cares?' Zoë says, sitting on her nominated bed by the window.

'Not you, obviously,' Edith points out, wary.

His interest resides on his steak, perfectly cooked to his taste, rather than the skin on her chest, clearly designed to catch his attention.

Celeste seldom treated him to much, certainly not evening meals, due to her supposed pitiful salary, so Briscoe jumped at the opportunity, only to remember that he did not think of her in the way he used to and that he has to explain that fact to her before the night is out.

Today, he isn't keen on his vegetables and moves the food around the square white plate, his thoughts drowned out by the light atmosphere in the restaurant. Quite upmarket, men are in suits, women in evening gowns, chandeliers hang brightly above and the waiters wait with expensive bottles of wine, hovering discretely beside tables when not going in and out of the kitchen. The top sphere of society dine to their hearts' content, money to throw away on three courses and intoxicating beverages.

'Stop playing with your food,' she orders, smiling.

'I'm eating,' he lies easily. He doesn't put anything into his mouth for the rest of the conversation.

'Is it work?' Celeste asks, concerned. She reaches over the table and takes his hand, her thumb rubbing over his skin.

'It's always work,' he says, distracted. 'When is it not work?'

She mutters agreement. 'More wine?'

'No, thanks.'

She already summoned a waiter to pour their white wine which had been on ice. He stares glumly at the full glass as he raises it.

'Cheers,' she salutes, clinking glasses.

He fakes a smile and sips.

'Fenella's on holiday again. If you ask me, she may as well leave. She said as much.'

'Who?'

'Fenella. My stylist. Her family are from Greece. Well, she was born there and raised here. Isle of Man, I think she said. Goes on holiday to see her parents and brother over there quite often and has said, many a time, that she might up sticks and leave. The economy's better, strangely, and there are job opportunities, apparently. I'd have to see that to believe it. Anyway, Steve is convinced she'll probably quit soon because she's not happy with the money but she's good and he wants her to stay. Unemployment is so bad, it's a wonder that she would risk it. I mean, I was so glad when you got your job back—'

'I didn't get my job back.'

'You know what I mean.'

'Sidra died and Dolly needed me,' he corrects stiffly. Perhaps this is going to be easier than he had previously thought.

'That's what I mean. You got lucky. She could have hired—'

'Lucky Sidra died?' He grips his fork tightly.

'No. God, stop twisting my words, Kevin. It doesn't suit you. Being mean doesn't suit you.'

'Having no tact seems to suit you. Someone died Celeste. She's not just a story, she's a human being. Was a human being.'

They say nothing for a few moments and Briscoe gulps his glass of wine whole.

'So, how is work going? Anything new going on at the office?'

'Not really.'

Celeste eats a sprig of asparagus. 'I was thinking, this whole mess with the court escapee probably won't be solved.'

'What do you mean?'

'I mean, it's been a couple of weeks now and no one has heard anything. I think it's a lost cause. Wouldn't be surprised if it was a false trail. What about you? Kevin?'

He suddenly catches on and smiles. 'I see what you're doing here. You're trying to get me to talk again, aren't you?'

'No. No, I said I wouldn't do that anymore. Kevin, it's just a conversation. I—'

'Since when was anything you said truthful?'

'Wow.' She puts down her cutlery and weaves her fingers together placidly. 'Do you really want to go there?'

'Do you want to go there? All you've ever really wanted from me was the inside scoop for your crappy news programme!'

'Will you keep your voice down?'

'No, I won't!'

'People are staring.' It is true. Those nearer their table had been able to hear the heated discussion, some pretending not to be taking in every word. She calms down and leans over the table, whispering. 'You are not a mean person, I'm sorry I said that, but you have got to get a grip.'

He leans over the table, mirroring her figure. 'So, you deny that half of our 'conversations' aren't regurgitated every night at six?'

'Oh, I wish,' she says, sarcastic.

'Why? Because it would give you a reason to be with me?'

'I don't need a reason! I love you.'

'No, you love my job and everything that comes with it. More importantly, you love your job and you'll do anything to keep it. Commendable though that is, it's not a good enough reason for us to continue with this relationship. It's just not fair. It's not fair on me and everyone else I work with.'

'Oh, let me guess, the D word is going to come up.'

'What, denial?'

'No, Kevin. Dolly! Precious Dolly. Almighty Dolly. The Queen of Law, the Keyholder of the effing City in your doe eyes—'

'What are you talking about?'

'There is not a day when her name does not crop up.'

'She's my boss and my best friend. We've been together – I mean, friends since we were twenty-one. That's a hell of a lot longer than we've been together.'

'How do you think it makes me feel when you talk about another woman constantly and mask it with your so-called friendship? Do you convince yourself that that's all it is? Is that it? Do you not even realise what it is that's going on between the two of you?'

'What the hell are you—? Nothing is going on between the two of us. Now I'm going to mention the bloody D word. Delusion!'

'I'm not the one who's deluded here.'

'Really? Instead of talking about what the real issue is, you're turning this on me. Classic avoidance tactic. Bravo. Well done. It isn't going to work with me. I have been so stupid over the past few months and the biggest mistake was seeing you. You're a lovely person, deep, deep down I'm sure, but you're selfish and unkind, sometimes even cold and you can't be cold in a world like this. Coldness equals loneliness and that's what you're going to be. Alone. Alone with just your defunct broadcasting, your only true love. Who knows, maybe Steve will take pity on you and not fire you in exchange for something else. I don't need to say it, you know what I mean. Maybe you'll get lucky too, but I refuse to let you use me like this, badgering me about investigations I'm not even part of. If you want dirt on things like that, find a policeman to manipulate because it won't be me. We can go Dutch on the meal but after that, the only place I want to see you is grudgingly on my 65-inch TV screen while I contemplate single life on the sofa.'

Her knuckles have gone white as she clutches the serviette, her eyes dark.

'You be very careful about the words you choose because I know I will,' she utters, menacing. 'The difference between you and me is that when you speak, the inside of a courtroom is where you make the most effect. Me? Hundreds of thousands of people see this face and hear the words from these lips daily. I might just mention, accidentally of course, the austere favouritism and blatant discrimination deep-set within the very heart of the legal system in England. Such poor management and misuse of power can only be down to one Dolly Mason, the attorney general who hires and fires more than human resources allow, constantly favouring her long-time best friend who, for all we know, doesn't know the difference between grand larceny and petty theft because he simply follows the bigger, better lawyers wherever they go, sniffing out the best jobs he can. Who needs interviews?

'Isn't it funny that as soon as Sidra Tall goes comatose that the dynamic duo are finally free to reign over the rest of the Crown Prosecution Service? It's the whole lion and lambs thing. You two work your way up into power, a scheme you've been working on for years, a plan formulated in the stuffy old libraries at the Inns of Court all those years ago which has finally come to fruition. Who cares if people die? Certainly not these two dictators. They spend their time laying off the little people – don't think I haven't been keeping an eye on those disastrous employment figures – and shagging each other in their offices when the wee little assistants aren't looking or working into the night for pennies because the wages are so poor. But yours aren't, sweetie. You have the money to have a swanky apartment in Islington with more rooms than you have friends while the people in this country suffer and die and are subject to the law you and your buddy MPs voted in and the laws you enforce and uphold. Criminals paying their debts to society, I bet that seemed like a great idea at the time, but the reality is so much more than anyone could have anticipated. People say the news is depressing and negative. I say it's the truth.

'Did you know that ninety percent of criminals who pay off their debts in society reoffend? Or that thirty-six percent of those who buy these people are injured or killed? Or maybe that seventy-odd percent of people can't find jobs, housing or rehabilitate fully without the aid of free counselling or halfway houses? They squat and steal and plummet further and further into poverty and despair. Homelessness and unemployment are only rife because of this system where the downtrodden are shoved into the dirt and those who aren't criminals become them. People I knew growing up, people who never would have done a thing wrong, are being thrown away for menial things, being ostracised by their families and their social circles all because of one little thing. Next thing you know, they're being shipped off to some stranger for a sentence. The worst thing is some people like it. Some people are so poor that they reoffend because it just might give them a home and a roof. People are happy with their fates. It's crazy. Bad luck if they end up with some heartless slave-driver instead of a caring family but people take that risk because that's all they have. Risk shouldn't replace hope or faith or clarity. Humans are made of tough stuff, but no one should have to suffer the things we have here. It's a mess and Wilson Frost tries to do the best he can while he's sat all cosy at Number Ten. For all we know, he's smoking cigars and playing slots while those on the outside who just about have lives need his help.

'Give the people a voice and they say what's on their mind. Choice is the real power these days. Choice and change. And I'm not saying I'm in any position to judge or empathise because I have a job and had a boyfriend and have a family and friends who love me, but I see things a lot clearer than you or Frost or your precious Dolly to know what the bigger picture is. England can't go on like this. Look at the beginnings of the United States or the Dutch Revolt. Rebellion will come sooner or later and I want to be on the front line when it all happens not tucked behind the skirt of my lover, best friend, whatever you want to call it, asking for a piece of the action because I stand my own ground. I don't let others tell me what to do or tease information out of me. More fool you for being so weak and ignorant just like the rest of your peers. Why, I think an exposé could be on the cards. I can see the headlines now! "Attorney General and DPP Sex Scandal. The former solicitor general and the most powerful lawyer in the country spend evenings at the office alone when they should be concentrating on justice, indifferent to those they claim to fight for." Your constituents would go crazy. No one likes a sex-mad politician. It doesn't sit well with the news channels either, Kevin. So please, don't be so full of yourself thinking that you have the power here because I think we both know that that rests with me.'

Taking a breath, Celeste grabs her bag and leaves Briscoe to pay the bill, her long blue dress floating behind her in her wake. He says nothing, soaking in her words, memorising them as much as he can before he relays the conversation in its entirety to the attorney general.

He finds Dolly the next day shut in a conference room with Freil, Michaels, Wendle and Waltz, George sat in the corner with a dictaphone and typing notes onto a laptop. She had beckoned Briscoe in to join her through the large glass walls, yet he waits patiently outside, not wanting to be drawn into other conversation lest he forget what he came to her to say.

He is more than nervous when he begins speaking, a predecessor to the bout of the shakes he develops midway through.

'You know when you said that breaking up with the Devil would be good for us? I wholeheartedly disagree.'

Briscoe recounts the sordid event, leaving out the wordier portions of her threat and instead stating what it is she really meant, the meaning shrouded within the metaphor.

'That's just brilliant,' Mason utters. She is smiling, although Briscoe cannot see why.

'Why are you smiling?'

'Because it's just funny. Dead MPs, one senior judge comatose, a convict worth more than all our salaries on the loose, a teenager in my flat and, to top it off, Celeste Lander out-manoeuvres us and threatens to spread lies to the entire country.'

'Not as stupid as we all thought she was,' George comments.

'I had the feeling it was an act,' Mason admits. 'Pity.'

Briscoe sighs. 'I'm sorry.'

'I don't think you understand. This could shut us down.'

'You can't get rid of Prosecution.'

'I mean us. Everyone who works here will probably be replaced. If the public don't trust us now, they won't after she decides what it is we're guilty of.'

'You're the one who said I should do it! And you!' He points a threatening finger at George.

'I meant in a nice way, a way that didn't get a backlash like this! And so the propaganda continues!' He had never seen Dolly this angry. In fact, he had never seen her angry at all. She usually supresses it, cries when she's alone and then gets back on track all within a day.

'Should I get Felton and Smith?' George asks, almost standing.

'No. Not yet. We'll call an official meeting with PR and HR if and when that cow follows up on her threat. I'll call Felton today just to warn PR and comms to keep an eye out, not naming any names. Then if it all goes to shit, we'll go to Frost. As if I don't have enough on my plate.'

Mason walks out of the room and through the corridors to her office. Briscoe and George follow.

'Shah is not doing well,' Mason confides in Briscoe as she stomps. 'Our guys are going back to help and as much as they can, but I might have to retract them if the work gets so light. We'll need them here for Rissington anyway.'

'Do we have a start date yet?'

'Yes. I had a word with the supreme justices and they advised we start in a week. And also that I take over and prosecute.'

Briscoe stops short of her office and she enters inside, hands in her hair, picking up her telephone.

Sera had decided on St Giles' School based on its proximity to Mason's apartment as well as the boys and girls it admitted without testing or money.

'I've never been to school with boys and I think I'm slightly overdue,' she had said that evening over microwave lasagne.

Mason, agreeing that it about time she mingled with the opposite gender, makes all of the necessary calls the next morning, has a lunch meeting with the headmaster and Sera, is late back to the office, managing to be subtle in taking over Briscoe's case as well as responsible in her 'adopted' child's education.

Sera's first day is the following Monday and she counts down the days until she is no longer bored with daytime television and snacking on anything she can get her hands on. Over the weekend, they go out shopping for her new uniform, which happens to be a very flattering slate grey. Sera comments on Mason's lack of sleep while she tries it on, twirling for her in the dressing room in her pale grey shirt, darker grey skirt and matching blazer.

'Don't worry about me,' Mason assures, rubbing her eyes lazily.

'I don't. You'll feel better once I get to school. One less thing to worry about.'

'A million more to go.'

'Is it really that bad?' Sera yells as she changes back into her blue trousers and hoodie.

'It's worse, but never mind.'

They spend the evening packing a delightful lunch for Sera, ensuring she knew the route over the field to the large school set within an early 1900s prison and letting her know that she should call her when she's on her way in every day.

'Okay, Mother,' Sera half-complains.

Mason's stomach feels hollow. 'Are you sure you don't want me to take you in on Monday? I can come back from work and drop you off and make sure everything is okay and then go—'

'Absolutely not! Do I look like I'm eight years old? I'll be fine.'

Dawn comes a lot quicker than Sera wants. By the time she yanks herself out of the bed in the spare room and tumbles over her messy belongings, Mason is already gone, as usual, traces of her presence seen in the use of the shower and the coffee cup by the draining board.

After twenty minutes in the bathroom, Sera changes into her uniform. It feels a lot tighter than it had yesterday. Despite herself, she was nervous and scared of this new thing she was embarking on. She had not travelled to and from school daily since she was ten years old. Ever since she was eleven, she slept, ate and did everything on the same site, saw her family every few weeks and did not have to make much effort in turning up every morning. The housemistresses came to her to make her attend classes and, in order to do so, she simply had to wander a few hundred metres to her left and down a few staircases to get there – not across a whole field.

And there was the boys thing. She had never been educated around them, had done school sports tournaments and events with local boys' schools but had never been involved with them in such a capacity. A chess tournament when she was twelve. Careers events at a university in spring. Lacrosse tournaments last year. Boys had been around and never concerned her much but suddenly she found herself checking the mirror three times to ensure that her mousy hair sat perfectly in a messy bunch over her left shoulder.

Is this really a good idea? Pulling a face and hoping she does not break out into recurrent sweats over the next few hours, she makes for the kitchen, trying to clear her head.

She fixes herself a bowl of frosted cereal while watching the morning news. She hears Mason's name once or twice, accompanied by the prime minister and other important MPs, but she switches off completely, swallowed up by her fears of stepping foot into St Giles'.

The clock says 07:45 so she grabs her backpack, full of stationery, paper, lunch and a book entitled *Exploring the Comatose Consciousness: A Study of Brain Injury,*

Physiological Response and Deep Sleep Consequence, leaving the flat behind her.

She runs back and pushes her finger into the lock pad; Mason had her programmed into the security system yesterday evening. As she climbs down the steps, she texts Mason, saying, *On my way*.

A moment later, Mason replies: *I told you to call me*.

Sera switches her phone off and tucks it into her bag.

The street is less quiet than usual, commuters rushing down to the transport below or crossing the green to get across to the buildings ahead. The fields are vast and threatening, frost of the night before transforming into fresh dew that wets her ankles through her tights. Earphones plugged in, Sera tries to ignore the group of kids ahead of her chatting, dressed in the same uniform as her. Humming along to a random track, she ignores the feeling in her stomach that tells her this group of ten are probably quite popular, a mixture of girls and boys around her age, a couple holding hands and others occasionally squawking at something Sera thinks is probably not that funny.

She follows them the rest of the way, keeping a large distance between them and her. The large gates are the same as she remembers them when she had briefly visited with Mason last week, silver and sharp, a building made to keep them in. The barbed wire and broad security gate had not been removed from the old prison since they utilised it as a school, perhaps something to add to the surroundings. The courtyard is vast and the outdoor concrete was reduced for a small playground while the fields surrounding the grey building are used for sport; a couple of rugby posts and football nets stand on top of manually marked pitches and a large track is to the side.

The sign to the reception is clear and she reports to a slim grey lady, who Sera figured looked more like a librarian than anything else, and receives her student identification and electronic pass, a homework planner, her timetable, a map and an instruction to get to room S11 for registration.

Do I have to? she wants to say, but does as instructed, following the map as quickly as she can.

S11 is a lab on the ground floor of the Science Block and Sera arrives at the perfect time, while the students are filtering slowly in, only three people in the class so far. Before going in, something makes her take a backward step. Her foot makes contact with something hard and she jumps.

'Watch it!' she yells.

Behind her, a dark-haired boy in a blue wheelchair glances at her and rolls back slightly. His graffitied bag is hung over the back and he is the only student Sera had seen in trainers. She can tell that he is taller than she is, perhaps older.

'Sorry,' she corrects, embarrassed, and she slips into the class, taking a seat at the back.

Unknown to her, he is right behind her, following her in and parking his chair beside her.

'What?' She is so used to saying this, there is no desire for her to change her diction for a stranger.

'This is my seat,' he says plainly. 'Dead giveaway as it's the only place without a chair behind the desk.'

Sera's eyes check that this is true and she cannot see any evidence to the contrary. She is silent and takes out her timetable and places it on the desk. She begins picking the skin on her thumb.

Pupils continue to enter, some staring when they realise that they do not recognise her. Sera is sunk halfway down in her chair when the teacher, Mr Peach, introduces her.

'Would you like to come to the front of the class? Or stand?' No response. 'Okay, well, class, you'll have noticed that we have a new student today sat somewhere to the right of Edwin, if you can make her out. Her name is –' He checks his register.

'– Seraphim Reid …'

'Sera,' she corrects quietly. Some of the class smile and wave.

'… Sera Reid, sorry, and she's from London but previously went to school in High Wycombe. Please make her feel comfortable, don't badger her or ask her any stupid questions. I see, you've already made friends with Edwin, so he can show you around for the time being, which works out perfectly as you share most of the same lessons …'

Mr Peach continues on about what is happening at school, a warning to keep phones off and out of sight, menial updates and reminders for homework clubs, stressing the importance of study in such a vital school year. Sera glances to her left at Edwin, who is picking stray pieces of material from his leather gloves and fiddling with his wheels.

He notices her looking and smiles at her.

'What?' he mimics, pushing a hand through his hair, making sure that it stuck up in the right way.

Sera can't help but smile and roll her eyes. 'Funny.'

'I thought so,' he replies, taking off his brake. 'Let's go. Looks like we both have Maths first thing. The bane of my existence.'

Edwin paving the way, Sera picks up her bag and follows him out of the classroom, curious.

She follows 'Ed, not Edwin' around like a puppy all day, from Maths to French, History and English. It is ridiculously easy for her to stick by his side. Everyone likes Ed, although he is not one of the obvious group of leaders they encounter in every class. He is middling, neither loved to the highest degree nor hated and this position is perfect for Sera. She sits next to him in every lesson, allowing him to explain who they teachers are, whether or not to take them seriously and how much homework they liked to dole out.

Lunch is in the large food hall, stairs leading down to it,

not much different, Sera supposes, to when it was a prison, only some of the walls were a bright vermillion with posters about healthy eating covering them. She had asked him why he was not sitting with his friends at lunch and he said he never did because they were out playing football or rugby on the field, so he eats inside and goes out to watch if he feels like it. Otherwise, he would go for a walk, or a roll, as he had said, listening to music or visiting the library.

'Well, you can always feel sorry for me at lunch times if you like,' she says, hoping he would take her up on the offer to stall her loneliness.

They separate during the final period; Edwin has double Art and she is timetabled in for Physical Education.

'I can meet you after, if you want,' Ed suggests.

'Oh, thank goodness for that.' She lets out a sigh of relief.

'You can't get rid of me that easily.' He laughs. 'Have fun doing your stretches or whatever.'

'Have fun painting butterflies.'

As Sera had not brought in her sports kit, she sits on the sidelines, watching the class warm up and play a politically correct game of handball. At the end of the class, they go over the rules. She knows nothing as she had never played it before, which people laugh at but she knew all the answers about nutrition and biology.

'Not laughing now, I notice,' she says to the class after her perfect answer.

She rushes out as the bell rings and the students get changed to find Ed wheeling towards her from the courtyard.

'How was it?' he asks.

'Dismal. Who plays handball anyway?'

'You played?'

'Didn't have my kit. Might do that next time, it was so dull. I can tell my lacrosse stick will not be of any use here.'

They head towards the windy field, strolling through cars with parents in them, who have arrived to pick up their children. Their hair blows about their faces.

'Lacrosse? You went to private school or something?'

'Is that a crime?'

'No. No. Just different.'

'No, it's not.'

'It is here. Be careful they don't drag you down. The teachers. Not particularly inspiring.'

'Don't worry, I do that enough myself. I wasn't exactly a star pupil. Are you coming this way?' She references the vast field ahead.

'Okay. I'll get my mum to pick me up on the other side.' He pulls out his phone and texts her. 'I'm one of the few people who is allowed to have this on during school hours. For obvious reasons. It's all on the manual.'

'What manual?'

'I call it my manual.' He pulls out a tag which is fastened to his bag and points out a similar thing on his wrist. '"Hello, my name is Ed and I am a paraplegic,"' he reads. '"If I fall, please help me back into my chair or find someone who can. If I am unconscious, please assist me by calling 999 and placing me in the recovery position. If you do not have a phone near you, please use mine, which you will find on my person at all times. If this phone does not work, please find another as soon as possible." They forgot to add, don't laugh at me or poke my legs to see if I can feel it,' he says, grim.

'Jesus, by the time they read all that you'd probably be dead.'

Ed bursts out laughing, holding his stomach and Sera concedes, chuckling too.

'Probably be dead …' He wipes his eyes with a final titter and watches her. 'Can I ask a question?'

'You can.'

'If you went to boarding school and your parents could afford to send you there, what happened? Why are you here?'

Sera looks at the blue sky in wonder, searching for the right words. 'My parents are … elsewhere.'

'Say no more. You don't have to tell me anything.'

'Tell me something I don't know, nosey.'

'Oh, there's Mum.'

A short woman is stood beside the subway entrances in a warm coat, hands around herself to stop the wind from blowing her away. Ed goes over to her and Sera stops a few metres away, instantly recognising her. Rosine looks into her eyes in the same way that she had before, full of pity and sadness.

'Mum, this is Sera. She started today and I was showing her around.'

Rosine nods. She steps forward and holds out her hand. 'Pleased to meet you.'

Sera takes her hand reluctantly. 'You too, Mrs Briscoe.'

'Ms Shaw.'

Sera notices Ed's discomfort.

'Would you like a lift home? I have the car down—'

'No, thanks. I just live in that building.' She points to the apartment block a few streets away which can be seen ahead. 'See you tomorrow?' she asks Ed.

He nods and leaves with his mother. Rosine looks back over her shoulder at Sera, meeting her eyes again as she looks over hers.

Ten

The farm is silent and foreboding when Clarke arrives. There are no animals grazing the fields, no streetlights to pave her way, no cars rolling through the single-track roads.

The concealed entrance is on the right, so she skips across the road and hurries down the dirt track which leads first to a large, old farmhouse, cleverly christened 'The Old Farmhouse'. It is empty as Ellis had said, awaiting his parents' return.

Clarke takes the key he had given her and opens the front door, heading through the old hallway with beams on the ceiling and to the back of the house where she finds the kitchen. An Aga range cooker rests against the back wall, a few pans on the surface beside it. The window shines a light on the large fridge-freezer and she yanks it open, filling her backpack with a small bottle of soy milk, a lump of cheese, tomatoes, bottled water and a chocolate bar before raiding the cupboards of crackers and biscuits and the pantry of tinned baked beans, tinned sweetcorn and tinned chickpeas. In the living room, she takes a throw blanket from one of the sofas.

Satisfied that she can carry no more, she exits the house and continues round to a series of outbuildings, some of which housed shifting sheep, restless horses and a variety of cows. The noises they make scare her, at first, but she soon ignores the feeling of unrest once she realises they are no threat to her.

Following his instructions to the letter, Clarke finds a barn on the edge of the green land, a shack too large for housing chickens with enough room for her to make a bed for the next few nights.

Paul and Oscar lay side by side in the makeshift ward. The curtains are closed when Dr Rissington allows them to enter. Paula is with Zoë upstairs having her afternoon meal while the other two are taken to see their partners for the first time in five days.

They had been wasting time waiting for them to be ready, eating decent meals that were not the consistency of porridge; they had meat and vegetables, soup and bread – basics, but lovely, fresh basics. There is a vegetable garden in the back and a small farmyard with sheep and cows that provide most of their sustenance. Paula likes looking at the animals when they walk outside and there is enough grass for them to sit outside for lunch on a good day. They are treated well and are grateful yet restless and anticipating.

Zoë wants out as soon as possible and spends most of her time helping Edith look after her daughter, a plan set in place by the new mother to convince her that having a baby isn't a bad idea. Edith did not know how well this plan was going, as of yet, as her mind rests on her husband and his wellbeing. For once, she and Molly have something in common, an ill partner on the verge of death.

They hold hands as they enter and their palms grow tighter

when they see them. Both men are pale and unconscious, a measure Dr Rissington assures is the safest. Oscar still has cuts on his face from the collision, slowly healing and no longer bright red.

'We don't want them to be under much strain if they'll be having surgery.'

Molly nods.

'When will they get surgery?' Edith asks as she takes in her husband's features. Her hands on his cheek does not feel the same as it used to.

'That all depends on you. Paul needs a donor, a complete transplant. I ran some tests at the beginning of this week and the damage is too much to simply fix. It would cost too much. Oscar is better but he needs just one little valve replacement from a viable heart.'

'Well, do you have anyone?' Molly practically yells.

'They're a perfect match.'

It takes a moment for them to realise what it is she is saying and to assess the gravity and sorrow of the situation they are in. The realisation of the doctor's true intention becomes evident and the tone in the room shifts from sadness to anger.

'What are you saying?!' Edith blurts.

'You know what I'm saying,' Dr Rissington responds, stiff. 'It's one or the other and we don't have a lot of time.'

Before every trial, she likes to turn up absurdly early to observe the smooth dark wood, to imagine the best outcome and imagine success before the distractions begin. The people and the lies leave a bad taste in her mouth and being the first to arrive reminds her that this is just a room and it has no power over her; the only power it has is over the person sitting on the other side of the room with the defending lawyer.

His name is Smith Colchester. Not the defendant, the lawyer. His notoriety comes from his distinct habit of defending the guilty and being very good at it. The 'smug son of a bitch', as Mason often refers to him, had won every case this year so far, slaughtering all of the best lawyers in the CPS. She is the best of them all and he is about to slaughter her next.

He arrives dressed in a suit that looked something like silk, his hair gelled back and, for once, looked solemn.

'What's wrong with your face?' Mason questions, trying to concentrate on her notes for the opening statement.

'Hm? Oh, me?' He sits back on his chair. 'I'm just so so deeply concerned about what you'll do with your time once I wipe the floor with you.'

'Whatever.'

For once, she has no witty comeback and instead focuses on doing up her white robe and fixing the black wig on her head. She wonders why on earth they still had to wear these archaic things but has to admit that the costume gives her a sense of power and purpose.

R v Rissington (2051) begins at 10:02 thanks to a delay with Judge Cunningham, giving Mason another moment to grill her second on the case, Andrew Friel, about the worst of it, the situation as it stands, a running tradition that the others lawyers learnt to ignore: 'For goodness sake, the simple fact that his wife has not turned up is proof in itself that they are still in operation and all you cretins do is tell me that you can't locate their damn headquarters or operating theatres or whatever. Absolutely disgusting. Then again, if she doesn't testify for us, she isn't testifying for them and the one person who can tell you a judge of character is a person's spouse, even if she is lying – which means they are down one count because they don't have the doting wife saying what a great man he is. We have victims, dead and alive and people willing so we should be fine, only we won't be because they know where he is operating and don't have to disclose it. They even have the disdain to plead 'Not Guilty' and I'd love to see how they explain away all of this evidence, I really would. You know?'

'You'll do fine, Ms Mason. You always do,' Andrew soothes.

'Thank you.'

'Here he is.'

Cunningham strolls in an hour late and begins proceedings, stating the charges of GBH and murder, meanwhile Mason eyes the defendant, a short and cheery-looking man with a growing waistline who looks strangely and unsettlingly relaxed. As suspected, he pleads 'Not Guilty'.

The time for her opening statement has come, her stomach somersaulting and her mouth going dry. She hates this part, the people staring at her, the expectation of being blown away. Everything rested here. This is the moment where people decide to take you seriously or not, decide whether or not you're a good lawyer and can carry the case through to the finish. She can nail this, but all she has to do was speak.

'Madam Attorney General,' Cunningham says for the third time. He is impatient but it is subtle in his voice.

She is still seated, staring at the ground, vacant.

'Ms Mason?' Andrew whispers.

When he touches her shoulder, she finally focuses.

'I'm sorry.' Mason stands from her chair and begins her rehearsed speech. '"I swear to fulfil, to the best of my ability and judgement, this covenant: I will respect the hard-won scientific gains of those physicians in whose step I walk, and gladly share such knowledge as is mine with those who are to follow. I will apply, for the benefit of the sick, all measures which are required, avoiding those twin traps of overtreatment and therapeutic nihilism. I will remember that there is art to medicine as well as science, and that warmth, sympathy and understanding may outweigh the surgeon's knife or the chemist's drug. I will not be ashamed to say "I know not" nor will I fail to call in my colleagues when the skills of another are needed for a patient's recovery. I will respect the privacy of my patients, for their problems are not disclosed to me that the world may know. Most especially I must tread with care in matters of life and death. Above all, I must not play at God. I will remember that I do not treat a fever chart, a cancerous growth, but a sick human being, whose illness may affect the person's family and economic stability. My responsibility includes these related problems, if I am to care adequately for the sick. I will prevent disease wherever I can, for prevention is preferable to cure. I will remember that I remain a member of society, with special obligations to all my fellow human beings, those sound of mind and body as well as the infirm. If I do not violate this oath, may I enjoy life and art, respected while I live and remembered with affection thereafter. May I always act so as to preserve the finest traditions of my calling and may I long experience the joy of healing those who seek my help."

'That was the Hippocratic Oath, circa 1964, written by Louis Lasagna, the Academic Dean of the School of Medicine at Tufts University in Medford, Massachusetts in the United States, an oath vowed, in some form, time and time again by medical professionals for decades. Dr Rissington has broken his promise, the promise he vowed to when he became this healer of the sick, this preserver of nature. He took this oath, spat on it and squashed all meaning from it, insulting all of those who have undertaken it in earnest. Rather than respecting previous physicians, he ridicules them by taking their ideas and practices and using them for horrific surgeries that mangle and mutate. He shares this knowledge with unregistered surgical doctors, placing lives directly in danger. He does not do this for the benefit of the sick. There is no art to what he does, only butchery and savagery. Understanding and kindness are out of the picture, just a question of how much he will gain in return for treatment. If he does not know how to heal an ailment, he will guess rather than get the person the real help that they need and deserve. He uses personal information as leverage to fund this occupation and, not only does he do it daily, he takes pleasure in playing God. Rather than prevent, he will risk further damage in order to get a payday, operating out of greed not necessity with no morals or obligations to care. Dr Rissington will not be remembered with affection. If I can help it, he will be remembered as what he is; Dr Ian Rissington is a murderer and an abuser of his power, using the sick for gain and the dying for profit, hurting people as he goes. I have never seen behaviour like it, behaviour so abhorrent and vile. I, with the full backing of the Crown, call for justice and for this man to be punished for his many wrongdoings, which sadly include violating his professional oath, fracturing and stealing lives and living as a man with no heart and no soul – not like a man at all. He should no longer be graced with the title of doctor. Mr Rissington is guilty through and through.'

Finally breathing, she sits and surveys the room. Some impressed nods but mostly stunned silence. To her, that is a result. She hopes she did not bore people with the technical speech but it gave the powerful effect she had intended.

Mason doesn't hear the Colchester's statement, she can't. She doesn't have to. His angle is that Dr Rissington is an innocent man whose surgeries simply did not go to plan due to low resources, no money and fate. The current climate is to blame. She is accused of a wild goose chase, prosecuting a man who is a healer of the sick, doing all he can to help others in such dire times. An adequate speech but not as good as hers.

Her first play is Lucas Winner, a father-to-be who died on

the operating table after the doctor attempted an experimental treatment for a blood clot.

'At the final moment, Mr Winner was missing both arms and a leg and died from blood loss. The scene was horrific.'

On the screen is the remains of Mr Winner.

'How do you explain this?'

Dr Rissington has nothing to hide, happy to be cross-examined. 'We had agreed with Mr Winner that we would remove an arm and a leg to increase this chances of survival. As all doctors are aware, what happens in the operating theatre does not always go to plan and we had to do what we could to save him.'

'We? We being who?'

'Myself and the other surgeon operating.'

'And who was that?'

'Another doctor.'

'A name, if you would.'

'That's not relevant.'

'Oh really?' Mason wonders. 'I hear the other doctor was your wife, Dr India Rissington, a doctor, yes, but a psychiatric doctor, a woman unfit to perform medical surgeries.'

'Interesting theory. My wife is a consultant.'

'And yet she isn't here being sentenced or to prove otherwise.'

'No,' he says, clear.

'Because we can't find her.'

'Interesting,' Dr Rissington utters, looking away from her.

'Where is she?'

'You'd have to ask her.'

Mason smiles but there is no joy behind her eyes. 'I just have a few more questions. Miss Rebecca Bridge, first degree burns to the face and chest, left severely deformed?'

'That's a question?' Judge Cunningham queries.

'Yes,' Mason assures. Her eyes float back to the defendant.

'No? How about Mr G. Merryfield, cured of testicular cancer but left half-dead with a number of debilitating breathing conditions and in need of twenty-four-hour assistance?'

Dr Rissington says nothing.

'Ms Penny Attis, blown aneurism? Alice Niro, almost killed after liposuction, same for Jenny English, except it was a breast augmentation. William Hines, defunct pacemaker. Nataly Njeama, irreparable damage after extreme skin treatment, not to mention psychological harm inflicted to all. Shall I continue?'

Mason finds that silence means she is able to take her seat, allowing the audience and Cunningham to muse thoughtfully on this man's actions. She is careful to take a sideways glance at Colchester before she sits; she can see him thinking from the vacant expression on his face, hoping that she can secure the entire case with the statements of three of the victims.

There is still time to go back to the office to check on Briscoe and the others, so Mason drops by at six to find mostly everyone still at their desks, as is the norm. Friel had gone home straight from court, exhausted and riddled with a nasty headache after all of the days' events. She is beginning to develop a migraine herself.

After spying on her friend in a meeting room with three interns and hoping he was bullying them into actually doing work, she slips into her office, removes her shoes and lies back on her chair, relaxing – that is, until the telephone rings.

'I'm not here,' she whispers into the microphone.

'I'll ring back later then.'

'Who's this?'

'The man you're going to dinner with tonight.'

She knows exactly who it is. 'And would he be buying the food or my help?'

'Just a few moments of your time, sweetness.'

She grimaces. 'What makes you think that I'll say yes after all these years?'

'You can never resist a bit of gossip. I know that.'

'What do you have?'

'You'll have to wait and see.'

'I hate enigma.'

'So that's why you became a lawyer!'

She chuckles and is angry at herself for doing so. 'Where?'

'The usual place.'

'You really pull out all of the stops, don't you?' She hangs up. 'George!'

Within seconds, he is in her office.

'Yes?'

'Could you do me a massive favour? I need you to go shopping for me.' She gives him her credit card. 'Get as much food as you like, use the spare override key for my flat and just stay there for a few hours until I get back. You'll understand once you get there.'

'Okay.' He is confused but Mason is sure he wouldn't mind keeping Sera company for a few hours, despite his mumbling about having plans. She just hopes the poor girl had not already starved to death.

Mason arrives at Aaja within half an hour, a pristine Indian restaurant with the best food and service for miles, apparently, the fragrant smell of warm spices filling her nostrils, her stomach gurgling with hunger. After giving her name, she is taken to a table in the corner where Shah is waiting for her, dressed in a bright shirt and bowtie, glowing in the candlelight. She blinks a few times to make sure she isn't hallucinating his supposed halo.

'Thanks, Hassan.' The waiter smiles and leaves while Shah stands to greet her. 'Looking lovely, as usual.'

After removing her jacket, Mason sits. She takes up the menu and browses. 'Good choice,' she states. 'Family restaurant, no brainer.'

'Especially when I don't have to pay.'

'Cheapskate.'

'Don't have to but always do. How are you doing?'

'You know how I'm doing,' she counters. 'The Crown versus Rissington is how I'm doing.'

'You've never let anyone down before.'

'I've lost six cases.'

'In your entire law career. I hardly think that's something worth complaining about.'

'This meal might be.'

'What are you having?' he asks, studying his menu.

She glances over the items. 'Laal maas, hot.'

Shah smiles and flags down a waiter. After having a conversation about how each other's families are, he orders: 'Your best white wine. Two laal maas, hot. Two peshwari naan. You want poppadoms?'

'Whatever.'

'Hold the poppadoms. Cheers.'

Mason glances at Shah with wonder and delight, grateful to have a pause from her busy life.

'You didn't come here out of pity. I suppose you want to know what I have to share?'

She shrugs. 'Maybe not just yet.'

He raises his eyebrows. 'Shock, horror! Ms Mason actually wants to socialise like a normal human being. Well, bad luck, because it's good news and good news always must be shared.' He leans forward and Mason does the same. 'We have someone in custody.'

'What? Who?'

They are interrupted by wine. They let the waiter serve them and disappear before speaking again.

Mason sips the sweet white, eager to hear more.

'She kind of just fell into our laps. She confessed that she was at the hotel and that she shot and killed everyone she could, blowing half of the place up. Bit of a nut job. Not surprising.'

'Oh my God. Who is she? Can you trust her word?' Mason can hardly hear anything other than her heartbeat in her ears.

'Can't say here, but all the signs look good. You better gear up for another big case once you're through with this one.' He grins, confident.

'I honestly didn't think you had it in you,' she says smoothly. Something in her heart steadies and relief washes over her skin.

'Well, it wasn't me. It was my team. They're the ones who put their lives on the line to get criminals. God, I miss those days. My knees don't, but I do …'

'Tell me about those days,' she encourages softly.

'Bloody fantastic. I was twenty and every day since I joined the police, I was excited about what was going to happen. Sure, there was some days where you're just patrolling and nothing happens except putting a few kids in their place but when something big happened, it was big. The running, the danger, the sweat, the heat. Sometimes, you didn't know whether or not you'd be going home that evening. Cup of tea and a Digestive or on a cold slab in the morgue. It was so exciting. It still is. Having elevated to the position that I have means the world to me. If I could be out in the field, sure, I'd do it, but my place is here now, managing hundreds of London's police officers, those people doing what they love most. We share the same passions. Nothing makes me happier than finding someone who's done wrong and making sure that their victims are safe or making sure that they don't hurt anyone else. I've caught rapists, murderers, thieves, locked up paedos and gangleaders, traffickers, the lot, and it makes me happy to be alive and proud to say I've done those things and saved so many lives. I suppose it's the same for you but, for me – What?'

Kissing him is easy, too easy, more easy than she had imagined and the enjoyment is foreseen. She doesn't remember what the wallpaper is like or if he has sculptures and ornaments, a rug or a dog but she remembers that the lamb curry was to die for and that his bedsheets are silken, soft and predictable.

He smells of Old Spice, the aroma entering her nostrils while his smooth beard is against her cheek and his lips are at her neck. Her shoes are off at the door and the clothing trail – the bowtie, her jacket, his jacket, her shirt – leads to the entangled pair at the foot of his large mahogany bed.

Mason yanks his shirt open, buttons showering the wooden floor and bouncing hard like pebbles, reaching towards his belt.

'Your pity is astounding,' he whispers.

'Stop talking.' The buckle smashes against the floor and he kisses her shoulder while he removes her bra, then his lips find her belly button.

'Why the change of heart?' he asks, out of breath.

Her fingers grip his shoulders. 'Why are you still talking?'

Shah picks her up and tosses her at the pillows. He meets her in record time and they spend the next eight seconds removing the rest of their clothes and pressing their bodies together. Her toes twitch and an electric heat passes through her stomach, resting in her navel. They find a rhythm, eyes closed in the darkness, focusing on every breath and pulse and feeling. Skin perspires, muscles tense, moans leak from their throats without permission or caution, minutes feeling like seconds, time passing into the night while the passion intensifies. They lay within one another, cradled and transitory, safe and coveted, bursting at the seams.

Eleven

Two nights previously

Apprehended inside the reception area of Scotland Yard, she was wrestled down to the ground, gaining two broken ribs in the process. It had been quiet inside and she had wondered why there was no more than two security members behind desk and one at the door, but she supposed it was the middle of the night. Putting out a cigarette, they let her in after she buzzed, saying she had important information about a case. It was only past six and there was sure to be plenty of people still at work for her to speak with. She requested the big dogs.

'I killed those politicians.'

A security guard at the desk rushed over and apprehended her, a gun in the face, then she was on the floor, winded and broken. She heard a commotion and people speaking into phones, a panic alerted. More men and more guns appeared and all she saw barrels and dark shoes, the squeaky white ground beneath it all.

'WHAT ARE YOU DOING?!' she yelled over and over again, a repetitive pleading. 'GET YOUR HANDS OFF ME! STOP!' She screeched and screamed to find no responses as she is forcibly taken upstairs.

She can feel their hands touching her, keeping her in place, despite her words. Fear was all she knew and sweat dripped into her parched mouth. The anger made it so that she didn't realise her chest was in pain or that her nose was bleeding until she was dumped into an interrogation room where she spluttered and whimpered for help.

Her whimpers turned to laughter.

'Unexpected. You want to go in?' The deputy commissioner asked, hands in his pockets, watching the greying young woman through the mirrored glass. He is tired and drawn but undoubtedly attractive beneath and with his spectacles.

Shah shakes his head. 'You're better with words. I'll just get pissed off. Go for it.'

Nodding, he takes caution on entry, where he finds her face-down on the table in front of her.

'Good evening. My name is Peter Dahl and I am here to help you. The only reason I'll help you is because I'm one of the few people who can and the reason I will is because I want to. The only way for me to do so is if you help me by talking and cooperating and then we can get this whole thing straightened out and hopefully you can go home. I would like nothing better. If that does not happen, we can look for other avenues but for now I'm going to ask you if you know why you're here. Do you know why you're here?'

Blood sprayed his face and with the squint of an eye, he gazed into her hanging red mouth. Using the sleeve of his shirt, he wiped his face.

She chuckled and then laughed hard, the blood in her teeth made her look slightly comical. 'I walked into this big, shiny building because I wanted to confess, not because I wanted to be assaulted.'

'Excuse me.' Dahl left her for a minute and retreated to Shah. 'Should we clean her up first?'

'Just see what she knows.' He is agitated and needs sleep but he presses for results that may take hours to reveal themselves.

Dahl returned to the woman, cautious. 'Can you tell me your name?'

'Why does that matter?'

'I'd like to formally address you. With respect,' he added.

'As if people like you have respect for people like me.'

'Murderers?'

'Citizens. You sit here on your high horse with your satisfying job and your satisfying money. You've probably never had to work hard to survive, have never had to be a waiter working below minimum wage to stay alive.'

'I used to work in a pub collecting glasses when I was sixteen. Then I served behind the bar to save some money before going to university.'

'Let me guess, Mummy and Daddy sorted that out for you, made sure you had the best education money could buy.' She laughed, reading his expression.

He said nothing more on the topic. 'Did you know that you were doing what you were doing? Did you have control over your actions?'

'I'd never held a gun before that day. Never knew how to make a bomb either. Still don't.'

'So it was like an experiment? Was it a way to exercise your power and a way to figure out your own limits of what you can do?'

'I felt powerful. People feared me. Isn't that what power is about?'

'Power is having the ability to influence others, to lead with compassion.'

'Is that how we live now?' she asked. 'No. Now, power is control and fear and sometimes hatred. I hate people sometimes, it's not a crime. But my family has been pushed to the brink since the world changed. All dead. They're all dead and it's just me. I have nothing to lose, no one to go home to. I only fight for myself and the memories they left behind. Life would be so much better if you people didn't ruin everything and I just … it's about time you people understood.'

Present day

Alex wakes at five-thirty as normal, showers and dresses, then take a brief look in the mirror before he heads upstairs for breakfast. Recognising himself became easier as the days passed. He sits with Cliff and Yi-Ling, going over the newspapers in their morning ritual over tea and toast.

'"Today the unveiling of Sidra Tall's memorial plaque outside Victory House will take place, commemorating the loss of the late director of public prosecutions,'" Alex reads.

'Tragic,' Cliff mutters.

'Wait. Listen to this. "A tree will also be planted."'

'Fat lot of good that'll do,' Yi-Ling muses. '"You died. Here's a tree."'

'It's symbolism,' Cliff says over their laughter. 'Represents eternal life.'

'Whatever. Next page?'

Alex flips over. 'More assaults and muggings. More people to go into the system. You know, they must really get a lot of money from this, selling people off. I wonder where it all goes? Certainly not into the social infrastructure?'

'Definitely not healthcare,' Yi-Ling says. 'I broke my ankle last year. Cliff popped it back in and I had to hobble.'

'Frost didn't pay for it?' Alex wonders, shocked.

'Too scared to say anything. Might cost a bomb.'

'I'm sure he would have. It's not like he's struggling for cash or anything.'

'I thought so too,' Cliff says. 'Best not to chance it though. He could have gotten rid of her, Recycled her and someone else could buy her.'

'They do that?' Alex is stunned. 'I really know nothing about all of this.' He had been too busy trying to make a living to read all of the literature that had come out about the Auction system.

'Not very often, I don't think, if at all,' Yi-Ling whispers. 'It's, kind of, an old rumour – like an old wives' tale, only it's not so old. People sometimes just go missing and we just figured that they get resold if people aren't happy with them. I just hope people don't end up in ditches. So, you have to be on your best behaviour.' She pokes his rib and he coils a little, grinning.

Yi-Ling had grown to like him these past few weeks and he isn't complaining. As his body grew stronger and firmer, she used kinder words and spoke directly to him where necessary, allowing him into her small friendship group. So far, he could not see a downside to living in service of the prime minister – except for the fact that he would have to take a bullet for him if need be. Beside that minor stipulation, life is good, better perhaps than if he had been on the run.

He often took a moment or two to think about her, the young woman he had escaped with, CA45JM. Combing through the newspapers, he was waiting to see if she had been caught, wondering what might happen to her but, so far, she had been as elusive as ever, making him happy that she was free. This life is not as bad as he had thought and, despite not being free, he is healthy and fed and alive. She might not be so lucky, scraping for food, homeless and downtrodden. He tries not to think about it too much and focuses on making it from one day to the next and staying in the prime minister's good books.

For Frost's weekly meeting with the King, Nico arrives early today, stealing a slice of buttery toast before heading upstairs with Alex.

'Excited?' Nico asks, while he dusts crumbs from his shirt.

'About?'

'The Palace. Your first trip.'

'I don't see why. You said I was good enough to go last week.'

'It's nice to have something to look forward to,' Nico says. 'It's nothing personal. We all have to wait a few weeks before we get to go there. And you don't actually get to go in.'

'Why not?'

'You'll be outside, I'll go in and wait for him until he's done. There's plenty of nice things to look at and the security don't say much so it's always fun to try and get them to do something.'

'Great. I'm so excited,' he utters, sarcastic.

In the locker room, they put on their bullet and knife proof jackets then dress in generic black suits and fix up their radios and earpieces.

By the time they are done, Frost is waiting for them in the ground floor hall, reading notes from a binder that his brunette personal assistant handed him.

'Wrong.' He shoves it back into her hands. 'I need three copies, Jackie, and you haven't updated the schedule like I told you to.'

'Yes, Prime Minister.' The young woman retreats into her office, scattered.

'What's her story?' Alex asks Nico. 'Jackie's his twenty-

year-old goddaughter. Yeah, he had friends years ago. Weird.'
Nico chuckles while Alex frowns at Frost's treatment of her.
'He pays her really well though, a favour to her parents,
apparently. He's a family man, obviously.'

'Obviously.'

'Finally,' Frost says when Jackie arrives again with the
correct documentation. 'Yes, yes, ready to go.'

'There's also this message from Mr Shah,' Jackie mutters,
handing out a piece of paper.

Frost snatches it and he smiles. 'Thank you. Shred it.' He
tosses it back to her and she snatches the air, hoping to catch
the floating thing on its way to the ground.

Within minutes, they sandwich Frost out of the building,
leading him into his car and past the row of news crews outside.

It takes longer than Alex thought to get into the City. He hadn't
been through the traffic in years and had mistakenly thought that
given there were less drivers these days that the roads would be
clearer. An additional ten minutes are added onto the journey; it
takes this amount of time to get from the front of the building,
through the gates and into the magnificent stone courtyard. The
sun beats down on them until they are covered by the masking
shadow of the large, monolithic building, the car pulling to a
stop. Alex jumps out of the car and gets the door for Frost, who,
as usual, pretends he doesn't exist.

Frost leaves them behind, with Nico following, goes through
the repetitive and brisk security checks, says hello to the people
he passes with a smile on his face until he reaches the interior
of this grand palace, his feet luxurious on the rich carpet, his
eyes greedily taking in the expensive fabric on the wall, the
carved fireplaces, vast dusty curtains and oil paintings set in
gilded frames.

Nico waits in the hall as he is given the usual jargon, call
Him 'Sir' and never 'Your Majesty' or 'Your Highness', try to

be as casual as possible but be respectful, sit before He sits not after, shake his hand instead of bowing. This is only his one hundred and sixth time visiting.

Frost does as he is expected, greeting the King with a 'Good morning, Sir', while gripping his hand firmly and sits down on one of the pair of tall chairs just a fraction of a second before He does.

They chat over the morning news, the dreadful weather, potential white papers, local elections and how their families are doing.

'My goddaughter enjoys her work,' is all Frost mentions, brief and short. He moves on quickly, checking the clock. Near to an hour has passed and he has one final thing to mention. 'Mr Shah sent news this morning.'

'Who?'

'The Commissioner of the City of London Police.'

'Oh yes. And?'

'He's got a full confession for the shootings in February.'

'How the bloody hell did he get that?' the King splutters. 'I didn't think he was very good.'

'He isn't. She came to them. They've just charged her and it'll be in all the papers tomorrow. I'll make a statement too, I think.'

'Yes, good idea. I suppose the trial will be huge.'

'Huge but quick. She's confessed. It should be fairly cut and dry.'

'Best get the attorney general in for a chat. I expect she'll be in for Prosecution on this one.'

Someone in the corner of the room scribbles a note. A security guard sniffs.

'Possibly. But really a judge could say otherwise. It's up to the New Supreme Court.'

'Those old farts? If you say so. Since Reid, their average age has shot up to one hundred and five. Either way, I shall have a

word, see how she is, you know? One can only be so distant.'
He stands and Frost follows the same action. 'Lovely to see
you again.'

'Likewise, Sir.'

'Maybe smuggle in some Mr Kiplings next time? The wife
has banned me.'

Frost smirks, shaking His hand. 'I'll see what I can do.'

When he gets back to the office, he makes sure that Jackie
sends His Majesty a box of sweet treats along with a note to
keep them from under the nose of His Queen.

'So how long do trials take?' Ed asks.

They are sitting under the shade of a large tree in the grounds,
a few yards away from one of the grey football pitches where
the boys played during lunch. They had been sat in the library,
Ed doing a bit of homework for an upcoming lesson and Sera
reading *Exploring the Comatose Consciousness* again but had
been thrown out for either eating too loudly or being too loud
while eating.

Sera finishes chewing her ham and cheese sandwich and
shrugs. 'Weeks? Months? Depends, doesn't it?'

'On what?'

'On how long it takes. How many witnesses there are and
how long cross-examination takes. Bear in mind there's weeks
of prep beforehand. Factor in the amount of evidence, the
complexity of it, the type of crime, whether it's more than one
offence and how many people are involved ...'

'And you know this, how?' Ed questions.

Sera's phone vibrates and she reads a text message on her
phone. 'Obviously.'

'What?'

'Mason's going to be home late again today. She's done this

four times already, leaving me to be babysat by this guy. He's great but we were supposed to go to the cinema today.'

'What were you going to see?'

'That superhero one. Bound to be a pile of bollocks but I was still looking forward to it. Oh well.'

'We're having pizza.'

'I'm sorry?'

'We have pizza on Fridays every fortnight. I can ask Mum if you can come over. Might make things less awkward.'

'Okay.' She ignores his last sentence and allows him to text his mother. Something about Ms Shaw intrigued her. They had an unspoken understanding that she was sure she had not revealed to her son. Perhaps, she could tell her more about her father's condition.

She replies after a few minutes, saying yes and Sera texts Mason.

The phone buzzes again as they walk to their next lesson.

'She said yes and she'll pick me up when I'm done.'

As soon as the final bell rings, they meet up in the courtyard and make their way across the field in light rain, rushing the last few metres before they go down to the road below where Ed's mother is waiting for them.

'Hey,' she says, smiling. She is already dressed in her work uniform – or she had not taken it off. 'Good day?'

'It was alright,' Ed says. He presses a button on the side of the car door and waits for the ramp to unfold. Sera gets in the other side while he settles himself in. Ed lifts himself onto one of the seats and folds his chair up, storing it horizontally and securing it.

'Ready?' Rosine asks.

Ed pulls on his seatbelt and checks Sera has hers on. 'Ready.'

The journey is a lot shorter than Sera expected, a good thing due to her inability to speak a word. Their house is smaller than average with a small grassy front garden where a bed of flowers had died some time ago. The door is wide, perfect for Ed to get through – although it looks as though a larger one had been fitted in at some stage – and the first thing Sera notices when she enters is the stairlift to the top floor, which is damaged and graffitied, probably like most of Ed's belongings.

After placing her blazer on a hook, she follows them into the kitchen and dining area where Ed's father is sat at the breakfast bar with a coffee, a similar face to his son but with ginger hair.

'Hello!' He gets up quickly, startling her. 'You must be Sarah!'

'Sera,' she mutters.

'S-E-R-A, Dad,' Ed corrects. 'How many times?'

'Sorry, sorry.' He grasps her hand and she allows him to shake it. 'Nice to have you. I'm Mr Briscoe. Rex. Whichever you like.'

'I was going to suggest we choose what we're having,' Rosine says, unimpressed. 'Get the flyers, then.'

Rex dives into the drawer on the right of the sink and pulls out two pizza takeaway leaflets. 'So, it's either pizza or pizza on Pizza Friday.'

Rosine rolls her eyes and leaves the room while Rex and Ed sit at the dining table, musing over their options.

'Mum always has the veggie one,' Ed says aloud. 'Meat for us. What will you have, Sera?'

'Anything. I'm not picky.'

'So, we get a regular veggie and a regular meat-loaded monstrosity. You can sit down,' Ed advises. Sera had been standing in the corner of the room, not moving.

'Actually, do you mind if I go to the loo?'

'Upstairs, first door opposite.'

'Thanks.'

She rushes up, squeezing by the other chair restricting access to the steps.

On the right, she sees Rosine sat on her bed looking out of the window, clutching her wallet.

'Are you okay?'

Rosine jumps and puts the wallet out of sight.

'I was going to the toilet,' Sera explains.

'I'm fine. How are you doing?'

'You don't seem fine, Ms Shaw. You seem … distressed. Like something is bothering you.'

'How old are you?' she asks the young woman through narrowed.

'Fifteen.'

'Ed's fifteen in three months. You should come over.'

'I have the feeling that that wasn't why you wanted to know.'

'You're a brave little thing. I couldn't imagine what you're going through.'

'No one's asking you to. I'm okay.'

'Are you?'

'I'm being looked after until my Dad gets better.' Rosine gives her a nondescript look from the corner of her eye. 'I have a question for you. I read somewhere that his chances get smaller the longer he is in a coma. Is that true?'

'I'm a nurse. Neurology is not my specialty.'

'But if you had to guess.'

'Guessing is useless but I would say that sometimes it is the case and other times it's not. In my line of work, you see the worst things and you also see miracles way beyond your imagination. I didn't believe in anything and I still don't really but sometimes there are moments when I question myself and the physical. I realised that you have to be a sceptic and believe in the ability to be amazed and thrown off your guard because life and nature are not that simple. It works in ways we'll never understand so we should stop trying to.'

Sera doesn't know what to say until she does. 'Are you going to switch him off?'

Rosine smiles. 'It's been nearly two months. If we were going to, we would have done it by now. The attorney general—'

'How?'

'Rosie, can I have the card?!' Rex shouts up the stairs.

'Excuse me.' Rosine picks up her purse and begins the journey downstairs. 'They'll cut my allowance if we're not careful ...'

'She didn't answer my question,' Sera complains to herself. She follows Ed's mum downstairs and waits with Ed in the living room, watching the television until the pizza arrives. His parents snipe at one another, mentioned words like 'liar', 'money' and 'divorce' until they re-enter the room. Ed gives Sera an embarrassed look, but she smiles back.

The meal is nice and amiable, mostly because Ed carries the conversation, something Sera supposes he has much practice in. Pizza is vacuumed up with haste and, before seven, Rosine departs, heading for work without saying goodbye to her husband.

Just when Rex offers to show Sera his model airplanes and ships in bottles, the doorbell rings and she quickly excuses herself.

Ed rushes to the door beside her. 'He's unemployed. He gets bored,' he explains.

'I get it,' she says, putting on her coat.

Ed opens the door to Mason.

'Hi,' she says.

'Hi,' Ed says cheerfully.

Mason turns to Sera. 'Ready to go?'

Sera nods and gives Ed a brief hug. 'Monday,' she says. Then she turns her back and yells, 'Bye, Mr Briscoe!'

She hears his vague response from inside while Mason does a double take.

'Thank you for feeding her,' she says vaguely to Ed.

'No problem.'

'Thank your parents for me?' she asks.

'Okay. Bye, Sera.'

They depart and drive home in the car.

'So, what does Mr Briscoe do?' Mason says, curious.

Sera frowns. 'Nothing, he's unemployed.'

Mason nods. 'Still up for going to Glos this weekend? My parents want to meet you.'

'Oh, if I must,' Sera says, joking.

The next morning, they are up bright and early for the car journey north to the South West. Sera's favourite part, like Mason, is escaping the Belowground, getting fresh air in her lungs and seeing what beauty England had left.

'I suppose this is the one thing I liked about school. It wasn't in an old prison. You know? It was nice.'

'And now?' Mason wonders.

'I wouldn't be able to function without Ed.'

Mason makes a noise which doesn't suit her. 'So, you're close?'

'No.'

They arrive at the Masons' large cottage after midday practically begging for lunch, so the four of them sit immediately to a warm salad, sausage rolls, bread rolls, cheese and chutneys.

Her parents are mad for Sera, asking her all about school and her family, happy for her to become a permanent fixture despite her only being in Mason's life for two months. Sera enjoys the attention, talking about herself and the sausage rolls that are not half bad.

The news is on the television and, above their chatter, Mason turns up the volume and listens intently to Celeste's words.

'… suspect has been charged with the murder and attempted

murder of multiple politicians, as well as the late Sidra Tall, Director of Public Prosecutions. The commissioner of the City of London police commented that the arrest has taken the police force to further successes, making him proud to hand this over to the judicial branch of this just society. So far, we are not aware of when the trial is set to begin but there are rumours that the attorney general, Ms Dolly Mason will be taking this case on with all guns blazing and with the backing of—'

Her parents and Sera look at her.

'Well? Mr Mason asks.

'You know I can't talk about it, Dad.'

'You can to us,' he counters.

'Yeah? And what makes you so special?'

'Just the fact that you came from my loins ...'

'Please don't say "loins"'.

Sera chuckles.

'I don't know what's happening until it happens,' Mason decides. Even still, she takes out her organiser, checking for emails. She had, at least, expected to hear something from Shah. She sends an email to all of his accounts, although one is undeliverable.

The doorbell rings and Mrs Mason excuses herself. 'Might be a delivery. Hang on.'

'No, wait, it could be mine.' Mr Mason follows her out quickly and the others can hear them chatting at the door, waiting patiently for their return.

'How are you finding it?' Mason asks.

Sera is beaming. 'They're lovely. I never knew my grandparents so this is all a bit new.'

'I'm glad you like them. Anyway, I didn't want you to be cooped up with just me all the time.'

'Yeah, as much as I like George and Toby.'

'Toby?'

'Toby. George's boyfriend …'

Mason's mouth is ajar for a moment and then it all clicks into place. 'Yeah, I know Toby.'

'I don't believe you.' Sera takes out her phone and jabs at it with her thumbs, an old model her father had been paying for but was taken over by Mason. 'I'm stuffed. Your mum is such a great cook and kind of like you, but you've never cooked so I don't know if you have magic hands as well …'

'I don't.' Mason clicks on a message from Shah which as just appeared, but from his personal email account: I'm being investigated by the IPCC for mistreatment of suspects. Talk soon.

'What the hell?' she whispers.

Her parents enter the room and something catches her gaze. Her eyes go straight to her father's left hand, which is bare, and her mother's where there is a ring on her finger. Her eyebrows knit together, heavy with suspicion.

'Why the hell aren't you wearing your ring? You've never took that thing off.'

They say nothing, looking at each other. Mr Mason sighs heavily.

'Are you getting a divorce or something?' Mason demands.

'Yes.' Her mother's voice is strong despite the worry lines near her eyes and she rubs the ring nervously with her thumb.

Sera sinks into the wallpaper, not making a sound nor moving a muscle.

'Well?' This time, Mason addresses her father.

'What would you like me to tell you? Everything little thing your mother and I have discussed in the privacy of our bedroom, every habit we dislike, how many times we've tried to make things work for ourselves and for you and for everything we believe in, the sanctity of our marriage and the lives we imagined for ourselves? Of course, this is not what we want but hopes and dreams aren't reality and we can't make this into something that it isn't just because we want it to. Willpower is not enough on its own to mend something that's already broken and has been for a long time.'

'This is not a 1972 Hillman Avenger or a 2000 Polo that you're trying to resurrect. This is your marriage.'

'And it's between us and nothing to do with you, Dolly,' Mrs Mason affirms, irritated.

'True. I'm not a child,' she agrees. 'Far from it. That doesn't mean that I'm not concerned about you and that I don't want to help. From what I can tell, you're not as convinced of separation as he is because you're still wearing your ring.'

'Do not talk to me as if I'm just part of the furniture, missy,' Mr Mason booms. 'What we do and do not do does not have to be run by the flipping attorney general. I don't care who you are—'

'And we get to it!' Mason yells, triumphant. 'I wondered how long it would take for you to show your utter distaste for my profession. Well, guess what, what I do and do not do does not have to be run by a mechanic and a housewife. I am the Attorney General of England and that is not about to change just because you think I'm too powerful or rich or whatever it is you care about. You're my parents, whatever you do. I know where I came from and where I'm going and being in a certain job will not change anything. I'm not butting in because I have amazing negotiation skills or because I'm excellent in a crisis, it's because I love you and I will never stop being your daughter, whatever job I have, so get over it and focus on the actual subject at hand, Father, because I don't want you to lose something which I can only describe as a hopeful, honest and enviable love, something someone as powerful as me would die for. Please, don't ruin my fairytale.'

She is almost laughing at the end of it, at her naivety and

youth. Her model for a healthy relationship had turned into rotten fruit before her eyes. She began recalling every dinner over the past ten years and whether there had been any hostility or awkwardness, dust settling on the cracks in their relationship. She sees it. Her father had been absent many times when she had visited or Mr and Mrs Mason would find themselves busy in their own projects, distracting her from the vacancy. Although the break-up will not affect her directly and is something she could happily accommodate, she is not sure that she can handle another disappointment in her life, the thought that love is not that strong after all and it can fade and break away with little effort or choice.

Looking up, she notices that her mother is no longer in the room, Sera too. Her father is standing with his hand on her shoulder and a distinct glistening light in his eyes.

'You'll find someone soon, honey.'

Tears stream from her eyes, a hollow noise echoes from her mouth, pain filling her chest. The comfort of her father's arms around her is just enough to keep her in one piece, for now.

Twelve

Number Ten as his backdrop, the prime minister addresses the press in his best voice and suit, looking them all directly in the eye while he does so, attempting to convince them as well as himself despite his hesitancy.

'Dutifully, I thank the police force for apprehending and detaining the person behind the February attacks. Personally, I thank them for my life. Some might think this unnecessary and unimportant but I live for this country. I love this country. You all know that I have no wife nor children. This is because this country is my partner and its people are my children. I want nothing more than for the people to be safe and for them to flourish and mature at their leisure, aware of potential dangers and able to make free decisions. We are just coming out of one of our most difficult times. Winter is passing and England is banding together. Seed is flourishing, plants are growing and the availability of fruit and vegetables should be rising, almost in abundance. Now is the time for celebration.

'This country has suffered severely because of the loss of life within the executive branch, names you know well. All they are guilty of, all we are guilty of is attempting to make change for the better, trying to make this country a better place for its people. If we put ourselves in danger, so be it. Dedication should not be punishable by death and neither should passion and the willingness to affect change.

'The person responsible shall remain nameless for now and details of the trial will be released when necessary. We have no secrets to hide from you. In the meantime, I would like the families of those who have been robbed of life and those who have been injured to rest assured that we will continue to seek justice for what has happened and put in place provisions to ensure that a tragedy such as this will not occur again. She will be brought to justice. Thank you.'

'That was the prime minister's statement given this morning after the news of an arrest was revealed to the public.' In the newsroom, Celeste turns to the person sat on a sofa near her, a guest. 'Today, we have Charles Hempfield, CEO of Hempfield Finance and the former Chancellor of the Exchequer with us. Good morning.'

'Good morning,' he responds politely. He is fifty-something, but looks sixty, in a tired grey suit and matching his grey hair.

'Obviously, this investigation is huge and rightly so; there's been nothing like it for centuries. But, I have many, many questions from viewers about what budgetary impact this might have, taxes already being high as they are. The current Chancellor declined to comment but what is your view on this, being so experienced within this field?'

She crosses her bare leg, the hem of the skirt outlining the slender shape of her thigh. His eyes do not follow it.

'What people must understand is these 'taxpayer pounds' are not their own, it never has been. Money must be fuelled into projects such as the police and the fire service. Otherwise, there would be uproar if there was no one to arrest criminals and put out fires so there has to be some perspective here. Just because it is the lives of those in power, it doesn't mean they are any less deserving. If anything, more so, because these people who have been brutally killed were simply doing their jobs and helping their constituents. As we have seen, the constituencies of those MPs killed have suffered, you know – people have not wanted to take up the mantle in Liverpool through fear of their lives and this is what they are trying to prevent with Bhavesh Shah, a safe environment where people can step up and lead and guide without fear.'

'It has been reported that Bhavesh Shah has been replaced by Peter Dahl after investigations by the Independent Police Complaints Commission.'

'If we believe every story, the attackers will get what they—'

'This isn't a story. The dismissal has been confirmed by the Commission.'

'As I was saying, the attackers are getting what they want, are they not? Shah is out, MPs are dead. Who next? What next? We've already had the dissolution of the Criminal Justice Act. Will they dissolve parliament? That sounds like terrorism to me. This can snowball, but only if we let it. We have to stay strong.'

'And how do you propose we do that?'

'Well, Wilson Frost has the right idea. Stop blaming members of parliament and start unifying society by focusing on fresh food produce, energy efficiency, boosting the economy, investing in education and rebuilding properties and so on, after such a terrible winter.'

'A solid idea. Just before we go, what do you predict for the Budget this year, in terms of defence.'

'One thing cannot be isolated and valued on its own. I cannot say how much they'll spend on defence or health care or anything else but money will be spent on England and this is what people should remember, that resources are being used here for the people in the best possible way, in a fair way, where the only goal is to ensure the growth of England as a country and an economy.'

'Thank you for coming in today. That's Charles Hempfield, ex-Chancellor of the Exchequer.'

His heart is the stronger of the two and that means he has to die. It makes no sense to Edith, but Molly knows it is logical. He could not live due to a combination of different things, too many different factors make the decision for her. A replacement for Oscar does not guarantee his life, but it is more likely for Paul.

'It's better to go for what would work based on the odds. The odds say that Paul wins.' Molly does not look at her, nor Paula, nor Zoë who is sat silently in the corner looking at the palms of her hands.

'I can't take away your boyfriend. I refuse.'

'You can't give him to me either.' She can taste the fear on her tongue as the words exit her mouth.

'What about your family?' Zoë suggests. 'Can't your brothers help?'

'Oh, I don't even know where they are.'

'They might be exactly where you left them,' Edith suggests.

'And how can they help? The only way they can do that is to find him another heart within the next few hours. They're not magicians.'

The truth is, she does not want to find them, for fear that they could have helped save him or fear that they couldn't. Either option is heart-breaking for someone.

'He's your husband,' she resolves.

'Yes, but it doesn't mean Oscar is less important to you. He's a human being, like the rest of us.'

'Only he's too far gone.' A tear drips down her cheek and she wipes it away fiercely. 'I've already lost him. The longer we discuss it the worse Paul gets. He needs to meet his daughter.'

'But your son—'

'I don't want to hear it.'

Selfish and yearning, Edith accepts and presents Dr Rissington with the decision.

'Do it,' she whispers.

Surgery takes place the next day, Dr Rissington assisted by her two sons, Nick and Clyde, aged nine and seventeen respectively. They hold instruments and observe willingly, not touching too much or stepping on their mothers' toes. They follow instruction and do no real work, watching and waiting, monitoring and praying. Dr Rissington had never done a heart transplant without her husband. She had done kidneys, a liver and a few amputations, but nothing of this magnitude. Never allowing her fear to show, she carves and plucks, stiches and sutures with steady hands and intense focus, hoping that the painkillers were enough so that he did not feel any pain, but not so much that he did not regain consciousness.

As Oscar's life ebbs, Paul's is reignited. His skin gains colour and warmth, the harvested heart finding a home within his chest cavity. They fuel him with antibiotics and immunosuppressants with haste and care, leaving Oscar to breathe his last breaths on the table opposite.

She smiles at her sons. 'We did it.'

After closing Paul's chest and stabilising him, Dr Rissington approaches Edith and Molly, who she had called down to speak with. They are sat nervously on a bench in the corridor near the operating theatre.

'It's done.'

'I'm sorry?' Edith questions.

'You did it already?!' Molly cries. 'I thought you were – I

didn't even get to say goodbye to him and – You decided to do it before I got to – How dare you?'

Molly is on her feet, a wreck, and Edith tries to take her in her arms.

'How dare you?!'

'Molly, don't. There's nothing we can do.'

'He's dead. He's dead.' She slides down the wall and cries like a child.

'Would you like to see him?' Dr Rissington asks, calm.

'She would have liked to have seen him before you killed him!' Edith retorts.

'Do you, at least, want to see your husband? He is doing well.'

Edith glances at Molly's auburn hair, which is all of her that she can see in her arms.

'No, thank you. I can wait.' She positions Molly so that she can see her eyes. 'Do you want to see him?'

Beside herself, Molly nods.

'Shall I come with you?'

Another affirmation amongst her sadness. The doctor leads the way down the hall to a cold room. In the middle is a table and him, covered in a sheet. Molly can see it through the crack in the door and whimpers.

Dr Rissington motions for her to enter.

Edith holds her firmly by the shoulders and steps inside, her face in her chest near Paula's small body.

Molly does not move until Edith whispers that she will wait by the door. She looks at her, panicked, and then turns to the cold thing waiting for her. Each step is heavy and unsolicited, weighing a thousand pounds and breaking the ground.

His face is unfamiliar and cracked, so different to the last time she had seen it. He is hollow and grey and looks more like his father than anyone she knew and loved, perhaps a different version of himself. This stranger used to love her and kiss her and gave her a child once upon a time, yet her eyes do not know him like this.

Edith thinks he is beautiful, this tranquil creature despite the scratches and scars on his skin. He is slight and handsome in his sleep, the curly dark hair on his head making him pale and precious as marble. His nose is broad and pointed, his lips full and his expression is peaceful as though nothing can hurt him where he is.

Edith is not afraid, but Molly feels nothing and is confused.

'This isn't him,' she whispers.

'What?'

'That isn't Oscar.'

Molly walks right by her and out of the room as fast as she can go.

'I'm leaving.'

Neither Edith nor Zoë try to stop her from packing her bags, walking out of the door, down the corridor, down the steps and out of the building into the fresh chill of the morning. She walks until she finds people and shops and houses. Perhaps someone would give her somewhere to sleep if she paid enough with the little money left on her card.

She is alone now, but she had the feeling that she was when Oscar became ill. Losing her baby as well made it clear that she isn't destined for a family. She had lost her parents, her brothers, her partner and son in her short, fractured life, left with only money and sorrow to keep her warm at night. She never knew why she let him die, why she had chosen to be selfless in the moment that she should have fought for him, but the logic was there. Karma had spoken.

Holding back tears, she stops in a newspaper shop, purchasing a large overpriced bottle of water that she planned to refill in a river or canal when she could. Just when she began wondering where the closest one is, she sees the front page of a newspaper where the heading reads:

RISSINGTON BARBERY TRIAL DRAWS TO CLOSE
Dr Rissington's fate to be sealed this week.

Molly purchases the paper and a ticket for the first coach to Central London.

The owners of The Old Farmhouse returned the previous night and Clarke is sleeping with the sheep, hungry and tired but still holding onto a promise.

Just as her eyes drop into slumber beneath her blanket, she hears a noise outside the door of the shack. A car door slams shut. Footsteps creep closer and her heart beats uncontrollably the louder they get.

Foolishly, she hides behind the closest animal.

The door rattles open.

'Clarke?'

She says nothing.

'It's me.'

'Me who?' she says back.

'Who do you think?'

She peers over and Ellis is standing over her wearing a suit and a tired expression. He hands her a bag filled with some sort of packed lunch; there are sandwiches, a chocolate bar, fruit and bottles of water.

Clarke chomps on the red apple hungrily. 'Well?'

His finger attempts to wipe mud from her forehead. 'Well, Frost seems to think you're did it.'

'I saw in the papers. Why on earth would he think that?'

'Well, did you?'

'No! I already had problems. Why would I kill people and

give myself even more to worry about? I wasn't even there.'

He stares at her, as if he trying to see deep into her soul.

'You don't believe me.'

'It's not that.'

'What is it then? Spit it out.'

'That look I was giving you was my thinking look. I'm wondering why Frost would think that you did this.'

'How do you even know that?'

'Have you read a newspaper lately?'

'Yes, Ellis, I stroll down to the paper shop every morning, get the broadsheets, a bottle of milk, a loaf of bread and skip on back to my sweet little cottage on my farm because I'm not a homeless criminal on the run from the government. I saw one paper, once.'

He rolls his eyes. 'You were the face of political assassination.'

'Am I not anymore?' She throws the apple core into the corner and wipes her mouth with the back of her hand.

'Someone has handed themselves in.'

'Oh, thank goodness.' She exhales loudly. 'So I'm off the hook for the shootings.'

'Not yet. The name hasn't been released so, to most people, it could still be you.'

Her eyebrows join in her confusion. 'How do you know all of this?'

'I told you I'd find out all I could.'

'But why does it matter to you?'

'I'm getting Alex out if I can. No one should have to serve, let alone for that man. Too many people have been locked away in these lives for something they didn't do or something so menial that they wouldn't even get a reprimand twenty years ago. I told you I would sort it and I have.'

'Wait … Did you tell someone to confess?'

'Why the suspicion?'

'Did you? Did you find them?' Her heart is racing.

'Of course not.'

'Who are you?' Clarke asks.

'A friend. Alex is mine, so you are too. But this is the end of the road. You have to leave before my parents realise you're here. If I were you, I'd travel north in time for summer, then come back south next winter.'

'What about Alex?' Her guilt weighs heavily on her shoulders and, despite her hopes of leaving and never coming back, she feels the need to hold true to her vow to help him escape the clutches of Downing Street.

'I can keep an eye on him.'

'Okay.'

'Okay.' He smiles condescendingly and pats her on the head like a small child. 'Now, I'm going inside for tea. Don't wait up.'

He leaves without another word and Clarke begins to let her intuition settle. Someone had taken the blame for the killings and now she has to disappear. A week in London and he has all of this accomplished. Money is his likely aid and money can help her get to Alex undetected.

Under the cover of the black sky, she slips out of the barn and sits close to his brand-new BMW. With a small push, she lifts open the boot and falls inside.

'Shit.' Only once she has shut herself in, waited and the footsteps come, followed by the hum of the engine, does she remember the big bag of food that she had left among the sleeping flock.

Inside the car, Ellis and his father sit in silence as they drive through the dark country lanes.

'Couldn't you get yourself to London?' the elder asks.

'Could have,' Ellis responds. 'I just wanted to talk.'

'I've told you enough, Ellis. Don't milk it. I'm not supposed to be talking about anything with you.'

'Well you shouldn't be forcing people to confess to crimes they didn't commit.'

There is silence between them, but it expresses more than words.

'What do you want?'

'I just want to know why you're doing this. Is someone forcing you? What are you mixed up in?'

His father maneouvres a roundabout and the continues. 'You know, things have changed in the last decade. More than you think. Things used to be fairly straightforward. People lived their lives but we all knew money ruled. Whatever you did, money was the culprit. Now? Who knows? We have money but time is what we all want, really.'

'What are you talking about? You were all for this whole government switcheroo.'

They fall Belowground into the brightly lit roads, avoiding a number of motorcyclists that were weaving around the cars.

'Things don't turn out the way you expect.'

'So why are you involved in all of this? What do you have to gain?'

'You really think I'm going to tell you?'

'If I didn't catch you talking on the phone—'

'You mean if you weren't eavesdropping.'

'So what if I was, Dad?'

'It was private business and I don't want you ever, ever poking your nose into my business again. You've got to understand that this is bigger than you, your mum and I.'

'I understand. You're fucking with the top people.'

'I am the top people!' he growls, gripping the steering wheel. 'I'm doing what I have to do. And if you ask me, those people deserved whey they got and I'll stand by that until my dying day. All you have to do is keep your mouth shut and know you place. Actually, you know what? Get out of my car.'

He pulls up at the side of the road at the nearest pedestrian exit.

'What? No, there's no buses at this time of night.'

'That's not my problem. Out.'

'It's ten miles yet until—'

'Now.'

Swearing, he gets out of the car and slams the door shut behind him. The car speeds off in the opposite direction and Ellis begins his walk home with hands in his pockets.

Breakfast is on the table when she arrives home. Her toast is buttered, although she prefers it dry, cut in rectangles rather than triangular and after a sip of the accompanying tea, she realises that it has two sugars rather than zero point five and far too much milk.

'Rex.'

Rosine finds him in the garden, half-hanging out of their shed with a spanner and a roll of black tape.

'What are you doing? It's before six. Not even the birds are awake.'

'You're awake.'

'I work.'

'Thought you'd have gone straight up.'

'What are you doing?'

He smiles through her impatience. 'Fixing Ed's chair. I think a bolt got loose last week. It started making a funny noise after we got back from town.'

'And your solution is cheap gaffer tape?'

'This stuff is not cheap. Twenty quid I had to pay.'

'Twenty quid!' she rages. 'That's my money and you waste

it on tape? I told you not to use the card unless it's necessary.'

'Ed's chair isn't necessary to you? He needs a new one. He's needed a new one for about a year. He's getting far too big for this one now, Rosie.'

'We don't have the money.'

'Yet you get mad over tape?'

She sighs aggressively, hair askew. 'I'll sort it! Like always!'

'You know, I'd actually do more if you'd let me.'

'What can you do with that thing on your wrist?'

Rex covers his tattoo defensively. 'I can get a job!'

'If you haven't gotten one by now, you never will. You've always been lazy. Same as eighteen years ago. You're only comfortable on your arse and in someone's else's wallet.'

'I try to help, I get abuse. I don't try to help, I get abuse. What do you want me to do? I love you and our son. All I want is for us to be happy like we used to be. I'll get a job – today if I have to. I'll try my hardest, but for now, I just want to fix this, for Ed. He's been so unhappy because of all of this mess with money and I just don't want to break up his family unless we need to. Ed would die without us.'

Rosine softens. 'He knows what's going on, doesn't he?'

'He's not stupid. At all. Gets that from me.'

She chuckles.

'Could you hold this for me?'

Rosine takes hold of the middle of the chair while her husband secures it with tape as best he can. She avoids his bright eyes and busies herself by looking at the neat illustrations her son had worked into the chair with permanent marker. Rex places a soft kiss on her mouth, unexpected, and her eyes close for a moment. This was their first real kiss for a long time.

'I'll take Ed to school,' he states.

She can't help but find his eyes. 'You said that last month.'

'I will. I don't do enough around here as it is. And I feel like a spare part after I do all of the chores.'

His wife chuckles. 'I do most of the chores.'

'Did you enjoy your breakfast?' he asks.

Rosine nods. 'I'll go and finish it now. Coming?'

'In a bit.'

She heads for the kitchen, looking forward to a morning of sleep, a rare thing, and wonders how long it will take for Rex to break his promise again. A day? A week? A month? The inevitability makes her heart sink. Instead of her sadness turning to anger, she throws her toast in the bin and the tea down the drain, resetting the toaster and kettle, making her meal all over again.

Having fallen asleep on the sofa, she had developed an ache in her neck, made worse by Ed's quiet laughter on the other side of the room. He is relaxed on the sofa, watching the television quietly and texting on his phone.

'We didn't know whether to move you or not. Sorry.'

'Why aren't you at school?' she questions, ready to lecture.

'I've already been. It's just six.'

'Oh, sugar.' She leaps off the chair and sniffs her underarms. 'I've got to go in fifteen minutes and I smell like a dead dog.'

'Nice.'

Rubbing her neck, she makes her way upstairs. Half undressing in the bathroom, she searches for something to tie her hair up with and rushes to her bedroom in her underwear.

Upon opening the door, she finds Rex splayed out on the bed with his trousers at his ankles, his pride in his grasp, a look of euphoria on his face while watching the evening news.

His head turns to her, fast, guilty.

'Rosie …'

She slams the door shut behind her and returns to the bathroom, locking that door too. She wants to cry but cannot, there is only anger boiling inside her chest and a yearning to punch something. She bangs her fists on the edge of the sink a few times, accidentally forcing a fingernail from the skin and howls in anger at the pain while he talks.

'Come on, baby, I need some kind of release … It's not like I was watching porn; it was the bloody news … stop overreacting …'

She steps into the shower, shaking.

'You haven't even touched me for weeks!'

The water fills her ears, rushing all around her, drowning out his excuses, the picture burned into her mind. She places her fragile hand under the drops the waterfall creates and counts to ten. She does not feel a thing, not the nail, nor her sore knuckles, nor the sorrow, a numbing sensation spreading from her heart right down to her toes, blood dripping into the drain.

Today, she calls the final witness, the final person who can show Dr Rissington for what he is. Amy Beard had been promised a safe place to live and work in exchange for her selling her organs and had been left on the street after she refused.

'Which organs did you donate?' Mason questions.

'Mostly bits of liver. You know, because it grows back. Lots of blood. Then I gave a kidney, provided skin for four skin grafts – which left me with scars on my thighs and back – and I flogged a bit of hair online. Apparently red hair is worth quite a bit in the Far East.'

Sick to her stomach yet holding her ground, Mason provides the courtroom with images of Miss Beard's scars, raw and rough.

'Were you ever paid?' Mason asks.

'I was given somewhere to stay while it all happened. They kept me for over a year but when I'd given too much and was anaemic and bald and wanted out, I begged to leave. But they carried on until I was literally useless and I was tossed out.'

When Colchester comes to question her, he spins his web as she knew he would, holding her breath and hoping that hostility he feeds her will not take.

'Good afternoon, Miss Beard,' he begins. 'You say that you were cared for during the fourteen months you were in the care of Dr Rissington.'

'Yes.'

'Is it not true that being housed and fed is payment enough? This man nursed you back to health. That is what you just admitted.'

'Yes, but I wasn't paid in the capacity I thought.'

'Well did you sign a contract?'

'We had a verbal contract.'

'Which is your word against his. What I see here is that you agreed to cut out your organs and sell your hair with full and unhindered knowledge, completely aware of what you were doing at the time. We couldn't even try Dr Rissington for assault because you agreed to him cutting you open. Did you not?'

'Yes, but—'

'And you were saving lives. Are you saying that you wish you hadn't given your liver and kidney to help another dying human being?'

'Judge Cunningham,' Mason said, raging. 'The witness does not need a guilt trip. She is not on trial.'

'Why not?' Colchester said. 'Every single witness here today has been given a deal of some sort to testify here today. Any other day, any other place, I'd have them all locked up for their part, perjurers and all.'

'Did you just accuse my witnesses of lying? Judge!'

Cunningham holds up his hand and allows Colchester to continue.

Dirty tactics aside, the day in court ends without Mason

knowing either way where the decision would lie. Reflecting in her office, she yells 'Come in!' after the door knocks and Briscoe enters with a box file under his arm.

'Howdy, stranger,' he says, smiling.

She tries to smile back but leaves her eyes on the documents she has to read and sign before the end of the night.

'Don't get me started. How was the meeting?'

'Serious Fraud is always a picnic.'

'You enjoyed it?' She almost laughs.

'Hated it. Getting a straight answer out of those people is like getting gold out of a turd.'

'What?'

'My mum used to say it.'

'Right.'

'Some high-ranking companies have been hiding and/or changing personal information for gain and—'

'What's new?'

'I know. And they're telling me that this case –' He pushes across the box file. '– which they opened in September 2046, won't be closed for another few months. Apparently, their effective work is based on the co-operation of various organisations.'

'Who's taking the mick now? I'll take a look. I didn't have anywhere to be tonight anyway. Except in my warm bed.'

'Did you hear about Shah?'

Mason flushes red. 'What? What about him? Wait – of course I heard about it.'

'Jesus, I was just asking. Don't bite my head off. Someone might have thought that I was intruding on a secret.' He smiles, coy. 'Dolly, you don't blush. What did you do?'

'Nothing.'

'Did you shop him in?'

'Of course I didn't, Kevin.'

'From my experience, you only flush when you've done something embarrassing, when you're on your period or when you've had sex. Which is it?'

'Kevin! Don't you even go there with—?'

'Has to be sex.'

'No!'

'Why else would you look as though you're about to throttle me?'

'I don't know. Maybe because I'm about to throttle you?'

'How many years—?'

'I said, do not go there,' she warns.

'How many years have we been friends? I was going to say.' He laughs, hard.

'Too many.'

'You can't be embarrassed. Not with me.'

'I'm sorry. I just have so much to do. I physically want to rip my own hair out.' She removes her glasses and rubs her eyes.

'You'd think sex would help.'

'Not with this workload.'

'Was it good, at least?'

'It was effing amazing.'

'At least Shah does something right.'

Mason smiles, unwilling. 'I've been avoiding him ever since. Well, I asked him about work and then after he said what happened, I just couldn't take our relationship from professional to personal. He's tried to call but I – I just can't. I don't love him.'

'Since when has that ever stopped anyone from having harmless relations?'

'After university, I told myself I wouldn't do that anymore. You didn't know me when I was eighteen. I was a mess, my thought processes were powered by peer pressure and my blood was more alcohol than anything else. I had a really close call and since then I decided I wasn't going to gamble with my life and I refused to have one night stands or to sleep with someone on a whim just because I like them. I wanted a love my parents had, but now of course, that isn't even a factor anymore.'

She explains her weekend, minus the tears.

'They didn't even tell me, I found out and interrogated them.'

Briscoe is shocked at the revelation but does not show how much, for the sake of her emotions. 'There's nothing you can do, Dolls. From what you've said, it's been in the pipeline for ages and if it's what they want, they'll do it with or without your permission.'

'I know they don't need my permission. I just felt left out and lonely. Sera said something before. That I should be happy that they're still alive. Things could be a lot worse. I suppose that's a way to look at it.'

'Yeah, a morbid way,' Briscoe utters.

'But all of a sudden I feel like a teenager again. I feel like I'm going to explode. Like spontaneous combustion.'

He ignores her last comment, smiling. 'I forget that I didn't know you before pupillage, but your mum did tell me that you were an idealist, that you loved your princess stories when you were young and wanted a fairytale romance or whatever. I didn't think it was naïve, I thought it was refreshing. I never would have thought that you slept around. I just figured you were a bit of a prude.'

'Thanks.'

'My point is, looking for love isn't as hopeless as you think. Shah could be it but you just squander the opportunity because you're not sure.'

'Bhavesh Shah is definitely not it.'

'How do you know?'

'I just do.'

'Dolly, you're not an ugly woman. You're accomplished

and driven and loyal and passionate and that is sexy to most people. Just give him a try. He can't take anymore rejection at the moment. Cheer him up.'

They chuckle to themselves for a moment.

'That really wasn't funny.'

'Was it too soon?'

'The man was sacked and is the subject of public shame as well as a thorough investigation of his actions and practices. Way too soon.' Her phone beeps. 'George, if it's Mr Shah can you tell him I'll call him in the morning?'

'It's not Mr Shah. You have a visitor,' George says from the phone.

'At this time?'

'It's about Rissington. I think she's homeless,' he whispers.

'Dear God, I cannot take in another lodger right now. Then again, they could have my room as I'm not using it and Sera could use a friend …'

Briscoe frowns.

'Give me a second, George?' She puts the phone down.

'What is it?' Briscoe asks.

'It never ends. I have a visitor. Come with me?'

'No.'

'Please,' she begs, putting on her jacket and slipping on her shoes. Briscoe flattens a bit of her hair that is stuck up in the middle. 'You see, I need you,' she utters, smiling.

'Fine. I'm on my way out anyway. I was thinking about getting a new car …'

Mason and Briscoe exit the office.

'Didn't you just get a new one last year? Keeping up with the Briscoes is so difficult.'

They head to George's desk on the other side of the corridor, arriving to find a young woman sat on a spare seat, looking gaunt and drawn.

'How can I help you?' Mason asks, not recognising the woman.

'Molly …' Briscoe holds his breath and freezes in his path.

'Hi, Kev.'

Thirteen

Kevin's apartment is messy and unprepared. A half-ironed shirt he had thrown over the sofa is where he had left it, the crusts of his toast are scattered on the chopping board and he had accidentally left the milk out of the fridge.

Her presence throws him into chaos and his heart palpitates uncontrollably.

'Sorry I can't offer you tea.' He throws the milk carton into the bin with disgust.

'You have tea? Fancy.' He says nothing. 'Water will be fine.'

'You're skin and bones, Molly.'

'Or bones and skin. Depending on what way you looked at it.' She hadn't noticed the way her clothes hung from her child-like frame these days.

He gives her a glass of water and grabs a packet of chocolate biscuits, settling her on the soft leather sofa. He wants to hug her and feed her and bathe her and wrap her in blankets. Safety and comfort is all he wishes his sister in this moment. He has to admit, he hadn't spent much time thinking about her, but had always assumed that she was okay. At least, that was the impression he got from the vague phone calls that ended about six years ago.

'I didn't think you'd still be there. Victory House. It has been so long.'

'Ten years almost, Molly.'

'I wanted to see the prosecutor on the Rissington case. I didn't come to see you.'

'Oh,' he says, hurt.

'No, it's not like that. I just didn't think …'

She reaches for the glass of water and lifts, but her shaking hand means she has to use both. Kevin helps her get the glass to her lips.

'When did you last eat?'

Molly shrugs. 'Monday?'

He practically shoves a biscuit down her throat but she takes it from him and wipes her mouth with the back of her hand.

'Calm down. I'll eat it.' She takes a nibble every few minutes. 'You've done well for yourself. Director of public prosecutions. What does a director of public prosecutions even do?'

'I'm still figuring that out at the moment. I was solicitor general, then I was fired, then got offered this job after the old DPP was murdered.' Molly raises her eyebrows. 'But really it's a fancy title. Just means I'm just another lawyer.'

'If you say so.' She smiles sweetly, reminding him of when she was five and had convinced their mother that he was the one who had drawn all over the sitting room walls with her ruby red lipstick.

Taken by the memory, he draws her into a hug.

'Where have you been?'

'Just away.' She tries to hold in her tears as her arms find comfort around his middle. 'After the fire, I kind of just …'

'We don't have to talk about that. Please, don't.'

'We don't have to talk about the fact that I killed our mother?'

'Do you have to say it like that? Like you're a cold-hearted nutcase that needs to be locked up!'

'It doesn't.' She wipes her eyes. 'Accidents make the worst regrets. That's because there is nothing you could have done to change them. It has eaten away at me for all of this time and it will carry on until I die. I could have stopped it. I didn't notice the cigarette. I know that you blame me for it, I see it in your eyes. You were such a mess afterwards, that's why I left. And I miss her so much.'

Their mother was a worker, too busy to admit she was tired and too proud to admit she was struggling as a single mother. They lived in a small house with three bedrooms near the hospital that Mrs Briscoe worked in as a cleaner.

'I do too.'

They talk of the lipstick incident, the potatoes thing, school trips gone awry and their mother's angry face – an expression which made her look part-pug, part-anteater. Conversation is almost normal and the empty decade in between is almost forgotten.

'Are you and Oscar still taking on the world one city at a time?' Kevin asks, smiling.

'Oscar's dead.'

'What? How?' His expression falls, sorrowful and honest.

'You know, I don't really want to talk about it right now.' She closes her eyes for a moment and focuses on not crying or showing any emotion of any kind.

'You should have told me straight away.'

'I didn't want any more of your pity,' Molly admits.

'What are you talking about? I don't pity you.'

'Don't you? I have nothing, literally nothing. I have no one and you have your fabulous job and this lovely apartment. You're okay and I'm really, really happy for you. I just don't want to feel – You're safe and happy and that means I'm happy too. Don't worry about me.'

Kevin hands her another biscuit. 'Well, I do worry about you. You're my little sister. Anyway, my job is a death threat in case you hadn't noticed. And just because I have a stable lifestyle, it doesn't mean that I'm happy.'

'You're not happy?'

'I am but the two aren't mutually exclusive.' She smiles at him and drinks more water. 'I want you to stay here,' he demands.

'Where else was I going to stay, pea-brain?' she whispers.

'You can have the bed.'

'What I really want is to help Dolly.'

'Well, why didn't you speak to her then?'

'I thought it might be better coming from you. Kevin, I haven't spoken to the woman in years. And no, I didn't expect you to still be here, but now that I know you are … I just want you to help me, please.'

'Okay.'

'I have information about the Rissingtons that might help.'

'Oh, Molly, you didn't? You shouldn't be involved with these people.'

'Do you think I had a choice? Listen, just please ask Dolly if I can help before the trial is over. I just want to say my piece.' Angry, she eats another biscuit in silence, not looking at him. He can tell that their time talking this evening is over.

Kevin sleeps on the sofa, while Molly takes the bed, enjoying its comfort and warmth, sleeping soundly without interruption. In the morning, he makes her breakfast and gives her one of his jumpers to wear. She doesn't eat much, but he doesn't expect her to. Over time, he is hoping to watch her gain at least twenty pounds to supplement her time spent hungry and desperate.

After leaving Molly to chat on the phone to Mason, he drives

Molly to the Crown Court the next day, a silent journey. He
wonders what she has to say and how she is connected to
Rissington. He thinks the worst but does not question her. He
makes sure that his morning schedule is pushed back or passed
on to Waltz, wanting to fully support his sister through this.
He would have to wait with everyone to find out what it is she
knows, information which could potentially win them the case.

They arrive early and Kevin seats Molly in the audience in
the front row by his side.

'You don't have to say anything you don't want to say,' he
advises, softly.

'I know,' she replies. 'I'm just here to tell the truth. If they'll
let me.'

'Sure, Dolly's sorting it.'

Patiently, they wait and, soon enough, Mason joins them to
confirm everything is going ahead.

'The judge has said that I can call you as a witness. He's just
telling the defence lawyer now so he can prepare.'

'Prepare for what?' Molly asks, worried.

'Cross-examination. He will take every word out of context,
so I advise that you say as little as possible about what you
know and, if in doubt, just repeat what you already said,
reinforce the idea.'

'Okay.'

Mason heads back to the front, leaving them alone while the
seats fill around them.

'She turned out nice.'

'Who? Dolly?'

'Yeah. Did she know about why I left?'

'She knew but we didn't really talk about … Well, because
she knows I don't discuss the fire and everything.'

'Isn't it weird how our lives can be categorised into pre-fire
and post-fire, like there is a huge crack in the middle?'

'I know. Life with Mum and life without.'

'Are you and Dolly an item yet?'

'Nope. Never have been. Never will be.'

'Why not?'

'We're just not that way with each other. I had a girlfriend but she turned out to be a gold-digger and the gold she was digging for was political secrets.'

'Unlucky.'

Kevin chuckles. 'Tell me about it.'

'I'm sorry.'

'It's alright. You're back now. I have Molly and Dolly to fight my corner.' He mumbles a rhyme he made up years ago about his two favourite women to attempt to soother her nerves. It works until quiet is called and the day starts.

Molly had never seen the other Dr Rissington. He looks harmless as he is brought out into the room, dressed in a grey jumpsuit. He sits beside the defending lawyer quietly not looking very guilty at all, perhaps just like a man waiting at a bus stop.

Shaky, Molly awaits her turn after the proceedings begin. She had never been to court nor done anything as important as this in her life. After the fire, Kevin had made sure that she was never questioned and the whole thing was put down to an accident, caused by the victim herself, something neither of them had been truly comfortable with.

Twenty minutes pass before she is called and her brother squeezes her hand before the takes the stand. She states her name and promises the judge that she will tell the truth or face prosecution.

'Could you tell me what happened to you?' Mason asks.

Molly explains the story as it happened, Oscar's accident, being approached at the hospital, the meeting, the journey to Reading, the decision and the operation – everything but her pregnancy.

Eyes full of sadness, Mason presses on, 'Was this operation performed without your permission?'

Molly takes a breath and states clearly, 'Yes.'

'Thank you.'

Colchester approaches, smiling. 'Sad tale, very sad. My condolences. I just have a question. Did my client here have any part in your boyfriend's death.'

'It's his business,' Molly counters.

'But did he find you, bring you to Reading and operate on your boyfriend?'

'It was his—!'

'Answer the question,' Colchester orders, combative.

'No.'

Colchester takes his seat and whispers something into Dr Rissington's ear as Molly returns to the crowd.

'I'm sorry,' Molly says to Mason. 'I thought it would help. I'm so sorry.'

'It's okay, honey. You did great.'

After closing statements, the verdict does not take long, only as long as it takes for the press to fill the rest of the room and get a good spot. In the back, Briscoe spots Celeste beside a photographer, looking as petite and slender as ever.

No jury to weigh in, Judge Cunningham returns from consulting with Judges Scott, Gwilliam and Rogers and sits at his podium.

'For the charges of assault, grievous bodily harm and murder, I find the defendant, Dr Ian Charles Rissington, not guilty.'

Mason's stomach feels as though it has hit the floor and her eyes glaze over. She uses her hand to steady herself at her desk and sits before she passes out. 'Not guilty' is all she hears echoing around her head.

Colchester holds his finger up as though it is a gun, blowing away the smoke from the imaginary barrel and stowing it inside his trousers, triumphant.

By the end of the day, India had arrived for him. Late, as usual, he had to wait in the reception area for her long after the trial was done. Tall and elegant, he smiles as she embraces him, kisses all over, their bodies close. Their family had always said that she was too young for him or he was too old for her, but an unknown decade in the past is not as important as a decade in the future that they could spend together.

Her touch makes him shiver and her voice is honey.

'Oh my God, Ian.'

'Told you,' he whispers into her hair.

'You did,' she agrees. Her eyes fall onto his faded jumpsuit and she laughs.

'I brought you some clothes.'

'Thanks. I was just starting to get comfortable.' He is allowed to change into the shirt and trousers she had provided and signs the final documents. He is given his watch and phone, which are the only items he had on him when he was arrested, although now the battery is dead in both items.

They sit in the car together, each one drinking in the other after six months apart.

'You shouldn't have come.'

'I know. I told them I was a taxi. As usual, the security guys aren't the smartest.'

'Where are the boys?' Ian asks.

'At the surgery. They thought it best to hold the fort and stay close to school. I didn't want them caught up in the media either. A couple of photographers have already followed us.'

A small man in sunglasses and a backpack on his shoulder steps out of a bush and takes another snap on his camera.

'Drive. Please,' Ian says.

She starts up the car and moves off, eager to get away from prying eyes.

'I know that I haven't called,' India mutters, apologetic. 'I just thought it would make things easier.'

'It's okay. I get it. I probably wouldn't have survived hearing from you regularly. The walls were my friends and I'd talk to myself, thinking about what I've done. Maybe it wasn't a good idea. We started out loyal enough; we were true to our vision. We wanted to help people who didn't have money. Just like it is today, people exchange one thing for another and we did the same. Not everyone has a credit card or any means to look after themselves. People are dying. We still have only limited funds. People knew what they were getting themselves into. Did we become monsters? Maybe. But we only did what people allowed us to do and free will means more than it ever has before.'

'Freedom is relative to its context,' India says.

'Exactly. Our patients were free to make their own choices and we acted on those choices. We have saved so many lives. If only they could see that …'

'Everyone needs a scapegoat, honey. You were theirs but they didn't get the better of you. Now you're free to continue your great work.' He asks how she has been doing since he left. 'It's been okay. Clients are few and far between but the clinic still provides. Women come to us more than men oddly enough now that I'm running things, perhaps I'm more trusting. I don't know. There is an abortion you need to perform when we get back too.'

'Why didn't you do it?' Ian asks.

'You know I don't like doing them.'

'You're stronger than you think, India.'

'I know, I just don't want to test my own limits.'

When they get home, it is almost evening. The old factory

that held the clinic and their apartment is the same as when he had left. Time does not seem real and being in London is a blur.

His sons greet him as soon as they get inside, hugs passed all around and they chat around him about all he had missed. Nick had his ninth birthday last month, was top in his class in science and had won a regional chess competition. Clyde had almost finished his final year at school, got a place at Bath University and had a girlfriend. Ian sighs at the time he had missed and how he would make up his absence. They knew why he was away and did not judge him; happiness consumed any anger they felt.

India cooks a roast dinner with the last of their vegetables and Clyde offers to pick some more from the gardens in the morning. The atmosphere is tense yet safe, their family complete again. They stay up all night until they fall asleep on the sofa. Ian carries Nick to bed and wakes Clyde, getting him to go to his room. The rooms had not changed and Ian smiles at this, happy he had not missed too much.

In the morning, he has a shower with his wife and, after they removed their hands from one another, decided he wanted to get back to work as soon as he could.

'Are you sure?' India wonders. 'There's a lot going on at the moment. I'm okay handling it.'

'You've been handling a lot since I left. I just want to help you and give you a bit of a break. You've done so wonderfully.'

They kiss one more time and India takes him around the building, updating him on their patients.

'We have fifty percent of our rooms full, quite a lot are still in recovery. There are twelve people in for organ donations and three need transplants. We have the blood bank going with fifteen people giving on rotation throughout the month. They're eating through our sweet treats. I performed six amputations in the last six months with Clyde's help. He's really good at bone resets and sutures. Nick mostly observes and keeps an eye on our surgical tools, makes sure they're clean but he has done a few cuts to warm him up. Hair sales are low but it is coming into spring so that's to be expected. Then, of course, that means we don't get bags of staple foods in return but the vegetables are doing their part. Next, is the milking suite. We have twenty women, seven new mothers, the rest on hormones, supplying milk to the rich. You wouldn't believe how much these people will pay just so that they can have a bowl of cereal in the morning since the cow famine. Crazy. One pregnant lady is here to give her baby to a lady who had ovarian cancer, a coincidence we are utilising. Had a hysterectomy a few weeks ago and is staying until the baby is born. She helps out by changing bedpans and sheets. Then we have the other lady wanting the abortion. There are three people in for skin grafts after a serious house fire, a bone cancer patient who wants us to try a new Hungarian treatment, seven bunion removals, five breast augmentations, one nose job, three dental implants, several botox patients, scar tissue removals, two cosmetic skin treatments and one old man on dialysis for which he is paying for by supplying us with drugs from his pharmacy.'

'And you've been handling all this by yourself?'

'I'm good at scheduling. And everyone knows they have to wait their turn. I worked it into the contract.'

'Verbal contracts only, remember? No traces.'

'Exactly.'

Ian meets Zoë after lunch. India invites her down to the consultation room. Zoë looks uncomfortable, not only because her stomach is growing, but because she is staring at Ian with mistrust and fear.

'Zoë, I'd like you to meet my husband, Dr Rissington.'

Zoë says nothing.

'He is going to be performing your operation today.'

'If that's okay with you,' he inputs, softly. 'I know you haven't met me before today but you can trust me. I will do you no harm.'

She shifts in her chair. 'It's my fault Molly left. All of this is my fault. If I didn't want this … Oscar wouldn't be dead.'

'Don't feel bad about that,' India orders. 'Molly agreed. She knew what she was giving. And they were both dying.'

'It doesn't matter.'

'If you don't want to do it, you don't have to,' Ian advises. 'There are other options to consider. You can see this through, give your baby up instead. We can try to organise something. Or you can keep it. See how you feel.'

Zoë's eyes glisten. 'I feel trapped. I always have. Sometimes I cannot breathe, like something is holding onto my lungs, pressing down on them and forcing me to give in. I'm almost twenty-five weeks. It's now or never.'

Ian frowns for a moment and then says, 'We can give you another few days to decide.'

India is confused and Zoë leaves the room in tears.

'Why did you do that?' his wife asks.

'You know as well as I do that a baby is more profitable than anything here. And anyway, she wasn't sure. Did you see her? She's torn. She's borderline as it is. I think you should give her a few therapy sessions, ease her into the idea of keeping it.'

There is loud noise outside the room, a harsh thud, then footsteps rushing on the ground and voices.

'Of course. I'll see if she wants to start tomorrow. What the hell is going on out there?'

Dr and Dr Rissington rush out of the room to find a patient looking down over the banister at a body at the bottom. People surround the figure and yell up to them. The doctors move as fast as their legs can carry them down the treacherous staircase to the body at the bottom.

'Dr Death Goes Free,' is what the newspapers say, along with, 'Attorney General Loses Clear Cut Case' and 'Rissington Calls Into Question The Strength Of Justice Today.' The newscasters verbalise the doubts of the people. The polls and the social media prove that society feels let down by the decision, anger hurled at Mason, rage brewing from the bottom up.

That evening, she yells down the phone at Briscoe, pacing in her pyjamas while Sera pretends to listen to music on the sofa.

' – goodness sake, why are they not pointing the finger at Cunningham? He's the one who effectively makes the decision! I'm not God! I display the facts, Colchester does the same, we wait for verdict. Simple!' She pauses, hands balled into fists, toes curling. 'How on earth can I relax? This was clearly a thrown case. I had him. I had him! Don't tell me that I didn't.' Another pause. 'I feel like punching someone, I really do. And now I have a meeting with Frost instead of the one I was supposed to have at the Palace tomorrow. What if he fires me? No, he could. It's a possibility. This whole thing is a mess. And I didn't even think – How is Molly? Is she alright? Good. Good. I'll try to but I don't think I can sleep tonight, I have too many things on my mind. Okay. I'll try. See you.'

Wailing, she melts into the space next to Sera. The teenager pats her head consolingly.

'Fancy an all-nighter?' Mason asks.

'I have school in the morning, but thanks for the offer.' She sits up and gives Mason a brief hug. 'You'll be okay. You did your best.'

'But my best wasn't enough,' Mason replies, miserable.

'Your best is what it is. As long as you know that, you'll be cool as a cucumber when you get to that meeting.'

Mason smiles at the corner of her mouth. 'I thought I was

the mother figure.'

'I've been known to be full of surprises.' Sera heads for bed, yawning widely. She falls asleep as soon as her head hits the pillow, before she has time to text Ed back saying goodnight.

She walks Sera to school the next morning, wanting to breathe in fresh air as though it was her last day. She has a bad feeling about her meeting and hoped that the earth would make her feel calmer. She is wrong.

She leaves Sera with Ed, hearing him recognise her face from the newspaper.

Sera says, 'She can hear you, idiot,' and then waves goodbye at her.

Everyone knew her face after it had been slapped onto the face of every tabloid. She considers changing her hair but she never agreed with chemicals and dyeing and gives up on that idea very quickly as she drives into London.

Within the hour, she arrives in Downing Street, unsurprised by the photographers climbing over one another to get a picture. Once inside, she goes through security and is told to wait in Frost's office until he arrives.

She feels like a pupil who has been sent to the headmaster to be reprimanded. It takes her a minute to realise that that might be what this is.

Behind her, the door opens and her heart beats uncontrollably.

'Tea?' The maid enters with a tray, setting down a teapot and two cups, milk, sugar and biscuits.

'Thank you,' Mason mutters, mouth dry. 'Peppermint?'

She nods. 'I find tea helps when you're nervous. At least, that's what people say and then it becomes a cycle. Everyone wants tea, whatever is going on.'

'Who says I'm nervous?'

'You've been biting your nails and fiddling with your hair.'

Mason coils her fingers after patting down her hair. 'Sorry.'

'Don't say sorry to me. I'm only here to serve. Tea, I mean.'

'How long do you have left?' Mason wonders.

'Maybe five years? I forget. But it can get exciting, I suppose.'

'Frost is exciting? News to me.'

She frowns a little, confused. 'So, it's not you.'

'What's not me?' Mason asks.

'No one. Nothing.' She heads for the door.

'Where are you from?' Mason asks, intrigued.

'Was born in Hereford then moved into Kent when I was small. I was a dentist and I was smart. There's a lot of money in dentistry. Well, there was more at one stage. There's only a select few who give damn about their teeth now, but they do pay big. I got into a bit of trouble with one of my colleagues, thought my only option was to fight my way out of it, then, all of a sudden, I'm in trouble with drugs and money. I lost everything. Now, here I am. Cinderella story.'

Mason is sympathetic, pitying almost. 'Don't you have family who could have bought you out?'

'I was too expensive.'

'What's your name?'

'Ling.'

'It's nice to meet you, Ling.'

'You too, Ms Mason.'

The door opens, almost hitting Ling in the face, something Frost is not aware of.

'Yes?' he asks Ling.

'Excuse me.' She exits with haste, leaving the two of them alone.

'Mason.' He sits behind his desk while she pours herself tea. 'Mason, Mason, Mason, Mason.'

'Are you actually going to say something or are you going to continue being condescending?'

'When you succeeded the post of attorney general you took

a vow. This vow involved your full committal to seeking the right way, to strive for justice, to be the voice of the country in the highest matters, to do your very best in legal matters concerning the Crown and State and to do so in keeping with our data protection rules, the laws of our country, to do so efficiently, in keeping with time and money, both vital factors while enforcing the law.'

'I don't "enforce the law." That's what the police do. I promote and uphold justice, analysing the evidence given to me by the police force and presenting this to the judiciary so that they can make an informed decision. Aside from that, I review a hell of a lot of cases, run the CPS, SFO and all of the other departments that sit under it, as well as all of the people who make up those departments. My job is more than just lawyer. If you have a problem with any of my cases, take it up with the judges.'

'I hate this blame culture we have here. It isn't just you. We don't have suspects on a big case, people point the finger at Shah –'

'Yes, and look where he is.'

'– and if there is a problem anywhere in England, people turn to me, not the education secretary or the defence secretary, not the people responsible for transport or health or whatever the issue concerns. Why? Because I am the figurehead. Someone must take responsibility somewhere along the line. '

'So why don't you take on the responsibility if you love it so much?'

'Because you've become the face of this farce. It's like someone has a vendetta against you and we have to be seen as taking this matter seriously.'

'I bet it's that Celeste Lander out to get me. I don't know what her problem is.'

'Her problem, it seems, is you.'

'So that's it? You're going to get rid of me because the media have something to say? If that was the rule, we'd have no MPs, no lawyers, no royals, nothing.'

Frost says nothing but he looks as though he is thinking deeply. 'The police have made some arrests following the trial. Some of your witnesses were apprehended shortly after closing.'

'What? Not Molly?'

'I don't know who. They have been taken for unlawful trading after Dr Rissington's verdict. Dahl believes there is still evidence of their misdoings. And the rest … they are suing the justice department because they aren't happy with the verdict.'

'Surely they could just petition for retrial so we can seek more evidence?' Mason wonders.

'They don't trust us anymore. This is in the hands of the civil courts now. Nothing we do will convince them that we are right. The papers and the television broadcasts have already begun showing their hatred for us and we need to lessen the burden.'

Frost pours a tea for himself and sips. 'You know, I have never fallen in love with anything other than my work—'

'Listen, I don't have time for this or any more of your damn stories. I should be in a meeting with the King as we speak.'

'Mr Briscoe has attended in your place.'

'In my place? I see.'

Everything is clear now. She is about to lose everything she had worked hard for, about to be devoured by the darkness of failure with no one but herself to blame.

'You are suspended for six weeks without pay.'

'You're not firing me?'

'Not yet.'

Fourteen

Mrs Cunningham likes garden centres more than she does gardening. She lives and breathes green, practically floating down the aisles, commenting on the seed variety, postulating her hedges and, for once, not worrying about spending too much on prettying up the garden when spring arrives again.

It is time, again, for Sera's fortnightly visit so, begrudgingly, she attends, music player in tow. It is far better than staying home with Mason while she feels sorry for herself and eats her way through the winter food stock in the pantry.

It is a sunny yet grey afternoon, so after claiming a few free samples and purchasing a new watering can, plant pots and fertiliser, they head home in a brand new black SUV Sera had not seen before. The lush cream interior provides both comfort and visual pleasure and the journey is smoother than she had ever experienced in her godmother's previous vehicle.

'Where did you get the car, Mrs Cunningham?' Sera asks, curious and melting into the passenger seat.

'Mr Cunningham bought it for me last weekend. He can be so romantic!'

'Was it your birthday?'

'No, he just likes to spoil.'

Sera frowns. From her experience, Judge Cunningham is a stingy bastard, a man hard-pressed to buy his wife flowers on a special occasion or spend disposable money on thrown-away items. He only invested in the house and his career, giving his spouse a menial non-negotiable spending allowance every month.

'How are you enjoying school on the other side?' Mrs Cunningham chuckles.

'You make it sound like the underworld,' Sera berates. 'It's fine. Better, in fact.'

'Friends?'

'Just the one.'

'What's her name?'

'Ed.'

'A boy?'

'Clearly.'

'Oh.'

They say nothing until they return to the Cunningham's home for lunch, another salad concoction, this time with cous cous and quinoa. Sera gets through it holding her nose and thinking of bacon. During their meal, she notices the new television, several shiny kitchen gadgets, new rugs, a lamp and a brand new grand piano.

'Been shopping?' Sera asks.

'Yes, just a one-off treat. I did buy you a little something too.'

She pulls out a bright pink bag with a ribbon. Sera delves through the tissue paper and finds a brand new music player and headphones at the bottom.

'Oh my God! Thank you so much!' She throws her arms

around her tightly.

Mrs Cunningham is almost in tears. 'Just a little thank you for putting up with me.'

'I don't put up with you,' Sera denies.

'If not for your father being unwell, we wouldn't have had our time together …'

Sera pats her back softly. 'It's okay. That doesn't make you selfish. I enjoyed it a little too.'

'Are you sure you don't want to come back here for a while?' Mrs Cunningham tries.

'I'm sure. But I'll be back soon, I promise.'

They talk about the past, present and future while Sera fiddles with her music player with glee. She does not remember where the time goes and soon Mrs Cunningham drops her off home – Mason is not in the mood to pick her up that day and no one can blame her.

When she returns, Sera finds Mason in the living room watching an old film called *Eternal Sunshine of the Spotless Mind*, a movie that she had never seen before and thought was way too depressing to make Mason feel any better and too ancient for anyone to enjoy.

'Get up,' Sera orders.

'Why?' Mason's hoodie is zipped all the way up so that Sera can only see her eyes.

'I know what happened to your case.' That catches her attention.

Sera tells her about the new car, her new gift and her theory that Judge Cunningham was paid off to say 'Not Guilty.'

'It makes sense…' Mason muses quietly. 'But what can I do about it? I don't have any proof.'

'Are you a lawyer or not? The car is the proof. This is the proof.' She references her music player. 'Surely it's enough to get your job back.'

'Frost didn't do this because of the case, it was public perception that got me suspended.'

'So you're just going to lie here feeling sorry for yourself?'

'I'm afraid so.' Mason flops back down onto the sofa, sending a wave of air towards Sera.

'What is that smell? Is that smoke?' Sera wafts the air as Mason's phone rings. Briscoe's name is emblazoned on the shiny surface.

'You can't ignore him forever,' Sera advises.

The phone stops ringing and this time it is Shah who is calling.

'You can't ignore him either.'

'Yeah? Watch me.' Mason pulls a cigarette out of her pocket, lights it and puffs away, watching the film.

'I cannot breathe in here.'

'Then go.'

'What about me? What about the people who depend on you, the people in your constituency?'

'I gave that up as of yesterday. They don't need me screwing everything up anymore.'

'I need you. But if you want to turn into a fucking hopeless recluse, be my guest!'

Angry, Sera heads for the door again, while Mason doesn't move a muscle.

'Where are you going?'

'Out.'

Taking Mason's credit card off the side table, she slams the door behind her.

She had never been out alone, even on a Saturday evening, so Sera makes her way to the shops and restaurants nearby, texting Ed as she walks. He agrees to meet her at a café nearby so she busies herself by purchasing two hot chocolates and a blueberry muffin until he arrives.

'You got here quickly. Expected you to have rolled down

here yourself.'

'Dad wanted something to do. I didn't want to let him down.' They grin at each other happily and begin to pick at the muffin between them.

'Are you alright?' Ed asks, picking at the black tape on his chair.

'Yeah. Why?'

He shrugs. 'You look upset. And your frantic text message was a bit of a giveaway.'

'My mum's dead and my dad's in a coma. So, on a scale of one to ten ...'

He is stunned. 'I – I don't know what to say.'

'You don't have to say anything, Ed.' She lowers her head and looks into her open hands on her lap.

'If it helps, that's kind of how I felt when I found out I'd never walk again. I got back pains a lot when I was younger. They put it down to arthritis, muscle weakness but, as it happens, there was irreparable nerve damage along my spine that just ate away at me bit by bit.'

'So, can you not feel anything down there?' Sera instantly flushes red at her phraseology.

Ed suppresses a snigger. 'It comes and goes. But, my point is, I've been through some things too and I'm here if you need me. If you want to talk.'

'I never thought your paraplegia was something I could possibly relate to, but thanks,' she mutters, slightly embarrassed. 'Most of the girls at my old school would pretend their bulimia issues were far greater than anyone else's. People have their own problems. You can't ever think your life is more important.'

'They sound just swell.'

'I used to be so jealous of them. Having parents. And I took it all for granted when I had them both, even though I was young, I should have been different. I should have paid more attention, maybe. Been less stroppy. Anyway, the past is the past. Those ghosts haunt my dreams no longer.'

Sera and Ed agree, without words, that only the future can be changed.

'So, shall we continue to pretend this muffin will fill us up or shall we relieve my father of his stalking duties outside?'

Sera looks over her shoulder at Mr Briscoe in the car across the street. 'Sounds crazy, but, shall we just go?'

'He's gonna follow us. He's in a car. He'll see us,' Ed says, smiling.

'Probably. It'll be fun! Come on.' She stuffs the muffin into her pocket, while Ed carries his coffee in his hand. Standing by the door, they stare out at his dad, watching patiently.

'Looks like he's on his phone watching videos,' Ed observes.

'Good. On three? I'll push.'

'Okay. One, two …'

Sera opens the door, getting Ed's wheels out and ready. 'Three!'

She sprints as hard as she can, forcing the wheelchair down the street at spend and, when she had gained enough momentum, he lifts herself onto the back, occasionally using her right foot to speed them up again. In the distance, the car outside the café sits in the same place, Mr Briscoe unaware of the location of his child.

Laughing, they cut across the park and under a shelter of bare trees, stopping once Sera yells, 'My legs! I can't anymore. Stop.'

'Sensitive,' Ed says as they stop sharply.

She chuckles. 'You know what I mean. I'm not fit at all.' She sits down on a bench to catch her breath and Ed swings around to face her, placing his coffee next to her.

'Then exercise, lazy git,' he teases.

'The keyword is lazy,' she says, pulling the muffin out of her pocket. She yanks and it falls to the ground, leaving her disappointed. 'Oh no.'

'Do you want my coffee?' Ed asks.

'No, it's okay.' She watches him finish it and throw the disposable cup into a bin five metres away. 'Have you considered playing basketball?'

'I used to.'

'Oh. Why did you stop?'

'I don't know. I guess I was bored? Wanted to focus on school. As shit as that is.'

'You should do it. If it makes you happy.'

'I don't know what makes me happy,' he responds.

She shoves her hands together between her knees for warmth. 'You sound like me.'

'What do you mean?'

'Nothing.'

He takes his fingerless gloves off and throws them at her. She catches and pulls them on. 'I know what you mean. You're not a happy person.'

'Thanks!'

'You know I'm right, Sera. I had the feeling. You didn't talk much in the beginning.'

'That's because I didn't know you. I wasn't about to tell you my deepest darkest secrets, was I?'

'How about now?'

She looks up at him and wonders whether her barriers were visible or crumbling. Her mouth opens but no words appear.

'You don't have to,' Ed revises, looking back at her with worry. 'It's okay.'

'It's not that,' she says. 'I trust you. I just don't think you're going to like what I have to say.'

'We'll get to that later.'

She closes her eyes for a moment and then turns away from him slightly, holding her arms around heself, protective. 'I'm so unhappy.'

'I already knew that,' he says, trying to smile.

Sera shakes her head. 'I don't think you understand. I wake up in the morning, wondering what the point of everything is. My mum isn't waking up, my dad isn't. Why should I?'

'Because they'd want you to,' he says. 'It's as simple as that, Sera.'

He tries to find her eyes again and sees the tears falling down her face. 'I really don't want to. I can't do this anymore. They're leaving me all alone and I don't want to be alone. I'd rather not be here at all.'

Ed's face changes instantly. Frowning angrily, he grasps her shoulders tightly. 'Don't ever say that again, Sera. You're not alone, you idiot.'

He holds her as she cries, cramp forming in his arms as he leans over. He ignores it for as long as he can to soothe her and calm her down. He shifts slightly so that she can rest her head on him. He can see every pore on her skin, the faded acne on her forehead, fluff in her hair, the water streaked across her nose and the misapplied mascara on her, eyelids, lashes and cheeks.

'What are you looking at?' she says, scrutinizing his face in the same way, watching the crease form in between his eyebrows and the beauty spot on his nose.

'How ugly you are.'

'Well, I know that's not true.'

'No, you're pretty disgusting.'

She smiles with small, knowing eyes. 'Then why do you want to kiss me?'

'I don't, but I'm gonna do it anyway.'

'I thought you might—' His chapped lips shut her up, a

perfect fit. They coast over hers slowly as he loses all feeling and simultaneously bursts with energy and joy, despite her snot and tears going all over his face. He feels her smile beneath him and then they separate, slightly embarrassed yet content.

'Are you comfortable?' she asks, looking at their quiet surroundings, breathless.

'No, but, that's okay.'

Sera sits up and wipes her nose on his gloves. He sighs and decides that she can keep them.

'Everyday, I've been living with the possibility that he might not wake up.'

'He still might,' Ed tries. He considers stroking her hair but decides against it.

'It's more likely that he won't. And then what?' She sighs and takes his hand. 'Would you do something for me?'

'Sure.'

'Will you please let me kill myself? If he dies.'

His skin prickles and his heart beats hard. 'You're being serious?'

'When have you known me not to be?'

He moves away from her. 'I can't let you do that. Why would you ask me that when you know what my answer would be?'

She turns to him, begging. 'I've got no one else!'

'I thought you said you were alone,' he utters, dark.

She grunts, angry. 'What is the point in you, if you won't help me? I'll just do it anyway. I just thought you'd help me. I'd feel better knowing I had you there with me.'

Clearly hurt, he turns away from her and begins to head for the main road. He pulls his phone out to find several missed calls from his dad and a similar number of texts. He ignores the incoming call that appears on the screen as he browses and makes his way home in the dark, a thousand thoughts running through his mind – enough to keep him occupied for his quarter-of-an-hour journey.

When he gets home, his dad isn't there yet, so he picks up the house phone and calls him.

'Where the hell have you been?' Rex shouts. 'I've been going out of my mind. Don't you dare leave like that again.'

'Chillout, Mum won't know. You can come home now.'

He puts the phone down and heads up to bed, burrowing himself beneath his sheets, stifling the fresh tears that fall from his eyes with the duvet. He considers texting her, or calling, doing something to change her mind but, instead, allows his sadness to rock him to sleep – something he imagines Sera is doing tonight too.

'I won't do it! I refuse!'

'Come on, Celeste, stop acting like a little girl. It's just one tiny interview.'

She stomps out of the lunch room and to her chair in the dressing room, Steve following like a puppy.

'It's not just a tiny interview. It's an interview with a man I have had lots of sexual intercourse with and also threatened with huge media bombshells that would ruin both his career and his life.'

'Which you have yet to drop!'

'Only because I was saving it for when it would make the most damage. I can't look him in the eye now.'

'This could be it. This could be when you do it. Highly suspect that as soon as the DPP is dead, he takes up the mantle and now the attorney general is out and he gets the job too? The public would want answers. Do it for the people.'

'No.'

'Well then, do it for the money.'

Unable to resist her only flaw, Celeste spends the evening

preparing questions for their interview while Steve organises the meeting. The words float around in her head all night as she tries to sleep. Her one-bedroom apartment is lonely and quiet.

When did you take on the role of attorney general and in what circumstance?

Is this an interim role or is it permanent?

What do you say to the public who have lost faith in the justice system?

How does promotion work within the attorney general's office?

Do you have the relevant experience to be taking on this role of acting attorney general?

Would you say becoming who you are today was easy, that everything was handed to you?

Does your office benefit from tragedy?

Who is taking on the role of director of public prosecutions now?

How would you have handled the Rissington trial? Do you think you would have gotten a different outcome?

Would you say that you work for the people or for your own selfish needs?

Are you proud of what you do?

What will you do as attorney general that Dolly Mason could not?

Do you have any insight into why there is a new MP for Vauxhall?

Are you a better person to take on the role because you are a man?

What, do you think, is the future of justice?

Each question more damning than the last, she knows that she will ruin her relationship with Kevin Briscoe forever and although this was always her plan, it doesn't mean that it isn't a difficult thing for her to do.

Even when he is sat before her on the plush blue sofa being

fussed over by the team, she softens and recoils slightly, watching him with wonder. All she can think about is when they first met in a bar near the studio, when her career was in freefall, at a time where she was looking for someone to add value to her life.

She had been sat at the bar with a shot of sambuca in hand, waiting for a man she had been fixed up with. Tall, brunette and greying with a smile on his face, Kevin had approached her, offering another 'student shot'. She wasn't offended and allowed him to buy her three more before they floated over to a velveteen sofa on the other side of the room. They talked for hours about their lives, not meaning to reveal so much and she fell asleep next to him, resulting in their being awoken and thrown out at the stroke of six. They laughed at their ignorance and fatigue and grabbed a tasteless morning coffee to get them going.

Since then, they had been on several dates and moved in together, loved each other but had a terrible ending. She both regrets it and is proud to say that she has stood up for herself and loves herself, despite her affection for this man.

'Ready?' Steve asks, coming out from behind a camera. 'We're live in thirty seconds.'

Celeste nods while he takes his place with the rest of the production team. Her stomach plummets and gurgles. Her heart beats rapidly and Kevin looks at her vaguely, unresponsive and calm.

'Good morning and welcome to The Breakfast Show,' Celeste begins. 'Today we are joined by the newly appointed attorney general, Kevin Briscoe, but before we talk with him, I'll take you through the morning's news.

'Former attorney general Dolly Mason has stepped down from her post as the country's lawyer due to backlash from the case of R v Rissington after the defendant was found not guilty for murder among other crimes. This case has caused a stir in public opinion as to whether or not our justice system is doing its best for its people. She has also been replaced as MP for Vauxhall.

'Border security is getting stricter than ever all over the world since the USA limited all ad hoc short-term visits to seven days. Holiday goers have been restricted to week-long holidays in Australia and China this week. Exemptions include business, political or medical trips or specific long-term purposes that go over three months in length such as migration, work or overseas aid. Many have protested and called for action. The president is yet to address this issue.

'Employment is up yet homelessness is still at a record high due to poor wages and lack of housing. The national living wage is the highest it has ever been at thirty-five pounds per hour but the price of living has also sky-rocketed, causing a rise in poverty, many people falling out of the so-called 'middle class' bracket. The price of a loaf of white bread is now just over seven pounds and a pint of almond milk is four pounds and sixty pence.

'On the show this morning is the new Attorney General for England, Mr Kevin Briscoe. Good morning.'

'Good morning,' he mutters, stiff.

'Many people have been speculating on the terms of which you have been appointed to this role. Some have said there is an element of workplace favouritism, others have agreed you were the best person for the job and there are some who believe there to be a hint of sexism in the workplace. What do you say to that?'

'The terms of my employment, as always, has been arranged by Wilson Frost and passed by His Majesty the King. Clearly, in such a fragile time for the department, a decision was made. Many directors of public prosecutions have then stepped up to become the attorney general. This is not unknown. As for the sexism, I don't know where that has come from because Ms Mason was, by far, one of the best attorney generals this country has had and by asking that question you're being sexist by implying any disparity between my role and hers based on our biology.'

There is nothing in Celeste's eyes. He guesses that years of poking and prodding to provoke a reaction and make good television has made her emotionless and submissive. 'So is this an interim role? Will Ms Mason be returning to her post?'

'Again, this is up to the prime minister. For now, you have me.'

'What do you think of Tomas Ciotti, new MP for Vauxhall?'

'I wish him the best of luck in his appointment.'

Celeste appreciates the change of topic. 'Who is the current director of public prosecutions?'

'At this point in time, I will be taking on both roles, backed by a very good, very supportive team until someone is appointed.'

'So, your department is in a state of flux at the—'

'We're doing perfectly fine.'

'What I mean to say is, things are not yet in balance.'

'Lawyers think on their feet and my department have been in worse situations than this one.'

Celeste frowns, heated. 'Have you? With all of the uproar and the reservations and lack of faith, do you honestly feel comfortable taking on the position? I mean, in terms of the Rissington trial, would you have handled it differently?'

'I cannot say now because that's all done and dusted. I won't say I would have handled it in the same way but we're all different people with different methods.'

'Very … diplomatic.'

'As always.' He smiles, annoyingly.

'What do you think is the future of justice, then? Will you all survive in the end?'

'That's a very harsh a punitive way to phrase it—'

'Just answer the question, Mr Attorney General.'

'The future of justice depends on the people allowing everyone to do their jobs without media influence, without prying eyes and with the support of society in terms of co-operation in cases and performing honest public duty when testifying as a witness to a crime or supplying evidence. Let us do our jobs and the streets will be safer.'

'Some beg to differ in that sense. Criminals are on the streets, irrespective of whether they are guilty or not. Dr Rissington would have been out in society if he was found guilty!'

'But he would have been serving his time and rehabilitating.'

'So, you think the verdict was wrong?'

'No comment.'

'The Attorney General of England here this morning, not commenting on recent public issues. Thank you for coming in.'

Kevin says nothing, and waits for the camera to go away from his face, exiting the set as soon as he can.

There is a chill up her spine, a vacant nudge called instinct which tells her to turn around as she walks to her car.

Nothing.

But she is sure there was footsteps or something in the wind.

Even the drive home is menacing and unnatural. Was the same black car following her all this time or is it her imagination? Caution implores her to check her rear view mirror every few minutes.

Nothing.

The street is quiet when she goes to her front door. Except the rumble of a car engine. Then nothing. Silence.

Shaking hands make her keys jingle excitedly as she shoves them into the door and hurries inside.

It had been a trying day; various talks and speeches, meetings and excuses, plans to figure out and stories to tell. Her job is always difficult but recently more so, a threat looming in the distance.

Smash.

Something falls ahead. She jumps.

The ceramic pot on the window sill that she was growing herbs in. It seems the wind from the open window had pushed it over. Except she never leaves her windows open; even in Kensington, you had to be careful.

Her body makes a circle. Everything looks as it should, she thinks. The fruit bowl sits on the table: three bananas, an apple and two oranges. The newspaper she half-read is on the breakfast bar, shoes by the front door and the rug slightly upturned after she slipped that morning, keys in the bowl ...

Where are her keys?

Panicked, she rushes to the mantle beside the door, opening all of the drawers and rummaging through. She only had them a second ago. She can't have lost them. Unless someone is in the house ...

Her heart suddenly relaxes and she breathes. Her hands had fallen into her pockets. There they are, safe and sound.

She feels better but light disappears. To her left, a shadow forms. A shadow from the glass in her front door, blocking out the pretty stained colours that usually danced across her face.

She bolts down the hall with her bag still over her shoulder. She could swear she heard a bang as she attempts to unlock the back door.

Footsteps.

She swears at herself, begging to pull herself together.

The door is open and she is gone, running around the house, jumping over a hedge to her neighbours' garden. Mr and Mrs Forster won't mind as long as she misses their flowerbed.

Chest burning, she pushes their gate open and tears down the concrete passage to the front of their houses, dashes to the car and drives.

'Do you realise what time it is, Renata?' are his first words.

It is just after seven in the evening.

'I know, Wilson, I – I know but I was so scared and I didn't know what to do. There was someone in my house. The window was open. T-then they were right next to me on the other side of my door. I knew someone was following me in the car when I was going home. I just had a feeling and when I got back I – I knew I wasn't hallucinating and I just thought of you. I didn't know where else I could go that was safe. I'm sorry.'

'You should have called the police.' He beckons her into the sitting room and sets her down on the edge of the powder pink pouffe by the window.

She is shaking. 'I know. I know I should have but I panicked. I ran out of the back and got to my car and just drove.'

'Well, there might well be someone in your house if you've left the back door swinging open.'

'I didn't – I did … Well, maybe I could call the Forsters. Ask them to close it?'

'Don't be ridiculous, it could be dangerous. I'll get someone to go over there and give it a sweep.'

'The police?'

'No. I don't want to cause any panic or get the media involved in any of this just yet.' He picks up the phone in the corner of the room and dials a quick extension. 'Jacqueline. Time to get up. I need you to get security over to Gibb's residence for a thorough sweep. No authorities please and get it locked up tight when they're done. Also, get Ling to bring some tea to the sitting room.'

'Thank you,' Renata says, sniffing. 'You didn't have to do all of that.'

'I told you that you should have moved into Number Eleven where I could keep an eye on you.'

'Keep an eye on me?'

'You'd be safe here. Ever since Hempfield decided not to live there, Coombe hasn't. I doubt any Chancellor ever will.'

'And I'm not living there for the same reasons they gave. It's an archaic tradition with no real purpose. You should get out of Number Ten and see the world, Wilson. You just might find out how fun it is.'

'Tradition is the real purpose.'

'Ceremonial pomp and glorification for the sake of vanity. The purpose is perception and counterfeit insight to fool the masses.'

'The glorification of tradition doesn't stay within the executive and judicial branches, nor just within the monarchy. Weddings, christenings, funerals, ceremonies stemming from the most archaic and unproven system known as religion, stretching on to 2051 where churches and temples are simply decorative and memorial. I know you're a believer, Renata, and I say nothing against it but is this not counterfeit?'

'Only for those who pretend. I know that when I get married, I want it to mean something.'

'Love itself means something. You're not married, engaged.'

'Neither are you.'

He is about to respond, but hesitates. 'Now isn't the time to argue.'

'Hear, hear.' She smiles for the first time that evening.

They are interrupted by tea, Ling entering with a smile.

'Evening, Ms Gibb.'

'Good evening.'

'Are you okay?' Ling asks, concerned by her bedraggled appearance.

'No questions,' Frost reminds her.

She sets the tray down without another word and leaves

quickly while Frost dispatches two cups of tea, pouring milk, doling sugar.

'So, do I get to stay this time?' Renata asks, staring into her warm beverage.

'You've had a scare. I can't send you home tonight.'

'Is that the only reason?'

The space between them is huge and small at the same time, damning yet delightful and all she can do is watch the brown liquid swirl around the china cup and listen to the sound of her own heartbeat while Frost contemplates her words.

He isn't a direct man but he is never lost for words. Until now. Instead of saying something he might regret, he says nothing, just kissing her softly, a sigh of happiness on her lips.

Just as she guessed, in the morning, she wakes with no one by her side. It makes sense to her because the clock reads eight-thirty and the day had more than just begun.

She dresses in her clothes from the night before and sneaks out of the prime minister's lavish bedroom without anyone seeing her, arriving downstairs as if she had been down there the whole time.

'Where's the prime minister?' she asks one of the security members in the hall.

'Erm ...'

Frost exits a room to her left and she instantly pounces.

'I've been waiting down here for you for ages, Mr Frost,' she says for the sake of their company.

The security guard says nothing but looks on with a raised eyebrow.

Frost strides towards the front office and Jackie.

'Sorry, I have things to do. Can it wait?'

Deflated, Gibb says, 'Of course. Yes. I should go home anyway.'

'Yes, it's all clear now. Jackie, is there any post?'

'Package just arrived, Sir,' Jackie responds, pointing at a brown box on her desk.

'Who's it from?'

Jackie frowns. 'There's no name.'

Gibb's hand closes around Frost's arm faster than he can register.

'Don't open it.'

'What? All of my post is thoroughly checked before it even—'

'Please? For me. I just have a really bad feeling. I can't explain it, but after last night …'

'Don't be silly. It—'

'Fine, open it.' Renata heads towards the door. 'But I won't be here when you do.'

She leaves, angry.

Frost and Jackie look at each other.

'Open it,' he tells her.

'I'm sorry?'

'Open it.'

'But I—'

He stares at her with ferocity. Automatically, her hand reaches towards the seal, quivering. She pulls up the tape on one side and then stops. Sweat has gathered on her forehead and her eyes water.

Nobody moves.

'You're going to have to fire me, Mr Frost.'

He smiles. 'Nico!'

'Sir?'

'Could you do me a favour and get a bomb squad down here please?'

They arrive within five minutes, the state's anticipation of violence not disappointing. Everyone in the room is evacuated, along with all others inside Number Ten and the Press Office at Number Twelve. Once they had moved along to the entire street evacuating, the police try their hardest to keep speculators and the media back and out of harm's way.

Sweating, an officer peels back the rest of the tape after scanning the box. It looks lethal, so the rest of the squad step away and he has been left in on his own.

He runs his finger down the middle flap. There doesn't seem to be any wires.

Moving with care, he pushes the flap upwards and peers inside to see a phone and plastic bottle filled with a clear liquid, penetrated by three wires.

'All was quiet in Downing Street this morning after a bomb scare at the prime minister's residence. Reports say that a mysterious package had been sent to Number Ten at around eight this morning, containing what appeared to be a fake bomb. No one was hurt and the press secretary had this to say.'

'A package containing an inactive and non-lethal bomb was sent to Number Ten Downing Street this morning, addressee unknown. Downing Street was fully evacuated and there have been no casualties. We do take these threats very seriously and the police will be taking on a full-scale investigation as to who sent this and why. Thank you.'

Mason had been wrapped in her duvet on the sofa, but raised herself up towards the television as the news story was revealed. The days following Sera's rant were quiet; they only spoke to confirm when she would be home from school and to negotiate the handing over of Mason's credit card. She received no apology for the theft but didn't expect one anyway. Sera had a point. Mason had given up yet, this afternoon, the idea of a threat to the executive branch sparks her interest.

She looks around to find her phone lying on the dining table. She trips over the linen hung over the sofa, gains a carpet burn on her elbow, stands and then retrieves it. There are twelve missed calls from her successor and five from Shah.

She dials Briscoe's number immediately.

'Kevin.'

'Dolly.'

'Have you seen the news? It can't be a coincidence. Right? Am I right?'

'Dolly, what on earth are you going on about?'

'The bomb scare on the news. Someone sent that as a message, Kevin. I know it. It has to be someone on the inside. How else do you explain the package getting in anyway? And Shah losing his job and then me and now this? I wonder who's next and I feel sorry for them, I really do. I literally have no money in my—'

'Could you stop talking about yourself for one minute? I've been trying to contact you for days and you couldn't stop feeling sorry for yourself for one minute, could you?'

'Kevin, what's the matter? What's happened?'

'The police arrested Molly three days ago. Charged her with perjury. Dolls, they're saying she lied.'

'Well, they can't do that. All they have to do is track down Oscar's body and they'd see it was the Rissingtons. Kevin, you can't let this happen. You're the attorney general. Do something!'

'What do you think I've been doing? Sitting on my arse all day? It's too late. Half of the other witnesses have been charged too. I reckon it's some back-handed scheme of Scott's to raise sales at the auction. I've tried contacting their department but they're shutting me out.'

'Now you know how I felt.'

'They're putting them on sale next week, Dolly.'

'Why do you sound so down about that?' she questions.

'Why do you think?'

'Kevin, all you have to do is buy her back.'

'They'll see that coming and charge a fortune for her.'

'Well, club together with your brother or any other secret siblings you have coming out of the woodwork …'

'How did you know about my brother?'

'Not from you, that's for sure. But we don't need to go into that now.'

He sighs down the phone. 'I don't know where he is.'

'Lucky for you, I do.'

Fifteen

Having no video evidence from the scene and using the eye witness testimonies, the confession and good old fashion instinct as well as trusty common sense, Dahl deduces the events as such.

A group of unknown troublemakers, social outcasts, anti-establishment pariahs, people who felt they had been let down by the system or working class, poverty-stricken, irrational, nonsensical fools had banded together to form a plan. This plan involved the inhumane massacre of members of parliament and whoever else they could get their hands on. Judges, lawyers, bankers, businessmen. Members of parliament usually come together at the Commons at the Palace of Westminster where there is too much security and no feasible way to execute a plan to slaughter. The ten-year anniversary of the Criminal Justice Act amendments was a perfect opportunity, a symbolic way to express the hatred of change and everything they hate about the new society they had been forced to live in. All manner of powerful people were in attendance, presenting a timely chance to act and be seen.

So, she gathered a team of like-minded individuals, willing accomplices, formulated the details. The when was already figured out. The question was how. It is clear a message had been put across. They wanted suffering, no quick easy deaths; they wanted pain. Guns are easy enough to get hold of these days, as they always had been. She couldn't do it alone and needed cover, found them a way in through the catering team and served a barrel full of bullets for the first course.

At least, this is what he would say during the meeting. Not in those exact words … *a barrel full of bullets for the first course* … a bit too graphic for the likes of the police. He is in charge, but he doesn't want to trouble them with metaphors, especially in terms of such a serious case. After all, the prime minister will be in attendance. He would be timid and professional with his words, careful and cautious so as to not be misinterpreted. The woman had been identified, but they were saving the grand reveal for tomorrow afternoon.

He wishes Shah were in his shoes, that he had to face this challenge. It was not his fault that he was overheard by an IPCC investigator in the lavatory while he relieved himself in the urinal, complaining that Shah spent more time depriving detainees of medical care than doing things the right way. Next thing, Shah was being marched out and he was in. He heard that his predecessor was interrogated and questioned for weeks, finally being suspended for three months pending investigation. He would probably be fired at the end of it all, mainly due to media speculation, but he enjoyed telling people that he was just filling in, modest man that he is.

There is no doubt that he enjoys the salary rise for less work and more responsibility. His caseload lightened while his face graces the television screens more often, facing the media on more occasions that he wished. People knew his name and an elderly couple pointed him out in the street once after work. His face was in the paper three times and his name more than that, all in a positive light, thank goodness, usually accompanying a slanderous comment about Bhavesh Shah, the irate and vehement ex-police chief.

The basketball net was gone from his office and replaced by Dahl's degree certificate. Also gone was Shah's old police uniform, nothing but the bare wall on show instead. The view is as splendid as ever, a captured moment of the City beyond. As the sun sets, he smiles, not believing his luck, in sheer amazement of his position and status. A smile creeps over his face, a precursor to the laughter, but he is interrupted by of the admin staff member who knocks and enters without a response.

'Come in,' Dahl mutters sarcastically.

'I'm sorry, Sir, but I was sent up to get you. She wants to talk to you.'

The drive to the City police station where she was being held takes twenty minutes in the traffic, but not too long. The room had already been set up, a chair opposite her and a glass of water for him. No doubt, there were other officers watching behind the mirrored glass. He would be stood there himself if she had not taken a liking to him.

'I'm here,' he says, undoing the button on his suit jacket and sitting down, leg crossed over the other.

She looks the same as last time, although healed and marginally healthy, less deranged.

'I've got a secret for you.' Her voice is so small that he can barely hear it.

He asks her to repeat herself anyway, just to be sure.

'I've got a little secret.' She laughs, throaty and deep.

'And what's that?' Dahl is nervous but sits up tall as if he were confident.

'There's a bigger fish in this pond, Mister. A bigger fish

waiting to swallow this place up whole.'

'What do you mean?'

'You'll find out soon.' She laughs until a tear drips from her eye. She is in tears as Dahl watches, sick to his stomach. 'All of this misery just for a voice and a chance to make things right. Do you know what it's like to be free? Does anyone? I'm a slave to the system and you're a slave to yourself. And, after all of this, I'll be someone's puppet, doing whatever they want, saying "Yes Ma'am, no Ma'am," in exchange for my life, trading my time for the day I can be my own person again. But what is it I go back to? Back to poverty and restlessness and trying to find a way while everyone else spends money on cars and houses and nice food and drinks. It's just not fair. And you'll pay. Not because you deserve to but because you don't back down. You refuse to lose the fight. Your character is too strong and unrelenting. It's not because of us. You don't have to die for this, but you will.'

'Well, we can be quite stubborn.'

'So can we.'

The other officers speak what is in his mind. He has to postpone the conference. Does this mean they have to investigate further? She may not be the mastermind behind it all. Mastermind or no, she must have been there and clearly believes in the cause. Who is this unstoppable being coming for them and how will they strike? When? How far will this possibly go before society itself must bend to the will of a few rebels? How far will this go before society itself becomes a rebel along with them?

The air is thin. She had missed her opportunity to escape on several occasions, left with no choice but to wait and wane inside the back of the car. Every breath is heavy and determined.

Hunger punishes each minute and the thirst is unimaginable, a small step away from dehydration.

Head banging, Clarke listens for a whisper of life. She has to tell herself not to scream, not to panic and shout for help. Tears fall down her cheeks as she places her hand on the roof of the boot. She can hear her weak heartbeat in her ears. How long had it been? Is the sun up or is it down? She is too afraid to sleep, too afraid of the darkness. Will she ever see anything again?

A pair of shoes are jammed to her left, along with an umbrella under her feet and a bottle of motor oil above her head. There is a blanket but the stagnant heat does not warrant its use. She had already tried to unfurl herself from her coat, finding some relief and had taken to sucking on the edge of the sleeve; the vague taste of washing powder and conditioner is sweet on her tongue.

What had she done? She convinces herself that she will die in here, that this will be her resting place and that her remains will only be found when she starts to smell foul, when he takes a look at what was rotting. The thought of maggots and flesh turns her stomach.

How long does a person go without looking in their boot? She has a sinking feeling that he already knows where she is. She had coughed once on a journey yesterday, trying her best to mask it within the noise of the traffic, the stuffy air tickling her throat.

Her back is twisted and uncomfortable. Every now and again, she attempts a stretch, shifting her position slightly, each movement barely relieving her pain. It hurts more than ever to close her eyes this time, fearful that she will never wake but she does, falling easily and fast.

She wakes when the car swerves a corner abruptly. A horn beeps far away as she is jostled about. Listening carefully, she hopes her location had not been revealed. At the same time, she longs for the fresh air.

Sweat drips into her mouth and her body shakes.

The car slows and swerves as her eyes close without permission. Her hand hits the top of the boot five times.

'Help,' she whispers.

Minutes, hours or days later, Clarke comes around. Smelling salts, she presumes, as there is a strong, sharp smell in her nostrils that almost makes her pass out again. Water is rubbed on both of her full lips and then tipped inside. Her throat now moistened, she sits up and looks around.

The garage she is sat in is completely empty, nothing on the shelves and no car kept safe within it. She is slumped on a mattress with her arms and ankles bound together by two pieces of rope; she may as well be back at the Crown Court.

In the forefront of her vision is a man, a man with a youthful face but with grey hair and a pair of small rimless glasses which reduce his eyes to a smaller size. The hair on his head is slicked back and his body is swallowed up by a large suit, at least four inches too large.

Clarke curls herself into the corner of the room, fumbling off the tattered mattress.

'Where is he? Where's Ellis?'

'So you're Clarke Manning, twenty-six, ex-photographer, instead of the woman with no name and a debt which far outweighs the cost of her own life.'

'How do you know that? Ellis …'

The man nods. 'He won't be coming to the rescue. Not today.'

Clarke sits up, uncomfortable. 'What do you want from me?'

'I thought you'd ask who I was first.'

'It doesn't matter. It doesn't change what you want and why you're keeping me here.'

'Let us cut to the chase then, shall we?'

'Please.'

'I'm going to let you go. Then, I will drop you off at the

home of Peter Dahl, the commissioner of the City of London police. You will threaten his life, frighten him a little and then leave, scaring him into action. He will believe that he is the next target and then will hopefully step up and take charge after what comes next.'

'Why should I?'

'Because, if you don't, I'll send someone else and tell the media that it was you. Young black girl with a record. It won't be hard to convince anybody.'

She holds in her frustrations, aware that she has no choice but to obey.

'And what comes next?'

The man takes a knife and cuts the ropes that kept her bound.

After two tall glasses of Dutch courage, Kevin drives the short journey and rings the doorbell. It is closer than he thought.

A dark-haired woman with honey-coloured eyes answers the door, dressed in a nurse's uniform and jacket, keys in her hand. It is clear that she is on her way out but is stopped in her tracks by the familiarity of his face.

'Hello.'

Kevin had never met her but thinks she is nothing less than stunning where some might think her plain.

'Kevin?'

'Yes,' he responds, shocked. 'I didn't think you'd—'

'I'm sorry. You two could be twins.' Her hand is on her chest as though she is short of breath.

'Yeah, our mum used to say that.' He smiles at her awkwardly. 'Can I come in?'

'Oh my God, yes. Sorry.' She steps aside and he enters the narrow hallway, caught under the coats hanging from the hooks. 'I'm Rosie.'

'Are you my long-lost sister-in-law then?' he asks.

She smiles, although her eyes are unhappy. 'Not too sure about that one, at the moment. Rex is out in the garden and I have to leave in a minute, but I'd like you to meet Ed. If you want to.'

'Okay.' Not one for kids, Kevin accepts anyway, interested to meet his mother's only grandchild.

They step into the living room where Ed is lying languidly across the sofa with a bottle of water in hand, watching a sports recap program way too loud.

Rosine picks up the remote and turns it down, just as he notices them enter. 'Ed, this is your uncle, Kevin. Kevin, this is Ed. Edwin after my dad, but just Ed.'

Ed sits up and allows Kevin to shake his hand. Kevin can see the confusion on his face but this boy is clearly too polite to verbalise the strangeness of the situation.

Kevin says the first thing that comes to mind. 'I found you through Dolly. Mason. She used to be the attorney general.'

'You mean through Sera,' Ed corrects.

'Well, yes. But it was Dolly's idea. Sera didn't make the connection. Well, she probably did but didn't say. Too clever for her own good really.'

'Annoying, isn't it?' Ed asks, almost smiling.

Kevin turns to Rosine. 'I'm sorry to intrude on you but I just need a quick chat with Rex and then I'll be on my way.'

Checking her watch, Rosine says, 'Well, I'm already ten minutes late. I have to go. Ed, can you get your father please?'

'Yeah, okay.' He leans over to get his chair, which had been on the other side of the sofa. Kevin tries not to stare and waits patiently as he seats himself.

'It was lovely to meet you, Kevin,' Rosine says in earnest.

'You too.'

'Come by whenever you want.'

'Thank you.'

'Bye, Mum,' Ed hollers before she leaves, settled in his chair and going out of the room. 'You know, she just wants to avoid talking to him.'

'Is that so?'

'Isn't it obvious?'

Kevin shrugs and is shown the garden. Ed stays inside but tells his new uncle to go down to the shed, so he does so, walking down a little ramp and walking across the matted grass. He hears banging and clicking on the inside, a cry of frustration and a small crash.

Kevin taps on the door lightly.

'I'll be ten more minutes. Bloody thing isn't co-operating.'

'I only have ten minutes,' he says in response.

Before Kevin can tell, the door is open and he is looking into the face of his big brother, a face that he has grown to resemble over the years. He has more facial hair than he does, then again, he doesn't spend as much time on the television than Kevin so it is understandable.

Rex doesn't look happy to see him, but he could be holding back despite himself, pretending that he isn't happy to see one whom he calls family.

He holds his hammer in hand firmly and leans against the door frame, seething. 'What do you want?'

'Nice to see you too,' Kevin mutters.

'Don't pull that with me. You could have come around sooner.'

'If I knew where you were. Rex, I'm the one who's lived in the same place for about a decade. You're the one who could have come around. Take some responsibility for your own life for once.'

'So that's it? You came here to piss me off? You came here to tell me how shit my life is and give me a good shake so that

I can bow to you like everyone else does?'

'What are you even talking about? I came for your help!'

'Well the shoe's on the other foot now, isn't it?' Rex says, smug.

'Just because you spent your life borrowing twenty quid every week from whoever you could, it doesn't mean that's what I'm here to do. It's Molly.'

'Bekah. What's happened?' He had taken to calling her Bekah, a use of her middle name, ever since he was a small child and it stuck.

'Do you remember, just before Mum and just before she left, she was with that idiot Oscar? Well, he died and they were taken for a ride by a pair of doctors who in the end convinced Molly to let him die to save someone else.'

'What the hell?'

'I know. I know. Just let me finish. Anyway, she came to London to try to help with the trial but he got off and now she's been done for perjury. She didn't lie and nor did any of the others, it's just some mad conspiracy to get money out of the situation.'

'And these are the people you work with? How could you let this happen?'

'Believe it or not, I don't have that much power.'

'Sure you don't.'

'I need your help to buy her back. They're selling her on Monday morning along with all of the other witnesses, only I know they won't let me buy her. It would be too easy. So, just in case I'm right, I want you to come with me and outbid me.'

'Good. At least you're not asking me for money.'

'Well, feel free to cough up, Rex. She is your sister!'

'How do they set the bid price?'

'However they want.'

'We don't exactly have much money going around Kevin. Unlike you.'

'I heard you were unemployed. How's that going for you?'

Rex shakes his head. 'You come in here, insulting me, and you expect me to help you?'

'I expect you to help your little sister. Or are you forgetting that she feels responsible for your little accident which cost Mum her life? You should have known better than to leave those things lying around. Molly took the blame because she thought she had to. The only reason she didn't get investigated was because she was underage and I let you go because you felt so bad about it!'

'I do feel bad about it! Every day, I think about what I've done. I'm trying to change.'

'Well, start by helping me with this. Free of charge, mate, just this time.'

'Fine,' he says, stubborn. 'Tell me what you want me to do and I'll do it. For Bekah, not for you.'

They organise their plan to deceive the judge in charge, the money transfer and the date and time, hoping that their sister would be okay this time, after all of her sadness and sacrifices.

It is another fine Monday for Judge Scott. His young fiancée makes him a full English breakfast to start his day, accompanied with a coffee for the road and a morning quickie on the marble breakfast bar.

He has a spring in his step all the way to the car and drives to the courthouse, happy as ever, singing to himself through the morning briefing with the administration. It is just another day in the office, another day of selling off the City's wrongdoers and he is perfectly fine doing so and taking in a percentage of the profits.

He changes into his robes before sitting in his chambers with his coffee, taking a look at today's crop on his tablet:

AA345B, Amy Beard, 31
Born November 2017, 6'0", 201 lbs
Convicted of perjury during R v Rissington (2051)
Sentence: 1 year
Debt: £10,000
Minimum sale: £10,000

M281RB, Molly Rebekah Briscoe, 27
Born January 2024, 5'10", 96 lbs
Convicted of perjury during R v Rissington (2051)
Sentence: 2 years
Debt: £20,000
Minimum sale: £40,000

WA84JH, William Angus James Hines, 68
Born July 1984, 6'0", 185 lbs
Convicted of perjury during R v Rissington (2051)
Sentence: 1 year
Debt: £10,000
Minimum sale: £10,000

AL35GN, Alice Georgina Niro, 22
Born January 2029, 5'2", 133 lbs
Convicted of perjury during R v Rissington (2051)
Sentence: 1 year
Debt: £10,000
Minimum sale: £10,000

NK66SN, Nataly Keziah Njeama, 41
Born March 2010, 5'7", 157 lbs
Convicted of perjury during R v Rissington (2051)
Sentence: 1 year
Debt: £10,000
Minimum sale: £10,000

His eyes catch the name 'Briscoe' and expects to find the new attorney general in the crowd filled with hope. He will not purchase this woman; Scott does not care whether or not it is his wife, sister or cousin. Not because they would be accused of a thrown bid, of favouritism within their department, but because of her value. Being a close relation of Kevin Briscoe means that someone would potentially pay more for her and he is not one to deny money, hence the price on her head.

Just when he begins a search for a few custard creams, the clock strikes eleven and he heads for the courtroom, tablet in tow.

As expected, Kevin is in the crowd, even more shocking is the sullen figure of Dolly Mason by his side; no one has seen her for weeks, her suspension drawing to a close. She is wearing casual clothes, a thing unseen but ultimately looks as determined and strong as ever.

Scott laughs to himself in his head, taking his seat at the head of the room.

He takes up his gavel and begins.

'Good morning, ladies and gentleman, and welcome to this morning's sale. We have just five lots this morning so this shouldn't take us very long. I hope you all have your tablets. If not, they are available in the hall along with bidder number allocations. Shall we begin?'

He nods to the security guards on his left and they bring out the lots for sale all of whom had been branded the night before. All five walk out in a row and into their spot where everyone in the room can view them easily. As usual, they are dressed in grey and morose.

He begins with AA345B. Usually a happy woman, she is dead in the face and does not look up once while she is sold off to a bespectacled old woman for seventeen thousand pounds. It could have been worse. A dark-looking man with a wiry beard had bid but backed down after a while. Amy hopes that the worst she will have to do is clean the woman's feet and read her bedtime stories. She is taken back to her cell to wait for her new life; she reminds herself that it is just a year and holds onto that prayer.

Molly is taken from the rest of the group and to the stand. Scott watches the bottled expression on Briscoe's face with glee.

'Next lot is M281RB, aged twenty-seven, five foot ten, ninety-six pounds. A bit skinny but once you feed her up a little, will be healthy as a horse. Perfect for a bit of manual labour or even to bear children, I expect. Not too old, this one. Good member of the family potentially. We have a two-year sentence for this one today and a starting bid of forty thousand pounds to begin. Do I have a bid?'

Scott watches Briscoe try to contain himself.

'If I have no bid, I'll just have to lock her up for another week and then another and another until she is sold. She's a real treasure, I bet. A nice wife, maybe? Get a divorce after the two years is up. Peachy. Who knows, she might stay …'

Briscoe's hand shoots into the air.

'No bids? How upsetting.'

Briscoe angrily takes his hand down after encouragement from Mason and the faith in M281RB's eyes is extinguished.

'Any bids? Any bids now please or I shall have to hold this sale. Excellent! I have forty thousand.'

A young blonde man enters the fray, bidder number 5411. He looks nice enough but the look on M281RB's face says no.

Scott speaks quickly. 'Any more bids? Going once, going twice—'

Another man in the corner nods.

'Is that forty-one thousand?' Scott hollers, grinning. The man nods again. 'Forty-one thousand bid. Forty-two? Forty-two I have bid, Forty-three. Forty-four. Forty-five. Forty-six?

No bid at forty-six. Perhaps forty-five and a half? Forty-six. And a half. Forty-seven. And a half.'

The bidding continues until they reach over eighty thousand pounds.

'That's eighty-two thousand, five hundred pounds. Going once. Going twice. Sold to bidder 8363. Congratulations, Sir.'

Scott notices tears on M281RB's face and sniggers, only to take a moment and realise that they were actually tears of happiness. There was a smile hidden beneath the salty water dripping down her face. He turns to the crowd.

Briscoe and 8363 shake hands and then look at him. They had beaten him.

His face steadily turning a shade of purple, Scott continues the bidding, selling off every person off at the highest price he could get, the thought of the profits being the only thing to calm him down.

At the end of the sale, Scott reminds buyers to confirm their personal details at the desk before they leave and organise delivery. He disappears as soon as he can, seething.

After dotting the I's and crossing the T's, Kevin, Rex and Mason stand in the entrance hall as people filter out behind them, happy and unhappy with the results of the day.

'I'd call that a success,' Mason says brightly. 'A well-executed plan. Scotty didn't see it coming, the dunce.'

'I'll have to sell my body to pay for this,' Kevin utters, smiling.

'God knows you've already sold your soul,' Rex says, honest.

Kevin throws him a filthy look but tries not to rise to his taunts.

'She'll be home by the end of the week,' Mason says. 'At least you have something to look forward to.'

'Was that a work segway?'

'Well, now that you mention it, my suspension is almost up and I have a meeting with Frost next week. You can tell I'm really looking forward to that.'

'I'm going to go,' Rex says, clearly not part of their conversation.

'No, you don't have to. I can go. Are you two doing something now?' Mason asks. Kevin gives her a look which says 'absolutely not'.

'I've got to get back to the office. I can give you a lift home if you like,' he says to his brother begrudgingly, not looking at him.

'No, Rosie's picking me up. Thanks.'

'Great! Bye.' He walks away, leaving him alone, and goes onto the street.

After saying goodbye and thanking Rex, Mason joins Kevin as he walks to his car.

'That was rude.'

'You didn't know it, but that was nice, actually.'

'Is it that bad between you?'

'I'm not even going to answer that, Dolls.'

Having driven separately, Kevin walks Mason to her car first, complaining about work.

'Well, good luck, soldier. And tell George that I miss him.' She sits in her car and starts the engine, the window down.

Kevin frowns. 'You don't know?'

'Know what?'

'George was fired weeks ago. He didn't want to work there without you.'

Mason swears loudly. He hadn't contacted her, which meant that he blames her. 'Dolly Mason, ruining lives since 2041.'

'It's not your fault.'

'Then whose is it?'

She rolls the window up and drives home, slowly growing numb with every moment that passes.

As she arrives home, checking her emails, she notices a secure message from Dahl, thanking her for her intelligence on Judge Cunningham, letting her know that his arrest is imminent.

Slamming the door behind her, she instantly gets Sera's attention. She stumbles out of her bedroom, removing her headphones. 'Jesus, who died?'

'So not only do you steal my credit card, you snitch on Cunningham by hacking into my email?'

Sera blushes, not expecting to be caught. 'I didn't have to hack it, you left your computer on. You should be more careful.'

'Come on, Sera, I'm not trying to be your enemy but you are pushing it now. I was going to sort it!'

'When? You were too busy sleeping and feeling sorry for yourself.'

'I'm back on my feet now. And don't tell me you haven't been moping about recently.'

'No more than usual,' Sera assures.

'And why haven't you been going out to see Ed?'

'Because I don't want to.'

'Fine. Clearly something is going on but that doesn't mean you do things like this. Did you even think about how Mrs Cunningham would feel? They're arresting him and he's probably going to be sold off.'

'She can buy him back then! God knows, they have the money.'

'It's not that simple, Sera. Any extra money he got from any dodgy deals will be void. We don't know how far back this goes. She could be broke.'

Sera stares sadly at Mason, tears coming into her eyes. 'She won't forgive me.'

Mason goes over and gives her a hug. 'Me, you mean. She doesn't need to know.'

Gulping down her tears, Sera whispers, 'I'm sorry.'

'It's alright Sera. Well, it's not but, you've gotten away with it this time.'

'Thank you.' They both smile until Mason separates them and locks herself in her office for the rest of the evening.

The feeling comes back before vision does, first in her toes then travelling up to her legs, through her spine, her hands and arms, her empty stomach, stuffy lungs and finally up to her aching head.

Frowning, she opens her eyes to find dimmed lights surrounding her, a beeping machine and the four walls of a private room enclosing her in. Her body buzzes strangely, as if hiding a secret pain.

In the corner, a camera moves over her face and, within minutes, Dr and Dr Rissington enter the room, looking morose.

As their eyes fall over her stomach, so do her hands.

Nothing.

'I'm deeply sorry for your loss,' the male doctor says. 'We did everything we could to save you both but he was too far gone.'

It was a boy. He was a boy. The thing she had killed was a boy. The feeling leaks from her body just as it came, leaving her numb and cold. She remembers the fall and that it felt longer than it was, the world spinning in her wake, a sharp crack in her bones and something that felt like a kick in her middle.

'You may be wondering why you don't feel much,' the female doctor begins. 'You sustained some damage so you have been given sedatives. A broken rib, pelvis, ankle and both wrists.' That isn't why she cannot feel. 'As you well know, payment must be received for us to continue treatment. We have decided, given the circumstances, that we will treat you in exchange for your help and confidentiality.'

Zoë frowns.

The male Dr Rissington speaks now. Zoë decides that she likes him more than his wife; he seems less callous and warm. 'If you wish, we would like to offer you work, a recruitment role, if you will, a chance to help others such as yourself with their medical and monetary issues. You will act as a consultant of sorts, taking on the meetings near the hospital while Dr Rissington helps me here in Reading. We are in high demand at the moment. You don't have to decide right now, we just hope that, once you're better, you see that our purpose was not to harm you but to help. We want to help you and others in a similar situation. We wished things did not end up this way but you can help us change the futures of other young men and women too.'

Zoë hardly thinks that she is in any position to help others. If recruit is another word for manipulate, she isn't sure what to do. It is clear that the doctors did not want her baby to die, or so they claimed, but freewill won out and promises persist. Just like Molly and Oscar, she would have to pay for a treatment she never wanted. Instead of freeing both herself and her child, she became a different kind of murderer whom no one would ever understand. She did not know if Edith had come or whether she had been too horrified to step foot in her presence; she has Paul now and little Paula. Zoë has no one but herself. Working seems a lot better than falling apart, so she agrees to short-term work to pay for the hours and resources they will spend treating her, sending her life onto a new tangent of employment exploitation and virtual prostitution, spiralling and menacing, painful and unwanted, lonely and devastating, yet she still does not feel a thing.

Sixteen

Rain accumulates overhead as she pushes the pushchair along the path, balancing white roses in her left hand. From a distance, she locks the car, pointing the keys vaguely behind her and then tucks them in between her teeth.

She did not mean to scream when she saw it. It was an overreaction, now that she thinks about it, a reflex her throat released without any thought, just a flick of a switch in her brain that told her something was not right.

Where once were the names of Kris Abdo, Orla Victoria Archer, Phillip Pagett, and Ezra J Tuminez, side by side, is now four names spray-painted in red across the memorial plaques: FROST, MASON, SHAH, GIBB. Unsure of what to do, she calls the police and tries to explain the strangeness and horror of what she sees.

The media are there by noon, members of the church standing aside helpfully, a crowd gathering outside Westminster Abbey, a sight unheard of, people attempting to claw their way to the front to see the damage for themselves. Cameras flash and reporters stand in line talking into microphones into cameras about the graffiti and its implications.

'Are you sure we should be here?' Mara Waltz mutters as they slink through the people to get a good look at the memorials.

Briscoe sighs. 'Frost wanted us to check this out so that's what we're doing. Remember, don't say a word to anybody or you'll be seeking employment elsewhere. It would be sad to see you go.'

Waltz had worked at the CPS for seven years and recently became Briscoe's assistant a year ago. Unlike George, Mara is a legal assistant rather than administrative, although it feels like the latter sometimes. When Briscoe was fired, her job may have involved a salary cut but as he was rehired within a day, it meant nothing changed for her except who she was suppressing her legal talents for; solicitor general, director of public prosecutions or attorney general – it makes no difference to her. She is a brilliant lawyer working under those best at what they do, a woman with high ambitions and spades of bravado – something she never forgets to remind people of.

'Briscoe.' She points towards Celeste, who is speaking rapidly into her cameraman's lens. Like everyone else at Victory House, she had heard about the break-up and its implications. Gossip was rare but it spread quickly.

'Focus, Waltz.' He squeezes between stricken family members and she follows. 'Picture.'

Waltz yanks out her phone and takes a quick snap of the tainted memorials.

The picture is laid between them on a tablet as they sit at the table in the meeting room in Downing Street, gold and red and binding. The television is on mute but the face of Celeste Landau is all over it, covering the days' events.

Frost is sat, left leg over his right, musing with a finger to his mouth. On his right is the director general of MI5, Nicholas Stein, thin and pointed, and Elizabeth Lewis-Hague, the astute and poised home secretary, then Dahl, who looks as tired as he always is, Mason next, wearing a composed façade, and then Shah who is quite agitated, a thing unheard of.

'Do you really think this isn't an external threat?' Dahl asks, unsure.

Lewis-Hague tries to hide her annoyance. 'As I have said, our previous enemies have operated in a much more subtle way in the past. Graffiti on graves says personal vendetta. I have a team working on this as we speak, ruling countries out one by one, if it helps.'

'Great. Really comforting,' Dahl responds, after gulping down water. He is beginning to sweat.

Shah is silent.

'Be that as it may, a threat on the prime minister's life should not be taken lightly.'

'We are not taking this lightly, Stein,' Mason states, arms folded. 'We're stuffed in a room discussing how best to act. Thank God he talked you out of locking us up.' She motions Frost.

'A safe house is hardly locking you up,' Stein retorts. 'The longer we stay here and you are all left in the open, the more likely you are to be targeted. If we're going to come to a decision, we have –' He checks his gold wristwatch. '– I would say, twenty-five minutes.'

'We're already so many MPs down,' Mason notes. 'We're gonna need more than twenty-five minutes to talk this through.'

'Twenty-four and a half,' Stein hollers over them all. 'They're not just after MPs. They want the most powerful lawyer in the country, the man who was the topmost policeman and, let's not forget, the prime minister and his deputy. The urgency of this situation is more than I can possibly articulate.'

'Articulate it then. One more time.' Mason is growing restless.

'I don't want to turn this into a slanging match, Ms Mason, but—' Stein replies hotly.

'Then don't,' Shah says, finally finding words. 'We need to figure out what we are going to do and if we're going to take these threats seriously.'

'Well, if you had any real suspects for me to investigate, maybe we could gather how serious this was,' Dahl throws at him. 'I don't even know what you're doing here.'

'I'm sorry,' Shah spits, 'what were you doing before you got your amazing promotion and these guys were being knocked off one by one?' He turns to the others. 'I was breaking my back trying to solve this while you guys mock each other like children in a playground on those plush emerald seats at the Commons. I used to eat, sleep and breathe this case and you seemed so grateful about that! Next thing, I'm thrown out for my efforts. There's no wonder someone wants to get rid of you all. Bloody ungrateful …' The last part he mutters under his breath.

Frost speaks for the first time. 'Obviously, we are all very stressed. We've all been gearing up to something big. Ever since that night, we knew we were in for a fight and I, for one, will not go down quietly nor behind closed doors because it's the correct thing to do. You three can do what you like, but I stay right here.'

He retreats back to silence, thinking to himself with a hand to his chin.

'You can't possibly—!' Stein begins.

'I think he just did,' Dahl says.

'Well, I suggest you take Gibb for safe-keeping,' Lewis-Hague tells Stein.

'Good idea.'

'Where is she?' says Frost.

'She was called in,' Stein confirms.

'If he gets to stay, why not the rest of us?' Mason asks.

'Because he's the only one who overrules me,' Stein says happily. He types something on his phone and puts it into his pocket. 'The rest of you are with me. You'll get communications to a select few on the outside but no one will know where you are. Because I'm the lovely man that I am, you get two hours and two members of security while you sort out your affairs. Snap to.'

The first thing Mason thinks of is Sera. Not her own life, but the life of the fifteen-year-old girl she had taken in. She is not her child but she is her responsibility. If someone is after her, she has to ensure Sera's safety too. For her father.

A security guard waits in the car and the other accompanies her inside the school grounds, waiting in reception. It was lunch time, but Mason is surprised to find Sera eating alone in the hall. She drops her food and runs to her beside the door to the hallway. They step outside and close the glass doors, the people inside watching nosily.

'I saw the news,' Sera says. 'And everyone's talking about it.'

'So you know I have to go?' Mason wonders.

Sera nods. 'What happens to me?'

'I was thinking ... I need you to be safe. Your head teacher knows everything. I don't want anything to happen to you. If someone wants me, they may hurt you or my parents. So, I was thinking you go to them. I have to get you back to your dad in one piece, haven't I? They'll have security and money and we can bring all of your schoolwork ...'

'I'll go if you retract that last part.'

Mason smiles. 'Thank you.' She looks towards the door at the end of the hallway.

'Right now?' Sera asks, confused.

'Right now, Sera.'

'Oh. Can I say bye to —?'

'Of course you can.' Mason sees Ed approaching on the other side of the see-through doors and walks a few metres down the hall with the tall, beefy men who accompanied her, giving them a few minutes alone.

'So what's the verdict?' he says, cheery.

'I'm off to greener pastures. Literally. Lots of people are in danger and she doesn't want me dead. Which is a relief.'

'Congratulations.'

They say nothing for a moment, glancing occasionally at the childish displays and the photographs on the walls surrounding them. The silent receptionist listens intently like a fly on the wall.

'I'll text you?' Sera says, a question in her voice.

'I'll respond. Give me a hug then. This might be the last time I see you.'

Sera dives down and embraces him in a warm hug, almost sat on his lap.

'Bye,' she whispers into his neck.

'Don't get murdered,' he whispers back.

She snorts and laughs, animated. 'I'll try, honestly.'

'It's a wonder no one's done it by now,' he jests.

'I'll murder you in a minute.' Sera jokes. 'Release me!'

He lets go of her and she fixes her hair, which he had apparently had his hands in.

'Godspeed.' Ed salutes her and she does it back, laughing and rolling her eyes simultaneously.

She leaves the room contented and graceful, following Mason and the burly security guards to the car.

When they get home, they pack up most of the essential clothing and belongings, no need to bring any of the food they had stocked up in the pantry. They do this mostly in silence, disbelieving of the situation in which they have found themselves – at least, not until it was their turn to say goodbye.

'God …' Mason looks up, trying not to cry. 'You have changed me.'

'Sorry.' Sera smiles.

'I honestly didn't care about anyone before.'

'Except your parents.'

'Oh, yes, them.'

'And Kevin.'

'I suppose.'

'And George.'

'Okay so maybe I did care. A little.'

Sera counters her argument. 'It was me who didn't care. I lost my parents so I just … lost it. I'd have driven Mrs Cunningham crazy if you hadn't saved her.' Mason nods. 'Why didn't you send me to her? She is my godmother.'

'Because that would be cruel. I know you couldn't live with yourself. It's a nice thought but it's less risky in the sticks.'

'Where will you be?'

'That would be telling.'

'You don't know, do you?' Sera guesses.

'Not at all.' Mason hugs her briefly and breathes a huge breath. 'See you soon?'

'I hope so,' Sera mutters. She gives her guardian another hug. 'You'd make a good mum. Not for me. You know … for someone else …'

'I know what you mean.' Mason scrunches her nose up until the fuzzy feeling dissipates and her eyes dry.

Security explain that Sera will not be able to contact Mason but can contact the usual people on a new phone they provide her with. Mason will get her briefing when she arrives at the safe house.

They separate into two black cars, one going north, the other going south.

Blood drips from a cut on his head, a good patch of grey hair gone from his head, as the doctor removes the red dressings.

'You're lucky to be alive, Mr Dahl,' the doctor tells him, solemn yet positive while looking at the wound. He had been moved from A&E to a private ward an hour previously, where the room was fairly busy but quieter than it used to be decades previously, mostly due to the lack of money. The clientele in hospitals tended to be those who could pay outright, or those who had something to swap in order to get the appropriate care.

'I don't think luck had much to do with it,' Dahl says quietly. 'If someone wanted me dead, I'd be in the morgue.'

'Either way, you're lucky. I'd like you to stay overnight, perhaps longer to see if there is any further damage. I've been informed by your security of the special measures and they will stay here with you until you are well enough to be moved elsewhere. Is that alright?'

'I don't really have a choice, do I?'

'No. The nurse will be in in a moment to change your dressing again and then I want you to rest. I'll see you later.'

'Bye.'

The doctor leaves and the nurse enters, carrying new dressings and wipes.

'Good afternoon, Mr Dahl.'

'Afternoon.'

'If it's okay with you, I'm just going to change your dressing. Won't take long. Be as fast as I can.'

He nods and she stands beside him, unpackaging the new dressing with care. They say nothing to one another until she wipes the bloody wound, causing him to flinch.

'I'm sorry. Just one more minute.' She wipes again and then begins to prepare the gauze. 'Can I ask what happened?'

'You're not the police.'

'They'll be here soon. You can practice on me.'

Dahl is uncomfortable but speaks nonetheless. 'I was at home organising some things. Security were downstairs helping. We didn't have much time so they were loading into the car while I finished up. I was going to take a case downstairs and then the next thing I know I'm falling and then I'm here.'

'You didn't see anyone?'

'No.'

'How horrible.'

Dahl looks at her. She is close to his face, wrapping his head a number of times before cutting the material with a small pair of scissors.

'I'm still alive. They can't get me. Not yet anyway.'

'Mr Untouchable?'

Dahl chuckles. 'Yeah. I suppose.'

There is a knock on the door and two police officers enter.

'Can we have a word, Mr Dahl?'

'Of course.'

The nurse smiles and excuses herself, certain that he would retell the officers the same story he had told her, in those exact words.

The safe house is situated inside an old airfield, not far from a small village within vast countryside. It reminds Mason of her parents' home, leaving her wondering how they and Sera are doing without her. She hoped that they were okay, but mostly that they would be able to stand one another for however long this was going to last for. The three of them had thick skin but worried more than anyone she knew. She hates the idea of causing them stress.

Remote enough not to draw attention and close enough to

civilisation to not feel detached from the world, the building she is staying is situated behind the main bulk of the site, underneath in fact, entry gained through an elevator.

Inside, the place is friendly enough, modern yet empty. There is an unimportant sofa and a box television in the living area, a cheap, bland kitchenette and breakfast bar, a well-stocked pantry full of food, drinks, toiletries and cleaning products, four bedrooms with one single bed and wardrobe in each room and one bathroom with a shower over bath. The apartment also included Shah.

He is in the kitchen fixing himself a cup of coffee when they enter. Upon seeing her, he turns and makes another mug, which she appreciates.

Mason throws down the backpack she is carrying, while the security guards set down two more suitcases and an overnight bag.

'Where are the others?' she asks.

'Gibb will be here A.S.A.P. Dahl has been hospitalised and will be moved as soon as we can manage.'

Mason and Shah connect for a scared moment. No mobile phone, no laptop, no contact. No contact except the secure landline telephone on the kitchen wall and no entertainment except the television and old-fashioned conversation. If they were to be returned to London, there will be a phone call. If they were to be moved to a new location, there will be a phone call. They can use the phone for emergencies only.

'Will you update us on what's happening?'

'I'm afraid you don't have the authority any more,' the plainly dressed guard says. 'Neither of you do. Not here.'

Mason shakes her head, incredulous. 'Go on then. Get out.'

'There's an emergency ladder exit which leads to a manhole on the interior of the site and a courtyard in the back with the waste disposal. If you want fresh air. It's in the manual. Should only be used in emergencies but it doesn't lock unless the alarm's going.'

They are left alone after the crunching sound of locked doors and isolation deafen their ears.

'Can you believe those imbeciles?' She joins her coffee at the breakfast bar and sips. 'I actually like instant coffee.'

'There's tonnes of it in the …'

'Pantry,' Mason fills in.

'Yes.' Shah watches Mason study his face. Admittedly, he isn't as groomed as everyone is used to. His beard isn't oiled and combed and shaped. He no longer has to wear his expensive suits and wacky bow ties and swanky pairs of shoes. Today, given the time he had to change, he is in a pair of utility trousers and a university t-shirt belonging to an educational institution he never attended.

'Weird, isn't it?' he says. 'After all of the avoidance, we're locked in here together.'

'Dahl and Gibb will be here soon. No need to worry about any awkward situations,' she responds quickly.

'I'm not the one who's worried. Why didn't you answer my calls?'

'In case you hadn't noticed, my career was falling apart also. I'm allowed to be selfish every now and again, aren't I?'

Shah nods. 'It would have been nice to have a friend, that's all.'

Unfortunately, she understands what he means. Since losing her position and part of her life, her reason for being, she had become a reclusive outsider with no one on her side. He probably felt the same, if not worse. She had lost a high-profile case, but he was being investigated for mistreating suspects, something far more detrimental.

'Will you ever get your job back?'

'Probably not.' He smiles although he is not happy.

'Why did you do it?' The look on his face said remorse.

'You know what it's like. You become so focused on finding

the truth that you stamp all over the rules and you lose it. It's almost an addiction, our branch of work. I was so obsessed with finding out who did this, I just wanted to squeeze the answers out of them as quickly as possible. The way I saw it, the door was open and I just had to step through and hold on and push through to get to what I needed. Speed equalled efficiency not caution and, somewhere in the middle, I forgot that there were human beings involved. I slipped up.'

'In other words, you lost your marbles.'

'Pretty much. And I only have myself to blame.'

'You have nothing to worry about,' she reassures. 'You know where you went wrong. You've admitted it to yourself. You did something wrong and you're willing to face the consequences. But me …'

'You didn't do anything wrong?'

'No! It's a bloody fix, is what it is, and I refuse to let my career go down the pan because of a few money-hungry judges and a prime minister focused on the optics.'

'Surely, he's supposed to worry about how things look to the public.'

'So he puts Briscoe in my place? That looks worse. Not to mention, it pisses me off too.'

Shah smiles. 'I thought so.'

'I'm not saying he can't do the job but …'

'He can't do the job?'

'No. Not as well as me. He's a softie at heart and you can't be soft. Not in this place. They ripped me to shreds but I'm still here.'

'Locked in an old airfield.'

'Briscoe won't last. And I'm saying this as a friend. I know him better than he knows himself. They will break him down until there's nothing left. They've already tried and they won't stop until they have him.'

'So you have a positive outlook on the whole thing then?'

'You're a funny guy.' She looks at the white ceiling. 'Perfect time to take up a hobby.'

'What?'

'A hobby. Never had time before.'

'I recently started golf.'

'Might try knitting. Do you think there's wool here?'

Shah frowns. 'There's a TV.'

They move over to the sofa and get the remote.

'They better not have scrimped on the channels. Please, let there be films.' She almost prays. 'Have you seen *Titanic*?'

'Never heard of it,' Shah mutters as she turns the television on.

On the first channel, breaking news:

'– her home in the Kensington borough where her body was found. It is said to have been there for a few days before the neighbours went round to the late deputy prime minister's home after noticing that she had not collected in six bottles of milk from her doorstep. It isn't clear what occurred inside the house. The police have already begun investigations and interviews to gather whether there were any witnesses or, indeed, who the last person to see her was. For now, it is clear that members of the executive branch are disappearing one by one.'

Mason and Shah connect, again, for another scared moment.

He thinks best in bed, sinking into the pillows, drowning in the duvet and drunk on comfort. He feels fine. Considering how his insides shrank, he feels fine.

He didn't love her like he thought. He loved her company, her body and her style, disliked her ambivalence and lack of confidence and that made them incompatible. She was great at her job and being his second mate, always covered for him when he was busy or tired or not in the mood, attended events he hated and warmed his bed when he felt empty.

Marriage is not his style, an unnecessary custom that is more symbolic than actual, more financial and legal than special and spiritual. He could have loved her without the symbolism, just as they were, as two people promised to each other without words, promised to each other with a gut feeling and an insatiable instinct. They could have loved each other the fun way, the dangerous way, no shackles nor pressure to perform, with the freedom to leave and say goodbye at any point without the red tape. But they never would. He could have stayed with her if he had the courage to love and find friendship and companionship.

Childhood is what he blames, the vacant period he doesn't even remember that makes him afraid to be open and powerful enough to take, a terminal orphan. To him, the difference between power and willpower isn't will, its means. The ability to take control and give into yourself is harder than he thinks. It is harder to be himself than who he wishes to be so he is glad for the relief and the opportunity to not fail at it. Now he does not have to be happy and he can pretend this is what he wanted all along. This is what he wants. He wants to lie in his bed and try not to cry and wallow in the things he has done, shutting out the world and all of those horrible thoughts he needs to suppress. Why stop now?

Despite Jackie having pushed back his appointments, he gets up, showers, changes into a nice, clean suit and starts on his emails, ignoring all of the insincere condolences and decides to take a walk.

He calls Nico into his office and tells him his plan.

'Prime ministers don't go for walks,' he says, calm. 'We can go for a drive instead.'

It does the job. Frost agrees and waits in the sitting room

for him to arrange the trip. No one speaks to him, they just walk around him with caution. He knows that the press office are desperate for him to make a statement and would advise against going outside if this was not going to happen.

Frost sighs to himself and makes his way to the front door, checking his watch.

'Where is he?'

'Who?' Jackie asks.

'Who do you think? Nico!'

Jackie flinches. 'I – I don't know.'

Nico appears with Alex and two others.

'Ready?' he asks.

Frost says nothing, he just steps back waiting for them to get the door.

The sun blazes down on him, almost blinding. This is soon blocked by the intense shadow of the media.

They walk to the right of the street, followed by reporters, who had broken down the barriers. Police officers muscle through the crowd, shouting, and Frost's security surround him like shields.

'When did you find out the news?'

'Who will be investigating this tragedy?'

'Was Renata Gibb a close friend as well as your deputy?'

'What happens now?'

'Do you admit there is now a serious threat to the lives of those in politics and justice?'

He catches just one question.

'Will you be replacing Ms Gibb?'

Frost turns towards the reporters, held back by Alex. 'A deputy will not be appointed.'

He is shoved into his car and driven away with haste.

When Alex arrives back at Downing Street, he heads straight into the kitchen for his afternoon meal where Ling and Cliff badger him for details to fill in the gaps which the rumours created.

'Nothing really happened. We went outside and he said outright that he wouldn't be having a new deputy. I suppose, it's out of respect for her. She's not even in the ground yet. I don't know if he meant for now or forever ...'

'Did he seem to be grieving, at least?' Cliff asks.

'She's not dead,' Ling utters, shaking her head, fork in hand. 'I'm convinced she's not dead.'

'He did, actually,' Alex admits. 'He was really quiet and he got out of the car for some fresh air down a quiet street. He just paced and looked really troubled.'

'Well you would do if you murdered your deputy,' Cliff says.

'She's not dead!' Ling shouts. 'You can't be murdered if you're not dead.'

'She is dead, Ling,' Cliff responds. 'They found her body.'

'The media have made up crazier things.'

'You can't fabricate a dead body,' Alex reminds them. 'And he can't have killed her.'

'Well, yeah, he was banging her three ways from Sunday,' Ling slips.

Alex and Cliff stare at her, shocked.

'What?' Cliff yells. 'Why didn't you tell me this?'

'I didn't know for sure until a few weeks ago. Jeez, give me a break.'

'So, he did kill her?' Alex wonders.

'Hold your horses,' Ling interrupts. 'This surely supports the argument that he didn't. He is clearly in love with the woman!'

'Wilson Frost does not love,' Cliff warns. 'I'm sure he must have said that once.'

'Yes, he does,' Alex says. 'He loves control and thinks he's untouchable. Why not kill her to have all the power himself?'

'Because he already has it? Listen to yourselves.' Ling rolls her eyes. 'If it was just sex, he'd only get dirty with her once. Right?'

Alex laughs. 'No, Ling.'

'No,' Cliff agrees.

'Either way, it serves no purpose to kill her. This isn't *Macbeth*. Frost is already the top dog. She was just a woman he cared for.'

'I thought she wasn't dead,' Cliff questions.

'I said "is."'

'Sure.'

'Woman or not, she's dead and sex is usually a huge motivator for committing a crime. Maybe she had something on him,' Alex suggests.

'Not forgetting the psychopaths out there who decided they wanted Frost, Gibb, Mason and Shah gone just days ago,' Cliff says. 'Feels like a war to me.'

'Exactly!' Ling yells. 'It could be an outside party.'

'Or Frost is using it as a perfect cover to commit murder.' Alex is satisfied with the theory and folds his arms over with confidence.

'The spurned lover takes fate into his own hands,' Cliff mutters.

'Who said he was spurned? You two are so dramatic,' Ling says with anger. 'You'll see. She'll turn up soon.'

Alex doubts this very much. Too much had happened already for him to believe that something so good could occur amidst all of the chaos. The bomb scare was the penultimate straw. The mayhem and the fear that ensued was enough for him to quit it all and go back to the Auction. If it had been a live bomb, he could have been dead and now he appreciates his life more, suddenly tired of following orders, less happy to follow the crowd than he used to be. This was a twenty-four-hour job, one where he is not able to go home at the end of the day, he is simply rewarded with a bed to sleep in, food to eat and newspapers to stall the boredom.

Living with a potential murderer does not make him feel safe that night when he goes to bed and he is left wondering what Renata Gibb felt like during her final moments, sure if he and his friends would be next in the firing line.

Although Yi-Ling is happy to hope and consume her unsettling version of the truth and Cliff isn't, he sleeps surprisingly well.

The next morning, Cliff uses the mainline telephone to call upstairs to Jacqueline, like he always did when he needed to confirm meals he would be cooking or vice versa.

'Morning, Jackie speaking.'

'Morning, Jackie. Cliff.'

'Morning, Cliff. You okay?'

'Yeah, you?'

'I'm alright, considering.'

'Difficult few days?'

'You could say that.'

'Sure, sure. I need a favour.'

'What is it?'

'My son needs a job.'

'Your son?'

'Yes. He just got fired.'

'How can I help him get a job?'

'Your godfather can.'

'He's fragile at the moment, Cliff.'

'Exactly.'

She sighs. 'What do you suggest?'

'He used to work at Victory House. I'm thinking Scotland Yard. Admin.'

'What do I get out of it?'

'Anything you want.'

She pauses. 'Do you still supply?'

'You know the answer to that.'

'A kilo of the good stuff.'

'Done.'

Six days later, Jackie confirms the role Frost had allowed her to enquire about through a formal letter. He had not questioned her deeply, as he was more concerned with filling empty job posts as soon as possible. 'Do whatever you want' were his specific words.

After giving Cliff the good news, he spent his weekly telephone call to speak with his son, hoping to earn his favour.

'Afternoon, son.'

'What do you want?'

'To talk to you. What's wrong?'

'I'm unemployed. I'm broke. Toby left me.'

'He wasn't good for you.'

'I'll ignore that.'

'Not in that way, George.'

'Whatever.'

'I have good news. I got you a job. Scotland Yard.' George says nothing. 'Really.'

'How did you do that?'

'I asked Mr Frost.'

'Oh my God, are you for real?'

'Yeah.'

'Thank you so much. Why would you do that?'

'You're my son and I love you. You don't need to worry anymore. I've got you covered. Don't forget it.'

No matter how sour his life, there are only two that he cares for; his son and his clients.

Seventeen

The number 77 bus is late and Molly sits with a small pink elephant in her hands, nervous. She scratches the palms of her hands anxiously and paces, losing her seat on the bus stop bench to an elderly woman with a shopping trolley. She doesn't mind. Looking at her soft folds of skin, her random blemishes and wonky smile is a welcome distraction until the large, noisy vehicle stops in front of her, clanking and spluttering as if it were about to give in.

The face she is looking for appears, happy and steady. Edith waves at her from afar and instantly, she notices the change. For one thing, Edith was being nice to her, which was a shock when she received the telephone call asking her to meet. She looked taller than before, less troubled. Her hair is combed and lays tidily by her ears and the denim dress she is wearing reminds Molly that summer is almost over.

'Hey, lady.'

Molly doesn't expect the hug but embraces Edith fully and with relish. 'Hey, yourself. Where's Paula?'

They begin walking along the street towards the park. 'At home with her dad. Didn't want to make her travel all this way. And, let's face it, it's easier for me if she doesn't.'

They both smile. 'How is she?'

'Good. Getting heavier every day, the fat little thing.'

'Adorable.'

'We've taken to calling her Po. Paul hates Paula. Sorry.' Molly was the one who suggested it in the first place.

'Really? Harsh. You thought you were going to lose him.'

'He was literally dying! The sentiment was there but it's annoying to him. He tried, don't get me wrong. Anyway, Po is cute.'

'It's far too cute.'

Edith nods. 'Are you alright? After everything?'

'Better. I'm living with my brother, Kevin. Do you remember me saying on the phone?' Edith nods again. 'Bit of a pain. He coddles me so much I want to scream. He tells me to eat and I don't want to eat. I just want my own life. A job maybe.'

She looks Molly over, at the bones beneath. 'You do look a little skinny.'

Molly shuffles beneath her baggy hoodie as they settle on a bench. 'I eat. Don't worry. I've never had more biscuits in my life.'

'Rich Tea or Digestives?'

'Now that I think about it, he really only has biscuits in that apartment. I'm half-tempted to do a weekly shop for him.'

Molly laughs and Edith joins in, if not to convince her that she believes the lie.

'Have you heard from Zoë?' Edith asks, curious.

'Nothing. I hope she's okay. And the baby.'

'Me too. Paul says thank you, by the way.' Molly's insides hollow and she tries not to think about anything, not even breathing. 'He wants to say it in person.'

'So why didn't he come?' Molly says airily. 'I don't bite.'

'We had a talk last week and we think it might be a good idea if you come and stay with us for a while.'

This is the last thing Molly expects and it reads on her face. 'I'm sorry?'

'Only for as long as you want. Or as long as it takes for you to get back on your feet. Or indefinitely. Whatever suits you.'

'Wow.' She runs it through her tired mind, taking into account her loving brother and how suppressed she feels around him. Then there was Rex, who has not said a word to her since 2040. Even after her brothers released her from impeding servitude, he had only muttered 'hello', 'how are you?' and 'goodbye'. At home, she is bored and restless; watching the sun rise and set is a daily habit, a tease of the world beyond.

'If you're worried about work, I could see if they'll hire you at the factory.'

She is suddenly aware of the infinity mark on her wrist and pulls her sleeve over it completely.

'Where do you work?'

'Well, you might not—it's a clothing factory. They make lots of stock items, school clothes, police uniforms, nurses and doctors scrubs and they do … they do the grey jumpsuits.'

'Oh.' Molly knows what they are like. 'They itched.'

'Is that a yes?'

Molly takes her friend's hand and accepts. 'Of course. We've come a long way, you and me, haven't we?'

'Yeah. I don't want to punch you whenever you talk.'

They part in good spirits, having decided that Molly will take the bus over in two days, giving her ample time to explain to her brother than this is something other than abandonment, it is progress and moving on from her past.

When she arrives home, to her surprise, he is already there, back from work, cooking a meal for them to enjoy. Pots and pans sizzles and steam and Molly smells something like fish as she crosses the living area and peeks in through the kitchen door.

'What are you cooking?'

Kevin jumps but soon laughs at seeing her brittle figure in the doorway.

'It was a seafood broth about ten minutes ago. Now, it's just prawns and mussels in mush, so I'm going to whack on some pasta.'

'Cool.' Molly folds her arms and watches him buzz around the room.

'Where have you been?' he asks.

'Just to see a friend.'

'Who?'

'Edith. I told you about Edith.'

Her brother burns himself on boiling water and runs for the tap. He finds relief and continues. 'So, I was thinking, this weekend, we should do something. I don't know, maybe do a hill walk or something. Then maybe the cinema? We haven't seen a film together in ages.'

'I don't think that'll be a good idea,' she says quietly, picking at her nails.

'There's a load of walks available since the underground road system. More walks than you can believe. We can look them up on the Internet later on, if you want.'

'I don't, actually.'

He frowns as he plates their meals. She sits opposite him on the small table and holds the fork he gives her with distaste.

Kevin speaks slowly, at first. 'Okay, well there might a good film on. We can get large popcorns and pig out.'

'I don't want popcorn.'

'Come on, everyone likes popc—'

'I'm going to live with Edith, Kevin.'

'What?'

'She asked me today and I'm leaving. I think it's a good idea.'

His expression darkens. 'Did you ever think of consulting me? Your brother? Why do you always do this? Why do you always leave when things get hard?'

'No offence, Kevin, but I do not answer to you.'

'I bought you. If I say you stay here, you stay here.'

Anger is not the first emotion, pity is, and she holds herself calmly when she speaks, reminding Kevin of their mother, with all of her strength and glory.

'I do not belong to you, Kevin, and if you think that, then you misunderstand completely what family means. It means that you love me and I love you and that's why we're here in this kitchen. The money you spent doesn't come into it for a second. If I did the same for you – which I would – I wouldn't expect you to be locked up like some hostage until the last day of the sentence is up. I'd want you to keep living and the only way I can do that is away from here.'

'But, I've already lost everyone else, Molly. I don't want you to go too.'

'You'll survive. Celeste, Rex, Mason … They mean a lot to you but who are they really? They don't define you. Rex is still here for you even though he might not say it and Mason'll be back soon enough. You can still be the same old Cheerful Kev, even without me.'

'I don't think that's true.'

Molly smiles a big smile. 'I'm going to tell you something.'

'Go on.'

'My life is tainted by this domino effect, one thing after another. First mum and now all of this … I had a son. Because of Oscar's situation, I had to give him up and I honestly don't know what to do with myself. Do I use the last of my money to look for him? Do I not? Will it make me happy? I don't know. But I do know that I have to figure it out on my own. This won't be the last you see of me.'

Kevin is on the brink of tears, holding his breath and looking into her dark eyes. She takes his hand. 'Molly …'

A tear falls from his eye and he wipes it away quickly, sniffing loud.

'God, it's a relief to see someone else cry,' she admits unwillingly.

Kevin smiles. 'Listen to us pessimists.'

'I know. Mum'd be disappointed.' She goes around the table and gives him a tight hug. 'Are you sure you're okay with this?'

'You already pissed off for ten years, what's another decade?'

She giggles. 'Just two years, tops. I'll be back before my sentence is up, Master.'

He laughs and cries into her shoulder some more while she pats his head sadly. They stay like this for as long as it takes for the seafood broth pasta dish to go stone cold.

When she is gone, the flat is unashamedly empty. There are no longer any little messes; they had a big clean to keep themselves from falling apart at the departure. Molly didn't bring many things in her backpack but he gave her some clothes and a food package for the journey which he knows she will not touch.

She stopped him from taking a day off work to make sure she got to Edith's okay, in exchange for a phone call he receives during lunch. They make small talk and laugh, ending with her encouragement to rekindle his relationship with Rex.

'I don't know.'

'And you won't until you call him.'

After a gulp of vodka, which he had poured into a water bottle early that morning, harking from his teenage days of smuggling alcohol into school, he plucks up the courage to ask

Rex, Rosine and Ed to come to his place for dinner in the next week when they are free, hoping they will refuse. Rex doesn't and Kevin knows this is probably due to the fact that he would never give up that which is offered for free.

They arrive the following Friday, having given Kevin time to plan and practice the meal he has cooked, a spicy paella.

'Good for some of us who have access to decent meat. The rest of us have to take the scraps.' Rex is clearly in the same mood as he always is and Rosine ignores him with style, dressed well enough to distract Kevin from his brother's arrogance.

'Well it looks really nice, Uncle K – Kevin? Kev? What do I call you?' Ed asks, confused, as he dives into the food.

'Kevin will do, I think.'

'It really means a lot that you invited us over. It's nice to finally get to know Rex's family. It was just me and my dad on my side before he passed,' Rosine explains.

'Where's Bekah? I only came because I wanted to see her,' Rex says.

'Yeah, I haven't met her yet either,' Ed adds.

Kevin sighs. 'Molly left. Temporarily.'

'You let her leave after all we did?' Rex is enraged.

'She's been through so much and she needs to get through it. She said she was coming back and I believe her. Have some faith in her.'

'You know I don't believe in anything I can't see, Kevin,' Rex says smartly.

'Well open your eyes. Not everything is tangible and palpable.' This time it is Rosine who has spoken, sipping on wine and not looking into her husband's eyes. She turns to her son. 'You'll meet your Aunt Bekah one day, Ed.'

'Why on earth do you call her Bekah anyway?' Ed questions.

'Just your idiot father and his idiot ideas,' Kevin utter briskly. 'More paella?'

Ed helps himself to more food, taking in three portions by the end of the night, after which he and his father recover on the sofa, enjoying the vast amount of channels on Kevin's television.

As Kevin washes up the dishes, Rosine watches quietly. She notices the dishwasher beneath the kitchen unit but realises he needs a reason to have some distance between himself and his brother.

'We'll go home and he'll complain and say that he doesn't want Ed coming here again. He'll say that he doesn't want him to want what we don't have.'

'It's a fair point,' Kevin says with his back to her and his fingers in the suds. 'You're his parents. Whatever you want to do with him is fine by me.'

'Two years ago, we were having a difficult time of things. Money was tight. Always is, but we fought like crazy over it. I don't know if you knew this but Rex used to have a job in management, nothing too fancy but he did well. He never really knew what he wanted to do long-term. Well, one day, I noticed a huge chunk of money had gone missing and he apparently had a working weekend. Anyway, I question him about it. He lies. So I search through his phone and find pictures and texts and ask him again at his work. He'd been seeing a woman and he'd been giving her our money. I tried not to be angry about it but I was, obviously. Next thing I know, someone he worked with had told the police and he's arrested and sentenced. As far as I know, she wasn't prosecuted for anything. Then I feel guilty, for Ed and our family and I run myself into debt to get him back and ever since, all he does is complain. I wish I left him to rot with some other family.'

'And you won't divorce him?'

'Either way, our son ties us together more than a piece of paper does. I'd have to deal with him for the whole of Ed's life anyway, so I'm taking my time to sort things out.'

'I'm sorry.' He wonders what is holding her back and if she is strong enough to take action. He knows that even a mother can bear the burdens of insecurity and doubt.

She shrugs. 'It doesn't even matter. The funny thing is the woman he saw is in a picture frame on your mantelpiece.'

Kevin's heart stops. He can see the picture in his mind, her bright hair over one shoulder and her bohemian-style dress blowing in the wind as she smiles at a picnic they had enjoyed in Cornwall. Her face is clear, neither he nor Rosine could mistake or forget it. Suddenly his hatred for Rex grows stronger and weaker at the same time.

They leave his apartment in heavy silence because he is too stunned for words. He saves them for her when he calls. She tells him that her life was different then, that it happened once, that he liked her more than she liked him, that it was just business and she didn't even know he had a brother. She is with a man named Hempfield now. True, all of the facts are circumstantial, but he wonders how many other men she wooed in her escorting heyday and how many had tasted her body.

Despairing, he fills his mouth with spirits, alone in his home, thinking it better this way, better to be alone and unhappy. Hankering for something stronger, he thinks of Mason, but is too languid to find his phone and too numb to talk. He drinks until he is lethargic, tongue-tied and mushy-brained, dizzy and falling until he hits the sofa face down.

At three in the morning, Sera rolls over in the warm duvet to find her phone glowing in the darkness. Eyes screwed up and blind, she peers at it to find his name in black on the screen.

Hi.

She messages back instantly, not wanting it to be made clear that she thinks of him:

Took your time.

Didn't wanna seem too eager.

Well, you failed.

How are you?

Getting by. Mr and Mrs Mason are okay. Sick of the security guards.

At least you're safe.

Suppose. How's St Giles?

Same. I miss you.

She holds her breath, staring down at the words she relates to. She doesn't have to wait long until he sends more.

Do you miss me?

Yes.

No sarky comment? Shocking.

I'm a changed woman.

Did you mean what you said?

Which part?

That you don't see the point of me unless I help you?

Of all of the things to question, why that? You don't want to know why I feel this way?

I know why. Is that all you want from me?

Her stomach lurches. She wants to write 'no' but instead types: I'm just so tired of this, Ed. I know you don't get it entirely. I just need a friend.

He seems to be typing for a while but eventually says, *Okay. Just make sure you text everyday. It's painfully lonely without you. And I need to know you haven't kicked the bucket while you're away.*

She smiles: I won't do it without letting you know.

Who knows, you may not have to at all. He could pull through. I hope he does.

Twenty-three days pass. The moment they found the marker pens signifies the moment their brains did not relent. Theories and ideas float around their mind, fly out of their mouths and mark the four walls around them, first the living room, then the kitchen and the dining area. Facts and opinions swim among them, both resilient and fragile, vague and secure, hoping to find a truth among the mystery.

The trigger was the celebration of the ten-year anniversary since the criminal justice act amendment, stating that that all crimes, debts and unfulfilled sentences could be traded for either the simple exchange of free labour, the exchange of personal favours for those in power, or for the increasingly popular exchange of a wholly domesticated existence measured by the severity of the previous outstanding liability. The event that changed the country is the reason dozens had been injured and killed, a statement of disagreement and rebellion hidden amongst the struggle of the people.

Ever since that fateful evening in February, risk and fear had been at its highest level and the more time passed, the more the people distrusted the ones who governed their lives.

'They've never trusted the government,' Shah argues. 'What's changed?'

'Someone's plucked up the courage to kill. That's the difference. Or that's the illusion.'

'What do you mean?'

Mason hops down from the breakfast bar to the spot above the sofa where they had written potential suspects in bold. 'Well, you said you exhausted all of your methods to find this person before.'

'Yes. It was a dead end until a suspect walked in and said she did it. But if they haven't released it to the public by now, something must be up.'

'Bhav, didn't you think it was a little convenient that just when you needed to pin it on someone, she just handed herself in. I mean, come on! It's genius!'

'Well, when you say it in that condescending way …'

'You've been had. Someone sent her in to lie or tell the truth or whatever. We'll never know if she was involved or not but, either way, she's not the mastermind. She's just an instrument and there's someone else conducting this piece.'

A light switches on in Shah's head. 'Frost?'

'Frost,' Mason says, beaming. 'It has to be one of us, someone who has the money and the means. It's not me.'

'How do I know that?' Shah asks.

'Because I'm telling you.'

'I hope to God it's not you.'

'It's not.'

'Everyone else has been targeted. Think about it, he has the most to gain here. The shooting; he miraculously survives an attack where it seemed he was the target. Bet he feels like Superman. Reid, the minister for justice, is down for the count, then Tuminez, Abdo, Archer and Pagett. Tall goes, then Gibb. We lose our jobs, next our lives are on the line. Dahl's in the hospital. Where's Frost? Where is he, Bhav?'

'He's on the outside with not a scratch on him,' Shah states, convinced. 'He killed Gibb. He killed them all.'

'And what is the common denominator? Most of us didn't vote for the CJA amendment. It all makes sense!'

'That could be a coincidence.'

'He wants to silence us in case one of us decided to try to get the law changed back. He expects us to rot in here until he's ready for us,' Mason utters, sick to her stomach.

'I'm sure if he wanted to kill us, he would have done it but now. Maybe it's just enough to ruin our careers.'

'Well, if he thinks I'm going away, he's got another thing coming.'

'You're forgetting the bomb scare.'

'Fake. It was all a fake. Trust me.'

'He could be innocent, you know.'

'Unlikely. But if he is, I'll be the first one to apologise. If he isn't … We need to figure this out before anyone else dies. I couldn't stand it if anything happened to Kevin.'

'What are you going to do?'

'I don't know yet. But we can't do nothing.'

'Maybe if we just see how it all plays out,' he suggests.

'I've spent my life waiting for the right moment. If I wait now, how bad does life have to be before I step up?'

Bhav smiles at her. 'That's what I admire about you. Not afraid to point out your flaws.'

'I haven't even started.'

He focuses on the stitching in the sofa, the colour of the fabric and softness and comfort it provides, holding his breath. 'When all this is over, I'd like to see you again.'

Mason makes her way to the kitchen again with her back to him. 'I guessed.'

'So that's why you were avoiding me?'

'Not to turn you down but … Listen, I don't want to let you down.' The worktops are very interesting to her, every crumb and stain and line.

'So what do you call all of this? If we weren't locked in here together, you would have never spoken to me again.'

'I emailed you.'

'In person, I mean.'

She sighs. 'You're probably right.' She hears his footsteps and feels his hand on her shoulder and then a kiss on her cheek. 'I'm just not … available. I'm sorry but please don't do that again.'

Mason leaves the room with her arms around herself, wishing that the phone would ring, wishing that she was back in the hive of Victory House, rather than trapped within this dungeon with a man she wants to love.

A letter she had written the previous day goes into the red postbox with caution. She did not know whether he would get it, whether or not he would believe her words, but she knew that stealing the pencil and paper was worth the risk. It is something a phone call could not solidify and she needs this note to stand as a promise and a reminder to him that she has not forgotten him. Clarke is unaware that the letter will drive a wedge in Alex and Ling's blossoming friendship due to the name she signs and the hope she tries to inspire. She is unaware that he has to explain away her words for months to come.

She quickly forgets what she wrote but knew it came from her heart:

Alex,

It's me. I can't sign my name but you don't know it anyway. Not even sure I do.

I said I would come back for you and that hasn't changed. I was on my way and going strong but I was thrown off track. I found your friend and he helped me but, like most things, life changes.

You looked well on the TV and that's how I knew where to send this. I hope you're okay and not too hard done by over there. I thought your way was harder, serving others, I mean, but being here is much harder. Every day is a struggle. Do I wish I was in your place? Never.

My mother used to tell me that I needed to grow up. Harsh, I know. If she hadn't, I probably wouldn't be here today but I also wouldn't be as resilient as I am. I'll bounce back, I always do.

When the time comes, I'll know how to get to you. Until then,

hold on. I'm holding on too.
  All the best,
  Mrs Spade

Looking around the derelict street, she finds shelter from light rain inside a telephone box down the road beside a row of shops. Glancing through the glass, she feels her insides shrivel as the water washes down in front of her, resting inside her stomach, causing her to curl up and hold herself, her head low.

A sound comes from her mouth, something she hadn't heard in a long time, something like a hiccough, while her body shakes. She questions why she does the things that she does, how her life had come to be this way and slight tears burst from her eyes in unison.

Her hands find the phone but she doesn't dial. Instead, her fingers are in her hair and then she is on the ground, curled up, hurt and alone, scared and wounded.

'Stop crying!' she yells at herself. 'Stop it.'

With the palms of her hands, she rubs her eyes and nose with fury, hiccoughs one more time and stands.

Eighteen

Lord Daniel Reid, Minister of Justice, the president of the
New Supreme Court, comatose victim, never had many
visitors. His daughter, Seraphim, used to visit as often as she
could, around school and so on with whoever is her guardian
at the time. Then, of course, there were the doctors who ran
the tests and the nurse who had been assigned to his care in
the intensive suite. He is given a bed-bath daily, his teeth are
checked every few days, his food fed through tubes in the
correct amount, along with the fluids that keep him alive.
Waste exits his body at intervals. His hospital gown in never
swapped, the filthy, torn and bloodstained suit he had entered
the hospital in is in the custody of the crime scene investigators
until further notice.

The count is one-hundred-and-seventy-four days, a house
record within these walls of despair, a place that does not
specialise in miracles. Doubt aside, the hospital had acquired
a new MRI scanner, scarlet fever vaccinations, sanitisers and
over two hundred new surgical tools thanks to the continuous

donations from the former attorney general. Things had changed so much, thanks to this gift, that the staff do not want him to wake and joke casually about their permanent guest and how they should decorate his new room.

A grey man visits with a bunch of lilies, waiting patiently for the nurse to finish up before going inside his room.

'I'll just be a moment,' Rosine promises, ensuring Reid's fluids are in order. She frowns at the gentleman, who looks tired and drawn.

He pushes his glasses up his nose quickly. 'I'm alright, yes. Just a bit under the weather.'

She smiles at Reid, the man she spends half an hour every day talking to about her problems at home. He is a good listener. 'Take all the time you need.'

When she is gone, he takes a moment to replace the dead flowers in the vase by his bedside, throwing the fragile things into the waste basket and looking around with curiosity.

His eyes look over his pale face, a face that had not seen sunlight for almost six months bar the sliver of light that passes between the curtains on a good day. He had missed the spring bloom and the heatwave in May, well on track to miss the high winds, stormy showers and icy evenings of the coming seasons.

'Daniel, Daniel, Daniel. It's all you, isn't it? You pushed through this new way of life we live today, thought your ideas were bigger than anything and anyone else, completely oblivious to what people actually go through and have gone through since. Ten years ago, I was a prison governor, working all hours under the sun, trying to find ways to make these men's lives mean something when they get out. Of course, I had to make sure they made it out first and that they didn't kill each other. But I learnt something before I was made redundant by your political takeover. You know what I learned? I learned that we're all prisoners, we're all in the same situation. Change the circumstance all you want but here or there, in prison, outside of it, we all serve the state and live at its pleasure. I'm not sure whether you understand why you did what you did, why you drew up that White Paper, but you started something. You were the voice that got things rolling. No public vote, just you and your friends.

'Now what? People are hungry and homeless and tired and jobless and all because of you, my friend. I changed careers, retrained. Thanks to you, promotion from within is easier than ever now that only fifty percent of the country are in work. And I tried my best to help those who offended and had finished their sentences to move on, unencumbered by their pasts. So anyway – where was I? I was saying that I changed as a person and realised that it's your fault. Yours and everyone else who claim to do good. You're the villains and it's about time that people realised. Who knows? Maybe we can go back to the way things were. Things weren't perfect, I'll admit, but it was better than this. You were the catalyst. It all comes down to you. After all of the blood spilled, the shooting was just not enough so I'm afraid I'll have to …'

He places both hands over Reid's face and presses down firmly. It is easy. There is no struggle.

For a moment, he feels joy and relief and anger, all emotions and none, devoid of any guilt or woe. The machine beside them lets him know when Reid is almost out of time and he watches it as each second passes, patient and content.

Behind him, the door flies open and the nurse on his back, yanking him backwards by the shoulder and yelling in his ear for someone to call security. Her nails dig into the skin on his arms until he releases Reid, tosses her away from him, causing her to smash against the wall, winded on the floor.

He looks for an escape out of the room but only finds four

members of security pointing their guns at him. He prays for them to shoot but they tackle him to the ground instead, ending his massacre before the final part could be executed.

Finally, the phone rings. Mason sprints from her room to answer it before Shah, who had been watching the news, waiting for some crumb of information.

'Hello?'

'Dolls.'

'Kevin! Why are you calling? What's happened?'

'I asked to speak to you. Thought it would be better coming from me.'

'What would?' Shah gets up and floats next to her, anxious.

Briscoe continues. 'It's all over. It was Dahl. He confessed to everything. He even gives out false IDs to criminals under a fake name. He tried to kill Reid.'

'Oh my God. Is he alright?'

'Yeah, he's stable. I think.' He sounds muffled and drowsy. 'Anyway, they're coming to collect you t-tomorrow so just hang on there. Okay?'

'Okay.' She frowns and lowers her voice. 'Are you alright?'

'Me? Yeah, yeah, yeah. I'm fine.'

'Because it sounds like you've been drinking, if truth be told.'

'Course not. I'll see you soon, honey.'

'Bye.'

Mason puts the phone down and relays the news to Shah. They are both relieved and bursting to get out into the world.

'So he must have shopped me in,' Shah says.

'Probably.'

'Well … it wasn't Frost.'

She gives him a look which says 'not necessarily' and sits on the sofa with him, allowing him to talk while she thinks about what has happened, glad that Sera had not lost her only parent, pleased to be released from the safe house – yet her mind is on Peter Dahl.

Interrupting Shah, she asks, 'Why do you think he did it? Dahl.'

Shah shrugs. 'Does it matter? Everyone's safe now.'

'There'll be more. Knowing our luck, he'll have inspired some other nutters.'

'You're right there. If there were no crime, I'd have been out of a job earlier than this.' He chuckles to himself and Mason does not join in. 'Sad you'll be missing out on the biggest trial ever?'

The thought had not occurred to her. 'Less hassle, isn't it?'

Unfortunately for her, after they are marched out of seclusion and driven back home, back into the world of mass struggle, she is summoned to Victory House, where she is told that Frost is waiting for her in Briscoe's office. Wherever she goes, people greet her with a smile and wave, making her feel welcome and as though she had been gone for a much longer time.

Her best friend exits his office just as she reaches the corridor.

'Kevin!' She leaps into his arms and he clutches her tightly, burying his face into her hair.

'How are you doing?' He smells like beer and his body seems to shake a little.

'Forget about me. Are you okay? I know you were lying to me yesterday.'

'I'm just glad you're back. I missed you.'

'Missed you too. Especially being locked up with Shah for a month.'

'I'm sure you loved it.' He smiles a fake smile and ruffles her hair slightly. 'Frost's waiting for you. Good luck.'

She rolls her eyes. 'See you in a bit.'

Mason finds Frost looking out of the window patiently, his

demeanour unsettling her slightly. He is always too calm for her to figure him out.

'Would you like a seat?'

She looks around her old office with foreign eyes. Her messy habits had been eradicated, no piles of paper all over the desk, no shoes in the corner, no takeaway food filling the waste paper bin. Instead, there is an old framed picture of Kevin, Molly and their mother, box files and neat paper trays.

'No.' Despite her words, she sits on the chair on the wrong side of the desk.

'This chapter is drawing to a close, Mason. I feel good.'

'Good that Dahl betrayed us?'

'Good that the truth revealed itself. My mother was a compulsive liar, telling me that she loved me, that I was more important that her search for undeserved riches and her gluttony for men. Her hatred spurred me on, so this is what we must do now. We need to steer ourselves towards a satisfying end to this tragic year and recover for 2052. There are 450 members of parliament. There's no getting rid of us. Cut one out and another grows in its place. Like a hydra, a terrible and feared creature with enough force and enough ruthlessness, we persist. You have to work like this to make a difference in the world we live in even if it's not the world that most people know they want. Fear is how you convince people of the misinterpreted truth.'

'Fear is an easy route. We need to learn from what's happened, not scare the people,' Mason says. 'So many people have died. Justice is being sued. Tall … Gibb …'

She watches his face become rigid.

'Those were tragic events.'

'You're talking to me, not the press, Wilson. Do they know anything about what happened to Renata?'

'Not yet. Only that it was a blunt head wound that killed her.'

'Right.' She looks at him, defiant.

Frost smiles. 'No, it wasn't me, but I'm touched you think so.'

Mason becomes flustered and heated. 'That's not what I—'

'You're very transparent. The only time I don't know what's going on in that head of yours is when you're neck deep in work and I would much rather not be burdened by your thoughts as well as mine.'

It takes a few seconds, but she catches on. 'Are you giving me my job back?'

'But not your constituency. You heard about the re-election? Tomas Ciotti took over Vauxhall when you were suspended, with lots of support and presence. They had been suffering previously.'

'I know, but I quit actually,' she takes this with ease. 'Admittedly, I was a pathetic MP but I was always made for this.'

'Open the door.'

'What?'

Mason opens the door and Frost follows her. The first thing she notices is that most people are smiling at her. There are a few moments of applause and a welcome back balloon is floating beside a lonely plant pot by the window.

Frost takes her shoulders and turns her around to face the sign on the door:

DOLLY MASON KC
ATTORNEY GENERAL OF ENGLAND

Her throat tightens and a huge dry lump appears.

'Oh wow … but Kevin …'

'He smells like a distillery.' Frost says. 'I enjoy a drink but he makes me want to abstain.'

'Will he get his old job back?'

'Yet to be seen. But for now, we need you for the Crown versus Peter Dahl. Notes are on the desk.'

After celebrations and a glass of wine in the office, Mason nominates Waltz as her new assistant over Friel, as they are the only two she trusts to get to work right away.

'No offence, Andy!' Sat at her desk, Waltz enters Mason's office and closes the door behind her.

'So, what next, Boss?'

'Yeah, don't call me that. Ms Mason only. You arrive at seven every morning and leave at four if all the work is done. The works is rarely ever done so make sure that if you work more than fifty hours in the week, we can organise a day off in the month.'

'That's hardly fair.'

'You won't get a pay rise just now but this invaluable experience you'll gain could see you reach my job in forty years.'

'Why forty? You're not even fifty yet.'

'I plan on giving up this job only when I'm dead. Is that clear?'

'Very.'

'Prep me on all of the retrials in the morning and organise a coffee with Tomas Ciotti. Good news is that you have the rest of the day off. I'm working from home.' She picks up her files and heads for the door. 'I have someone to see.'

Finally herself again, Mason sees the beauty of the world again as she drives home. The sky is very blue, the grass is unnaturally green and she feels that she has found her place again.

Her apartment welcomes her back again and she makes herself a large cup of coffee as she waits impatiently.

When she had given in waiting and began flicking through her files and checking her many emails on her organiser, the door opens and Sera rushes in, grinning.

Mason stands from the breakfast bar with her arms wide. 'Come here.'

Sera timidly embraces her, realising she is happier to see her than she assumed.

Mason takes her shoulders and looks into the teenager's amber eyes. 'How was it?'

'Great, actually. We had a great time. Your mum and dad helped me with my school work. They're still divorcing but they're going to live together for a few years.'

'What? What the hell?'

'Don't ask.'

'No, I'm going to have to ask about that one.'

Sera laughs. 'I came back to do my exams …'

'How did you do?'

'Don't know yet but I'm sure I only failed three subjects.'

'Brilliant!'

Sera's faces falls slightly. 'I saw Dad yesterday after I heard what happened. He's okay, I suppose. Looked the same as usual.'

Mason attempts a smile. 'He's not giving up, Sera. That's the important thing.'

'What about Scott and Mr Cunningham?'

'What?'

'Will they get away with what they've done?'

Mason takes her in for another hug. 'I don't know, darling. That's out of my control for now.'

'Still unemployed?' Sera asks, organising her luggage from Mason's, which had all been dumped in the middle of the living area.

Mason snorts. 'As if. You know I'm the only one who can ensure that guilty verdict.'

'Strangely, I do.'

They had missed each other sorely and spend all night

talking about her strategy over takeaway Chinese food, Sera using all of the legal knowledge her father had imparted upon her, giving Mason faith that she would make a fabulous lawyer, doctor, teacher or whatever she wanted to be in the future. The night winds down with the girls sleeping top to tail on the sofa, sharing a duvet with the television flashing beyond their closed eyes and vibrant dreams.

Lady Justice watches London from her pedestal.

The Old Bailey is as it always was, grand and menacing, worn by weather and time, taking no heed of the rusting bars and scratched balustrades, the crumbled cornicing nor the chipped columns. Retaining its glorious edifice is no longer a concern. Inside, marbled walls and painted ceilings are gently crumbled, mosaics break form and murals are incomplete, and the bare cold halls precede the frenzied and intense scene taking place in the courtroom ahead.

Uproar. The audience cry out in response to an audacious comment, some standing and three people leaving, too offended to continue the observation. Disregarded, a gavel smashes against varnished wood in the distance, a whip cracking like thunder. Behind it, Judge Weaver and his dark, shining head sit troubled and disapproving at the top of the room overseeing the discord.

In the middle of the courtroom, Mason laughs. She is dressed in her robes with a familiar grey trouser suit underneath, her mousy hair tied into a ponytail, thick brown glasses on her nose. Opposite her in the stand, is Dahl, equalling her five-foot-eight stature from his place on the stand. He, too, is in grey, only he sports a fraying jumpsuit with the letters PP73LD stitched perfectly into the right breast pocket. His glasses are rounded and reflect the falling sun that shines through the large windows beyond.

Testing, he repeats himself: 'It wasn't an act of God nor am I playing God. I just lay outside of your jurisdiction. "Be strong, do not fear, your God will come with vengeance, with divine retribution he will come to save you."'

The attorney general waits for the last of the people to leave, their echoing footsteps fading. 'So, you're religious?' she asks, curious, recognising the quote from her youth and all of the forced church sessions and Sunday School lessons. She always thought the 'divine retribution' part to be of particular interest.

'No,' PP73LD responds.

'Well read?' she says instead.

The accused utters, '"A good decision is based on knowledge and not on numbers."'

First Isaiah, now Plato. Mason knows her literature and so do the audience. They are sick of the inference and games from the defendant.

Mason goes to her desk and picks up a document. 'Numbers. I have a few here actually. Since the second of February 2051, six members of parliament have been killed, three critically injured and one in intensive care, leaving hundreds of constituents abandoned, the government in turmoil and families devastated.'

'The government was already devastated.'

'So you plead Not Guilty to battery, assault, ABH, GBH, attempted murder, murder and sedition? Do you deny your actions?'

'I didn't do anything any other ordinary citizen of this heinous and farcical country wouldn't have done. Though … they wouldn't admit it.'

Mason hesitates, thinking.

Weaver prompts her. 'Madam Attorney General.'

PP73LD speaks up. 'I didn't shoot anybody,' he says very

matter-of-factly.

'You didn't have to,' Mason says clearly. She addresses the audience and Judge Weaver, no jury in sight. 'Ladies and gentleman, please take into consideration that accountability is not synonymous with whoever pulled the trigger. In this case, guilt is knowingly overseeing the execution of a plan and the execution of six people. Your Honour, I know that you will come to the right conclusion in light of reviewing the massacre the executive branch has survived, which the people have survived. Taking lives is a crime. Some call it a sin. You've seen the consequences. Now you must decide whether or not you want this man to walk among the people in the street as a free man or serving his debt. Thank you.'

The audience, having listened intently, wait patiently as Mason takes her seat and Weaver prepares to proceed.

PP73LD awaits the verdict without fear, despite the shackles on his wrists and ankles. He looks into Mason's hazel eyes and she stares straight back, holding his glare.

Meanwhile, Weaver leaves the room and there is a considerable break until the verdict is reached, forcing the court to disperse and go home, anxious.

Three days of speculation later, court is called to commence and every person in the country is eager to find out the decision. Bets had been placed, wagers made, sick days taken, appointments postponed and news channels and radios blare out in most workplaces.

England draws in a simultaneous inhale.

'For the charges of assault, battery, assault, ABH, GBH, attempted murder, murder and sedition, I find the defendant, Mr Peter Dahl, guilty.'

Mason cannot smile this time, cannot boast to Dahl's nameless and frankly terrible defending lawyer, she simply takes a well-deserved seat and folds her fingers together, grateful that she had not been stitched up again. Waltz whoops with joy and pats her on the back. The reporters at the back of the room applaud with glee.

'Sentencing and sale will be set in due course. For now, Mr Dahl will be detained.'

Wiry-haired and bedraggled, Dahl is led from the room smiling, delighted with his fate.

Waltz is discomforted. 'Why is he smiling like that?'

'Because he's going to be released, isn't he? When he's sold. He can't be contained.'

Her fears are expressed in every newspaper and on every news broadcast and daytime television show, pressuring Frost to no end, causing protests every day the following week outside Downing Street and Victory House calling for change to the justice system.

Had this been what he wanted? Was this his message, his parting gift? Mason has no choice but to place her trust in Frost and Cunningham and all of those in power who have the ability to change this. She had lost her status. No longer a member of parliament, she has no weighting in political affairs, no internal vote or inner perspective and is one of the others, an outsider who has nothing to do other than trust.

Her dreams were often empty and dark and although Sera hadn't spent much time thinking about how she would do it, just that it needed to be done. That feeling in her gut and the voice in her head knew that the time is drawing nearer. Her eyes are drawn to sharp objects and tall buildings, deep water and long sleep, so infactuated that she has to actively distract herself on a daily basis. With Mason busy with work and taking a few days away, opportunity reveals itself.

It is a Tuesday, the same day she was born, so she thinks it poetic and just. She invites Ed round to the apartment and he smiles at the simplicity, although his face falls once he realises why he's there.

She beckons him to the shower room, where the water is already splashing against the hard warm tiles and she sits on the ground before he can say anything about the shiny glint of the object beside her.

Instantly, he gets onto the floor beside her, pushing his chair away slightly. He doesn't care that he is soaking wet.

She smiles at him and holds his hand. A large intake of breath and she raises her face up to the flow of the water.

Beautiful and content, complex and obstinate, fractured and slow, the words coming from his mouth never reach her ears and her skin breaks into a crimson river.

'Prime Minister, the press secretary wants to know what you're going to do about the seven people squatting on Downing Street,' Jackie says from the door, while Frost is lying dramatically across a chaise longue by the window. She holds her clipboard tightly and her pen poised, scribbling fanatically whenever he speaks.

'Tell him to make up something good and inform me in the morning.'

'Still no call to nominate a deputy?'

'We've been fine without a deputy prime minister on many occasions in the past. Leave it alone.'

'The New Supreme Court judges have refused the second date you proposed for the meeting you wanted.'

'I didn't want it, I demanded it, Jackie. Make Mr Weaver aware of who he is and who I am, please.' She flinches instead of scribbling. 'Bastards.'

'What is going to happen to Judges Scott and Cunningham?'

'That's up to the other judges, isn't it? Goes without saying they'll be disbarred and not work again?'

'All of your autumn trips abroad have been booked and paid for. China, Milan, Vietnam and then the US. In that order. Security are all booked in to travel with you.'

'Good, good. Don't forget to remind me to get the press office on it when need be. And reschedule big meetings around my schedule not everyone else's.'

'You'll soon receive news from the investigators on the progress of Gibb's case. For now, her mother wants you to attend the service in her hometown, Norwich.'

'Pencil me in.'

'I found out that the person paying for Daniel Reid's care is the attorney general.'

He sits up. 'Interesting. Thank you, Jackie.'

'What would you like for lunch tomorrow evening?'

'Cliff is very good at deciding, but perhaps lamb.' His servants remain ever loyal and he wonders whether or not to wake Ling for an evening drink and a lecture. 'Anything else?'

'Steven Kingsbury called this morning.'

Frost pauses and then crosses the room for the telephone on the table beside the fireplace.

'Thank you,' he says. He begins dialling and pauses, calling her before she leaves the room. 'Jackie? Any news on CA45JM?'

'No, Sir. No sightings, nothing.'

'Goodnight.'

'Goodnight, Sir.'

She leaves him alone to continue on the phone. He waits for the ringing and then the voice on the end of the line.

'Hello?'

'Who's this?' the phone says.

'Your biggest fan,' he says softy down the receiver.

'Oh! Evening, Sir. Wasn't expecting you to call this late.'

'Me neither, I just wanted to check in.'

Steven sighs. 'Mostly covering the protests this week, just wanted to see which take you wanted really. Failing freedom-fighters or the desperate homeless using the opportunity to have better sleeping arrangements? Your call.'

Frost muses for a moment. 'Go for the former. We have to boost the morale occasionally.'

'And the trial?'

'You'll have the statement I released after the verdict. That's good enough for everyone else, should be for you too. But … keep an eye out for me tomorrow afternoon, perhaps get someone outside to pick up my speech live?'

'Yes, Sir. Thank you, Sir.'

'And keep the public interested in the Crown Court Convict as much as you can. I have an idea of how to find her but I still need her to be relevant.' Frost thinks of Alex, building his trust and biding his time, waiting until the perfect moment to strike.

'Sir.'

'Oh, and, before you go. I really think now is the time to drop the bomb on Mr Briscoe. He liked to drink more than anything else and he's been far too lucky in his occupations than most of us are in a lifetime. Shake things up a little. Be creative. Or honest. I don't care.'

'Is there any particular reason?'

'I've just never liked people who get things for free,' Frost reasons. 'Goodnight.'

Nineteen

'We are drawing to the end of a very trying year in England,' Celeste begins that grey afternoon in the studio, looking as perfect as usual in deep green. 'What began with a tragic event this past February, which ended many lives and injured others, is finally finding resolution and peace since the guilty verdict of Peter Dahl, the former Deputy and Commissioner of the City of London Police. The open court revealed that Mr Dahl had in fact lived a double life as a man named Edward Grier, aiding ex-offenders in leading new lives after their sentences had been served. Some have speculated that these people were involved in the attack in February, with one female accomplice detained and charged.

'We have been advised to still keep a keen eye out for the escaped convict, CA45JM, who also disappeared in February and has yet to be seen. Sources believe that she may be an accomplice to these attacks and we desperately want anyone involved brought to justice. The police advise that she may still be in London or the surrounding areas.

'The interim attorney general, Kevin Briscoe has been permanently dismissed from his office due to an apparent drinking problem, a statement from the justice department has revealed. He has been replaced by former attorney general, Dolly Mason, causing uproar to many and allegations of workplace favouritism. He has not been offered any other job in the department but has in the past. The favouritism claims have surfaced as it has been found that Ms Mason and Mr Briscoe had been students together when studying for the Bar, working their way up to the top in a record number of years, both breaking records as the youngest attorney generals this country has seen. Some have called into question the status of Ms Mason and Mr Briscoe's personal relationship and whether this has affected any decision-making. We will update you if there are any further revelations.

'Protests continue up and down the country from newly formed groups fighting for a new way of prosecuting the guilty. Especially after Dahl's verdict, the public have agreed that placing such a violent and perhaps mentally disturbed individual back into society puts everyone in danger and will lead to reoffending, making rehabilitation less likely. Historic cases have been brought forward in debates within parliament where murderers and rapists have reoffended and been continuously put back into the system, whereby they end up hurting others or themselves.

'Controversially, in response to the protests, the prime minister had this to say earlier this morning.'

A visual of Frost behind the podium outside his home appears. 'Following the guilty verdict of the Crown versus Dahl and the urgent cries of those protesting around the country and on my doorstep, I propose radical change. It breaks my heart that serious crime fractures society as it does and that our vision of peace and rehabilitation is not working in the way we hoped for those who harm the most. There was always this chance and we are working through a trial period. I say this is, therefore, the perfect time to put to you another change which safeguards our children, mothers, fathers, friends and family from men like Peter Dahl. Today, I am submitting my plan to draw up an historic capital punishment for the worst offenders, those who cannot be reasoned with, those who do nothing but destroy. I propose we reawaken the death penalty.'

The crowds on the video roar with intrigue and disdain, flashbulbs erupt, capturing the moment for years to come.

Celeste falls back into view. 'Various human rights groups and organisations have commented on this brash suggestion, all of which you can find on our website.

'Although many had begun to lose faith in the government, what is clear is that the City of London and the rest of the country can continue to sleep better after the capital has found a brief sense of normalcy since the culprit behind the February attacks has been found guilty with no hope of retrial.

'That's all for now. The time is almost one pm. I'll be back tonight at six for the evening broadcast. Have a lovely afternoon. Goodbye.'

It is dusk when she wakes from her sleep in the spot she had chosen the night before, under a dark bridge on a commercial road.

Clarke picks ups her blanket and rolls it ups, stashing it on the side of her backpack while glancing around suspiciously at the few people walking by her. She walks in the opposite direction.

At the back of a local pizzeria, an employee exits the back door into an alleyway, carrying a load of rubbish bags over his shoulder.

'Give me a minute!' he yells. 'God! I'm taking the – I'm doing it now!'

He throws the bags down on the ground and turns to go back inside, where his boss can be heard saying, 'Did you take the bags out?'

'What did it look like I was doing? Christ!' The door slams behind him, highlighting his apparent frustration.

From the side of a neighbouring building, Clarke sprints over to the bags, grabs the first one she can cling to and begins running back to her hiding place, however, a man flashes past her, grabbing the same bag from her arms as he goes, sprinting down the near-deserted street.

'Hey!' She runs after him was fast as her hungry legs can take her, a surprising speed powered by desire.

The unidentified man notices her pursuit and glances back at her. Through his curiosity, he trips over something ahead of him, rolls and continues to run, bits of food and rubbish falling out of the bag as he flies ahead.

'Hey!' she shouts again, furious. 'Hey! That's mine!'

Still running, Clarke quickly bends to pick up something that had fallen out of the black bag. A small box in hand, she throws it at the man as she chases.

'Stop!'

He stumbles.

Clarke grabs a glass bottle from the pavement, aims it at his head and pelts it in his directions. He drops to the ground, yelling out in pain.

She runs up to him, crouches over his fallen figure and carefully picks up a piece of the broken glass from the ground. Winding one arm around his neck, she puts him into a headlock while the other hand has the glass to his face, her legs pinning him to the ground.

'That bag was mine,' she spits.

'No, I was just—'

She yanks his head back forcefully and strokes his cheek with the shard of glass. He too has an infinity symbol on his wrist, a mark of his past, although it is different. There is a strike right through it.

'Don't think I won't use this.'

'Please,' he whimpers. 'I'm sure you're very capable but I honestly just want to eat. This figure takes some upkeep.'

She watches him for a moment, sees that he is not as skinny and hard-done by as the other homeless she had come across, perhaps a very good scavenger. He has a young chubby face and kind eyes, a bunch of hair grown over a rosy complexion. She is soon satisfied that he is no threat.

Clarke tosses aside the glass while he wipes the blood from the back and side of his head. Still sitting on him, she grabs the bag and searches through it. Irritatingly, there is nothing but empty packaging.

'Jesus,' she exclaims. Annoyed, she shakes her head and slaps him sharply on his head.

He flinches and holds his hands over his face. 'What the hell?!'

'There's nothing left!' Clarke wipes the blood on her hand onto her jacket then stands.

The man on the ground sits up slowly, dusting himself off.

'Which means,' she complains, 'I ran after you for no reason and, if there was any food back there, some other needy soul will have had at it. Thank you,' she adds sarcastically.

'Kyle,' he says happily. She looks at him, frowning. '"Thank you, Kyle." Just in case you wanted to – My name is Kyle.'

He stands. She walks away from him down the street and soon becomes aware that he is following her.

They reach a car park and Clarke walks swiftly between vehicles, checking through the windows for valuables while

Kyle follows timidly.

She carries on through the street to an overflowing bin directly opposite. She dives right in, searching, Kyle standing beside her quiet.

He tries to smile at her but she isn't looking. 'You looking for somewhere to stay?'

Clarke sniffs half a sandwich she has unearthed but drops it because she spots moulding on more than half of it.

'Not this second,' she responds grudgingly.

She picks up a fast food restaurant cup and shakes it. It is moderately full. 'Why? Have you got somewhere?' She sips the drink and uses her other hand to scour the rest of the bin.

'Maybe,' he admits, floating around the bin, teasing almost.

'Don't get all secretive now, Kyle.'

'If you knew me, you'd know I'm actually terrible at keeping secrets.'

'I never plan to know you. Keep your secrets.'

'Fine. I will.'

She squeezes a whole apple which falls apart, smashing bruised fruit between her fingers.

'Why are you even asking me?' she wonders.

'I don't know,' he replies honestly.

Kyle walks until he finds a bench and Clarke follows, curious. Both grateful for company, they sit and look at the small patch of grass before them. Kyle yawns and Clarke holds out the drink to him.

'Want some?' she asks.

'What is it?'

'Some dark, once-carbonated, caffeinated beverage.' She notices a backpack beneath the seat. 'So, is this it? This is your place?'

Kyle takes the drink and sips. 'Home sweet home. But at least I have somewhere to sleep at night. Right?'

'You shouldn't sleep at night.'

'Okay …'

'I don't. Daytime only.'

'Nocturnal?'

'Nocturnal. That way, I can protect myself when the sun goes down.'

'Protect yourself from who?' he asks.

'Everything.'

'Ah. Not a fan of this new system, are we? It's been like this for ten years, so—'

'And everything's gone down the effing drain. Years ago, the government complained that the prisons were too full and now they're empty or schools or hospitals. I mean, that's fantastic for people who are sick and dying and that's fine for kids in deprived areas who need to learn maths but to have murderers out on the streets? How does trading time equate justice? Since when was that something the whole country should agree with?'

'It's not,' Kyle mutters.

'But?' She hears the hesitation in his voice.

'You can see the appeal.'

'I really can't.'

'This way, the criminals have to work for their freedom rather than lazing about in a hole on their Playstations and starting fights. They owe the people who bail them out. Assuming they have a sense of morality.'

'Which is not something anyone knows for sure. It's just … no one is ever free. Criminal or not, we do what we are told. Fact.'

'Maybe some people like it that way.'

She nods. 'Maybe they do. I'm Clarke.'

Kyle shakes her hand politely. 'You can stay here tonight, if you want.'

'You don't even know me.'

'No but I'm good at judging character. You don't seem like an axe murderer.'

She holds her breath for a moment and says, 'You don't know the things I've done.'

The noisy car pulls to a stop outside the house. A quiet street, she thinks they will be heard miles away, but there are other cars and other people on the street going about their daily lives who do not even blink when she slams the door shut.

Clarke walks around the adjoining streets for five minutes, psyching herself up for her task. Just scare him. But how? What scares a middle-aged man? A shadow, the fear of something unknown.

If she could, she would be unseen. He had given her a balaclava just in case and told her that the back windows were always left open until around nine or ten at night when the house was locked up. That gives her an hour or so.

Courage prevailing, she pulls on her black balaclava, slips down an open gate to the backs of the houses and uses a strength she did not knew she had to climb three high garden fences to get to the one she needs, avoiding a flowerbed of peonies in the last house but one.

A light is on in the kitchen and one upstairs but she sees no one. Taking her chance, she creeps to the back wall of the house, peering inside while using her fingers to find a slot around each window base.

She moves sideways to the door and slowly pushes the handle down, the door freeing and moving inwards.

A television is on in the background. She freezes.

Thinking again, she moves around the dining space to crouch by the table. She leaves the door open, allowing a cold wind to enter. Her body slides under the table and shrinks into a ball as footsteps enter the room.

The door is closed and locked. The feet she can see wait anxiously, perhaps looking out of the kitchen window for a sign of life.

Clarke slips around the table and runs quietly up the stairs.

On the landing, she listens. The living room is accommodated yet again. She decides to wait upstairs until bedtime, giving herself more time to think of a plan. Was this already enough? Was an open door enough to scare a man? If it were her, she would be appropriately spooked for sure, but she could not just leave it like this. She had to be seen.

It is almost two hours before the television is switched off. Checking the rooms, Clarke hides in the office, hoping that the bedroom or the bathroom would be the next place to go.

Footsteps climb the staircase languidly and it sounds like the room next door is the destination. The shower turns on in the bathroom. No one feels more exposed than when they are completely laid bare, so Clarke makes this her moment. She can barely breathe through the constricting fabric, no hole to breathe out of, only tiny slits for her to see.

The trickle of water lets her know that the person she needs is in there; she can hear feet splashing and steam emits like smoke out of the open door.

Clarke slowly slips inside, watching the shadow behind the glass. It is a very nice bathroom, modern and dark, large tiles on the walls, a roll-top bathtub and a large wet room at the back.

She steps closer.

Soon, the shrouded figure behind the glass stiffens. She has been seen.

Clarke does not move.

There is a colossal high-pitch scream that could not belong to a man. The door slides open and there stands a naked woman with her dark hair tied back. In her panic, she launches at her and Clarke is forced backwards, almost falling over. She holds her arms up and they are tangled, pushing one away from the other, panicking inside the stuffy, warm room.

Water drips on the floor from the woman's skin and hair.

Clarke takes one step backwards as her arms fly forwards.

A crack signifies the woman's ankle slipping on the water. It breaks, she wobbles, trips backwards, her mouth releases a hollow yelp, arms grasp the air and then her head smashes against the dark tiles.

Time slows.

Blood washes down the fissure in her head as she twitches, then down her body until it gathers in a pool by her leg, unable to go down the drain that she is dying on top of.

Clarke runs. As soon as she is away from the house, she pulls off her mask, breathes, vomits and runs, fear in every step.

Kyle shrugs. 'I trust you.'

Clarke responds with stunned silence and distantly watches the dark sky fill with stars above them.

Reverence and celebration is not what she is used to, but it is the reception she receives when she arrives at the hospital on a bright autumn morning. Her money meant more than she realised and she notices the many improvements around the building, guided on a grand tour by three nurses on lunch, before heading to the room she intended to visit in the first place.

He is still where she left him. She had just wanted to check that all of her hard work had not been taken for granted, wanted to see with her own two eyes that Dahl had not hurt him and that his heart is still beating.

The machine sounds in the background, easing her mind.

Mason takes the only seat beside his still body and sighs heavily.

'We haven't spoken in such a long time. It's hard to update you on all that you've missed so I won't even bother trying to remember it all. I'll tell you all that I can remember off the top of my head. I'm sure you'll tell me if I'm talking too much.

'Sidra died. And Renata. I don't know if anyone told you that. I don't know how often people talk to you. You were friends so I thought you should know. Other MPs lost their lives so I guess … we're the lucky ones. You don't know it, but you're lucky. You're, kind of, safe in here. At least, you were. That's the thing, things change in the blink of eye, these days. One second someone is your friend, then they're your enemy or someone is alive and then they're just not.

'Tall really looked up to you anyway, believed in everything you did and said. It was so annoying. You were like a superhero to her. I think, secretly, she wanted to be a judge ultimately. I know it was her end goal. That's why she was so happy when you took her under your wing. God, she was happy when you'd look at her. Knowing you knew that she existed changed her, made her a confident, strong woman with ambition. The best gift you gave her was success, which manifested into jealousy and courage. She wanted your job and was happy to befriend you to get tips, that was the truth of it. The ambitious cow. I'm sure you knew that though.

'She wanted my job too, but it was Kevin who got that. There has never been a reshuffle like the one we have just been through, I tell you. Then again, this is unprecedented. No one's pulled off what Dahl has. Makes me sick, really, that he made a plan and waited ten years to execute it. Makes you wonder what else people have locked away in their heads. Especially Frost.

'So I just recently got my job back. It's been a long time coming and I finally feel like myself again because this is who I am. You know me. I'm not satisfied unless I'm drowning in the most horrific and morally challenging cases there are. What's the point in playing safe? It's paid off and now I'm still the attorney general. I'm on the right side of history, the side where I can count all of my achievements and be proud that I've made a difference and I'm proud of that.

'I was seventeen when I decided I was going to be a lawyer, so it wasn't always my dream. Before that, I had wanted to sail ships and be a fisherwoman in the Pacific. I'd changed my mind because I watched the news and became aware of all of the scary things that seventeen-year-olds barely thought about. People were dying but, more importantly, people were being killed and robbed of their lives over the silliest things. It shocked me and it still does now. I'll never forget that moment. I wonder when you knew what your fate would be. I never asked. I just assumed that you always had your life figured out. You seemed wise and aged to me, a generation ahead, even though there's less than ten years between us. I feel like a child in your presence, like I still have so much to learn.

'Sera's doing well. She's an amazing girl. She got all the best parts of you and Adrienne. She's smart and level-headed, kind, honest, fiery ... Sera is everything I think you hoped she would be. I'd be so happy if any of my fictional children turned out as good as she has and it's been a pleasure looking after her for you. She misses you like crazy, even though she doesn't say it, but she gets on. Her exams are done and she did great. She made out that she would fail everything, of course, but she sailed through. Finished her fourth year recently. Did someone tell you she switched schools? I forgot to say. She's actually happy at state school, has a best friend called Ed and isn't so sad anymore, I think. She's happier now. I had a feeling she was depressed, an inkling. She reminded me of how I used to feel at certain points in my life. She was so sad at that school, that's why she was acting out. Because you weren't there and she was lonely. Now, I feel like she's coming out of it. Still eats like a horse but there's nothing I can do to change that. I think she's might taken up tennis or something. Her lacrosse days are over. Funny thing is, I don't want to give her back. I almost don't want you to wake up.'

Mason looks at the ceiling and then at his unmoving face. 'We're stocking up for winter now. Started earlier this year. It's usually just me and doesn't take as long but I buy two of everything and fill the pantry before stocks get low and we can't get a tin of baked beans for two months. It's stupid that trade is so horrendous and food companies make too little. The new regulations were supposed to limit waste not rob half of the population of a decent meal. Oh well. We have plenty of tinned and frozen fruit and vegetables for when the time comes and we can't get them from overseas. Apparently, it's going to be a really cold winter. Do you remember, about eleven years ago, temperatures went to about minus ten degrees and I got snowed in? You stayed up on the phone talking to me every day and every night so I wouldn't feel lonely. You even had time for me during your lunch breaks, making sure I was still alive. Then you came over when it subsided and dug me out with a spade.

'I hate talking about it, really. It reminds me of how lonely I am now. I might get a dog, maybe a stray. Some kind of Husky mix, I think. I think Brutus is a good name and it might be nice to have someone come with me when I go for a run even though I know it's probably not good for their joints. Sera might want to take it for walks too after school. I need something to take my mind off things when I spend too much time thinking. Once you told me that the more I think the less the world can take me by surprise and you are so right. I get so caught up in the details, worried or nervous of the future or the past and I don't get time to just live. For some reason, I just cannot relax and I think it's because of you.

'For twenty years, I haven't been able to live my life the way I've truly wanted to. My life has been in the shadows, tucked behind my job and my family, the people I care about most in the world. I don't like to think about myself and my needs, afraid to become a narcissist and right about now I'm beginning to believe I've left things too late. For so long, I've been fixated on our past, unable to move on and breathe and say, "now it's time for you." I can't be me without us. I still remember the dates in my head. The day we met. The day you kissed me. Singing and dancing in the kitchen. The day you left me. The day you said you loved me. The day you met her. Your wedding day. The day you said you needed me. The day Sera was born. The day I told you that I do not ruin relationships. The day I ended it. You own me. I can't even function. I can't go on a date without thinking about this amazing love I had and how nothing will ever compare to it. We were cordial at work, almost friends. No one had any idea of the things we've been through. I never even told Kevin. Now everyone thinks I'm some frigid old spinster or closet lesbian because I haven't found love. But I did with you. My parents have given up on me finding someone. I see it in my mother's eyes, my age, my ticking timebomb. I convince myself that no one will have me now, to make myself feel better on the surface. I'm too busy. I'm a working woman. I don't need men.

'Everything is falling apart. We tried to make the world a better place, maybe you did it slightly differently ... But it's falling apart from underneath us. For a period, I hated what you did. I really, really hated you for it. Time has changed everything. The truth is, I'm still young. I can find someone else. The question is, do I want to? I know the answer to that. For ten years, we stayed away from one another but worked together where necessary, blocking out any thoughts or feelings we might have had and now that you're here, in this bed, I wish we hadn't.'

Tears stream down her face and she takes his hand in her own. 'I don't want to lose you, Daniel. I want ten more years of loving you from a distance, if that's all I'm allowed. Your daughter needs you to come home. I need you. You're the best thing about my counterfeit life, the only truth I've had for myself. After all these years, I'm still so in awe of you. You have to hold on. I'll spend my money on keeping you here because I have to. What is money anyway? These days, not much. You mean more to me than wealth or power or my own happiness. If anything happens to you now, after all of this, after all of the blood … You breathe, I breathe. Please, Daniel, I don't want to be alone and I don't want to regret the wasted years.'

Mason opens her eyes and realises that she had been lying face down next to his arm, fingers wound tight around his. She sits up and uses the sleeve of her woollen cardigan to wipe away the traces.

She laughs to herself. 'I am so glad you can't see my face right now. I'm an embarrassment.'

Standing, she glances out of the window, where she can see her car parked in one of the bays beyond the building. The wind howls through an air vent in the corner of the room and a few drops of rain begin to fall outside. She smiles and turns back to him, professional and direct. Mason is herself again and the past half an hour is tucked into a memory in the back of her mind.

'Well, it was lovely seeing you.' Her gaze finds his mouth, her stomach fluttering between heartbeats. 'I'm going to go.'

She heads towards the door, unwilling, trying to distract herself with planning the day ahead.

The slightest movement commands her attention, a hand brushing over linen. Via the machine, his heart takes a different tone. Mason swivels and watches his body shift delicately, life pouring back into his skin, redness in his cheeks and some strength to each muscle.

Daniel Reid takes in a shallow breath between cracked lips and his olive eyes adjust to the light.

*

CRIMINAL JUSTICE
ACT 2041

Be it enacted by the King's most Excellent Majesty, by and with the agreement and advice of the Lords Spiritual and Temporal, and Commons, in this here Parliament assembled, and by the authority of the same, as follows:–

AMENDMENTS OF POLICE AND CRIMINAL EVIDENCE ACT

An Act to make provison of criminal justice (including the powers and duties of the police) and about dealing with offenders; and the amend the law on custodial sentences.

1	Arrestable offences
2	Codes of practice
3	Removal of grant of bail
4	Warrants and cautions

AMENDMENT OF CUSTODIAL SENTENCING

An amendment was made dissolving the process and function of custodial sentencing, barring use of prisons for sentences. All custodial sentences are hence replaced with the Auction and its proceedings.

RETRIALS AND APPEALS

The right to appeal and the conditions are hereby set, including the limitations of resale, retrial and reallocation.

SENTENCING

Rights and conditions of sentencing and custody are detailed, along with the calculation of sentences, and the organisation and enforcement of roles.

MISCELLANEOUS

About the Author

L. Stanley started reading and writing at the age of nine and began writing this book at eighteen. She graduated with an English degree from the University of Birmingham and works in publishing. She lives in the UK with her partner and cat, Sulu.